SOUL KEEPERS

— OF —

GLENORMISTON SOUTH

Copyright © 2021 by Mickey Martin
First published in Australia in 2021
by MMH Press
Waikiki, WA 6169
www.mmhpress.com

Edited by Velvet Tea
Proofread by Amanda Schubert
Cover art by Jess Fowler – jebbers@live.com.au

Because of the dynamic nature of the Internet, any web addresses or links contained in this book may have changed since publication and may no longer be vaild. The views expressed in this work are solely those of the author and do not necessarily reflect the views of the publisher and the publisher hereby disclaims any responsibility for them.

 A catalogue record for this work is available from the National Library of Australia

National Library of Australia Catalogue-in-Publication data:
Soul Keepers of Glenormiston South/Mickey Martin

ISBN: 978-0-6453359-0-3 (Paperback)
ISBN: 978-0-6453359-1-0 (Ebook)

Martin has created an engaging, immersive world that captures your interest from the very beginning. With characters who quickly feel like old friends, you soon find yourself lost in the magical world of the Soul Keepers, and their role as guardians of Mother Earth. As a Glenormiston South native, Martin paints an exquisitely-detailed picture of the landscape of the area, which binds the entire story. It feels as though we are walking beside Angel and her family as they navigate their world, and the setting is rich with the magic of nature.

The plot itself is a delightful blend of 'good vs. evil', paranormal entities, and gripping romance. The characters are all unique and realistic, each with overwhelming strengths, yet flawed, as all people are. Their relatability grounds the story and makes the magical elements all the more believable, as well as creating deep attachments to them and the journeys they go on.

Overall, I was thoroughly hooked on *The Soul Keepers of Glenormiston South,* and cannot wait to read not only the sequel, *Obsidian Souls,* but the entire 'Victorian Collection'.

Amanda Maynard-Schubert ~ author, *The Bards of Birchtree Hall*

Soul Keepers of Glenormiston South is hands down one of my favourite books ever!

Right up there with Trudi Canavan and, in my opinion, even better than Sarah J. Maas.

It has been months since I've read this book and I still talk about the characters like old friends, and cannot wait to get my hands on the second book.

I was actually a little sad for days after I finished reading it that I couldn't dive back into this world that Mickey Martin has created.

The characters jump off each page as you turn them, seeming so real.

I am a highly visual person, and the whole book just played out before me like a movie.

The story is strong, the characters remain true to themselves, and the plot is fantastic.

I absolutely need to know what happens to Max. I want prequels. I want sequels.

These people became part of my own world. It is so rich in magic, but you really believe in all their powers.

It is an absolute killer of a novel.

Five Stars all the way for me.

Kelly Clark ~ *Garden Babies Fine Fairy Art/Portraits and Photography*

A rollicking adventure with an important message, this book had me hooked from the start. Just when I thought it had run out of twists and turns it took me down a new, unexpected path, fuelling my imagination and nurturing my romantic heart along the way. In *Soul Keepers of Glenormiston South,* Mickey Martin transforms a natural landscape and normal human beings alike into superheroes that do amazing things, while at the same time showing the depth of their humanity. This book is darkness and light, tragic and victorious, graphic and uncompromising in its telling. I loved the use of magical realism to show us Mother Earth and the problems she faces, as well as providing insightful solutions that are within our grasp, if we only listen.

Julia Kaylock ~ Author, poet, editor, and publisher

A must read for lovers of fantasy and romance who love and respect our planet. Mickey does drama and tension so well, making Soul Keepers a great read with memorable characters and themes. But, mostly, the overall message is relevant and so important today. We can all do more to be healing souls to our precious Mother Earth.
Danielle Hughes ~ *Four Moons Publishing*

Soul Keepers of Glenormiston South is a truly an incredible experience. This dark, paranormal romance will immerse you completely into its world. You. Will. Not. Want. To. Leave! As a local, I was thrilled to read that the Glenormiston landscape was woven so exquisitely into the life-blood of the story, and I could honestly not stop reading. Amazing latest work from Mickey Martin.
Jess Fowler ~ Artist

When the characters of a novel stay with the reader long after they've closed the book, you know the author is onto something special. Through Soul Keepers of Glenormiston South, Mickey Martin brings the landscape of the Noorat region to life and takes her readers on an epic adventure as they follow Angel, Bowie, Michael, Sam and Max on their quest to protect Mother Earth.

In a salute to her beloved hometown, Martin uses landmarks such as the Glenormiston Agricultural College, Quicks' paddock, and the Gatekeeper's Cottage to transport her readers to a world unknown. Those who know the region will look at the scenery around them for evidence of portals or the healing powers of the Elementals following the destruction caused by the Veins after reading Soul Keepers. They will feel the energy around them as they experience the change in climate and wonder if it is in fact merely a play of good versus evil. I cannot wait to see what Martin does with the next book, Obsidian Souls, featuring Maxwell Black. I look forward to another fantastic read from Martin.
Sally Taylor

Soul Keepers of Glenormiston South is set in the beautiful grounds of the Glenormiston College, Glenormiston South; a quiet farming community in the Western District of Victoria.

Martin weaves a fantasy world which is uncannily similar to our own, where the world is slowly dying and suffering at the hands of greedy humans; taking what Mother Earth provides but giving nothing back to nourish her. Martin has created a cast of intriguing characters that take us on a journey, where good battles evil, as the Soul Keepers of Glenormiston South do their all to fight the growing disease that pollutes and destroys Mother Earth: The Veins.

I loved everything about this novel and was invested in each character from Bowie Storm to Maxwell Black, and I so look forward to reading the next instalment!
Sue Croft ~ Historian

SOUL KEEPERS

OF

GLENORMISTON SOUTH

MICKEY MARTIN

MMH PRESS

Also by Mickey Martin:

The Given Trilogy:

The Given

Dark Angel

The Guardian

The Victorian Collection:

Soul Keepers of Glenormiston South *Glenormiston South 3265*

Obsidian Souls' *Noorat 3265* (COMING 2022)

Chilling Summer in Inglewood *Inglewood 3517* (COMING 2022)

Sweet Water Creek *Frankston 3199* (COMING SOON)

•

Sweet Delights – A GUMNUT PRESS ANTHOLOGY

MESSAGES from the EMBERS – BLACK QUILL PRESS

Writing as Michelle Weitering:

Thirteen and Underwater

The Power of Knowing – K P WEAVER – MMH PRESS

The Colours of Me – with Kez Wickham St George – MMH PRESS

Acknowledgements

Writing *Soul Keepers of Glenormiston South*, set in the picturesque areas of Glenormiston South, Noorat, Camperdown, and Terang, has been an absolute delight, and my way of celebrating and paying tribute to my childhood home, where my heart lies still.

Growing up in a tiny country town in the '80s and '90s had so many benefits, and gifted my twin, my cousins, my high school friends, and me with a real sense of freedom in a time where life had less stresses than the kids growing up today, who are saturated with technology, have.

To all my high school friends who helped make my childhood that much more special, and to those who have supported me with great enthusiasm in bringing this book to life, I thank you dearly. Trips back home now, without my darling Mum, are made enjoyable because of your friendships. Ashely Quick, Kylee Robertson, Brendan Clark, and Kim Krajewski. I love you all.

P.S. Ashley, thank you for answering every research question for Souls that I couldn't find the answer to on Google!

To the woman behind the scenes, who always has my back with every project I put forward - the most divine publisher, and my friend, Karen McDermott. Your support is everything, and I will never be able to thank you enough for being such a bright spark in my life. I adore you.

Heartfelt thanks to my editor, Velvet Tea. Your expert guidance and advice has been greatly appreciated, along with your unwavering support in respecting the direction I took SK. Working with you has been effortless and rewarding. Thank you.

To my proof-reader, and 'Crom Castle Cousin', Amanda Schubert. It has been an absolute delight watching you flourish as an author, Illustrator, editor, artist, candlemaker and all-round entrepreneur. Thank you for taking the time out of your very busy schedule to proofread SK. Have loved having you along for the ride.

Jess Fowler, my cover artist and fellow Glenormiston local. Working with you on this project has been an absolute delight, and I feel like the luckiest girl in the world to have met you and formed a friendship with you. Thank you for creating such a gorgeous piece of artwork that has captured the storyline so beautifully and celebrated our love for Glenormiston. Soul-sister.

To my sprint buddy, Peta Flanigan - you are partly the reason this book was completed in 39 days! I love our sprinting sessions and conversations. Thank you for all of your support. And Carolyn Wren – no matter how enormous your work load, you have always been so gracious and generous when it comes to helping me with every sized writing query. Thank you my *Darling* big sister.

To my thorough and wonderful beta readers—each and every one of you helped shape this story with your honest feedback, and I thank you for celebrating this story with me. Because of you, I know we have something pretty special within these pages.

Massive thanks to my local writers' group for all your ongoing support, and the most fabulously-creative writing days ever: Sue Croft, Kelly

Clark, Coreena Le Gallienne, Julia Kaylock, Liz Hicklin, Elise de Little, Rebecca Fraser - and ALL my fellow PWC writers.

And to all the connections I have made within the writing community across Australia, thank you for your support and friendship; it makes being in this industry one big celebration.

Kez Wickham St. George – our conversations over the past twelve months during our project together, have added highlights and laughter to days that would have otherwise been, just days without extra sparkle. Thank you. Danielle Line, Danielle Aitken, Kelly Van Nelson, Jennifer Sharp, Andrea Peterson, Sonia Bellhouse and too many other fabulous souls to mention. Thank you for adding to my diverse writing community.

To all my most fabulous readers who have reached out and expressed how much you love the stories I create for you – Thank you. Your feedback and support means the world to me.

To my absolute greatest loves, who make my soul smile every single day—my darling Jade, Jesse, Zane, Tommy, and Ireland. You make my green world sparkle and shine… xx

Finally, to all my everyday loves who adore Glenormiston as much as I—Leah Martin, Louise Manna, Sally Taylor, Nadine Mendoza, Rachael Hecker, Aunty Pamela, and Kylie Slane. Thanks for all the memories we made… xx

Forever and always—Lynette Martin… xx

Glossary of Terms

Angel Cloud – heavenly soul, and soul-sibling to Samantha Storm.
Michael Cloud – heavenly soul, and soul-sibling to Bowie Storm.

Heavenly souls have the power to heal.
Heavenly soul children are born with a protective amulet around their heart,
which gives them the power to heal the innocent without diminishing their
own life. However, when they use their gifts, they do become weakened, until
restored via Mother Earth's help, or aided by another heavenly soul, or an
elemental-soul.

Samantha Storm - elemental-soul, and Angel's protector.
Bowie Storm - elemental-soul, and protector to his soul-sibling, Michael
Cloud.

Elemental-soul children are born with the power to conjure and command
the elements. Their role in this world is to save it, and protect their Heavenly
soul-sibling. Elemental-souls have the power to protect and nurture the in-

nocent and Mother Earth, and have the sole responsibility of protecting the heavenly souls.

When Heavenly and Elemental babies are born, coinciding with one another's birth, a powerful connection is formed between their two families.

Pure-souls: Animals and Humankind. While they are mundane, with no special gifts, their presence on Earth is required for balance to flow in harmony.

Veins: Parasites in the form of humans, who grow stronger with the demise of the earth and pure-souls alike, and who have the ability to influence the pure-souls' actions. They feed off chaos, death, and destruction, and also have an insatiable appetite for the essence of heavenly souls.

Chapter One
Seven Years Ago

The grade-six students at Noorat Primary School eagerly followed their teacher, Mr. Kemp, along the narrow path on Mount Sugarloaf, in Camperdown. The excursion to explore the flora and fauna had been going smoothly, until the unexpected weather change.

Thunderclouds wrapped storm-filled arms around the sun, sending a chilly downpour onto the students below.

"Careful everyone, the path will be slippery," Mr. Kemp warned, focusing on his head count as the students made their way down the path towards the bus.

Twelve-year-old Angel Cloud was following at the back of the line when, suddenly, her stomach roiled. A feeling of dread and despair enveloped her, halting her in her tracks. She sucked in a quick breath as a burst of pain shot into the middle of her spine, increasing unpleasantly, as if her back were about to break. She had the overwhelming urge to vomit; this was the strongest pull she'd ever felt to any pure-soul needing her help. She paused for a moment, before turning to leave the path and follow the call.

1

She fought against the illness as she ran in the dark rain, almost stumbling down the steep slope of the mountain, to where she felt the energy calling her. That's when she saw the ewe, bleating miserably, its life dwindling; its back had broken after falling and landing awkwardly in a crevice of earth, where a deep tree root had once lived.

Above the ditch, two tiny lambs were bleating to their mother, whose life was waning. Angel quickly glanced over her shoulder and, seeing no one about, slid down the wet grass to reach the dying animal.

She knew that if she didn't save the ewe, the lambs would die, and her young heart couldn't bear that. Angel placed one hand gently on the suffering creature, her fingers curling into its damp wool. She placed her other hand over her heart, and whispered an incantation of healing, hoping she was strong enough to heal its broken back. She also hoped her brother, Michael, wouldn't find out about her illegally using her gift, as she was underage.

Samantha Storm was the last student to dash past Mr. Kemp, who immediately noticed her usual shadow was missing. "Where's Angel, Samantha? And where's Max?" he asked.

Sam spun around, expecting to see her soul-sibling behind her, but her heart sank when she noticed she wasn't. She frowned as an energy charge pulsated in the surrounding air. The pure-souls wouldn't have noticed it, but her soul-sibling radar was on full alert; Angel was doing something she wasn't supposed to, and Sam knew she would be in a whole world of trouble if she didn't find Angel, and find her now.

Sam held in a curse as she took off in the direction of the energy charge, praying she could reach Angel in time.

Mr. Kemp called out to their bus driver, "Mr. Kidd! Give me five minutes, please?" before racing after his young student.

Angel felt the amulet around her heart glowing, sending a pleasurable tingle all over her body as the sheep's bones snapped and popped back together. As the healing spell completed itself, a rainbow wave of energy knocked Angel backwards onto the wet grass. The ewe struggled out of the ditch before meeting Angel's eyes for the briefest of moments, then ambled off, her two hungry lambs chasing after her, waving sodden tails behind them.

Angel expelled a deep sigh before pushing herself to her feet, then began the climb back up the steep slope, slipping occasionally on the wet grass. She felt equal parts depleted and exhilarated after helping the pure-soul. When she reached the top, it surprised her to see a fellow student, Maxwell Black, standing above her, hands shoved deep in his pockets. He seemed unaffected by the rain as it pelted its icy fingers across his dark, handsome features.

"What were you doing?" he asked quietly, curiosity shining in his brooding eyes.

She stared at him, gobsmacked. It was the first time he'd spoken to her. Ever.

He'd been at the primary school all year, after being away at boarding school since the age of five. His family, of the estate Blacks in Noorat, was one of the area's most successful, and they had been known as the finest stock breeders in the southern hemisphere since 1804.

They stared at each other silently for a handful of minutes, before Samantha breathlessly screamed out, "Angel, come on, I'm getting soaked!"

Angel felt a flash of guilt as she looked up into Sam's eyes. She could see the irritation and fear on her soul-sibling's face; Sam knew what she'd done.

If Sam knows, does Michael?

"Angel, Maxwell, can you please get on the bus now?" Mr. Kemp yelled, trying to be heard above the thunder, impatience lacing his voice.

3

Angel nodded as her teeth chattered, waiting for Max to move.

Samantha's arm brushed against Max's as she held out her hand to grab Angel's. As she pulled Angel up onto the path beside her, she whispered, "What have you done?"

Angel shook her head; she didn't know what to say. It felt so good doing the right thing, helping the innocent soul. Unfortunately, she hadn't thought too much about the consequences that would follow.

"Come on, Max," Mr. Kemp said when he reached them. He ushered the drenched boy in front of him, with the girls following close behind them.

"What the hell were you thinking, Angel?" seventeen-year-old Michael Cloud yelled at his younger sister. Furious, he paced up and down the entranceway of their 19th century, double-storey homestead, where the two elder soul-siblings lived with their younger blood-siblings.

He tried to ignore the pull on his heartstrings as he stopped pacing to look down at Angel. She was sitting at the bottom of the stairs, hugging her knees, looking small and guilty. He took a deep breath, halting the string of curses he wanted to release, before turning away to resume his pacing, hoping to pace out his fear and anger.

ANGEL was smart enough to keep quiet until he got most of the anger out of his system. She also knew that his anger was masking his worry; she'd done the wrong thing, casting the healing spell. And she knew she'd put their entire family in danger…including Samantha and Bowie. She glanced across at her soul-sibling's brother, who'd already admonished Samantha before sending her to her room.

BOWIE STORM stood silently near the window, observing the exchange as he ran the sharp blade of his pocketknife through the crisp, Granny Smith apple. He placed a juicy piece into his mouth, chewing as he watched his soul-sibling become more and more frustrated. His liquid-amber eyes met Angel's baby-blues as he ran the blade through the apple's flesh once more.

He watched her eyes follow the juice of the apple as it fell to the polished floorboards, her eyes remaining on the shiny droplet as Michael fumed, "What do we do? I'm sure every Vein from here to Melbourne felt her incantation, how can we conceal her actions?" He wasn't asking—he was still venting. "She's underage, she hasn't learned how to cloak her powers...there's no doubt the impact would have been felt!" he cried, running his hands through his hair.

Bowie held in a sigh, wiping the juice from the blade across his jeans before flipping it shut and shoving it into his back pocket. Throwing the core out of the window, he looked at Michael, waiting for him to calm down; he knew him well enough to know that he was close to the point of expelling his worry.

He saw Angel cringe at Michael's words, before turning her eyes to the Prenzel-carved possum etched into the staircase. Like every panel leading upstairs, the etching of a native animal or plant told a story about the rich, Australian bush life. Was she hoping that, if she stared long enough at the little creature's wooden face, it would give her some advice on what to say to her blood-sibling? Bowie knew Angel hated causing Michael any grief.

"I'm so sorry, Michael," she whispered, her tears not yet falling.

And there it is, Bowie thought. One gentle apology from Michael's beloved Angel, and all was centred again in the universe.

Michael's bright, blue eyes met Bowie's briefly, before he sighed and knelt in front of Angel, staring for a moment, before reaching out to tug gently on one of her honey-blonde pigtails. He expelled a deep breath, then said, "Mum and Dad put me in charge of you, Angel. Samantha, Bowie, and I all have a job to do, to protect you. And none of us can do that if you don't follow the rules. Tell me you understand that?"

"I do, Michael. I do," she implored. "But no one was around. I couldn't let the mother die, I couldn't! I felt her pain, her fear for her lambs…I felt sick at the thought of leaving her when I had the power to do something."

Michael took a deep breath, as if searching for patience. "Angel, it doesn't matter if no one was around to see it, our enemy may have felt your power; your energy, even in its early stages, is extremely powerful. You know…"

"What do you mean you felt sick, Angel?" Bowie interrupted. "You felt sick at the thought of leaving the injured soul, or did you actually *feel* sick?"

Michael frowned at the question, turning his gaze towards Bowie.

Bowie knew Angel was an empathetic soul, but if she actually became physically ill when another soul needed her help, then that was a whole other ball game; a big, complex game, where they didn't know what all the rules were. It was times like this that he missed their parents being home.

Chapter Two

It was always complicated when a heavenly soul began the transition towards their powers, as the extent of their gifts were unknown. Which is why Angel using them underage was illegal; if a Vein were to be alerted to her powers, she'd be hunted down, then have her powers extracted from her in the most excruciating way. The Veins would keep her alive, so they could harvest the power from her beating heart, powered by her divine amulet, but she would suffer, and so would the pure-souls.

If she'd performed the act on the college grounds, their protection wards would have prevented her energy from being detected. But the fact that she'd used them outside their property gave Michael cause for worry; it was his role to protect her, and he'd never forgive himself if anything happened to her.

He waited with Bowie for her answer.

"I was walking back to the bus when it started, the call." She frowned at the unpleasant memory. "I felt a burning pain deep in my back. It was so intense, it frightened me for a moment, and I thought I was going to throw up." She looked up at Michael, then across at Bowie as a breath whooshed from his lungs.

"She's too young to feel all of that…" Bowie started.

Michael looked at him and shook his head once, signalling for Bowie to stop talking. She *was* too young—too young to hear the rest.

He stood. "Angel, that's all for now. Take your school bag upstairs and get out of those wet clothes. Mrs. McGoldrick will have afternoon tea ready by now."

"Please tell Samantha that she can join you," Bowie added.

Angel nodded as she stood, reaching for her school bag. She glanced at Bowie, then at Michael once more, before running up the stairs. Once she was out of sight, Bowie turned to Michael, wearing a grim expression.

"We have to contact our parents. Now."

Michael ran his fingers across his lips. "Yeah, I believe we do."

"If she has the ability to be impacted by the call of an injured soul in the physical sense, her powers will be off the chart."

"If the Veins get their hands on her, they could extract her essence and wield it in the worst kind of way. Her power in the wrong hands…?" Michael shuddered.

"The world would be in chaos," Bowie said, before heading down the wide corridor towards the study, which was rarely used by the professors at the college after-hours.

Most of the staff and students who taught or studied at the college were pure-souls, with no idea that the world of royal-souls existed. They blended in with each other as they thrived in a community that was collectively working towards reducing humanity's impact on the natural world. Their goal: making sure the world had a future.

Humanity needed these lessons now, more than ever; messages of healing needed to be spread far and wide, as technology and humanity had wreaked havoc on Mother Earth. It was time to begin the healing, not just for the sake of nature, but, since nature kept Earth stable, for the sake of all; it was time to rewind the damage, and re-wild the wild.

The pure-soul teachers taught with passion, under the guidance and instruction of the royal-soul professors, before they headed out of the college gates at the end of the day. Then they went back to their mundane lives, oblivious to how much work went on behind the scenes at what appeared to be a simple agricultural college. The pure-soul students slept on campus, absorbing so much more than what was spelled out in the college's brochure.

Tom Liam, an elemental-soul, stood gazing out of a window framed with one-hundred-year-old ivy, which overlooked sweeping gardens. He turned as the two younger men walked in. Tall and often broody-looking, Tom took his role at the college seriously. He, along with his soul-sibling, Jess Callum, were in charge of this young family whilst their real parents were off doing their part to heal the world.

Tom raised a dark eyebrow when he noticed the look on the younger men's faces.

"You've a right to be concerned," he said in greeting. "Where's Angel?"

"I sent her off to get afternoon tea." Michael crossed over to the six-foot-wide desk, where a glass globe of the world sat in the middle, three feet in circumference.

"Probably for the best, for now." Tom folded his arms, nodding to the globe. "I felt a shift in the energy."

Bowie nodded, "Yeah, so did we. We need to get our parents back."

"It's too late for that." Jess Callum strode purposefully into the room, his long locks tied back at the nape of his neck, revealing a trustworthy face, with solemn, dark-blue eyes filled with remorse. "I've just left the Gatekeeper's cottage. Red has called for the Light Accords' High Council to meet at midnight tonight."

"Why 'too late'?" Bowie mirrored Tom's stance, watching Jess closely.

"You will see," Jess said as he reached out and touched a location on the surface of glass. The globe spun, stopping after only one rotation. All the continents slid into the centre of the globe before vanishing; a clear picture presented itself inside.

Bowie exchanged a look with Michael, before stepping closer to see both of their parents, along with other Soul Keepers, struggling to maintain balance in a country to the north. Chaos seemed to reign of its own volition, without too much persuasion from the Veins. Yet the destruction was on such a scale of misery, the Veins were sure to be involved.

Riots in the streets…massacres…street gangs who were out of control…substance abuse and addiction ruining lives…a plague wiping out innocent, young pure-souls…the list was endless.

Jess tapped the globe again to reveal a disastrous wildfire eating up an entire state. Bowie frowned in concern, seeing the lines of exhaustion etched into his father's face as he conjured torrential rain to battle the wicked flames engulfing everything in its path. His mother, trying to heal those who'd fallen victim to the flames…

Jess tapped it a second time, and Michael, too, could see the strain on his mum's face as she posed as a volunteer nurse at a hospital. She placed her healing hands on the ailing young souls, who'd been purposely inflicted with the man-made virus conjured by the Veins.

Jess tapped for a third time, revealing Michael's father, kneeling on drought-stricken earth where pure-souls, both human and animal, were dying of thirst and starvation. Hands buried in the dry soil, he poured energy deep into its crust to form a layer of moisture. His spell allowed nature to grow through the soil and hold water in its cracked water beds. These images, and more of the other Soul Keepers, showed they were doing what they were designed to do—to heal a world where the Veins' poisonous ways corrupted the pure-souls into performing their wicked chores, enabling them to grow stronger.

"Why are my parents separated?" Michael asked, feeling uneasy as his pulse raced.

When an elemental- and heavenly soul were joined as soul-partners, they were to never be separated while they performed their Soul Keeper duties. This ensured their safety, as they protected one another, and were stronger together as a team.

Jess looked across at Tom, who nodded, knowing it was his turn to share some information that would be difficult for the younger men to hear.

"That country is out of control, and the Veins have been feasting on the negative energy, growing stronger; they are thriving there, unlike any other place on Earth. The destruction is so great, Michael, that your parents thought they could do more healing if they separated for a short time." He reached across and spun the globe at breakneck speed, before it suddenly stopped of its own accord and filled with blood, along with an image of Michael's mother and father.

Michael sucked in a shocked breath as his parent's eyes smiled into his. "What is this?" he whispered.

"Unfortunately, the Veins detected that your parents were separated whilst performing their duties. As they were unprotected, and focused solely on their task, they were easy prey. I'm so sorry to have to tell you this, Michael…but your parents are dead."

The room fell silent as Michael stared into his parents' bright, blue eyes, suspended in the ball of blood. He reached out to stroke their beloved faces, only to have them disappear as his fingers brushed against the glass surface. The world map reappeared across the globe.

Michael felt numb, fighting the overwhelming emotions that were rising to the surface, until a sob gushed from deep within his chest. Feeling a hand on his shoulder, he turned and met Bowie's eyes, filled with sadness and regret. The boys stared at each other in pained silence, as fat tears fell from Michael's eyes.

"How am I going to tell Angel?" His voice broke, before he cleared his throat.

"I suggest you don't for a while, Michael," Tom said. "There's no point at the moment, they've been away for two years; she's been doing fine with all of our support."

"I disagree." Bowie shook his head. "She needs to be told. She's mature enough to hear it, and young enough to heal."

Michael took a deep breath, drying his eyes on his t-shirt. "She needs to be told. It might also help her obey our rules; knowing our parents were killed for not following them, it may encourage her to think before she acts." A note of bitterness hung in the air as all eyes rested on Michael's grieving face.

Jess nodded. "That's a great way to look at it, Michael. If you need our support in any way, you know where to find us, okay?"

"Sure, Jess, thanks. Are we required to attend the Council meeting tonight?"

"Yes. As you are both Angel's protectors and handlers, you will be given instructions on her training from here on out, as we trained you."

"Training already?" Bowie raised an eyebrow. "She's too young."

Tom shook his head. "It's time. You'll receive instructions from Fletch tonight."

Bowie and Michael shared a slightly-terrified glance; Fletch was a High Council member from Warrnambool, and he unsettled them both with his dark looks and quiet, all-seeing eyes. Even when they hadn't done anything wrong, Fletch made them feel as though they had. Bowie shuddered as Jess told them what time to be at the Gate-keeper's cottage.

"See you then."

Michael and Bowie nodded as Tom and Jess walked out of the study and off towards their overseers' cottage, which was a three-minute walk down the road.

Once they were alone, Bowie turned to Michael. "I'm so sorry, mate. What a mess."

Michael ran his hands over his face before meeting Bowie's sympathetic gaze. He shook his head, sighing, as he wandered across to the window.

He leaned against it, stared at nothing for a few minutes, then said, "We are born into roles we aren't just *expected* to perform, we must have a burning desire to perform *only* that role; to heal and restore, with the utmost respect for each other and our rules." He turned to his soul-sibling. "Why did they separate? Why leave themselves unprotected?"

"I wish I knew." Bowie could hear the frustration in his friend's voice and felt for him. Twice in one day, Michael had shouldered a burden that only one in their circle could understand; firstly, his sister had performed an illegal healing spell, and, now, his parents were dead at the hands of their mortal enemy.

Was it only this morning they were at school, flirting with the Kavanagh twins, Elizabeth and Patricia? Michael had been dating the pretty, dark-haired Elizabeth for fifteen months now. Her blonde, vibrant, outgoing sister, Patricia was Bowie's good friend, despite both Michael and Elizabeth wishing they would form a romantic connection.

"When are you going to tell Angel?" Bowie asked.

"I'll let her have her afternoon tea and feed the ponies first." He dropped his head back to stare at the ceiling for a moment before saying, "I'm going to ring Beth."

Bowie nodded. "Are you okay?"

Michael looked at Bowie as he walked towards the door. "I will be." He headed to his room, hoping Beth would be home, and wishing, not for the first time, she wasn't a pure-soul. Then he could unburden himself of the fear he had regarding his sister, and the truth about how his parents died. Instead, he'd have to make up a story, like they'd perished in a car accident overseas or something. He sighed loudly as he closed his bedroom door behind him, feeling a hundred years older than his actual seventeen.

Angel dried off before dressing in her warm clothes, feeling a little guilty for not mentioning that Max may have seen her rainbow wave of energy…but he was just another harmless kid from her class. Taking a deep breath, she headed off to Sam's room to beg her forgiveness. She waited outside her soul-sibling's door for a moment, before raising her hand to knock.

"Come in," Sam called.

Angel pushed the door open and hesitantly stepped inside, wondering how cross her soul-sibling was with her.

Sam was lying on the floor, sketching, before looking up. Seeing Angel, she dropped the pencil, rolled over, and sat up.

"So, I hope you know I'm expecting you to do my chores for the rest of the week after your performance today?"

Angel leaned against the doorjamb and nodded. "Of course. Anything you want, Sam."

"Mm, *anything*?" Her eyes gleamed mischievously.

Angel nodded, smiling.

"You do know Bowie chewed me out good and proper, don't you?"

Angel nodded again, before saying, "I really am sorry, Sam."

Sam pushed herself to her feet and sat on the end of the bed, tucking a long, blonde strand behind her ear. After a quiet moment, she asked, "Was the pull really that powerful that you couldn't ignore it?"

Angel considered the question. "I don't know," she said, her voice quiet. "I just couldn't ignore the pure-soul's agony, her pain completely overtook me." She shrugged.

Sam nodded, getting up from the bed as her tummy rumbled. "I get it. But, seriously, Angel, you put both of us in danger. You can't do that again; not until you're allowed, okay? Promise me. Because if I have to listen to Bowie yell at me one more time, I'll be the one performing the illegal act because I will zap him with a lightning bolt!"

"I promise," Angel laughed, seeing the spark return to Sam's eyes at the idea of performing a punishing act on her blood-sibling.

"I'm starving after our day of hiking and getting drenched, but he said I have to stay in here."

"No, he sent me to get you, so we could go see Mrs. McGoldrick for afternoon tea before chores."

"Oh, yes!" Sam fist punched the air. "I could smell those Anzac biscuits baking the moment we got home. Let's go."

She grabbed Angel's hand and they ran downstairs to dip the golden treats into warm mugs of milk. After that, they'd do their chores of feeding the ponies and picking berries for the school fete's muffin bake the following week.

Chapter Three

The small Gatekeeper's cottage sat at the corner of Trufood and Blacks Road. There was nothing extraordinary about it at all, with its cream-coloured cement weatherboards and its slightly-charming-yet-plain exterior. Its picturesque gardens gave shelter to the petite Jenny Wrens and finches.

It sat, with nine other houses, along the isolated country road situated at the back entrance of the Glenormiston Agricultural College, and overlooked views of the Quick family's land and Mount Noorat.

One of Quicks' paddocks had cattle grazing, in a field as green as a shamrock. Five English oaks stood in the centre, whispering secrets only the mindful could hear. But what the pure-souls could *not* see was the portal of electric-blue wild wind dancing at its centre; a portal ready to whisk any royal-soul away at a moment's notice, to any location in the world where their gifts were needed to heal Mother Earth and save any pure-soul in danger.

Past Quicks' paddock was the old Glenormiston store. It provided a Wednesday morning, and a Sunday afternoon, High Tea, but otherwise sat dormant throughout the week. Mount Noorat stood to the south, guarding all it overlooked. The old Trufood factory, which had operated as a butter factory in 1934, now housed the most elite breeds of horses, as a front for the pure-souls. For the royal-souls, though, it was a lookout for signs of trouble in the shire.

The Light Accords' Council meeting of Soul Keepers from around the Western District and beyond was as formidable as Bowie and Michael had imagined. They arrived on time, then walked down the Gatekeeper's pot-holed driveway, past a lemon tree in desperate need of a prune. Sitting under the rose bushes, the tiny snout of a red fox appeared.

"Hey, Alana," Michael called, patting his leg for the shy animal to come forward. She was a rescue fox that Red cared for, along with other wounded, abused animals.

The fox stared, blinking her eyes before tucking her head back under her bushy tail. Her reluctance to greet them was a sign of what was to come.

Bowie pushed the Indian-red picket gate open, then knocked once on the back door. As his hand lowered, the sliding glass door immediately opened, revealing the sweet, friendly face of Red.

"Hello, boys. Come in."

"Thank you, Red," they chorused, as they followed the tiny lady with bright auburn hair into her small backroom. During the day, her large windows revealed views of a gardener's paradise; Glenormiston South was lush and rich, thanks to the weather, and travellers often compared the green, moist land to the likes of Ireland.

The boys stood on the brown, square carpet tiles, which should have been removed back in the '80s, and looked at the frosted, orange glass door that led to the inside of the house. They could hear a chorus of deep voices from behind it. The small grandfather clock, which sat above Red's organ, was ticking down the seconds until they were expected to go in, making them nervous.

"Bring them in, Red."

Fletch's voice automatically made Michael jump, causing Bowie to chuckle quietly as he slapped his friend on the back.

Michael shook his head and attempted a grin, which looked more like a grimace.

Red smiled softly and pushed her little framed glasses up onto her nose. "It will be all right, boys; I'll be waiting here for you when you're done." She nodded once, before sliding the frosted door open for the boys to step into the room beyond.

They had been in the Gatekeeper's house before, for a spot of tea and a friendly chat, and twice for a Council meeting. The inside of the house was open-plan, basic and cosy…except when there was a Soul Keeper Council meeting. The air held such power, and the quaint lounge room, with kitchen opposite, transformed into a cavernous hall filled with Soul Keepers dressed in dark-amethyst capes. Fifteen elemental-souls lined one side of the hall and, opposite them, fifteen heavenly souls; all were wearing worrisome expressions.

Fletch stood at the opposite end of the hall, adorned in a black suit, his dark eyes pinning the boys in place.

"It appears we have a situation," he began. "Angel Cloud has illegally performed an underage healing act, which has caused a wave of energy to be felt as far away as Melbourne. This is unacceptable." He stared unblinkingly at the boys for a handful of moments, as if they were solely to blame for this crime, before motioning to a Council member. "Phillip?"

Phillip cleared his throat before addressing the hall. "The energy has been flowing smoothly the past month, with no incidences occurring during our patrols, until the moment Angel cast the healing spell. We felt a major shift in energy and saw the rainbow." He nodded towards the three Soul Keeper members who worked in the city of Melbourne and outer suburbs with him. They all nodded towards Fletch.

"If the Vein seekers saw it, or felt it, they could be trying to locate her even as we speak."

"The surge didn't extend further than Melbourne," a Sydney member confirmed.

"Yeah, the wave stopped just out of Warrnambool, too," Justin Scot said, folding his arms.

Fletch nodded as the Soul Keepers from around Australia reassured him that they hadn't detected Angel's surge.

"What do we do now?" Vanessa Light asked, her voice filled with concern. "How do we protect Angel?"

Fletch turned to Bowie and Michael. "It is time to begin Angel's training."

"She's too young!" Michael burst out in fear for his blood-sibling.

"That may be so, but if the wounded energy from a pure-soul in need calls to her, causing her to become debilitated, we have no choice; she needs to be taught how to cloak herself, to shield her gifts."

"Who'll be training her?" Bowie folded his arms, frowning.

"You will be," Fletch said. "No kid gloves."

Bowie sent Michael a sidelong glance; it was against their nature to train as Fletch was implying. But he was the head Soul Keeper of their district, and their elder, who must be obeyed.

"Seriously?" Bowie asked, not meaning any disrespect.

"Deadly," Fletch said. "No pun intended."

The air in the hall vibrated with an uncomfortable silence.

"Samantha's training will also begin immediately. That will be all. May you keep the souls safe." Fletch waved his hand and every Soul Keeper in the hall bowed towards the boys, bidding them goodnight.

Michael and Bowie returned a deep bow, replying, "With every breath that we take," before retreating from the hall. Stepping through Red's little sliding door, they walked into her small backroom to find her sitting at her organ, playing an old tune called 'Danny Boy'. Alana lay curled by her feet.

Hearing the boys enter, she turned towards them, then rose from her seat to open the back door. Alana hurriedly got up to slink out the back door and head down to Red's potting shed. "Goodnight, boys."

"Goodnight, Red," they chorused.

As Michael walked by Red, she placed her small hand on his arm and said, "I'm so sorry about your mum and dad, love. If you or Angel need to talk, I'm always here." She smiled kindly.

Michael bent and wrapped his arms around her petite frame, kissing her soft cheek, catching her comforting scent of 'Oil of Olay', and Chanel perfume. "Thank you, Red." He smiled into her tired blue eyes before following Bowie out of the driveway, across the cattle grid, and onto the college grounds.

They walked in silence, both filled with apprehension regarding the girls' training.

"We can't start Angel's training until after I tell her about our parents," Michael said, his voice quiet.

"Agreed."

"None of this is going to be easy."

"It's going to be brutal," Bowie blurted out.

"Yeah, I know." Michael sighed.

"She's going to hate me!"

"Yeah, she will."

"Bloody hell, this sucks a bucket-load of hairy dogs' balls!"

"Agreed."

"Shit, Michael!" Bowie was beyond frustrated, knowing what training meant for a young heavenly soul. It wasn't pretty. And for a sensitive heart like Angel's, she would end up hating him. He almost wanted to cry.

He felt Michael's hand on his shoulder as they walked by the old, blue-stone stables. A relaxing energy swept through him as Michael gifted him with a calming spell.

"I'm okay, thanks." Bowie said. He hoped they would all be okay once Angel's training began.

Angel had been inconsolable after learning of her parents' deaths and did not speak a single word for a fortnight. Towards the end of the third week, Mrs. McGoldrick had packed her up, under Michael's instruction, and taken her to the Gatekeeper's for some therapeutic baking. She'd found the motion of punching dough and forming loaves of bread calming.

After several days in the company of the two elderly ladies, she had experienced the first flickering of happiness since she'd heard the tragic news. After baking, chatting, and some more crying, she would lay out on the grass under the sun's gentle rays, with Alana by her side. Everyone was relieved to see her return home lighter in heart and soul.

"Do you want to come over tonight?" Elizabeth held Michael's hand as she walked him to his bus. She smiled prettily up at him as he bent to drop a kiss against her cheek.

"Yeah, let's do a movie marathon." Patricia nudged Bowie's shoulder as they walked behind the others.

"No can-do, girls. Sorry, we've got family from out-of-town visiting," Bowie lied smoothly, thinking about Angel's training, which would begin that afternoon.

"You are coming to the footy on Sunday though?" Elizabeth looked over her shoulder at Bowie, frowning. "It's going to be the game of the season, us against Mortlake."

Michael dropped a second kiss, on her lips this time, before stepping up into the bus.

"I'll call you, Beth, okay?" He flashed a bright smile in her direction.

She looked up at him, and the irritation she'd been feeling at not seeing him tonight suddenly dissipated. A calm, joyful feeling filled her instead. "Okay," she sang brightly before grabbing her sister's hand. "Come on, 'tricia."

"See you!" Patricia winked at Bowie before her sister dragged her off.

Bowie chuckled as he sat behind Michael on the bus. "Nice one. Contentment spell?"

Michael sighed, dropping his head against the chair, and closing his eyes. "Yep."

"Keep it up—you may need to use it on Angel, later."

"Don't I know it," Michael whispered.

Their fellow Terang College students filled the bus, pleased it was Friday afternoon, with the whole weekend ahead of them.

Chapter Four

Angel and Sam finished their chores for the afternoon, then headed to the haystack to check out the month-old litter of kittens Mr. Duncomb had told them about.

"Hello, girls!" Mr. Duncomb's daughter, Rhiannon, a pure-soul, sang out as she headed off for the afternoon.

"Hi!" they called as a busload of college students drove by, heading out for the weekend.

"Did you see the way Max kicked that goal from behind the line at recess?" Sam gushed as they walked by the gardening centre, bustling with the afternoon crew of pure-souls.

Angel smiled at Sam's adoring tone, trying to ignore an uncomfortable burning sensation building in her throat. She swallowed as a dizzying red haze flashed across her eyes, as Sam continued chatting happily about how cute Max was before yelling, "I'll race you!" then sprinted the rest of the way to the twenty-foot-high haystack.

Angel tried not to panic as she struggled to breathe; a gross sensation of thick, sticky fingers with sharp nails clawed up her throat. She gagged as she hastened, on shaky legs, towards the pull of energy coming from the haystack, before Sam's blood-curdling scream froze her heart momentarily.

She ran around the corner, not believing the scene before her, her throat on fire.

Samantha was screaming at Bowie to stop what he was doing; tears poured down her face as she struggled to escape Michael's tight embrace. Desperately, she tried to reach Bowie as he stood, still as a statue, with his hand around the tiny bundle of fur, which was meowing pitifully for its life.

His eyes met Angel's.

"Bowie!" she screamed. *"STOP IT RIGHT NOW!"* Tears fell from her eyes, which were wide with terror and astonishment. She watched in horror as the tiny kitten stopped struggling…stopped breathing…

She felt a flood of mixed emotions before she flew towards Bowie and punched him as hard as she could in the stomach, crying in rage.

He was shocked for a split second.

"I'm going to *KILL* you, Bowie!" Samantha screamed.

To Bowie's horror, Sam placed her hands on Michael's arms, still bound tightly around her waist, and sent an underage, illegal bolt of lightning straight into him.

"*Samantha*!" Bowie yelled, dropping the kitten at Angel's feet as he rushed forward.

Michael dropped Sam, looking stunned, as he staggard backwards, trying to remain upright.

Angel fell to the ground, scooping up the lifeless body, and closed her eyes. She took a deep breath, then poured all her positive energy into the tiny kitten. As she whispered frantically, she wished away the unfamiliar hate and fury that she felt growing towards Bowie.

As Bowie reached Michael, a rainbow wave of energy knocked them all backwards, before lighting up the sky as Angel gifted the kitten with life.

What happened next surprised them all.

An unknown force lifted them off the ground, suspending them in mid-air. Angel dropped the kitten, which fell onto the soft hay before trotting happily off towards its mother, who was sleeping soundly with her other kittens. Michael had induced their sleep, so as to not disturb them, when he and Bowie had started their first lesson.

How had it gone so horribly wrong, so quickly? The aim of this lesson had been to help Angel fight the sickness, resist the urge to heal, and practise self-control; Michael would have healed the kitten once the lesson was over. Yet, now, they found themselves trapped in a force field.

"Who the hell is doing this?" Bowie frowned at Michael, who shook his head.

Moments later, they found out.

Fletch stepped from behind the hay shed, calmly inspecting his nails as he approached them. He dropped his hand, and they were all lowered to the ground. He looked at the girls, feeling a little sorry for them as tears ran down their unhappy faces.

"Silence, and listen," he began. "Firstly," he nodded to Bowie, "good job with the concealing barrier you placed around the area, it was strong enough that I barely felt Angel's energy wave at all, even from close-by."

Bowie nodded his thanks, feeling slightly proud, yet concerned, that Fletch had felt the need to spy on Angel's first lesson.

Fletch turned to the girls. "You," he said to Samantha, "have just broken a rule by performing an illegal act. Not just because you are underage, but because you know you are *never* to shock a heavenly soul. Ever." He stared at her silently, watching the anger dance behind her eyes as the tears dried on her face; she would make an extraordinarily-strong elemental-soul, no doubt.

"And you," he said, turning his dark eyes towards Angel, "should know better. Your parents died because they did not follow the rules. Do you want the Veins to find you? Or your family, here? Do you understand what they would do to you, if they found you?"

Angel returned his stare, not really understanding yet what a Vein could do to her. She briskly wiped the back of her hand across her eyes, glaring. Bowie and Michael were silently hoping she'd remain respectively quiet...

She disappointed them.

"If this was supposed to be a lesson for me not to use my gifts, it wasn't a good one, was it?"

"Angel!" Michael gasped, before Fletch held up his hand.

"No, it's all right. The point is, young lady, that it is all about controlling your emotions. Grief, anger, helplessness. You must refrain from using your gifts, no matter what. You need to build a resistance to the sickness that consumes you, until you can learn to shield your powers. Surely you knew, deep down, that your blood-sibling and his soul-sibling would not allow the pure-soul to be permanently terminated?" He waited.

Angel glared first at Bowie, then at Michael, before nodding. She was glad that Sam had zapped Michael, only wishing that she had the ability to do the same to Bowie.

"Right, girls, know that, from here on out, Michael and Bowie have the High Council's full support in instructing you in your lessons. You will do *exactly* as they instruct you, and you will trust the process. Is that understood?"

Angel and Sam exchanged a look, knowing they didn't really have any choice but to agree.

"Angel, once you have learned to absorb the sickness, then you will learn the power to shield, and to heal. Make sense?"

Angel nodded once more.

"Good. Off you go, so I can speak to your brothers."

Angel grabbed Sam's hand and they ran off towards the homestead, both resenting that their pleasant afternoon with the kittens had been stolen from them.

Fletch looked at the boys, understanding their peeved expressions. "I needed the girls to hear that, no matter the lessons you choose, they are to submit to you during this process. I didn't mean to undermine you in any way." He shook his head. "I think it would be a good idea to create a Vein vision for Angel, so she can understand the importance of why fighting the urge to use her gifts is so vital."

Michael shook his head. "With all due respect, Fletch, she's only twelve."

Bowie quietly agreed; that would be too cruel.

"As were you both. Just do it, you may see an improvement in her attitude. Tom and Jess will keep me appraised. May you keep the souls safe."

"With every breath that we take," the boys replied.

Fletch bowed before heading toward Quicks' paddock and the portal, which would take him back to Warrnambool in a flash.

"Well, that all sucked as much as I thought it would." Bowie kicked a stone and sent it flying.

"Yep," Michael agreed. "Now I know how much it all sucked for Jess and Tom, teaching us back in the day."

Bowie shook his head. "It feels like a lifetime ago, not five years."

"Mm. Well, time to go see if the girls can get over a grudge faster than we did."

"Ha. Good one," Bowie said darkly, not looking forward to seeing the furious looks on either of the girls' faces.

Dinner was a quiet affair, with both Samantha and Angel shooting the boys dirty looks throughout the meal. Mrs. McGoldrick tried to fill the dark atmosphere with bright chatter about her son, Sean, who was coming to visit her from Scotland, as she dished up shepherd's pie, followed by a chocolate pudding with cream.

"Well, my loves," she sang in a chirpy voice, "I'll be off for the weekend. I'll see you bright and early before school Monday." She dropped a kiss on the top of the girls' heads before giving the boys a hug as they stood to clear the table, which they did every night after the meal.

"Thanks, Mrs. McGoldrick." Bowie dropped a kiss on her cheek as she gathered up her bag and car keys. "Have a great time with your son."

"Oh, I shall indeed. Bye, girls."

"Bye, Mrs. McGoldrick." The girls waved as they headed towards the stairs and up to their separate rooms.

As Michael filled the sink with water, Bowie jumped up to sit on the butcher's block, snatching up a pear and slicing it in half with his pocketknife. The kitchen filled with the noises of dishes being washed and the crunching of pear, both boys deep in their own thoughts.

"Are you doing it tonight?" Michael asked Bowie, referring to the Vein vision.

"I don't want to."

"I don't think you have a choice."

"Clearly." Bowie threw the core into the corner bin, the top swivelling around for a few beats, flipping back and forth, before coming to a standstill.

"I'll make sure Sam's sleep is influenced, so she won't wake with the screaming."

"No need, I'll cast a silence barrier around Angel's room."

"Good idea." Michael pulled out the plug before wiping his hands on a tea towel, then flung it over the dishes left to drip-dry.

"Could it have been this stressful for Tom and Jess?" Bowie wondered, sliding off the butcher's block to follow Michael out of the kitchen and up the stairs.

"We'll have to ask them." Michael placed his hand on his doorknob as

Bowie walked past. "I'll be here if you need me. Good luck." He pushed his door open, feeling bad that Bowie had an unpleasant task ahead of him.

Bowie saluted as he continued down to the end of the hallway to bide his time before inflicting yet another horror on poor little Angel.

Angel woke at three-a.m., needing to go to the toilet. She shoved her feet into her fluffy pink slippers before heading down to the end of the hallway.

With the door shutting behind her, she sat on the seat and closed her eyes, feeling like she could fall asleep right where she was sitting. A scraping sound on the floorboards, followed by a wet, slapping sound, made her eyes pop open. Her hand, halfway to the toilet roll, froze, as did her next breath.

All was silent. She sighed, finished in the toilet, and washed her hands, before heading back to her bedroom. Halfway down the hallway, she froze, hearing the disturbing sound again, the hairs on her arms standing to attention. She spun around, blinking in the darkened hall-way, heart racing as she imagined a figure behind her. But no—it was just the tree branches, dancing in the wind, the moon casting shadowy arms around her.

"Silly," she whispered, relieved. But, as she walked away, so, too, did the shadowy branches, stepping right off the wall and towards her, reaching for her with long, sharp, bony fingers.

She stumbled back. A scream caught in her throat before she bolted to her bedroom. She slammed the door shut behind her, only for it to burst back open, as though a wind gust from hell had opened it.

This time, she screamed, as it threw her backwards. She fell onto the ground, pinned down by an invisible force, unable to move.

The figure of branches started to snap and pop in jerky movements as it moved towards her, forming into the shape of a spider the size of a horse. A torn cape, drenched in blood, hung over its twiggy form, making the wet, slapping sound against the floorboards as it dragged behind.

It terrified Angel to the point that she couldn't find her voice, could barely breathe, as the enormous stick-like-spider loomed above her. Its razor-like-twigs suddenly lurched forward, slicing her wrists open, before several long, tentacle-like veins pierced her flesh and began sucking her soul-essence from her. The pain was excruciating. But it was the tiny, leering porcelain doll's face, with hollow eyes protruding from its stick form, inching closer to her face that truly terrified her as it grinned macabrely.

The scream bursting out of her shocked even her own ears; it rang with absolute power because of her terror. In a flash, the Vein vision disappeared.

Angel sat up, breathing heavily, before sobs of fright escaped her as she scurried towards her bed, slapping on the lamp and diving under the covers. She pulled them over her head and cried into her pillow, wondering what had happened. Her arms were aching, yet not bleeding.

A knock at the door had her frozen with fear. She didn't move an inch, didn't take another breath. She jumped in fright as arms wrapped around her bundled body and she heard Bowie say, "Hey kiddo, bad dream?"

She cried noisily, then, grateful for his comforting arms as the vision played behind her eyelids. In that moment, she even forgave him for what he'd done to the kitten earlier.

Bowie felt her nod as he rubbed the bump that was her back. Riddled with guilt, he cursed Fletch, and the role into which he was born. He felt tired already, and they hadn't even truly begun the valuable lessons Angel needed for her protection. To say he wasn't looking forward to any of what was to come would be an understatement.

"Go to sleep," he whispered, his tone kind, in a desperate bid to ease the guilt consuming him.

Chapter Five

"Okay, Sam, here's the deal: I'm going to send a wave of tiny darts toward you, and I need you to visualise a shield protecting you, evaporating the darts once they hit that shield. Can you try that?"

"Sure," Samantha shrugged. "Sounds too easy."

Michael and Bowie exchanged a look, hiding their smiles, as Michael took a deep breath, preparing to send a small wave of invisible mind-darts towards her.

Angel was sitting at the desk, watching as Michael instructed Sam. It was the morning after her nightmare, and she was feeling washed-out and grumpy.

"Here we go," Michael said as he sent the first wave.

An enraged squeal burst from Sam as she threw up her hands, trying to physically stop the assault of Michael's darts pricking her flesh.

"Angels above!" she screamed, causing Bowie to laugh his head off.

He'd experienced that exact feeling when Tom had assaulted him with this method years ago.

Samantha spun around, glaring at Bowie, before screaming again as the darts pierced her back.

"Focus, Samantha!" Michael yelled. "If this were a fire, or a tsunami, would you allow yourself to become distracted, putting yourself and the pure-souls in danger? Concentrate."

Sam sent a dark scowl towards Michael, who'd halted the onslaught of piercing darts. They stared at each other for a moment, before Sam nodded.

"I just wasn't ready."

"I get it. Now, get ready. Again."

They continued for another hour, unsuccessfully, before Michael whispered encouragingly, "You can do this, Samantha."

Sam took a deep breath and closed her eyes, imagining a thick silver cloud drifting around her, protecting her.

Michael sent another wave, feeling her nerves as a couple of darts eased their way through her shield, pricking her skin. She gasped in pain, but remained focused on holding the silver cloud about her, and, within minutes, there was no more pain.

She opened her eyes and saw, by the look on Michael's face, that he was still sending the darts toward her. She beamed across at him, impressed with herself. "I'm blocking you."

He grinned back at her. "Well done, lower your shield."

Sam sighed, relieved that it was over. "I feel so tired."

"Of course, it takes a lot of energy and concentration to be able to do what we do. These are just baby steps, Sam, but a good start."

"If I just used my power, won't it be detected?"

"No. Remember, the college grounds have protective wards around the perimeters. But, as we train you over time, we will teach you how to conjure a protective barrier to prevent the Veins from feeling you out. Until then, we will continue shielding your gifts when we are off the property." Bowie said, sliding off the window seat. "Right, Angel, your turn."

Angel met Bowie's gaze. "I'm not feeling well."

"I'm sorry, kiddo, but too bad; we've got a job to do, no matter how we are feeling." He slowly rubbed his palms together...

"It sorta sucks though, doesn't it?" Sam looked at her blood-sibling. "How can Angel fight whatever it is you're going to do to her if she feels sick before you've even started?"

"You're just tired, right, Angel?" Michael asked, slightly concerned about his blood-sibling.

Angel shrugged. "I guess."

"Okay, Angel." Bowie pulled his pocketknife out of his back pocket and flipped open the sharp blade. "First lesson: I'm going to bleed, and you're going to feel it. Remember, I'm going to be fine, Michael can heal me. Okay?"

Angel looked from Michael to Bowie, then nodded.

"Focus on your breathing, the energy that each breath pulls towards your heart. Feel your amulet as it seeks to protect you from harm, from pain. You can do this, Angel. Ready?" Bowie asked.

She nodded, hoping she was.

Bowie took a quick breath, anticipating the pain that would follow, before slamming the blade into his thigh.

Two things happened simultaneously.

Bowie dropped to his knees, the pain almost blinding him. He went stark white as he gritted his teeth, trying not to make an anguished sound, knowing what that would do to Angel. As he dropped, so did she; being so close to the initial impact of a soul needing her help overwhelmed her senses. Her thigh was throbbing in a punishing dance, along with the pain in her head as her blood pumped like acid in her veins. She cried out, grabbing her temples as the sickness in her belly grew and spread.

"Concentrate on your breathing, Angel," Michael encouraged in a soothing tone, kneeling beside her on the carpet as she curled into the foetal position, crying.

"Come on, Angel!" Sam cried. "You can do this!"

Angel tried to ignore the pain emitting from Bowie; she could feel the lifeblood flowing from his femoral artery, hear his breathing becoming shallow as his organs tried to preserve the loss of blood. Angel squeezed her eyes shut, and could feel the flesh of his wound, his nerves, sliced open and raw. She envisioned stroking along the edge of the wound, sealing it with her fingertips, healing him. She whispered a loving incantation of wellness for Bowie's body. The pain within her eased, the sickness creeping away as a tiny rainbow glowed around her.

"Stop it, Angel!" Bowie cried, his voice wavering. "Focus on *your* body."

Her suggestion of wellness had begun healing his wound without her touching him physically. Angel gasped as her healing spell snapped back, and she was once again filled with pain.

"Stop it! Stop it *right now*! I can't do this!" she cried desperately.

Michael rushed over to Bowie and lay a hand on his leg, placing his other hand over his own heart as he hurriedly whispered a healing incantation. Within moments, a wave of energy washed over them all as the pain dissipated and quiet resumed. Bowie clapped Michael on the back in thanks as he pushed himself to his feet, before walking over and holding a hand down to Angel, who was uncurling herself.

"Come on, up you get."

She took his hand and let him pull her to her feet. He placed a hand gently on the top of her head and ruffled her hair. "Good start, kiddo."

She looked up at him, frowning. "Why do we come into our powers so early if we're not supposed to use them? Why can't you just put a spell on me, so I don't feel anything or do anything I'm not supposed to do?"

"Wouldn't that be cool, hey, if it worked that way? You were born into power, Angel, for an exceptionally good reason. You are one part of a lock and key, and, one day, you will gift wellness to the world. When you are joined with your equal, together you will create unimaginable power that will heal the pain in this world, both physical and mental, and keep the pure-souls safe."

"But why do I have these gifts now, if I'm not supposed to use them?"

"Because you finding the strength to block a pure-soul's pain now is what can save all in the long run. The Veins are everywhere, Angel, undetected by us, which is why we must never disclose what, and who, we are to the pure-souls; because we will never know if they are one of them until it is too late. You both understand that, don't you?"

The girls nodded.

"Does Mrs. McGoldrick know?" Sam asked.

"No," Bowie answered shortly.

"So, me using my gifts sends a wave of energy, and the Veins can feel that, too?"

"Yeah." Bowie walked backwards out of the study as the others followed. "And if they find you, Angel, they will keep you prisoner and use your amulet and your Heavenly essence to destroy this world."

"Why can't we find them, if the Council can feel when they create a negative disturbance?" Sam asked.

"Good question, and one we have been trying to answer for thousands of years," Michael said as they walked into the kitchen.

He crossed over to the fridge and pulled out a container of Mrs. Quick's famous apple slice. He popped the lid open and placed it on the butcher's block, before reaching back into the fridge for the milk as Bowie grabbed four mugs. Sam grabbed a piece and took a mouthful, before saying, "So, Angel has to become *mentally* strong to stop the physical pain?"

"Pretty much." Bowie grabbed a piece, too, as Michael filled the mugs with milk, pushing one towards Angel.

"Think you're up for the task, Angel?" her blood-sibling asked.

Angel took several swallows, emptying her mug before placing it on the butcher's block, and reached for some slice.

"I'll give it my best shot," she said.

"It's a start," Bowie said, trying not to laugh at her milk moustache.

"This key to my lock, how will I know how to find it?"

Michael swallowed his milk. "It's actually not an 'it'—it's a 'who'. The Council will select thirteen elite elemental-souls, and bind them all to you in a ceremony."

"All?" Angel looked confused.

"Yep, all thirteen." Bowie finished his milk and reached for another piece of the slice.

"But how will we know which is the right key?" Sam asked.

"Because he'll be the last one standing," Michael said.

"Standing?" Angel raised an eyebrow.

"Yeah, the others will become pure-essence, carried away by the breeze, sent around the globe to add joy to the mindful pure-souls around the world."

"You mean…they just *die*?" Sam asked.

"In a nutshell…yes," Michael answered.

"What does that mean, 'they become pure-essence'?" Angel was interested in this, wondering if her parents' essences would have been released after the Veins murdered them. It was a thought that gave her comfort and strength for the first time since she learned of their deaths.

"You know that feeling you get when you hear a black cockatoo cry, or the song of a blackbird? Or when you see a butterfly in the garden, or a random memory that makes you smile, or the scent of rain in the air before it falls?" Bowie smiled.

The girls nodded.

"Well, when an elemental- or a heavenly soul dies, they become the essence of joy and comfort for any soul who is mindful of the world around them."

"A rainbow?" Angel asked, thinking that would be wonderful.

"No." Michael shook his head. "When any pure- or royal-soul sees a rainbow, it's a sign of a heavenly soul healing another without shielding their gifts."

Angel thought of the rainbow wave of energy that had knocked her backwards after healing the sheep, and the sparkle of one earlier.

"So, this key, the last one left standing; what happens if he's one-hundred-years-old and greasy?" Sam frowned, not wanting her soul-sibling to partner up with someone gross.

"Ew," Angel muttered around her apple slice.

Bowie chuckled. "I really don't think you need to be worrying about all that right now. How about a trip into Terang to watch the footy tomorrow?"

Sam screwed up her nose. "No, thanks, you guys go; Angel and I are going to ride the ponies."

"Once we're back, another lesson will be happening for you both, got it?" Michael put the milk back in the fridge, hearing a groan from both of the girls.

"Hey," he said as he turned. "You won't improve if we don't practice."

"Still," Angel said, wiping the icing-sugar dust off her fingers and onto her jeans. "I know it's our duty, and we should be honoured that we were born into these roles, but..." She didn't know how to finish the sentence without sounding ungrateful.

"Look, how about tomorrow, we do a rewarding lesson?" Michael said. "Sam, you'll get to see what Bowie does, and what you will get to do for Mother Earth in the future. Angel, you and I will do the same. Okay?"

The girls nodded, more than happy to have a lesson that didn't involve pain.

"Right, let's go enjoy the rest of our Saturday then, shall we?" Michael smiled.

Bowie shoved the lid on the container and slid it across the bench towards Michael, who swooped it up and put it in the fridge. "Enjoy three hours' worth of legal studies and humanities? Oh, yeah, can't wait," he grumbled, as he headed off to grab his schoolbooks to take upstairs into the octagon-shaped study.

"Wanna visit Moonie and the other kittens?" Sam asked Angel, who nodded eagerly. Angel had named the kitten whose life she had saved 'Moonie'; Sam was still thinking up names for the others.

Michael watched the girls leave, feeling like they'd made a good start on their lessons, and wondering if Fletch had tapped in and watched them.

Fletch and his Soul Keepers spun their globe back to the world map, after viewing the girls' lessons.

"Samantha Storm did well," a softly spoken elemental-soul commented. The others nodded in agreement.

"Angel Cloud has a long way to go," another said.

"She'll be fine. She's just extremely sensitive, as we would want any Soul Keeper who will have the power to heal all to be," another heavenly soul defended.

Fletch listed to the Council around him as they discussed the girls. He was happy enough with how the boys were instructing them. Time would tell, and tell them soon enough, if all would be safe from the growing wave of evil the Veins were conjuring. And if Angel Cloud could listen to instruction clearly, and do what she was born to do, then they may just have the answer to destroying the Veins once and for all. Hopefully before they dug their wicked fingers into the pure-souls' hearts, causing the world to fall.

Several weeks later, Bowie and Sam stood in the study, looking into the globe and feeling out any negative energy from within. The globe stopped spinning, and, as Bowie tapped a finger against the glass, the continents disappeared, before revealing the small country town of Woolsthorpe, which was a little over sixty-five kilometres away.

"Are you ready for your first portal experience?"

"Really?" Sam couldn't contain her excitement.

"Let's go." Bowie led the way to the four-wheeler, and they set off to the Gatekeeper's house in minutes. A flock of corellas called noisily from an old gumtree as they sped over the back-entrance cattle grid. Red greeted them with a smile as they parked on the front lawn. She led them to the back gate, then they walked through the Quicks' property to reach the portal in between the English oaks.

"I'll see you both soon," she smiled. "Good luck, Sam."

"Thanks Red," Sam said, smiling as she jogged after Bowie towards the five enormous trees, which whispered a thousand secrets the closer they got.

Bowie reached out and grabbed Sam's hand. "Don't let go, whatever you do, okay?"

She nodded, feeling nervous for the first time as Bowie clasped her hand before stepping into the centre of the trees.

In a flash, a whirling energy spun them in an electric-blue circle of wild wind, consuming them. To Sam, it was both exhilarating and terrifying, despite her eyes watering, and feeling like her stomach had ripped through her spleen.

Within five heartbeats, it was over, and they were standing in the middle of an out-of-control grass fire, eating through a field of wheat. It was heading toward a shearing shed full of pure-souls who were waiting to be shorn.

"Are you ready, Samantha?"

She met Bowie's amber eyes as nervous energy consumed her. Taking a deep breath, she nodded, and raised her hands towards the flames, imagining a fire retardant falling on the wicked flames, suffocating their breath. Bowie could see the strain on her young face as she projected both the suffocation spell and the protective shield around her, blocking her energy from any Vein who may be in the area; he was ready to jump in at any second if her energy weakened. It thrilled him to see the flames die down for a few minutes before they flared up once more.

He raised his hands either side of his body, and summoned the air away, suffocating the flames in moments, leaving a scorched trail across twenty-five hectares. He was proud of his blood-sibling; she'd done well, using both the protective shield and the suffocation spell. Her gift was gaining in strength, and he knew their parents would be so proud. He whispered for rain, and a gentle shower fell, snuffing out any remnants of heat from the earth.

"Good job. Time to go." He reached for her hand, and within moments they were flying back into the electric-blue whirlwind, and through the portal.

Samantha's laugh whooshed from her as they crossed the paddock towards Red's house. Bowie smiled and slung his arm around her shoulder, hoping Michael was having the same success with Angel.

Sitting in the waiting room at the Headscope reception area in Camperdown, Michael was pretending to read a magazine as he focused on Angel's breathing. He reached into her mind to see how she was doing. Her lesson today: to see if she could tap into a nine-year-old pure-souls mind; one who was suffering terrible depression to the point of self-harming. Her aim was to gift him with peace, calm, and hope, whilst maintaining a strong shield.

She also needed to ease the mother's mind. The woman paced the corridor in a fit of silent tears and helplessness as she worried about her son and doubted her abilities as a mother.

Angel could hear Michael in her mind.

Shield yourself now, and begin.

He saw the nod of her head as he focused on the magazine, and felt her conjure her shield before touching the mother's mind. It was a mess, just like the boy's; both were in a world of anguish. Angel closed her eyes, dropping her head against Michael's shoulder, pretending to sleep as she focused, first on the boy; she'd heard the receptionist call him 'Simon'. She focused on his name as she pushed calm, loving energy towards him, down the corridor and through the door of the room in which he sat.

Poor Simon was shielding himself against the helping hand of the kind Headscope counsellor. He sat there, listening, as the man asked him questions, trying to get him to open up. The boy occasionally nodded noncommittally, answering with a simple "yes," or "no," as his thoughts drifted back to his black cave. Lit only by the light of one candle, its warm glow gave him the slightest hope that things could get better. He felt safe there, in his dark cave, where no one could reach him. But then he imagined taking a final breath, then blowing the candle out, blowing all the pain away, to leave him in utter darkness, forever safe.

Angel jerked back in her seat, as if he'd physically shocked her.

Seeing the expression on the receptionist's face, she forced a smile and muttered, "I was falling in my dream."

The receptionist smiled as she watched Angel push her face into Michael's arm, getting comfortable again. Angel focused on her shield, before reaching back out to touch Simon's mind, feeling his utter devastation and his decision to end his life.

This is it, Angel—you can do this.

She saw an image of another young boy, who Simon hung out with at school. A lonely boy, who only had one friend: Simon. She pushed an image of the boy, lonely and friendless, towards Simon, showing him what would happen if he went through with his decision to take his own life. She showed him the boy grieving for his one, true friend, who understood his home life wasn't perfect—that the friendship he shared with Simon was the only true reason he was still alive himself.

Angel could feel Simon move away from the darkness, to light the candle and carry it towards his friend. She could hear their laughter as they planned a camping trip, a bike ride to the Terang pool, a visit to his grandmother at the May Noonan Hostel. And a future at Terang College, making new friends and discovering their happy, strong selves. She could sense a calm wash over Simon's mind, which eased the pressure in hers as she focused loving intentions towards the mother. Angel showed her all the wonderful, supportive things she did every, single day for Simon.

Angel could feel the mother take a deep breath, dry her eyes, and nod her head, sensing the moment that she changed her thought process from one of guilt to one of hope.

"Good job," Michael whispered, feeling so proud of Angel. He nudged her 'awake', and said out loud for the receptionist to hear, "What a dill I am, I've got the wrong time. Let's go."

He grabbed Angel's hand and smiled apologetically at the receptionist, before pulling Angel out the door with him.

Angel felt tired, but not as washed out as she'd been over the past several weeks, when she'd been learning how to shield and use her gifts.

"That was really great Angel, I could see what you did in there." He smiled down at her as he led her to the car, where Tom was waiting to drive them back to the homestead.

She smiled up at him. "That felt really good."

"How did you go, pet?" Tom asked as Angel jumped into the back seat of the Ranger.

"Good, I loved it!" she enthused, clicking her seatbelt in as Michael closed the passenger door.

Tom pulled out onto the Princess Highway, taking the long way home so he could drop Michael off in Terang to spend the afternoon with Elizabeth.

"Well done. After we drop Michael off, how's about we grab a few litres of ice-cream to celebrate? It will go nicely with Mrs. McGoldrick's butterscotch pudding, that she's made for afternoon tea."

"Yum!" Angel looked out the window as they flew along the vibrant green countryside.

At Elizabeth's house twenty minutes later, Angel watched as the tall, striking girl walked up to greet Michael.

"I'll see you both later." Michael smiled. "Beth's dad is going to drop me home."

"No worries. See you then!"

Tom reversed, and Angel watched Michael and Elizabeth share a sweet kiss before they drove out of sight.

After stopping by Alf's store to grab the ice-cream, they drove down Terang Road towards Noorat, before turning up past the mountain and along Glenormiston Road. Tom chatted to Angel about the newly-en-rolled college students who had toured earlier that morning.

"They sound nice," Angel said as they drove past the old iron gates of Maxwell Black's house, opposite Lover's Lane. It was as pretty as a picture, both sides lined with the trademark elms of Glenormiston.

Tom grinned at her in the review mirror. "It looks like it will be an interesting year ahead, with all the new personalities."

His eyes left the road for a split second, and Angel gasped as a black truck appeared out of nowhere. The narrow country road could handle two cars if they both veered closer to the shoulder of their side, but the truck was enormous, and wasn't moving an inch.

Tom had one second to react when he saw the truck, yelling, "Hang on, Angel!" He yanked the steering wheel sharply, avoiding the truck, causing the Ranger to fly through the barbed wire fence, and into the paddock, narrowly missing a large cypress. The Ranger flipped over several times before violently stopping on its side. Angel was suspended sideways and the pink, white, and chocolate Neapolitan ice-cream was smeared across the windows and in her hair.

She blinked hard, feeling okay, before a blinding-white, searing pain stole her breath. "Tom…" she whispered around the pain.

"Angel, are you okay?" Tom's voice was rife with agony.

Angel reached for her seatbelt and struggled out of it, falling to the door. She tried to orientate herself, before climbing up through the front seats to get to Tom. The pain in her lungs intensified. A buzzing in her head threatened to consume her, and she forced herself to concentrate and not pass out. She gasped when she saw why her lungs felt as if they were on fire; a rusty star-picket had pierced the windscreen, and the tip point had gone into Tom's chest, puncturing his lung.

"Tom?" She touched his cheek, which was paler than the vanilla ice-cream dripping over the back of his head.

His eyes fluttered closed, then opened again as he felt her hands on his chest, her finger encircling the pole.

"Don't," he choked out. "You're not strong enough."

She knew he meant mentally, as she'd just completed a nurturing spell back at Headscope, but she would not let Tom die here in Maxwell Black's paddock, which was where they'd landed. Surely she had the strength to project a shield as well as heal Tom?

Well, she was going to try.

Angel closed her eyes and whispered a prayer for the Angels above to give her the strength she needed to save her friend.

She focused her energy on creating a shield around the vehicle. She felt it pull back, then took another deep breath as she drew it over them once more. Placing a hand over her heart, the other firmly against Tom's chest near the wound, she whispered a removing, healing incantation. She could feel Tom's chest muscles push at the fence picket, trying to force it out. After a few moments, Angel knew she wasn't strong enough to hold the shield and do the spell.

While a pure-soul medic would have advised against her decision, they didn't have her abilities; Angel took a deep breath, positioned herself closer in front of Tom, and placed both hands around the picket. Placing her feet on the passenger chair for leverage, she pushed her legs with all her might, sending herself and the picket back towards the windshield, removing it from Tom's chest. He gasped in pain. His eyes flew opened for a second, before he passed out. Angel forced herself not to cry as she, once again, pushed a hand firmly against Tom's bleeding chest, the other over her heart.

"Please, please," she chanted. "Let me do this… may I keep this soul safe."

She poured her intentions toward his wound as she whispered a healing incantation over and over. Angel was so focused on healing Tom, she didn't see the dark figure walking towards the overturned vehicle; so focused that she hadn't felt the shield around them lift slightly, until a small rainbow filled the car. She took a deep breath and forced the shield firmly down around them, blocking the rainbow wave of energy.

The pain in her lungs eased, and the colour on Tom's face returned. His eyelids fluttered open before staring at Angel's young, sweaty face, with ice-cream dripping in her hair.

"Hey," he whispered. "You did it, Angel, you did it."

She laughed weakly as she fell against Tom's chest at an awkward angle, since he was still on his side, held in place by the tight seatbelt.

"We have to get out of here," he said, looking up. "Can you climb up and out of the window?"

"Yes." She used different parts of the car to climb through the window, only to find Max Black standing beside the old well and tattered windmill, hands in his pockets.

"Are you all right?" he asked, looking worried.

Angel leapt down to the grass as Tom began to climb out behind her.

She spotted Max's father racing towards them, a concerned look across his face. As Tom landed beside Angel, Max's father joined them, out of breath.

"Thank goodness you're both okay. Is anyone else in there?" He nodded to the car.

"No, sir. And, luckily, we are all right, just a little shaken."

Tom put his arm around Angel's shoulder, feeling a little more like his healthy self.

"You're Tom Liam, who heads the wellbeing team at the college, aren't you?" Max's father said. "I'm Rob Black." He reached out his hand to shake Tom's.

"Nice to meet you. Your son goes to school with our Angel and Samantha." He shook Rob's hand.

Rob smiled down at Angel as he released Tom's hand and reached out to offer her his hand. "How do you do, young lady?"

Angel wasn't sure why she got a greasy feeling in her stomach being close to Max's dad. She forced a calming breath, holding up her ice-cream covered hands as her excuse as to why she didn't shake his hand, before running them back through her sticky, ice-creamed hair.

"How about we give you a lift home? You must both be in shock. I'll ring Aitken's tow truck on the way."

"That would be great, thanks."

The party of four walked back to the Blacks' mansion, with Angel and Max a few steps behind the other two. The men were chatting about the upcoming Noorat Show as Max and Angel walked in awkward silence, before Max asked, "What made you run off the road like that?"

Angel looked at him and raised an eyebrow. "There was a truck heading straight for us."

"No, there wasn't," Max frowned in confusion. "I was out by the stream looking for tadpoles; I saw you guys driving past, and then straight through the paddock—there was no truck."

Angel didn't know what to say to that as they approached Rob's car.

"Jump in, kids." Rob opened the back door for them as Tom got into the passenger side.

The drive to the college was quick, and as Rob pulled up to the rounded driveway in front of the blue-stoned homestead, he let out a low whistle.

"The craftsmanship of this homestead astounds me every time I see it," he said appreciatively, looking up at the bell tower as Angel opened her door and got out.

A panicked-looking Bowie, Jess, and Samantha rushed out the front door as another car pulled up behind them; Michael leapt out of the car before it came to a complete stop. When Michael had felt Angel's shield drop, and the desperate energy she'd poured into Tom, he'd immediately asked Elizabeth's father to drive him home, claiming he was feeling unwell.

Elizabeth reached through the open window to grab Michael's hand. "Call me later, let me know how you are."

"Sure, Beth. Sorry about today." When he saw that both Tom and Angel were okay, he turned and bent, brushing a quick kiss across Elizabeth's pretty, pink lips. "Call you later," he promised. "Thanks, Mr. Kavanagh," he called as the car turned around the driveway.

Angel turned to Max and said goodbye, before shutting the car door.

"See you." She heard his muffled reply from inside the car as Tom thanked Rob for the lift.

"Take care, then." Rob waved jovially before following the other car down the long, winding driveway.

"What happened?"

"Are you all right?"

"How did this happen?"

"My God, but you are lucky to be standing here!"

The four worried family members blurted out over the top of each other as they looked at the pair of sticky, rumpled, beaten individuals in front of them.

Tom held up a hand. "I think, if Angel and I can have a shower, and wash four litres of ice-cream off us, and relax for five seconds before we answer any questions, it would be appreciated."

"Of course," Jess nodded. "We'll meet in the study."

Sam grabbed Angel's hand as they headed up the staircase towards their bathroom.

"Are you okay?" Sam asked, her voice cracking, before she cleared her throat.

Angel squeezed her hand as she closed the bathroom door and turned to run the faucet.

"I am now. We ran into the Blacks' paddock after a truck was heading straight for us—a star-picket pierced Tom's chest and punctured his lung. I had to use my gift, but I did shield us first."

"Good job." Sam nodded as Angel stripped off and got under the spray of water.

"Max saw us run off the road; he said he saw everything, but claims there was no black truck."

"How weird is that?"

"That is a bit weird."

Angel lathered her hair, rinsing the sticky cream from her honey-blonde locks.

"So, I guess that means we are eating ice-cream-less pudding tonight, then?" Sam watched as a swirl of ice-cream floated towards the plug hole.

Angel giggled, thinking that was the funniest thing she'd ever heard, considering the events of the day. Meeting Sam's eyes, they burst into fits of laughter.

Chapter Six

"Max didn't see the truck?" Bowie folded his arms, looking at Angel.

"Or there *was* no truck." Jess slid off the window seat and walked over to join Tom at the desk.

"Yeah, that's what Fletch said, that the truck was a vision, summoned by the Veins to provoke a royal-soul to tap into their gifts. They're trying to seek us out; apparently there were one-hundred so-called 'trucks' on the road in Victoria alone. And there were four heavenly souls involved, including Angel, who had to use their gifts." Michael passed Samantha and Angel a cordial as they sat together on the opposite window seat.

"Did I shield us properly, Tom?" Angel sounded worried.

"I hope so, pet," Tom smiled, wishing he hadn't been so close to fading into essence; he could have somehow helped her shield them.

"In all our years of evolution, it astounds me that we can't bloody-well locate these bastards!" Bowie shook his head, amber eyes blazing.

Tom put a hand on his shoulder to soothe him. "Fletch has summoned a Council meeting in Warrnambool tonight, we're all to go through the portal at midnight." Tom looked at the girls. "That's you girls, as well."

Samantha jabbed her elbow into Angel's side, excited her soul-sibling would get to experience the portal finally.

"So, we won't know anything 'til then?" Bowie nodded. "I'll go see if Mrs. McGoldrick can serve dinner a bit earlier."

"Thanks, Bowie." Jess called as he left the room. "Okay, we may as well try to relax until tonight. Who knows what is going to happen?"

Samantha and Angel drained their cordial, not sure if they wanted to find out the answer.

Michael gripped Angel's hand as tightly, as Bowie held Samantha's, when they stepped into the wild wind of the portal. Angel nearly laughed at the shocking pull of energy that flashed around them, but the feeling of leaving her entire body was too unsettling for laughter; it was over too soon to become comfortable with it.

Tom and Jess stepped forward, looking impressive in their dark-amethyst capes. They led the way into a massive hall filled with hundreds of royal-souls, all dressed in Council attire. Angel, Samantha, Bowie and Michael were all dressed in white, and were the only young royal-souls in attendance, which made the boys proud, and the girls nervous. It seemed as if the entire Council was waiting for their party to arrive. Once they stepped through the large, curved doors, which stood thirty-feet high, the hall fell silent, and all eyes turned to look at the newcomers.

"Alrighty, then…" Bowie whispered to Michael.

"Welcome, our young royal-souls," A cheerful cry rang out from the end of the great hall.

Tom and Jess nodded to their group and, together, they walked down the centre of the crowd, which parted for them as they made their way toward the voice that beckoned.

Stopping in front of several elders, including Fletch, they watched as the owner of the cheerful voice stepped forward and shook Jess', Tom's, Michael's, and Bowie's hands, before smiling down at the girls. "It is such an honour to finally have you with us, girls. Let me introduce myself, I am Uriel."

The impact of his declaration made the young group exchange side-long glances. If this was *the* Uriel, Soul Keeper of Wisdom, then they were, indeed, in excellent hands.

He spoke over the heads of the girls as he addressed the hall of Soul Keepers. "My dear royal-souls, our duty to Mother Earth and her pure-souls has always been to heal, restore, and protect, whilst shielding our identity from not only the pure-souls, but our mortal enemy. The Veins' reach has grown far and foul; the time has come where we must be most vigilant in our hunting of these parasites, whose cloaking abilities are almost as supreme as our own."

Hundreds of heads nodded in agreement, before Uriel continued, "A trap was set for us this day, creating chaos, and, on this day, they were successful. A powerful, young energy was detected when this heavenly soul used her gifts. Gifts that she did also use a few months ago, illegally." He paused for impact.

All eyes went to Angel.

Sam protectively reached out and grabbed Angel's hand, casting frowning eyes around the hall, almost daring anyone to say a negative word against her soul-sibling.

Uriel continued. "This heavenly soul will one day be a match for the most lethal of the Veins. A Vein who has walked this earth a thousand times over. Once young Angel here comes of age, and meets her soul-partner, she will, in time, have the power to destroy this Vein. This, we believe, will cause all other Veins who have chosen to leech off the pure-souls to bleed out and die, once and for all. But, until that day comes, we must remain vigilant."

"With the Veins' cloaking abilities, we must grant a royal-soul permission to use the ancient method of essence-flight," Vicki Light, Vanessa's mother, called out from further down the hall, creating a few disagreeing murmurs.

"This is true, dear Vicki, and for this ancient method, we must use our most powerful Soul Keepers. And, as we all know, the most powerful are our Soul Keepers of Glenormiston South."

Bowie, Michael, Tom, and Jess felt every set of eyes in the hall fall upon them like a weighted blanket.

"Tonight, Bowie Storm and Michael Cloud will be gifted with the grace of essence-flight to search for our enemy."

The hall filled with a quiet flutter of gasps. This method of essence-flight had been forbidden hundreds of years ago, because of the dangers it brought to any royal-soul who found themselves unable to re-enter their bodies if things went wrong.

Angel and Sam looked up at their brothers, not exactly sure what was going on. But, from the looks on the boys' faces, they were.

To be gifted with the ability to hunt a Vein this way was a great honour. It was also incredibly dangerous.

Uriel continued. "This grace will also elevate their young powers to the greatest of heights, in order to continue the protection of our young royal-souls." He nodded down to Angel and Samantha.

"Bowie Storm and Michael Cloud—please kneel."

The boys knelt. Tom and Jess took the girls' hands and led them towards a break in the crowd to stand alongside the other Soul Keepers.

The room fell silent, then, after a few moments, a sweet chime filled the room and gifted everyone in the hall with the most enchanting song. It stole the breath from their lungs and brought tears of joy to their eyes.

A white light, so bright and ethereal, forced everyone's eyes shut as it approached the kneeling boys, before enveloping them in its loving arms. It then poured its essence energy into both boys' hearts before vanishing completely, along with the chime.

Michael and Bowie felt as though someone had plugged them into an electrical socket, the charge of energy making their hearts beat furiously, the blood in their veins to flow in a fashion that tugged them in a million different directions. They looked at each other, wondering if the other was feeling exactly as he was.

"Rise, Bowie Storm and Michael Cloud." The hall erupted into thunderous applause.

Angel and Samantha joined in, each wanting to ask their blood-sibling exactly what had just occurred.

Uriel stepped forward and placed a hand on both the boys' shoulders. Looking at Michael first, he said, "Your parents would have been proud."

Michael nodded, swallowing the lump that formed in his throat before Uriel turned to Bowie. "Your parents will be notified shortly, no doubt they may make a quick visit to you and Samantha."

Bowie smiled, feeling proud of them both, and sympathy for Michael. He could sense his soul-sibling's pain at not being able to share this honour with his parents. He'd do everything in his power to be there for Michael. Everything.

"May you keep the souls safe," Uriel said.

"With every breath that we take," the boys responded.

"Goodnight, dear Soul Keepers," Uriel called before glancing at Samantha and Angel, then, with a wink, he disappeared in a flash.

Bowie and Michael walked over to Tom, Jess, and the girls, before reaching for their blood-siblings' hands. "Time to go," Bowie said.

Tom nodded. "Well done, guys. I think we will all sleep well after the eventful day we've had."

"You better believe it," Michael agreed as they headed out of the hall and into the portal to take them back home.

Max

Max walked into his father's formal lounge room and took a seat, as instructed by the family's butler, Francis.

Francis poured Max a glass of soft drink before exiting, leaving Max to sit alone and wait for his father, who'd left to greet his nephew, who was coming to stay with them. Max looked around the room, with all its stately masculinity, and wondered if it would have had a softer touch if his mother were still alive.

He drank half of the fizzy drink before placing it on a crystal serving tray as he heard footsteps approaching. He checked he'd tucked in his shirt as he sat up straight on the edge of the seat, placing his fists on his lap.

"Here he is, Brendan, meet your cousin, Max." Rob stepped aside to allow Brendan to walk over and shake Max's hand. He was supposed to be the same age as Samantha's brother, Bowie, but Max knew he was much older, from the stories he'd heard from his father. He looked young, though, which confused Max, as did much of their family history, revealed to him only in quiet whispers and confusing innuendos.

Max stood and shook Brendan's hand.

"Good-looking boy you've got here, Uncle Rob." Brendan smiled down at Max. "Nice to meet you, Max."

Max shook his hand and nodded. "You, too."

"Max, your cousin is here to start your training; he is one of the stronger influences in our business." Rob said proudly, clapping Brendan on the back. "Your parents would have been so proud."

"Thank you, Uncle Rob." He turned to Max. "It is always great to start your training in the country. There's a satisfaction in honing your skills in a smaller community, seeing the outcome of your work before coming of age and graduating. But then, boy…the fun you'll have, causing mischief in the city." Brendan laughed, smiling over his shoulder at his uncle.

Max presumed he was talking about going out to party and getting drunk. He didn't think it sounded like fun.

Brendan turned back to Max. "And the best part about training here at home is you'll be undetected by any Soul Keeper that may be in the area."

Max still wasn't sure what all this talk about 'Soul Keepers' was about; his father had never been clear what it was they did for their business. He assumed it was something to do with the prize stock they owned, bred, and sold for a fortune around the globe.

"How about we start his training this weekend, at the Noorat Show?" Brendan suggested to Rob.

Rob nodded, watching his son's expression; he knew his son also carried his mother's kind soul. It was unheard of in their circle, for a Vein to have lain with a royal-soul and produce a child. Which is why he'd kept her identity a secret from the others, and why he'd killed her once his offspring had been born.

She'd never known what he was. Not until the moment he'd slid under her skin and consumed all her glorious, sweet essence. She'd been too weak, after twenty-four hours in labour, to fight him off.

He blinked away the glorious memory of consuming his wife's essence and focused on the conversation at hand. "Right, Max, your cousin will be in charge of your training from here on out, you understand?"

He didn't, of course, but replied. "Yes, Father."

"No matter what he asks you to do, for the next several years, you will do it. No questions asked."

"Yes, sir." Max nodded, knowing he'd no other option. He never thought he'd miss the strict life of boarding school, but, when he'd returned home to a house icily ruled by a father who spoke in riddles, he did often miss it. At least during the school week he got to enjoy the few friends he'd made; he was certainly enjoying the connection he was making with Samantha Storm. There was something about her that just made him feel complete.

"I've a gift for you, Max. It was your mother's."

It intrigued Max, as always, that the mention of his mother evoked a calm feeling inside of him.

"Here you go." Brendan passed him a long, dark-blue velvet box.

Max took it, wondering why, if it was his mother's, his father wasn't giving it to him?

"Open it up, son." Rob smiled.

Max ran his fingers over the soft lid before opening it. A large, blood-red ruby gleamed up at him, sitting in a four-clawed casing surrounded by ornate onyx, attached to a thick leather strap. A weird kind of energy rushed towards him, but he figured it was just from having his father and cousin stare at him so intently, waiting for some kind of reaction from him.

"Here we go." Brendan took the leather strap out of the box and placed it around Max's neck. "You will not be able to take it off, so it's like you'll have your dear, departed mother with you always."

The leather bound itself together, like skin meshing, holding fast around Max's neck.

"What do you say, son?" Rob smiled.

"Thank you." Max touched his fingers to the cold stone, feeling an energy hum pleasantly. *That's better.*

"You are welcome." Brendan smiled at Rob, knowingly.

"Okay, then." Max's father interrupted his thought flow. "Brendan, why don't you settle in? Nothing has changed since your last visit, so, please, make yourself at home. Max, why don't you go for a bike ride, visit your friend down the road?"

Max nodded and got up to leave the room.

"I look forward to training you, Max," Brendan called out.

"Yeah, me too," Max lied, before leaving the room, feeling more relaxed when he was out of the men's line of vision. *Training?* It didn't sound like anything he'd be interested in. He was happy to reach his room and get out of the stiff slacks and shirt. He threw on a pair of comfortable track-pants and a Carlton footy jumper before getting his bike and pedalling off to his best mate, Eddy Argyle's, house.

Angel

The Noorat Show was always a thrilling event for the entire community, and those attending from the surrounding districts. There was an assortment of enjoyable rides suitable for the young children, then the more adventurous and hair-raising, for those who had a strong stomach…or not, which induced a good hurl afterwards. Wood-chopping, an art expo by the town's very own award-winning artist, Jess Fowler, an assortment of craft stalls, animal competitions with fabulous prizes for the best-groomed pet, food stalls, and a variety of entertainment for all, from sun-up to sun-down.

The sun was setting when Michael suggested they take a final spin on the Ferris wheel before heading home.

Michael, Elizabeth, Patricia, and Bowie took one carriage, while Angel and Samantha got in another with their friends from school, Joanne and Kylee.

"My God, if I eat one more bite of this hot dog, I think I'm going to puke," Kylee said, passing the hotdog to Joanne.

Samantha laughed. "If you're gonna puke, wait 'til we are up the top and aim for Bowie!"

All the girls laughed their heads off at the thought.

"Nah, your brother is too cute to vomit on," Joanne said. Kylee agreed. Angel chuckled as Samantha rolled her eyes.

"Speaking of cute…" Samantha nodded to the carriage opposite them, watching Max, who was sitting with a tall guy none of them had seen before.

Kylee smiled, "The guy beside Max isn't too bad himself."

"Kinda is," Joanne agreed.

The Ferris wheel was finally full, and had begun its slow cycle, giving all the joyriders the most magnificent views as twilight kissed Noorat and beyond.

They'd circled around twice when Angel felt an uncomfortable stir in the air. Fear gripped her stomach and blood pumped uncomfortably loud in her ears; someone was about to jump, and that 'someone' hadn't been thinking about it until just now—it had come out of the blue, unexpected, and, deep down, they did not want to die.

Her breathing grew shallow as she felt the pure-soul's confused and frightened adrenaline kick-in. She gripped the rail of the cage for dear life.

"Are you scared of heights, Angel? It's going to be okay. Look, we're going back down," Kylee reassured her friend, who had been fine a few seconds ago, but now looked pale and terrified as she clung to the cage of their carriage.

Samantha could feel Angel's energy, and she tried to reach out to Bowie with her mind. Angel tried to search for the pure-soul who was getting ready to jump, knowing if she could source them, she could persuade them to sit. She forced a shield around all the carriages as her mind flew to each individual, trying desperately to locate the one in need.

Max

The Ferris wheel had taken off not long before Brendan said, "See that bloke with the red cap, sitting by himself?"

Max nodded.

"I want you to see if you can feel my energy, tell me what I'm thinking." Brendan forced an image of the man jumping from the top of the Ferris wheel into his mind. He heard Max's gasp and smiled proudly. "Fast learner."

Max sat forward and shook his head at his cousin, confused and terrified. "No, don't, please!"

Brendan pinned Max with an unpleasant look, which had Max scuttling back into his seat.

"Focus on my thoughts, the images, the feelings. Don't close your mind off." He stared unblinkingly, waiting for Max to acknowledge him.

Max nodded, heart heavy, an unhappy expression on his young face.

Michael

Michael felt the disturbing, negative force the moment Angel did. He darted worried eyes towards Bowie.

Luckily, Elizabeth was tucked under his chin as she snuggled into him, and didn't see his expression. Patricia was too busy taking photos of the activity below to notice anything untoward.

There's a Vein here. Michael pushed into Bowie's mind.

Bowie nodded once, worried about Angel and Sam.

Michael sensed his train of thought as his eyes moved to search the carriages, finally spotting his blood-sibling. Her eyes met his, her face stricken as the wheel turned again. They could both feel it, the sickness growing as the jumper grew desperate and confused.

We'll do it together, Angel—just calm your heart, search with love.

Angel nodded to Michael and closed her eyes, feeling for the confused, frightened pure-soul. Finally, she found him, as the wheel turned for the third time; he was approaching the top, and his thoughts were a maze of miserable confusion. Angel pushed into his mind, but felt a block. She couldn't pour any good intention or positive thought towards him at all. Instead, she felt her own mind become a murky puddle of disarray, her heart heavy as a different kind of sickness leaked into her soul.

Michael was stronger, and the evil disease making Angel ill had no effect on him. But it shocked him that he had no influence at all over the man contemplating jumping.

Max

Max felt ill as he saw his cousin push horrid images towards the man's mind. Then, as the man approached the highest part of the ride, he climbed onto the outside of the carriage, and, ignoring the gasps and screams from the onlookers, leapt to his death.

Overwhelmed with what had happened, Max froze in disbelief, feeling as though he might vomit, as the desperate cries and shocked screams around the fairground reached his ears.

Brendan reached over and put a hand over Max's, whispering fiercely. "This is the moment you take it all in, Maxwell. Feel the energy, the sadness, the heartbreak, the fright. Can you feel it? Let it in, let it fill you. Close your eyes."

Max stared at him defiantly, snatching his hand out from under Brendan's and folded his arms.

"Do it." Brendan commanded.

Max closed his eyes, trying not to freak out, as his cousin had instructed him. He tried to focus on what Brendan was saying. Yeah, he could feel the darkness swirl around him. And yes, it absolutely felt like a bolt of amazing energy, unlike anything he'd ever felt. His veins throbbed in a pleasant way that he almost wished wouldn't end. But, then, he felt something else. A beautiful sadness he wanted to make feel happy again—would do anything to make happy again. He knew, without a doubt, it was Samantha Storm who was feeling so forlorn.

Looking over as her carriage hit the ground for her to exit, he watched as she ran to her brother, and saw how relieved she looked when he wrapped his arms around her shoulders. He wished he could be the one to comfort her.

He looked back at his cousin, who was watching him carefully.

"If you don't embrace the humans' downfall, it will be the demise of you," Brendan said softly.

Max nodded stiffly and was grateful when their carriage hit the ground so they could leave. The fairground filled with emergency workers try-ing to figure out how it had happened as they closed down the Show. It bothered him greatly that Samantha's worried, sad energy had filled his heart with a most delicious need of wanting more.

Chapter Seven

Once the police had checked everyone's statements, Mr. Kavanagh drove them home while his wife raced Patricia and Elizabeth to the sanctuary of theirs.

An hour later, they were sitting in the lounge, holding hot Milos and rehashing the event.

"I've never felt anything like it." Michael rubbed the back of his neck. "It was like trying to see through a mud puddle full of twigs."

Angel shivered; Michael was right. It had been beyond horrible, and his description reminded her of the nightmare she'd endured a few months ago. She didn't know whether she would sleep tonight.

"I couldn't locate the source. So much for these amazing, amplified powers," Bowie spat in disgust.

Michael shook his head. "It just means that, whoever it was, they're older than us, has been doing it for longer."

"Still." Bowie shook his head. "It sucks."

"We just have to train harder, every day. We've got this, Bowie, don't worry."

"Michael, we have a Vein right here in *our* town. He made a pure-soul jump to his death, causing a negative ripple effect throughout the crowd, which would have fed his energy. I'm sorry, soul-sibling of mine, but I *am* worried, and you should be, too." Bowie's eyes went to Angel before he got up to pace.

Michael followed the direction of his gaze. "She was shielded. I felt it."

Angel nodded, trying to reassure both of them. "I was, Bowie, you really don't have to worry."

"The worrying thing is not knowing who it is." Sam said, finishing her Milo and reaching for a piece of Vegemite toast.

"We will figure this out. Even if the Vein is an ancient one, I know we will find a way to source who it is." Bowie stopped in the middle of the rug, looking pointedly at Angel. "I think it's best, for the moment, that you stay completely under the radar. No using your gifts for anything, anything at all. You got me?"

Angel looked across at Michael, who nodded before meeting Bowie's intense look.

"Angel?" Bowie wanted to hear her say it.

"Yes, I've got you."

"My God, this show is deep." Sam rolled her eyes. "Angel, you want to bunk in with me tonight?"

"Yep." She didn't hesitate. She did not want to be alone tonight with all those murky feelings floating around in her head; it was like something dark was still touching her, making her feel grimy.

"Sleep well. Tomorrow, I don't want either of you leaving the college grounds," Michael said.

"We're meeting Kylee and Joanne at Kenna's Lane, to go for a pony ride." Angel looked at him.

"Call them in the morning and tell them they're welcome to come here. I want you on the estate only."

"Sure," Angel agreed sullenly.

63

Samantha reached for her soul-sibling's hand and pulled Angel up the stairs towards her room, leaving the worried-looking boys behind them.

They brushed their teeth, got into their cosy pyjamas, and snuggled under the thick quilt, which smelled divine, as Mrs. McGoldrick always poured homemade lavender softener in the wash.

"Are you okay?" Angel asked Sam.

"Yeah, I will be. You?"

"Yeah…I guess I will be, too."

"Goodnight," they whispered together, grateful to be warm, safe and sound.

The following morning, while the girls went on their pony ride, on the estate grounds as Michael had instructed, Tom and Jess took him and Bowie up to the bell tower.

"You've both been gifted with the ability to locate a Vein, and, if we have one in the area, you should be able to seek it." Tom indicated that the boys should stand facing each other.

Bowie pulled in a slow, deep breath as he stood opposite Michael, who was looking calm and ready.

Jess rang the bell, causing a ripple to flow through the air, brushing against their skin, similar to Uriel's chime. "Your bodies will remain here, safeguarded by the tower. Your essence will take flight, leaving your body to be carried away by the wind, which will protect you whilst you're away."

"Is this actually safe?" Michael asked.

"Yes, as long as the bell continues to ring every minute, on the minute."

"And if it doesn't continue to ring?" Bowie raised an eyebrow.

Jess and Tom exchanged a glance, not wanting to tell either of the boys the answer.

"Come on, we can handle it," Michael sighed, feeling slightly apprehensive.

"Then your essence will drift, sightless, trying to find its way back to your body," Tom said.

"Oh, is that all? Well, in that case, carry on." Bowie rolled his eyes towards Michael.

Michael wanted to chuckle, but the thought of his essence floating sightlessly around Glenormiston and beyond wasn't a comforting one. "Well, it's simple, isn't it? Just don't stop the ringing."

Jess smiled. "I don't intend to."

Michael and Bowie nodded to each other, knowing their soul-trainers would never allow anything to hurt them.

"Focus your energy on the darkness; you should be able to feel it within moments of my wind carrying you." Under his breath, Tom whispered, "If we're lucky." The jumper from last night had shocked them all, along with the entire community, and that shock wave of despair would have strengthened the Vein they couldn't detect.

Bowie and Michael each stared into their soul-sibling's eyes and felt their power magnify to seek the evil.

Jess rang the bell again, the vibration raining over them, stroking their flesh and reaching out tiny hands to collect their essence for flight, as Tom conjured a calming wind to carry them away.

Within seconds, Bowie and Michael felt lighter than air and, before they knew it, were drifting up and out of the bell tower. They glanced down and saw themselves standing as still as statues, before looking at each other in their essence form. They were both surprised at what they saw.

Michael was a vibrant, shimmering aqua, who became iridescent with every shift of the wind.

Bowie was a deep, glorious amber, who resembled a warm flame of candlelight.

To a pure-soul's eye, they would appear as small, bright birds.

"By the Angels…you're beautiful," Bowie said to Michael, who laughed.

"I was about to say the same thing about you."

"Great, now when Elizabeth calls you her 'beautiful-boy', I'll just see you like this." Bowie chuckled.

Michael grinned. "Let's do this." He focused on their mission as the wind carried them in the direction they needed to go.

They flew over the college grounds, then past the Glenormiston store towards Noorat. Bowie felt a weak throb penetrate him before they were whisked past the Black's mansion and suddenly pulled over Mount Noorat. It felt like the wrong direction, as the wind carried them further, as if it were taking them towards Mortlake, before suddenly spinning them back toward Terang.

"This doesn't feel right?" Bowie felt like a magnet being pulled in the wrong direction.

"How do we know? We've never done this before."

"Focus on the dark, a sickness. I felt a touch of something before." Bowie focused on the energy in the air.

The wind carried them back again as they drifted in a flash across fields of green where cattle were grazing, past Dalvui Lane and a property called Dimora; they both felt a warm energy of good vibes before they were whisked away again. Suddenly, the wind picked them up and perched them on a branch outside the iron gates of the Blacks' mansion. The wind gentled to a calming breeze, waiting for their soul-essence to dictate their next move.

"Can you feel that?" Bowie whispered.

Michael paused, feeling out the energy before replying, "I feel… something."

Below them, Max was walking with his friend, Eddy, as they pushed their bikes down the driveway. Both Michael and Bowie sensed a positive glow radiate from Max's soul.

Eddy was as pure as they came, no issue there. But it was the other feeling they felt uneasy about—deep, bloody thoughts were reaching out, like razor-sharp tentacles, searching for them, right at that moment.

"We're undetectable, right?" Bowie frowned.

"Absolutely. Uriel's gift should increase our cloaking abilities tenfold." Michael sounded confident.

Bowie felt a slimy probe brush his thoughts and gasped in shock at the invasive touch that filled him with pain.

"What is it?" Michael sounded worried.

"We have to go. Now." Bowie imagined the wind collecting them and carrying them back towards the homestead. Within a flash, their essence returned to their bodies, and, as soon as they did, Bowie raced to the edge of the bell tower, and hurled up the acid-like contents of his stomach.

"What happened?" Tom was relieved they'd returned within the hour. His dark eyebrows drew together as he watched Bowie vomit.

Michael shook his head, unable to answer for Bowie.

Jess walked over and placed a hand on the clearly-shaken young man's back. "Bowie?"

Bowie wiped a hand across his mouth after spitting out a piece of carrot that always seemed to be there after he'd vomited. Placing a trembling hand against his chest, he frowned, his forehead beading with sweat. "Something touched me."

Michael stepped closer. "There wasn't anyone else around, Bowie."

"Something *penetrated* me." Bowie's voice caught, and he took a steadying breath.

Tom grabbed the hem of Bowie's t-shirt and tugged it up, revealing a firm, youthful chest with a red-raw welt running across it.

Michael gasped and stepped forward, placing a finger against the welt.

Bowie sucked in his breath; the pain was intense.

Michael drew his hand away, and a slimy residue came away with it.

"I need a shower." Bowie tugged his t-shirt down and started down the bell tower stairs.

The others followed behind. "Nothing touched you?" Jess asked Michael, who shook his head.

"Bowie, after you shower, meet us in the study," Tom said. "We'll contact Vicki Light. Her son, Andrew, had a similar experience whilst on recon a few years ago."

Bowie nodded as he left, hoping the water would wash away the throb, which intensified with every breath he took.

Thirty minutes later, Vicki Light stood with the worried group as she ran a finger over Bowie's red flesh, still slimy to the touch, even after his shower.

"Yes, I've seen this before," she said, her voice quiet. "It takes an ancient one to inflict this type of wound on a soul's essence. An extremely dangerous Vein."

"I can understand why this method of flight was forbidden in the end." Bowie frowned.

"Is there something we can do for the pain? For whatever reason, I haven't been able to lift it." Michael didn't like to see his soul-sibling suffering.

"Yes. Take him to the Gatekeeper's house, Red will have an ancient remedy for this." Vicki lowered Bowie's t-shirt.

"So, the gift that Uriel gave us didn't do squat," Bowie spat, not meaning to sound ungrateful.

"On the contrary." Vicki turned her warm, brown eyes towards the handsome young Elemental and smiled. "First, you found the location of a Vein, an immensely powerful Vein indeed, by the looks of things. And second, you're not dead. When Andrew had been inflicted with a similar wound, he was in his solid form. I'm amazed that you are not dead."

"Well, when you say it like that…" Bowie ran a hand through his damp hair.

Michael nodded. "Not bad, when you consider the odds."

"The Blacks have been in our area for hundreds of years, it's not them. We've never had any problems 'til now." Tom was trying to figure out what all this meant, considering Bowie was just attacked on the outskirts of the Blacks property.

"Yeah, we got a read on Max. His soul is light, pure. There was no dark energy emitting from him whatsoever." Michael folded his arms. "It doesn't make sense."

"I'll take this news to the High Council, and we will let you know what we find. Until then, no more essence-flights." Vicki turned back to Bowie. "Come, I'll take you to Red's before I portal back."

Bowie nodded, always enjoying the older woman's calm, loving vibe. It made him miss his own mum all the more.

She addressed the room before leaving. "Your shields must be strong. Be on the alert, and protect the girls. Whatever has arrived here, it only has one desire, and that's to destroy everything it comes across. May you keep the souls safe."

"With every breath that we take," the room chorused in farewell before watching her leave.

Bowie nodded to Michael. "I'll see you later." He followed Vicki out the door, looking forward to Red making him feel better. As the throb increased, fingers of pain drew closer to his heart.

Rob Black had strengthened the wards around the estate once Brendan informed him of their uninvited visitors; he thought it was about time to double security. The thought that royal-souls had come so close thrilled him.

Oh, if only he'd known who they were! He rubbed his hands together gleefully, remembering the sweet, sweet taste of his dear, departed wife as he'd drained her pure-essence from her body. He closed his eyes, savouring the memory.

"Uncle Rob?" Brendan called out.

Rob turned, smiling. "Dear boy, you're a hundred years older than I! When we're alone, please, just call me 'Rob'."

Brendan smiled, his eyes black and pupilless, like a shark's. "Rob, Max has an excursion tomorrow, and I thought I'd volunteer as a parent helper? I feel it's time to see if he has what it takes. Otherwise, I may need to take him to Europe with me. Maybe the Black Lords can inspire him to embrace our way of doing things."

The Black Lords were the highest order of Veins, marginally older than the Blacks themselves. Rob nodded. "I'd been considering that option myself. I think a few years with our brethren will only enhance Max's ability and desire to become great."

Brendan nodded, delighted it was this easy to take young Max away, to mould him as his shadow. The boy was too soft, too kind…that had to change. His potential for greatness was immense and, under the right instructor could even exceed Brendan's power.

"Right, well, I'll ring the school and sign you up for the excursion."

"Excellent," Brendan smiled, looking forward to the mayhem he would create tomorrow, hoping Max would understand the importance of why they did what they did.

Max

"All right, everyone, time to release your tadpoles," Mr. Kemp called to the grade-five and -six students, who'd been studying the life forms around Castle Carrey Creek. Max smiled as Samantha passed him a jar of creek water, filled with tadpoles. They'd paired up with Angel and

Eddy, and had made a good team, being the first to recognise twenty items off the list of local flora and fauna.

Max could hear Brendan laugh as he flirted with one of the mothers, and suppressed a groan of embarrassment.

"Is that your uncle?" Sam asked.

Max tipped the tadpoles back into the creek. "Cousin," he replied. He tried not to blush as Sam stood close to him. Her eyes looked so bright, almost orange, against her green t-shirt. Her long, blonde hair, which was tied into double-ponytails, smelled like strawberries.

Sam watched Max's cheeks glow red and wished she could say something to let him know she liked him, too.

"I like your ruby," she said instead.

"Thanks, it was my mother's."

"It's masculine-looking. Did her father pass it down to her?"

Max looked down at the ruby, shrugging.

"Hey, Sam," Angel called. "Mr. Kemp said we could make a bouquet out of the grasses, to give to Mrs. McGoldrick."

"Okay." Sam smiled and ventured off to pick some wildflowers.

"Listen up, everyone." Mr. Kemp called out. "Five more minutes, then Mr. Kidd wants everyone back on the bus."

Max picked some bright purple statice flowers from the ground, and, as they walked to the bus, passed them to Sam.

This time it was her turn to blush. "Thanks, Max."

He smiled. "Sure."

"Good job, everyone," Mr. Kidd called cheerfully, offering a bright, comforting smile to each student as they climbed aboard the bus, giving their favourite bus driver a high-five as they walked by him.

Brendan followed Max to the back of the bus and sat beside the pretty, young mother who'd just finished handing out orange slices.

As the bus got into gear and backed out of the parking area, Mr. Kemp congratulated his class on their excellent behaviour.

71

Max could feel a strange sensation as the bus ambled along the road and towards the old, rickety Castle Carey Road bridge. Samantha's sweet voice faded away as he tuned into what he knew was his cousin sending him a message.

Brace yourself.

For what? But Max didn't have more than a second to think on it. The terrifying sounds of concrete shifting, wood splintering, and horrified screams filled the air as the bus plummeted through the centre of the old bridge, falling into the creek bed below.

The screaming of the frightened students above the waterline filled Max with a pleasant, tingly feeling, which confused him. Why would he feel so good when chaos was brimming around him? He looked around, worried for Sam.

The top end of the bus was being sucked into the blackness of the deep creek bed. Those souls who were terrified and gasping for breath before they were totally submerged under the water, were sending out the most euphoric energy, filling Max with the most mind-blowing sensation he'd ever felt.

That's right—feed off the fear. Let it enter you, strengthen you, Brendan's voice whispered into his mind.

Max blinked for a second, wondering what the hell was happening. He was clinging to the back of a seat as bodies all around him were fighting to get out through the back window the mother had opened.

Mr. Kidd was constantly diving back into the murky water, pulling out the small bodies. He pushed them towards the seats above water, yelling, "Climb up and out, go, go!" before diving again.

Angel

Angel saw the deep gash across Mr. Kidd's forehead before he dove back into the murky water, where orange slices bobbed on top – the bright orange skins looking way too cheerful amongst the chaos.

Mr. Kemp and the mother were helping kids climb up and out of the back window as Mr. Kemp caught Angel's eye.

"Climb out, Angel, now! Come on!" he cried.

She nodded, feeling a heavy fog consume her when she turned to see Sam, lying on the back of a seat, a large bump forming on the side of her temple. Angel gasped, and struggled across to her soul-sibling, feeling her heart throb miserably with the pain and terror of all the surrounding souls.

She focused on breathing deep breaths, and imagined each breath making her heart swell, which charged her amulet with positive energy. She glanced around, then, cupping Sam's face and placing her other hand over her heart, whispered desperately to revive her. With the chaos erupting around her, and her worry for Sam, she forgot, just for a split second, about her shields. A small, bright rainbow glow seeped from under her fingers, and she shut it down quickly, chanting her healing incantation.

Brendan was halfway through the back window, as a charge ran through him. He glanced over his shoulder, but seeing nothing out of the ordinary, continued climbing out.

The fog lifted from Angel's vision when Sam's eyes fluttered open, just as a hand was thrust in between them.

"Take my hand!" Max yelled. He grabbed Sam's, pulling her towards the back window, with Angel following.

As they jumped down into the cold water below and began to swim across to the bank where their fellow students sat huddled and crying, they could hear a siren. A passing truck driver had pulled over and told the teachers he'd called triple-zero.

Max patted Sam's back as Mr. Kemp and Mr. Kidd did a head count. Everyone had escaped, and, thankfully, although there were injuries and bruises, there were no fatalities.

Brendan placed a hand on Max's shoulder and led him a few feet away. Bending, he said against his ear, "You can still feel the fear. Absorb it."

Max jerked away from his cousin and hissed, "I don't want to."

Eddy looked curiously at Brendan before he asked Max. "You okay, mate?"

Max nodded, looking away, not meeting Eddy's concerned eyes. "Yeah, I'm fine."

Angel put her arm around Sam's shoulders as the emergency vehicles arrived. She reached into her traumatised fellow-students' minds and pushed warm thoughts of healing and calm towards them.

Sam leant against Angel's shoulder as her head throbbed, wishing they were home in their fluffy warm beds already.

"Soon," Angel whispered, hearing Sam's wish. "Won't be long."

And, thankfully, it wasn't. Tom arrived with a swarm of parents, collecting their kids to either take them to Camperdown hospital for a check-up, or home.

Chapter Eight

When Mrs. McGoldrick saw the bump on the side of Sam's head, she bundled her into the car and took her to the hospital for a scan, before Michael, Angel, or Jess could put their healing hands on her.

It was a bit of a wait, as the emergency room was full, but, thankfully, the scan revealed Sam was okay. Afterwards, Mrs. McGoldrick took her back home and tucked her into bed.

"Thanks so much for staying back, Mrs. McGoldrick. Head home now, and take half the day off tomorrow if you like." Tom thanked her.

"Goodnight, dears," she called before pulling the front door shut behind her.

After Jess and Tom made sure Sam was fast asleep, they headed down to Angel's room to say goodnight.

"You okay, pet?" Tom smiled as Jess kissed the top of her head.

"Just tired is all." She hugged Tom back as he squeezed her.

"See you in the morning. Sleep well."

She nodded as they left, heading off to their overseers' cottage for the night. She closed her eyes for a moment, sighing heavily. It had been one hectic afternoon.

She heard muffled voices downstairs as Tom and Jess talked to Bowie and Michael. The front door shutting indicated their departure, as footsteps headed upstairs and towards her room.

Bowie knocked once before pushing the door open to see Angel sitting up in bed, hugging the teddy bear her mother had given her when she was a toddler. She was too old for it now, but he knew it contained traces of her mother's perfume, and she needed some comfort after the afternoon she'd experienced.

Michael walked in and sat at the end of her bed as Bowie strolled over to the window and remained standing.

"How are you, Angel? No headache?" Michael squeezed her foot through the blanket.

"No, I didn't really hit my head."

"Good, I'm glad." He smiled warmly, which she returned.

"Did you sense any dark energy before the accident?" Bowie asked.

Angel met Bowie's worried amber gaze, thinking he looked tired. She shook her head.

"Nothing at all?" He sounded frustrated.

"No."

"Afterwards?"

She shook her head again.

Bowie let out a frustrated groan as he paced. "They are here somewhere, causing mayhem, and we can't find them!"

Michael stood and crossed over to Bowie. "We will find them, relax."

"When? How?" Bowie threw his hands in the air. "Both of our sisters, along with a busload of kids, could have been killed today because our supposed '*fang-dangled*' powers couldn't even bloody-well find who we're supposed to be able to find!" He made quote marks in the air as he spat out *fang-dangle*.

Angel slipped lower under the covers, watching as Bowie paced. She'd always found it fascinating, observing him when he became frustrated. When Michael got upset, she usually felt upset, too, but with Bowie's frustration, it was always entertaining somehow. He was like an animal—sleek, wild, and unpredictable. She sensed an energy from him she hadn't felt before, and she curiously reached out to touch his mind, wondering if she could help calm him.

He turned on her the instant he felt her reach toward him. Still feeling uneasy about the 'thing' that had probed him whilst he'd been in essence form at the Black's property, having Angel intrude now did not sit well with him.

"*Cut* it out, Angel!" he practically screamed at her, eyes blazing in anger.

The venom lacing his voice shocked Angel, before her hurt kicked into defensive mode. She bolted up in the bed and flung her teddy bear at his head. "I was only trying to help, Bowie!" She yelled back. "Get out of my room!"

Michael held up his hands. "Calm down, the two of you." He shook his head, wondering about the pair of them at times.

Bowie looked at Angel, and, seeing her angry, hurt expression, forced himself to take a deep breath and apologise. "Sorry, kiddo. I'm just a bit on-edge."

She folded her arms, frowning stubbornly.

"Forgive me?"

She thought for a moment, before holding out her hand for the flung teddy bear, which he bent and scooped up. He crossed the room and placed it into her hands, saying, "You do know about the rule that you should never tap into an Elemental's mind, don't you?"

"Yes. Sorry." She dropped her eyes.

He sighed, wanting to say something else, but said instead, "It's okay. Get some sleep. We'll see how you're feeling for the end-of-year picnic we're hosting this weekend."

"I'll be fine." She looked up at Michael as he crossed over to her and bent to give her a hug.

"Goodnight, Angel."

She hugged him back as Bowie reached down and ruffled her hair.

"Sleep tight, kiddo."

"'night, Bowie." She watched as they left the room, feeling exhausted, and snuggled under the flannelette sheets scattered with bumblebees, and was asleep in seconds.

When the girls went downstairs on the morning of the end-of-year picnic, the atmosphere was festive, the chatter bright and constant.

Mrs. McGoldrick had hired some of the most proficient bakers in the district to help feed the army of people arriving in under four hours' time. The homestead's kitchen was filled to its capacity; Edna Royal, Mrs. Quick, and Vicki Light were there, along with Red, accompanied by her niece, Jane Irish, who was staying with her over the Christmas break.

Samantha and Angel walked into the kitchen and saw Jane sitting on a stool, legs swinging to and fro, listening to the happy conversations around her. They squealed in delight before launching at each other, jumping up and down as they hugged, talking all at once.

Red laughed. "All right, girls, why don't you grab a roll and make yourselves scarce for a few hours, so we can get organised before half the town arrives?"

Angel snatched up three rolls with ham, cheese, and relish as Sam asked Jane, "Want to go see the kittens at the haystack?"

"Absolutely!" Jane grinned as she looped her arms through Sam's and Angel's.

"I want to hear all about who's coming today, and if there are any cute boys," Jane gushed happily. Her dark hair glistened as they walked out into the sunshine.

Tall for her age, most people assumed she was the same age as Bowie and Michael, but she was only a year older than the girls. They'd gotten along like a house on fire ever since they were toddlers.

"Well, Samantha can certainly fill you in on the cute boy scenario." Angel grinned.

"Oh, do tell!" Jane bumped her hip into Sam's as they strolled along.

"Maybe I'll just let you use your honing skills to see which one my attraction floats out to." Sam fluttered her eyes at Jane.

"I may do just that," Jane laughed. "How's the training been going? I've heard you've had an interesting few months."

"You could say that," Angel answered, passing the girls a roll each as they walked down the long winding driveway; it followed the ancient volcanic rock wall, standing as solid as the hands that built it hundreds of years ago.

Walking under the shade of the elm trees, a black cockatoo let out a mournful cry in the branches above, startling the girls for a moment. They all laughed.

"Well, now that I'm here for the Christmas break, hopefully I'll get to join in on the action," Jane said.

"Well, we're pretty eager for a few days *without* action, aren't we, Angel?" Sam shook her pigtails, trying to ward off the flies taking an interest in her bread roll as she went to take a bite.

"That would be nice, actually, a few quiet days. Both Bowie and Michael have been a bit grumpy lately."

"Bowie and Michael? Grumpy? Never!" Jane scoffed as they approached the haystack, where they could see the kittens playing amongst the bales of hay.

Sam grinned at Angel as Jane dropped the girls' arms and ran towards the six kittens, who were falling all over each other as their mother slept.

The girls spent the next few hours in constant laughter as they shared stories, catching up on the year they'd all had since they'd last spent any length of time together.

When the townspeople arrived, the end-of-year picnic got into full swing in a swirl of activity. After Mr. Kemp, along with the other primary school teachers, gave out their awards for the year's work, they all partook in a BBQ lunch, followed by the tastiest desserts.

There was a treasure hunt for young and old, trail rides, tennis matches, and a golf tournament. The pool was in peak condition for the summer crowd, and most of the teenagers flocked to that activity, where a massive inflatable slide was set up. Michael and Elizabeth were running the snow cone booth in between enjoying the water activities, and Patricia was helping Bowie monitor the younger kids in the shallow section of the pool.

Samantha introduced Max and Eddy to Jane, who immediately picked up on the tell-tale flush on both Sam's and Max's cheeks with the introduction.

"Nice to meet you Max, Eddy." Jane smiled. "Should we pair up on the treasure hunt?" she asked.

"Sounds good," Eddy said enthusiastically, liking the fact that Jane was almost as tall as he was, and her pretty smile was sweet to look at.

"What about Angel?" Sam asked, hating that her soul-sibling might feel left out, since it was a pairs game.

"No, I'm good," Angel said, hearing Sam's concern. "I'm going to join the trail ride with Kylee and Joanne."

"Are you sure?" Max asked, knowing Sam would be more comfortable with Angel joining them.

"Oh, yeah. I'm actually really looking forward to it, but you guys have fun, seriously." She flashed a bright smile before turning around and bumping straight into Brendan, who had come to find Max.

A greasy ball formed in the pit of her stomach as he placed his hands on her shoulders to steady her. She swallowed the bile that crept into her throat.

"Whoa! Where are you off to in such a hurry?" He smiled charmingly down at her as he removed his hands from her shoulders.

The uneasy feeling disappeared as soon as he took his hands off her. She looked up at him, trying to get a read on him and the unexpected greasy feeling, but there was nothing now.

He, too, had felt something—a delightful, pulsating glow of energy when he'd placed his hands on her. He stared down at her curiously; he'd never felt anything like it in all his years. Such a spark...her essence seemed to flow through her baby-blues. On closer inspection, he realised her glossy, honey-blonde hair shone like a halo.

He almost laughed out loud. The fact that he'd come across a heavenly soul so accidentally, and one who exuded such power at such a young age, was pure luck! He wondered if the royal-souls themselves had any idea how powerful she actually was?

Sam didn't like the way Max's cousin was staring at Angel. "Can we help you with something?" She sounded rude, even to her own ears.

Jane held in a laugh; she'd never heard Sam be rude to an adult before.

Max wanted to cheer for her; he was liking his cousin less and less as the time they spent together grew.

"Yes, young lady, in fact, you can." He concealed his grin. "Max, I just wanted to let you know that I'm heading home. Tom said he will drive you home after the party."

Max nodded, "Okay."

"Splendid. Enjoy the party, young people." He looked down at Angel once more before turning on his heel to head for the car park.

They all looked at each other for a second, before Eddy said to Max, "Your cousin is a real creep, mate."

Jane snorted a laugh at Eddy's honesty.

"Yeah," Max said, his voice quiet. "He is."

"Right, let's go gang," Samantha said brightly. "I want to win this so-called treasure. Angel, you're sure you won't join us?"

Angel smiled as she walked backwards. "No, have fun, I'll find you later."

She headed for the stables where old Rocky's memorial stone was the starting point for the trail ride. She could hear her friends laughing behind her as they ran off to catch up to the competition.

An hour later, Angel was completely in her element. Corellas screeched merrily in the afternoon sky as the thirty-odd horse riders cantered over fields of green, sewn with snowbells and dandelions.

It felt good to get away from all the noise of the festivities for a little while; as fun as they were, there were still plenty of people in the community feeling overwhelmed with the suicide at the Noorat Show. And some kids from the bus accident were still shaken and suffering trauma.

It was all of their combined emotional responses which tugged at Angel's nurturing, heavenly heart, and drained her energy. As was expected, she was still young and wouldn't be able to shield herself from the emotional needs of the pure-souls until she came of age. Even then, she would always respond to an innocents' suffering.

To be out in the open, with fewer souls around - and only content souls, at that - filled Angel with a peaceful heart, which beat happily.

"Time to turn back, gang!" Penny Welch, head of the equestrian team, shouted to be heard above the flock of corellas overhead.

"Perfect timing, I'm starving!" Kylee cried gleefully.

Joanne laughed. "Seriously? We ate before the ride."

"Yeah, over an hour ago. I need sustenance before I pass out." She winked at Angel, who laughed.

Joanne rolled her eyes towards Angel, before she gently nudged her horse into a canter after Kylee.

"Angel," Penny called, watching the younger girl drop back. "Catch up, sweetie." She nudged her horse to the side as the other riders cantered by, waiting for Angel to reach her.

"Penny, I'm going to ride the long way back." Angel looked at the pretty, dark-haired lady, hoping she'd allow her to have some free time.

Penny thought for a moment, knowing she couldn't really say no, it was Angel's home, after all. "Okay, just be careful. Do you want your friends to join you?" She looked over her shoulder, seeing Kylee and Joanne cantering off ahead of the group.

"No, thanks." Angel wasn't ready to give up her inner calm, and was looking forward to being around no one else's feelings but hers and her pony's for the ride back.

"Just be careful, Angel. Tom and Jess will fire me if anything happens to you." She smiled.

"I won't let them." Angel smiled back as Penny nodded and turned her horse to follow the others. She sighed, content to be alone at last, and turned her pony along the track that would meet up with the old cattle track and take her past the equestrian centre.

With the school year over, she thought about all the things she wanted to do with Sam and Jane during the holidays. She wondered if the boys would portal them somewhere fun for a day? Although she knew the importance of the portal, and that it was only supposed to be used for royal-soul business, surely there wasn't any harm in asking? She daydreamed for twenty minutes about the locations Sam might like best, knowing Jane was well-travelled, being the Gatekeeper's niece, and probably wouldn't care where they went, as long as they were all together.

As her pony rounded the track lined with thick bushes and dappled with shadows of the branches above, the hairs on the back of her neck stood up. Whatever it was, her pony felt the ominous presence, too—it shuffled its hooves and snorted.

"Hey, there," Angel soothed, rubbing the animal's neck, trying to calm her both physically and mentally as she pushed a calming intention towards her mind. It didn't work. The 'thing' that was making the pony nervous, was far stronger than Angel.

A greasy ball of fear grew in the pit of her stomach as she looked at the track behind her...

Nothing there.

She nudged the pony forward, seeing the equestrian centre up ahead. If she could just get inside, she'd feel much better. "Come on, girl, come on," she cooed, running her hand over the pony's velvety neck. But the pony would not settle, flinging her head up, eyes wide in fear. She kicked her back legs out furiously, pig-rooting and throwing Angel to the ground, before bolting off.

Angel lay winded and temporarily unable to conjure a calming spell. She rolled over onto her side, desperately pulling air into her lungs, not too worried about her pony, knowing she would head straight to where her basket of lucerne would be waiting.

Finally, she could suck in a lungful of air as she pushed herself up onto her hands and knees. Relived she could breathe again, she wanted to get as far away from this unusual, dark feeling—one that she'd never experienced before on the college grounds. That was...until Max's cousin touched her earlier. Before she could dwell too long on that thought, a pair of brown, Italian-leather shoes filled her vision. Looking up, she gasped in fright. *Speak of the devil!*

"Hello, there. Are you all right?" He smiled coldly.

What was he doing here, when he'd told Max he was leaving?

"I was taking a call when I saw your pony throw you," he said, offering her a hand up.

She sat on her haunches, not wanting to touch him at all. "I'm fine, thanks," she said begrudgingly. Standing, she dusted off her dirty bottom and back before wiping her hands over the front of her jeans, taking a nervous step backwards. *Sam,* she pushed out into the breeze. *Michael? Bowie?*

Her fear was sending the most delicious thrill through him. He pinned her in place with his stare, his eyes going completely black, as he conjured a dark ring around her, from which she could not escape.

Her heartbeat accelerated at an alarming rate as she reached out, trying to push through the transparent black barrier that imprisoned her, only to have it burn her fingertips. Gasping in fright, she looked up at Max's cousin. "What do you want?" She hated that her voice quivered with fear.

"Just a little taste," he whispered, and, to her horror, he stripped off his shirt and opened his arms.

What is he doing?

He smiled eerily and whispered once more, "Be still."

Angel nearly cried out in horror as her entire body froze. She couldn't even close her eyes to the terror that filled her vision.

Brendan's outstretched arms revealed lines of pulsating veins that looked like a mass of thin snakes sliding around under his skin, looking for an escape. Suddenly, they protruded from his flesh like long, skinny leeches attached to their host, inching closer and closer to her.

She wanted to scream, to cry, but even without Max's cousin freezing her in place, terror held her immobile.

Her breathing quickened as the long, wet veins approached her, sliding through the black barrier, and brushing against her exposed flesh.

The ice-cold, bloody ends chilled her as they caressed her face, her arms, her throat. Then a world of pain infiltrated her soul as they pierced her flesh and slid under her skin to latch around her veins. An unimaginable agony filled every nerve ending as each individual vein sucked the blood essence from her.

Michael, I need you! She screamed silently. The surrounding barrier blocked the cry for help that she so desperately tried to push towards her blood-sibling.

Ecstasy filled Brendan; her blood was unlike anything he'd ever tasted in all his one-thousand years. He dropped his head back, smiling up into the sky as he took and absorbed more than he should have. He sensed the vibration of her silent call within her blood, and, after greedily taking another sweet mouthful, he regretfully called his tiny mouths back to his body.

He knew once she reached maturity, her essence would provide the most elite power to those who ingested it. He laughed gleefully as she collapsed, and marvelled at his luck, running into her this day. Brendan bent down and scooped her small, limp body up in his arms, determined to take her with him back to the mansion. He'd keep her imprisoned for the remaining years that it would take for her to reach her full potential. This way, Max would have company with someone he knew, being the same age and all. It might soften the boy towards him once he'd had a taste of her himself.

Michael had been underneath the pool's water, kissing Elizabeth soundly, when Angel's first call for help rang out.

Samantha heard it as she and Max found their second treasure, a bundle of comics, which thrilled Max, as he knew Eddy loved them.

Sam froze for a moment, but the second she'd heard Angel's call, it dissipated. No feeling of fear or dread reached her as calm resumed. She tried to call back to Angel but received no answer. She frowned—should she be worried? It was time to find Bowie and Michael.

"Are you all right?" Max asked, not liking to see her frown.

"I have to find my brother, right now. I'm sorry..."

"It's all right, I'll come with you."

Sam nodded as she ran from beyond the tennis courts, across campus, and towards the swimming pool where she knew all the teenagers liked to hang out.

Bowie was sitting on the pool's edge when he heard Angel's first call.

He sat for a second before diving back under to get Michael's attention.

When he breached the surface, Michael raised an eyebrow in question as Elizabeth joined them, pouting that her delicious lip-lock with Michael had been interrupted.

Something's wrong with Angel, Bowie pushed into Michael's thoughts, but said aloud for Elizabeth to hear, "We've got to say goodbye to Red's friends, they're heading off." He tugged on his t-shirt and tossed Michael his.

Michael caught it, before running a hand over Elizabeth's hair. "Be back soon, gorgeous."

"Okay. I'll be right here, waiting." She pushed off from the edge and floated backwards, smiling radiantly up at him.

As they approached the pool gates, they both saw Sam running towards them, concern etched on her young face. Seeing Max with her, they didn't say anything as they pushed the gate open.

"Hey, Sam," Bowie said. "We've got to say goodbye to Red's friends."

"Oh, yeah, of course." She played along.

Michael turned to Max. "Max, why don't you go find your friends? Sam won't be long."

Max could tell Michael wasn't *asking* him to find his friends, he was telling him to.

He looked at Sam. "I'll see you soon?"

"Yep, quick as Maccas chips." She forced a calm smile before she turned around and ran after an already-disappearing Bowie and Michael.

"Bikes," Bowie called, sprinting past the dairy shed to where the bike shed stood, opposite the haystack.

"Where is she? I can't get a read on her! Sam?" Michael asked as he got on a bike, starting it up, patting the seat behind him.

Sam shook her head as she leapt on behind Michael and wrapped her arms around his lean waist as Bowie shot off in front of them.

"Anything?" Michael called over his shoulder.

"I'm not sure!" Sam yelled above the roar of the bike's engine as Michael followed Bowie past the stables. The earlier group of riders had already returned and were walking back towards the festivities.

Bowie pulled up in front of Penny, yelling, "Where's Angel?"

"I was just coming to find you all. Her pony returned ten minutes ago."

"And you didn't think to go look for her?" Bowie yelled in disbelief.

"I'm sorry, Bowie, but we had another young rider fall, and we've only just finished bandaging her up and settling the horses. Something spooked them all."

"Well, where was Angel when you left her?" Michael asked, calmer on the exterior than Bowie, not wanting to further poor Penny's guilt. She worked hard, going above and beyond in caring for the college horses. They were lucky to have her on staff.

"Beyond the equine centre, probably off the old cattle track?"

"Thanks," Michael called as Bowie revved the bike and took off, leaving a trail of dust.

"I can't feel her!" Sam cried nervously to Michael.

He patted the top of her hand before gripping the handlebars and flew after Bowie. He couldn't feel her, either—couldn't sense her at all.

And it worried the hell out of him.

Brendan deposited the unconscious royal-soul at Rob Black's feet.

"What's this? Young Angel Cloud, Max's friend?" He looked at Brendan, confused lines running across his face.

"Yes, young Angel Cloud. Taste her," Brendan said, stepping back.

"What?"

"Taste her. She's a royal-soul." Brendan nodded. "And, trust me, she is divine." He grinned wickedly.

Rob bent down and scooped the soft, warm body up in his arms and crossed over to the couch, placing her down. He took a deep breath and released the veins in one wrist. The moment his veins broke through her skin and wrapped around her veins, to taste her Heavenly blood, he pulled back, surprised.

He looked across at Brendan, as a sunny smile broke across his features. "How did you discover this? I've met the girl before and never felt a thing."

"She was shielded, no doubt. I ran into her at the picnic. The moment I placed my hands on her, I felt her energy, her essence. She's young, but she is powerful. I'm going to take her with us when we leave for Italy tomorrow."

Rob titled his head. "Why take her?"

"If her family is looking for her, you won't have the power to shield her as I do. I can conceal her overseas until she reaches the age of full power. Then we will harvest her essence, made all the stronger by her mature, amulet-beating heart."

Rob nodded, "Of course. Where's Max?"

"Still at the picnic. Tom Liam said he'll drop him home."

Rob turned back to the small unconscious figure on the couch, not believing their luck. A royal-soul, finally in their grasp. Good fortune was smiling upon them once more.

Bowie, Michael, and Sam had circled the property trying to locate Angel, and, by the time they returned, it was late afternoon and almost everybody had gone.

Tom pulled into the driveway, after dropping Max home, at the same time the boys parked their bikes. He could feel the tension draping heavily around the three young royal-souls and frowned in concern.

It had been a massive day, entertaining and hosting the three-hundred community members, and he was exhausted before he'd even heard what the problem was. "What's happened?"

"Inside," Michael said, seeing Elizabeth and Patricia walk towards him.

"I've got this," Bowie assured Michael as he grabbed Sam's hand and tugged her into the homestead behind him, leaving Michael to get rid of the girls.

"Michael, where have you been? I missed you, babe." Elizabeth raised a dark eyebrow.

"Sorry, we've been helping out up here and we got caught up. Forgive me?"

She smiled, wrapping slender arms around his neck, stretching up for a kiss. "Only if you kiss me."

He dropped a sweet kiss against her rose-petal-pink lips as her father called from the car, "Come on, girls."

"See you, Michael," Patricia called as she ran to the car.

"See you, Patty." He looked down at Elizabeth. "I'll call you tomorrow?"

"I'll be waiting." She brushed a kiss across his cheek as her father good-naturedly honked the horn.

Michael forced a smile. "Talk soon."

He waited one heartbeat as Elizabeth took off to the car before turning and bolting inside to see what the hell had happened to Angel.

Chapter Nine

Max stood at the end of his driveway with Eddy, who was excitedly flicking through one of the comic books as he cheerfully rambled on about how cute Jane was.

"She sure is nice," Max replied absently, feeling slightly distracted since he couldn't say goodbye to Sam before he left.

The sound of a Harley Davidson reached their ears before they saw the dust trail blaze down Lover's Lane.

"Your dad's so neat." Max smiled at Eddy.

"Yeah, he's the best."

As Eddy's dad, Steve, pulled up, he passed Eddy a helmet, yelling out, "Hi, Max!" over the engine's roar.

Max grinned and waved as Eddy tucked his comic books into a side-pocket of his bag before jamming the helmet onto his head and jumping on the bike behind his dad. "See ya, mate!" he yelled.

Max smiled and waved again, watching them speed off, back along Lover's Lane, before he let out a sigh. He turned and walked along the gravel driveway up into the mansion, wishing, not for the first time, that his dad was as cool as Eddy's.

Pushing open the butler's entrance, he walked into the kitchen and across to the fridge. Looking inside, he contemplated the contents before grabbing a small, red apple from the crisper, to chase down the fairy floss he'd pigged out on.

As he headed up towards his bedroom, he could hear his father and cousin talking. He tiptoed, so as to not disturb them, hoping to make a quiet escape to his room to be left in peace.

The ancient floorboards on the staircase betrayed him, groaning loudly under his weight.

"Max? Is that you?" his father called.

He wanted to yell back, '*No, it's someone else*,' but his boarding-school manners told him otherwise. "Yes—Eddy just got picked up."

"Yes, we heard Steve's bike. Please join us in here."

Max rolled his eyes as he bit into the apple. He sighed and walked down the hallway and into the open lounge room that doubled as his father's office.

When he saw the small figure on the couch, he dropped the apple and rushed to her side.

"What's wrong with Angel?" He shook her shoulders, trying to wake her.

Feeling a large hand clamp down on his shoulder, he frowned as he looked up at Brendan.

"Max, you can't wake her, otherwise she'll be frightened. You don't want to frighten your friend, do you?" The thought of how delicious her royal-blood would taste, being pumped with fright around her body, nearly convinced him to allow Max to wake her up. But they'd already consumed too much of her blood; she needed time to rest, to allow her amulet to heal her.

Max looked confused, but shook his head. He looked across at his father. "What's going on, Dad?"

Rob smiled. "Son, tomorrow you're heading off to Italy for a few years to complete your training, so that, one day, you will be able to run the family business. Brendan will take good care of you, and you'll be trained by our elders. We thought young Angel here would make a fabulous travelling companion for you."

Max stared at his father, not knowing what to say to this absurd statement.

Rob stared back at his son, waiting.

"What about Angel's family?" Max asked.

"What about them?" Rob took a deep breath, trying to keep his patience.

"Won't they worry about where she is?"

"Oh, they know, of course." Rob forced a tight smile.

Max knew that was a lie.

Brendan could see that Rob might make the situation worse at any moment by losing his patience with Max's questions, so he placed a hand on his shoulder to get his attention.

"Max, we are leaving early in the morning. Why don't you pack a few things, then get an early night, hmm?"

Max looked up into his cousin's dark eyes. They reminded him of one of Eddy's cartoon shark posters on his wall, eyes that were both empty and terrifying. He knew he had to play his next part exactly right.

He looked across at Angel, then forced a smile before looking up at Brendan. "Sure, this will be fun having a friend come with me."

"That's the spirit, Max. Now get some sleep."

Max nodded and forced a big yawn. "Goodnight." He nodded to his father, who was looking more relaxed. He concentrated on leaving with a casual air, collecting his dropped apple and walking unhurriedly along the hallway before noisily running up the stairs, banging his bedroom door shut.

Max dropped the apple into his corner bin before falling forward, placing his hands on his knees as his thoughts swam in a pool of confusion.

What was Angel Cloud doing here? And why was she unconscious? And what were his cousin and father going to do to her? He thought of Sam, and how worried she would be that her friend was missing.

He stood up, turned to the mirror, and whispered to his reflection, "You have to do something!" He nodded to himself once, before grabbing the spare pillow and an extra blanket from his closet. Rushing to his bed, he pulled the covers back and shoved them in. Then he wrapped the quilt around them, forming a body shape.

Max grabbed his old Halloween costume bag, pulled out a black wig, and shoved it over his bicycle helmet. Then he propped it onto his pillow, shoving it down and pulling the cover almost all the way over it, so it appeared as though he'd snuggled down nice and tight.

He hit the repeat button on his white-noise CD before grabbing a black hoodie out of his drawer. He pulled it on as he rushed over to the window, then climbed out on to the roof. Max slid it shut behind him, then scrambled down the gutter, and onto the dark lawn for a stealthy get away.

"This is *absurd*!" Bowie yelled. "Why can't we find her?"

They'd spent the last few hours casting a locator spell, but, even between all their powers, could not locate Angel.

Anywhere.

Bowie was growing equally as frustrated as Michael was becoming anxiously quiet. Six hours has passed since Angel's disappearance, and it had them all on-edge.

Jess shook his head as they all looked toward Fletch, who'd been summoned as soon as the boys had returned from searching the property.

"Whoever is cloaking her is an ancient one."

"Well, he'd have to be, to be able to cross our wards without alerting us to his presence," Tom said in agreement.

Michael had his arm around Sam's shoulder. She'd been crying silent tears for the past four hours. She felt so guilty that she hadn't been with Angel. It was her duty to protect her soul-sibling, despite them both being underage and still learning to use their gifts. Her guilt was growing stronger by the minute, and she thought she might explode with every second that passed, with them still failing to find Angel.

Michael sensed a charge in the air. He assumed it was Bowie, who hadn't stopped pacing angrily since the location spell had failed. But the hairs on the arm he had placed around Samantha's shoulder rose stiffly. An uncomfortable feeling hit him, but before he could remove his arm, Samantha's anger shot a bolt of lightning around her, impacting all in the room. Bowie counteracted it and shut it down, but not before it knocked everyone else over.

The air sizzled around them as Fletch got to his feet, running a hand over his dark hair, which was standing on end like someone had rubbed a balloon over his head, creating static.

Samantha cried out, "I'm sorry! I really didn't mean to do that!" She burst into further tears and ran to Bowie, pushing her face into his chest. "I want Mum!" she cried repeatedly. "I just want Mum!"

"Shh, it's okay, Sam. It's all going to be okay." Bowie rubbed her back as he watched Jess help Tom up from the floor, and then Michael.

Hurried footsteps approached from the corridor before Mrs. McGoldrick burst worriedly into the room. "What's going on in here, my loves?" She looked exhausted after the big day at the picnic, but had still stayed on after learning of Angel's disappearance.

Michael shuffled his feet restlessly as Tom answered, "Just one of the bulbs exploding, nothing to worry about. Why don't you put your feet up with a nice cup of tea?"

"How about I make *everyone* a nice cup of tea?" she replied, just as a banging noise sounded at the front door. "After I answer that, of course." She hurried from the room as the banging persisted.

Bowie smoothed a hand over Sam's face, wiping her tears as she looked up at him.

"She'll be okay," he said. "I can feel it."

Her amber eyes were staring worriedly up into his when hurried footsteps running towards them had everyone turning toward the door.

Max burst into the room, breathless and, by the looks of his clothes, had taken more than one tumble on his way to them in the dark.

"What is it, Max?" Michael asked the breathless boy as Mrs. McGoldrick rushed into the room behind him.

Jess walked over to her, placing an arm around her shoulder and steering her out. "How about you and I get that tea going?" He smiled down at her.

"Good idea." She patted the top of his hand as they walked along the hallway and into the kitchen.

Everyone in the room turned their gaze on Max, waiting for him to catch his breath.

He turned to Sam. "I'm so sorry, Sam, I don't know what they've done to her, but they've got her, and he plans on taking her to Italy with me in the morning!" He blurted out between breaths.

Bowie strode forward after seeing the blood drain from Michael's face. "Who, Max? Where?"

"My cousin and father, at my house." He dropped his hands onto his knees, panting and beyond relieved he had made it here to share his burden.

Sam walked over and rubbed his back. "Thank you, Max, thank you for coming here to tell us." She looked over her shoulder at Michael, who'd turned to address Fletch.

"The Blacks. Of course! We should have known, after what happened to Bowie."

Fletch shook his head, looking grievously troubled as he folded his arms. "The Council cast a detection spell over their property after that incident, they felt nothing." Glancing at Tom, he said, "Their wards must have been conjured by someone with ancient power."

"As were ours, but, apparently, ours weren't strong enough, if one of theirs got through it today without a single one of us feeling it." Bowie pulled out his pocketknife and nervously flicked it open and closed repeatedly as he resumed pacing.

Tom put his hands on his hips. "We don't know what this ancient one is capable of. But we do know that both Bowie and Michael can create enough of a disturbance for us to get inside that house and get Angel out."

Fletch considered this for a moment, concerned that time was ticking, and wondered if Max's father was aware that his son had run off to get help? Looking at Max, he saw the reason why he'd betrayed his own family—Sam was clasping his hand with both of hers. There was something familiar about the boy, something that shone through his dark eyes...

"Come here, boy." Fletch held out a hand, waiting for Max to take it.

Max looked at Sam, who nodded, releasing his hand. He stepped forward to take the hand of the tall man, who, although he looked as forbidding as his father, held a certain note of light about him.

Fletch held the young boy's hand as he stared deeply into his soul, frowning in confusion at what he was feeling. This was unheard of...

"What is it, Fletch?" Tom asked, seeing Fletch frown.

"Max is half royal-soul, half Vein." Silence followed Fletch's statement.

"What does that even mean?" Max finally asked, feeling braver than his twelve-years of age usually afforded him.

Once again, all eyes turned to Max.

"What that means, young Maxwell Black, is that your mother was one of our kin. There is such lightness in you, and it overpowers the shadows that want to consume and guide your instincts." Fletch released him. "Heavenly, I believe." He addressed the others.

"What does that even mean?" Max whispered, stepping back.

Sam shook her head, letting him know now wasn't the time as she reached out and took his hand. Immediately, a calming warmth filled Max. What was it about her that made him feel complete?

"Has this ever been heard of, a Vein producing a child with a royal-soul?" Tom raised an eyebrow towards Fetch, who slowly shook his head.

"As intrigued as I am about this situation, what are we waiting for?" Michael asked Tom. "Let's go and get my sister."

"Yeah, let's do that." Bowie marched towards the door, a dangerous glint in his eyes.

"Bowie, stop!" Tom commanded.

Bowie didn't listen as he marched down the hallway.

Tom turned to Michael. "You have to stop him. We can't just waltz in there, thunderbolts and mind control won't work on an ancient Vein's property; we won't know what we're dealing with. The only thing we can do…is trade Max for Angel."

"What? *No!*" Sam cried. "He'll be punished! He's betrayed his father, and that cousin of his is evil!"

Tom took a deep breath, then looked at Sam before saying, "Michael, get Bowie. Sam, come here."

Sam clung to Max's hand, but, finally, stepped towards Tom, who bent down and said in a calm voice, "I know you want to protect your friend here, but please don't make this any more difficult than it already is, okay?"

Sam looked up into Tom's eyes, hers filling with tears as she whispered, "I just wish I could keep Angel *and* Max safe."

"I know, pet, I know." Tom straightened as Michael walked back into the room with a furious-looking Bowie, followed by Jess and Mrs. McGoldrick, who walked in carrying a tray of tea, and sandwiches.

"Here you all go." Mrs. McGoldrick smiled warmly, noticing the tension on all their faces, wishing she could do more than bring tea and food.

"Thanks, Mrs. McGoldrick. You may as well head home now, we've found Angel. She went home with Max without telling anyone, and Max, not knowing our phone number, came all the way here to let us know that she fell asleep there."

"Oh, what a relief!" Mrs. McGoldrick beamed. "I was hoping it would be something as simple as that. Well, I'll see you all in the morning." She bent and dropped a kiss on Samantha's cheek before waving to the room and heading out.

The room remained silent for a handful of moments as everyone took a cup off the tray and had a few mouthfuls of tea. The sandwiches remained untouched; no one could think of eating until they had Angel back, safe and sound.

"Time to make the call. Michael, are you ready?" Fletch asked.

"Like you wouldn't believe," Michael said calmly, placing his cup on the desk and walking to the phone. Picking it up, he turned to Max. "Your number, please, Max."

Max gave him the number, and, as Michael dialled, the room held its breath.

Michael waited, feeling more and more nervous with every unanswered ring.

"Good evening, Black residence," A formal voice finally answered.

"Mr. Black?"

"No. Please hold for one moment."

Michael waited for the two minutes - which felt more like an hour - before a voice he recognised called, "Hello?" through the phone.

"Rob Black, I want my sister returned to the corner of Trufood and Black's Road in ten minutes, or you'll never see your son again."

Silence ensued.

"Hello?" Michael said into the receiver. It sounded as though someone had dropped it onto a hard surface.

He could hear muffled voices through the receiver, then what sounded like hurried footsteps and yelling as Rob Black called out his son's name and instructed Brendan to check Max's bedroom.

Another minute passed before a cold voice reached Michael's ear. "What have you done with my son?"

"Nothing. And I will continue to do nothing to him, if you return Angel, unharmed, in…eight minutes, now, to that location."

The phone went dead. Michael held it away from his ear as he looked around the room.

"I think that's a 'yes'?"

"What about Max?" Samantha cried, worried for her friend.

"It sounds like Rob thinks we took Max, Sam, not that he ran away and betrayed him. He'll be okay." Michael looked at Max. "Are you fearful of your father?"

Max shook his head. "Not really. My cousin is a creep, though."

"I'm sorry, Max, but we can't be worried about your cousin right now. We have to meet your father and get Angel," Tom said. "If there is anything we can do for you in the future, just know we are here, okay?"

Max nodded, wishing he could stay. There was a lightness in the air here, a calm inner peace he'd never really felt until now.

Fletch turned to the group. "We don't have much time, let's move. Samantha, you stay here."

"But…"

"There's no time, Sam," Bowie cut her off. 'It's okay, we've got this. We don't need to worry about you, too. Come on." He made for the door as Michael watched Sam and Max hug goodbye.

"Be safe," Sam whispered, before Max turned and hurried along behind the others to get into Jess's jeep.

They flew down the driveway and towards the corner of Black's Road. Bowie grew calmer the closer they got to Red's house, and Michael could hear his intention.

Not until Angel is clear.

Of course, Bowie replied.

They pulled up before crossing the cattle grid. The exchange-party stood beside the signpost that pointed to Black's Road and Trufood Road, where they watched as Rob's high-beams shone up the sloping road.

"Are you okay, Max?" Tom asked.

"Yeah, sure," He replied uncertainly.

Bowie put his arm around Max, shifting his small body in front of his own, holding him close. "I'm not going to hurt you, but I need your father to think that I could, okay?"

"Okay." Max could barely whisper the word. He didn't really know Sam's brother that well, but, in this situation, he sensed a dangerous energy flowing from him.

Rob Black pulled his car up along Red's sweeping side lawn and got out of the vehicle. Standing still, he stared at the group of men holding his son for ransom.

"Are you all right, my boy?"

"Yes, Father." Max made his voice sound small, like he'd been through a hard time and was grateful his dad had come to his rescue.

"Where's my sister?" Michael yelled. He could see Red's front-bedroom curtain shift as she heard the commotion, hoping she'd stay inside and clear of Rob Black's radar.

Rob nodded to the car and another figure climbed out, with Angel in his arms.

The hairs on Max's, and almost all the other men's hair, stood on end. All but Bowie's.

Brendan stepped forward, Angel looking like a broken ragdoll in his arms.

"What have you done to her?" Michael's voice cracked in anguish.

Calm down. Bowie brushed against his mind.

"Let's make the exchange and be done with it, shall we?" Fletch commanded.

"Right, then." Rob nodded to Brendan.

Brendan and Bowie walked into the centre of the road, Michael one step behind Bowie.

"Like gentlemen," Bowie said, holding Max in front of him.

As Brendan stopped a foot away, Bowie nodded to him, then gestured to Michael. "Pass her to him."

Brendan stood motionless for a moment before saying, "I'll be back for her one day, this I promise you." He smiled coldly.

"Just give her to me," Michael spat, then reached for Angel.

Brendan practically dropped her into Michael's arms, then reached out, grabbing Max sharply by the arm and dragging him towards the car. He'd seen the dummy in Max's bed and, unlike his father, wasn't fooled that he'd been taken against his will.

"She was delicious," Rob called to Michael's retreating back, grinning like he'd already won and this exchange was nothing more than a slight hiccup in his grand plans.

It filled Bowie with disgust and rage. He didn't think twice about his next action and threw a lightning-bolt straight into Rob Black's chest. It sent him flying several feet into the air before he thudded to the ground like a broken clay figure, the bloody, charred hole in his chest smoking.

Brendan cursed as he tossed Max in the car's direction, spinning around to throw a handful of razor-sharp veins out of his wrist and towards the retreating backs of the royal-souls. "Like gentlemen—*really?*" he screamed.

Bowie whispered to the wind, sweeping the vein-arrows off-course before running behind Michael to shield him as he headed towards the jeep. "Go!" he yelled as they all ran for cover.

Brendan flung out another handful of vein-arrows as Max screamed over his dead father's body. Bowie turned to see if the boy was all right, worried for his sister's young friend, and gasped in surprise as the vein-arrows pierced his chest.

"Bowie!" Michael cried, feeling his soul-siblings pain.

Fletch dove to snatch up Bowie's stricken body, and hurled a gust of wild wind towards Brendan, sending him back twenty feet.

Red ran out of her front door, waving madly at Fletch, indicating he get them all out of there.

He climbed into the jeep with Bowie before they took off at break-neck-speed towards the homestead.

Tom watched Red through the rear windscreen as Vicki Light and Jane rushed out the front door. The three of them sent a blue ring of wildfire around the college grounds, before placing a protective barrier around Red's house.

Fletch looked down at Bowie's ashen face, which was covered in sweat, his breathing shallow. Moving his t-shirt aside, he saw a mass of wriggling veins moving under his flesh.

Bowie gasped in pain before gritting his teeth together, preventing the scream that wanted to escape.

"Will he be okay, Fletch?" Tom asked shakily.

Fletch clenched his jaw and briskly nodded once.

The jeep screeched to a halt in the driveway, and it was all-hands-on-deck getting Angel and Bowie inside and into the lounge.

Sam rushed to Angel's side as Michael laid her on the couch. Fletch cleared a space on the tall side-table to lay Bowie on.

"Oh no!" Samantha cried in despair at seeing her brother in such a state. "Michael, what happened?"

"It's okay, Sam, I'll heal him with everything I've got, I promise." Michael squeezed her shoulder before he raced to Bowie's side and placed a hand on Bowie's chest, the other over his own heart. He chanted a healing incantation, filled with loving intention, and an extraction charm, to rid Bowie's body of the invasive parasites.

Sam looked down at Angel, wishing for the first time that she was a Heavenly Soul and not Elemental, so she could heal her soul-sibling. Tears fell from her eyes as she placed her hand on Angel's chest and pushed her thoughts towards Angel's mind. *Wake up, Angel. Wake up and be well, please.*

Jess put his arm around Sam. "I've got this, little one."

She nodded and stepped aside so Jess could pour his Heavenly healing energy into Angel.

It took longer than Fletch would have liked for both Bowie and Angel to regain consciousness.

Angel gasped in fright when her eyes opened, unsure at first where she was. Then she cried with relief and rolled onto her side, reaching for Sam's hand.

Sam took her hand and squeezed it, worried about how limp Angel's grasp felt.

Bowie sat up and put his arm around Michael's shoulder. "Thanks," he whispered shakily.

"No—thank *you*. Those things would have grabbed onto Angel and I if you hadn't protected us."

Bowie smiled weakly. "That's my job."

Michael hugged his soul-sibling before walking over to Angel, then placed a hand on her small, sweaty back as she cried, clinging to Sam's hand.

Michael focused on her body, feeling out any injuries. Jess had done a great job healing and reviving her, but whatever Brendan and Rob Black had done to her had weakened her considerably. Her amulet needed her heart happy and strong to recharge her essence.

"Angel?"

She looked up at her blood-sibling, tears running down her face as she reached her arms out to him.

He gathered her up and said to the rest of the room, "I think Angel can answer questions in the morning, a healing bath would do her good."

"That is correct, young man," Red agreed as she breezed through the doorway, young Jane at her heels.

It relieved Michael to see Red, knowing Angel was at the age of wanting her privacy, and, since Mrs. McGoldrick had gone home, Red's female, helping hands were welcome.

He smiled in relief. "Thanks, Red, I'll carry her up for you,"

Red nodded as she said to Sam and Jane, "Girls, get the bed ready for the three of you to snuggle into. But, after I tuck Angel into bed with you, no talking, she'll need healing sleep."

"Yes, Aunty, of course," Jane said, while Samantha nodded enthusiastically in agreement.

As Michael carried Angel out of the room, Red called, "I'll be up in a moment!"

Sam crossed over to Bowie. "Will you be all right?"

He nodded, knowing he shouldn't be lying to his blood-sibling. But she'd been through enough today as it was.

Tom saw the strain around Bowie's eyes. "Time to get ready for bed, Sam. Goodnight, Jane." He smiled at the two girls, dismissing them.

Sam looked at Bowie one final time, worried about the pallor of his skin, before giving him a quick hug. "See you in the morning."

"Goodnight, Sam." He forced a smile as she walked from the room. As soon as she was out of sight, he doubled over in pain. "They're still inside me, Jess!" he cried to his elder.

Fletch, Tom, and Jess rushed to Bowie's side just as he collapsed.

"What is this?" Jess cried to Fletch.

Red hurried over to place her hand over Bowie's chest. Grimacing slightly, she shook her head. "I've seen this before," she said. "Prepare yourselves for a long night ahead, gentlemen."

"Red?" Fletch turned to face the respected healer.

She met his concerned gaze. "We are dealing with a parasite that can regenerate, even when there is only a single molecule remaining. We must drink a blend of energising healing herbs, cut a cross in Bowie's chest, and chant a extraction incantation to lure the parasite out."

"And to destroy it?" Fletch raised an eyebrow.

"Tom will need to vaporise it."

Jess nodded. "I'll prepare the herbs." He looked at Bowie, who was writhing in pain, a slick sheen of sweat coating every inch of his skin. Jess shot Tom a worried look before quickly heading out into the garden to gather the required herbs.

Red turned to Tom. "Keep him cool, I'll be as quick as I can with Angel."

Tom nodded, placing his hands on Bowie's fevered flesh, sending a gentle wave of icy air across him.

Once Red had attended Angel, and tucked her into bed with the sleeping girls, she joined the others.

They drank the healing herbs that Jess and Michael had prepared, cut a cross into Bowie's chest with a sharp blade, before each placed a hand on his feverish flesh. It pained them to witness Bowie's torment; he thrashed and moaned in agony as their extraction incantation began.

Michael was beside himself with angst, terrified that the blasted parasite would do more damage to Bowie's insides before they could eradicate it.

The minutes ticked by as they repeated the extraction chant, whilst simultaneously, they attempted to push healing energy into Bowie's afflicted body. The parasite seemed to be blocking their good intentions. Every cry of pain he released as he thrashed about on the table struck their hearts. Finally, after several hours, as the first bird of the morning greeted daybreak, they vanquished the parasite from Bowie.

It crept in a repulsive, slug-like manner from his chest before falling to the rug below with a wet splat.

Tom raised it up with a whisper to the air and sent it out the window in a swirl of wind, before obliviating it with a fireball.

Checking Bowie was completely free from any toxicity, Michel sent a healing wave through him before sealing his flesh together. The healing party sighed as one, before disappearing to their own quiet space, scattered throughout the household, and collapsing in an exhausted heap.

They managed an hour of sleep before the cheerful Mrs. McGoldrick arrived, bustling around to serve pots of tea and coffee, along with a hearty breakfast.

Chapter Ten

"Bowie, if Max's dad is dead, you can't let Brendan take him away to Italy, you just can't!" Sam cried in despair.

Bowie, still not feeling one-hundred-percent restored, sat in the chair as Samantha paced up and down the length of his room. "I don't know what you want me to do, Sam? That's his cousin, we can't just waltz in and demand he hand Max over."

"Why not? Fletch said that he's part royal-blood. Shouldn't it be our responsibility to look out for him?" She begged with liquid-amber eyes, her top lip wobbling.

"Oh, please don't cry, Sam…" He trailed off, wishing he had more energy to comfort her. *Where's Michael when I need him?*

"Right here," Michael sighed as he walked into the room, sensing this was all a bit too overwhelming for Bowie in his healing state. "Sam, we understand your concern for Max, we do. But his cousin is dangerous and…"

"Exactly!" Sam spun around, cutting Michael off with glowing eyes. "He *is* dangerous, and Max put himself in a dangerous position to help Angel, to help us. Don't you see? It's *our* turn to help *him*."

Michael met Bowie's gaze. They knew she was right.

"Sam, I promise you, as soon as I'm feeling better, and we have the High Council's blessing, Michael and I will rescue Max. Even if we have to portal to Italy, okay?"

"But how long will that be, Bowie? Max needs us *now*, while he's still *here*." Samantha did something she'd never done in her life; she stamped her foot.

Bowie raised an eyebrow.

Michael hid a grin.

They could see how profoundly serious she was, and they didn't want her to think that they weren't taking this important discussion seriously.

Bowie ran a hand across his forehead, hating the fact that it felt damp with fevered sweat. His hand shook with lethargy, causing his handsome features to frown in frustration. "Michael, can you please pour some energy into me? I hate feeling like this!"

Michael walked over and ran his hand over Bowie's shoulder, easing him back against the chair before resting his hand over Bowie's chest where Brendan shot the veins into him.

He smiled at Sam before closing his eyes, and began whispering a nurturing, energising incantation.

Sam forced herself not to pace. She knew, deep down, that she couldn't expect Bowie to rescue Max in the state he was in. But it was hard to be still, to not cry or scream; she was completely desperate to rescue her friend from someone who'd hurt both her blood- and soul-siblings so terribly.

"I feel better, thanks, Michael." Bowie didn't want to drain Michael any further; last night had taken a toll on them all.

"I can keep going," Michael said, concern lacing his voice.

"No, all good." He forced a smile and stood up, turning to Sam. "Let's go talk to Jess and Tom. See what they think."

"Absolutely no way in *hell* am I letting you out on a rescue mission, Bowie."

"But Tom…" Bowie began in frustration.

"Bowie," Tom interrupted. "You've not fully recovered from last night!" Tom didn't yell, but he may as well have.

Sam stood beside her blood-sibling, hands fisted at her sides as she begged Jess to say something that would help her cause.

"I don't know, Tom, I think we have to make the most of this funeral situation delaying their departure; the fact that Max is still here in the country is to our advantage." Jess downed the banana smoothie Mrs. McGoldrick had whipped up for him before ripping into a Snickers bar. He was on a quick break before the afternoon run to feed the cattle.

Tom folded his arms, mulling over what Jess said. "Yeah…I hate to admit it, but you're right. I just don't trust Brendan Black as far as I can throw him."

"He's not going to make a scene at a country funeral, Tom," Michael jumped in, as it looked like Tom was considering their plan.

"Mrs. McGoldrick said the wake is going to be held at the Blacks' mansion. It will be packed to the rafters with townsfolk wanting to come and pay their respects." Jess nodded. "By all pretences, Rob Black was a popular man."

"And that makes it easy for us to get in and get Max out," Bowie finished, driving the point home. "No fighting necessary, just a simple identification spell and a smooth extraction."

Sam looked up at Bowie, hope in her eyes. He winked at her before giving Tom his attention.

Tom nodded. "Okay. I'll check in with Red, she'll have all the news on any unexpected arrivals from out of town, as she and her ladies are preparing the food for the wake."

"She'll obviously be using an identification spell, too, after last night?" Michael asked,

"Of course." Tom replied.

Bowie felt at ease at the thought of Red being safe.

"All right, then, it looks like we're doing this. Bowie, you're not going anywhere until you are fully healed, so I suggest you go lay out in the healing garden and let Mother Earth restore you. Michael, go ask her for some healing assistance. Take Angel, too."

"But she's not fully healed herself." Michael was concerned about both his soul- and blood-siblings.

"I'm fine!" Angel called from the doorway, where she'd been standing with Jane, listening to the conversation.

All eyes turned towards a still-pale-looking Angel, but her eyes were bright with determination.

She'd pour every bit of energy-essence into Bowie, if it meant it would help to rescue Max. For Max, and for Sam.

Sam crossed over to her soul-sibling and took her hand. "Are you sure?"

Angel smiled as she nodded. "Absolutely."

"All right, then," Tom sighed. "Let's do everything we can to be as strong as we can be, and as prepared for the unexpected."

"Can Sam walk me home?" Jane asked.

"Sure," Bowie answered. "Why don't you stay with Jane for the afternoon, Sam? Help Red and the ladies do some of the food prep?"

"Oh, yes!" both Sam and Jane agreed enthusiastically.

They turned to hug Angel, Sam whispering, "Will you be all right?"

"Don't worry about me, we'll get Bowie strong enough to rescue Max, I promise." Angel hugged Sam back reassuringly.

"Come on, Sam." Jane smiled at Angel before waving to the boys, then, hand-in-hand, the two girls dashed into the kitchen to say goodbye to Mrs. McGoldrick.

Michael crossed over to Angel and dropped his hand on her shoulder. "Are you feeling up to this?"

"Yeah, I've just had a pot of lucerne, oat straw, peppermint, rosemary and rosella tea to energise me." Angel met Bowie's frowning eyes; she knew he was worried about her stamina, too. "And I've just made one for Bowie to drink, with chamomile, jasmine, lavender and rose-scented geranium to relieve exhaustion."

"Yuck." Bowie grinned good-naturedly, letting her know he appreciated her efforts.

"Come on, are we doing this or what?" she called as she headed towards the healing garden.

Tom got Michael's attention as Bowie followed Angel out through the kitchen to get the teapot, before heading out the back door. "Feel them both out as you perform the spell, Michael. Don't overdo it."

"I won't, promise." Michael nodded to Tom and Jess before he headed out into the garden.

A drooping She-oak offered a patch of shade as the Australian sun beat down. The Kangaroo Apple's purple flowers scented the air, along with the wattle tree and Old Man Weed. All the plants in the healing garden uplifted and energise one's soul. A bed of chamomile flowers smiled up at the sky, surrounded by a curving aisle of fennel, rosemary, French tarragon, basil, parsley, mint, sage, and chives that twisted around the healing bed.

After Bowie finished the herbal drink, he pulled his t-shirt over his head and tossed it onto the lawn, then lay down on the bed of chamomile.

Angel and Michael knelt either side of Bowie, whispering thanks to Mother Earth as they each took one of his arms and placed his palms against the bed of flowers.

Next, Angel took a teacup filled with healing herbs, which were always steeping in a barrel in the kitchen, and poured it over Bowie's chest. He gasped at the coldness of it.

"Sorry," Angel laughed, feeling better in that moment than she had since Brendan Black had taken her.

Michael grinned at Angel, loving that her eyes immediately brightened with laughter.

"Let's do this, little sister."

She smiled and nodded. They each placed a hand against the wet, scattered herbs that lay against Bowie's chest, and, placing a hand against their heartbeats, took a deep breath. Feeling their amulets charge their beating hearts, they thought good, healing intentions, closed their baby-blue eyes, and whispered,

"Mother Earth below and angels above,
Hear this prayer for our beloved,
Help us heal this ethereal soul,
To avoid despair, a gaping hole,
Let us shine our healing Light,
Remove the foul touch of damnations blight."

They sat there, fingers pressed against Bowie's smooth, firm chest, their essence flowing into his soul from theirs.

Bowie looked up into the faces of the two heavenly souls he'd loved since the first moment he saw them both. He could feel their charged energy wrap around his heart and flow through his blood, cleansing him of any remnants of the toxic touch of Brendan's veins. It was a little painful, yet exhilarating, having both souls' positive energy swirl inside and around him.

He could see a light sheen of sweat on both their brows as they sat under the summer sun, repeating the chant over and over again. An hour passed, and he could feel Angel's exhaustion.

He whispered to the air and waved his fingers, sending a breeze to kiss their faces cool. Their eyes opened, connecting with Bowie's as a rainbow wave of energy washed over them all, making them laugh.

"I'll never get used to that!" Bowie smiled.

"How do you feel?" Michael asked, his hand still on Bowie's chest, beside Angel's.

Bowie placed his hand on top of theirs and squeezed as he beamed up at them, his amber eyes glowing. "I feel great, thanks."

He picked Angel's hand up and kissed the back of it noisily, making her laugh. "Special thanks to you, kiddo. I know you must have been feeling worse than me, what with both of the Blacks taking your essence. Are you okay?"

He sat up, brushing the dried herbs off his chest, watching Angel. He and Michael waited for her reply.

Angel wiped her palms together, sitting on her bottom to stretch out her legs, considering telling a white lie. But she could feel Michael brush her mind—*Don't lie.*

"I am tired, but the herbs helped, truly."

"You know you're not coming to the funeral tomorrow, don't you?" Bowie stood up, looking down at her crestfallen face, wishing now that he'd let Michael be the one to tell her.

She looked up at him, shielding her eyes from the sun. "I need to be there for Max."

"No." Michael stood, reaching for her hand, pulling her to her feet. "You can be here for Max when we bring him home, okay?"

As she stood, she squeezed Michael's fingers before releasing his hand. "Sure," she replied quietly.

Bowie retrieved his t-shirt, teapot, and cup as Angel turned and walked away, heading in the opposite direction of the house.

"Where do you think you're going?" Michael asked.

"I'm going to lay in the sun with the kittens," she replied.

"That sounds like a good idea." Bowie smiled as he walked backwards to the house. "Do not step one foot off the property. Red's wildfire has been amped up for protection, so you're safe in our boundary. Got it?"

"Yes, I've got it." She waved as she took off around the side of the garden gate lined with rose bushes.

She sighed once she was out of the boys' line of vision and allowed her shoulders to drop as she wrapped her arms around her stomach. Exhaustion draped around her like a weighted blanket. By the time she reached the haystack, she could have wept with relief. She curled up on the scattered hay, bathed in sunlight, falling asleep instantly. The mother cat and now-grown kittens rubbed against her before wrapping around her and sleeping the afternoon away.

"I'm spending the night, Angel, so when Sam goes to the wake tomorrow, you and I can hang out." Jane was happy to see Angel's face light up with that piece of information; she hated seeing her friend unhappy and drained after her horrific ordeal.

"Oh, I'm so glad. The thought of waiting here on my own sucked." Angel smiled at Jane.

"Come on, let's watch a movie before lights out." Sam headed up the staircase.

"Angel, can you please come in here a moment?" Tom called down the hallway as Angel's foot hit the bottom step.

"I'll see you up there." Jane smiled before following Sam.

Angel walked into the study and was surprised to see Red standing at the end of the desk. In front of her was a deep metal bowl and a wickedly-sharp looking blade.

Michael, Bowie, Tom, and Jess stood to the side, arms folded, each wearing a serious expression.

What now?

Michael stepped forward. "Angel, Red has an idea about how to distract Brendan tomorrow, should anything untoward happen."

"Oh?"

Red smiled. "Come here, my dear."

Angel crossed over to Red and smiled up into her sweet face. Her gold-framed glasses glinted as they caught the reflection from the old pendulum-light hanging low over the desk.

"Many years ago, there was an enormously powerful heavenly soul, who'd been captured by the Veins. They extracted his essence to power their forces for three decades before we had the opportunity to rescue him."

"How did you rescue him?"

Red smiled. "We used blood from another heavenly soul and infused it with an elemental-soul's lightning bolt, which made it extremely potent and irresistible to the Veins. It was like an overpowering drug to them, you see, and, once they'd consumed it, they went into a frenzy, searching for more. We left them a blood trail, leading them away from their fortress, and were able to get inside and rescue our own."

"You want to use my blood to distract Max's cousin?"

"Correct. We'll just take enough to make a sweet, irresistible cake, which will distract Brendan, and then we will whisk Max away."

Angel beamed. "I'm so happy to be able to help."

"Come here, please, Bowie." Red smiled, holding out her hand.

Bowie grinned at Tom, pleased they'd asked him to assist in adding potency to Angel's blood.

"Take Angel's hand," Red instructed Bowie.

Bowie took Angel's small hand in his as he looked down at her. "You feeling up to this, kiddo?"

She nodded as she watched Red move the bowl in front of them and pick up the wicked-looking knife.

"Angel, the cut will not be deep, but it will hurt, I'm sorry to say."

Angel looked up, seeing regret fill Red's eyes. "It's okay," she smiled, trying to make her dear elder feel better.

Red returned Angel's smile, before saying to Bowie. "Bowie, as Angel's blood flows into the bowl, I want you to continuously light it up until the last drop falls."

"Of course." Bowie nodded, knowing how important his role was.

Michael turned out the lights. Tom snapped his fingers, creating a small flame that flickered at his fingertips. He sent the flame towards several thick, white candles placed around the room, lighting the wicks.

Jess opened the windows, and Bowie whispered to the night. A cool, sweet breeze drifted in, making the candlelight flare and shoot a powerful white light around them.

Red nodded to Bowie and Angel before whispering, "Ready?"

They nodded. Angel took a deep breath as the blade glistened in the candlelight. Bowie flexed his fingers and held them above the bowl, waiting.

The blade drew along Angel's wrist, making her gasp. She squeezed Bowie's hand, trying to focus on his fingers wrapped around hers, not the pain throbbing along her wrist.

He returned her squeeze, and as the first few precious drops of blood fell towards the bowl, Bowie whispered to the breeze that caressed him. When the first drop contacted the metal bowl, so, too, did Bowie's lightning bolt.

The blood sizzled in the bowl as a steady stream flowed from Angel's wrist.

She held Bowie's hand tight, marvelling at the beauty and magic of an elemental-soul as she watched his outstretched fingers continuously light up her blood.

Red nodded to Bowie, smiling once the bowl had a cup full of lightning-blood.

Bowie stopped the flow of lightning, but clasped Angel's other hand as she swayed with fatigue and blood loss.

He cursed under his breath, feeling her exhaustion as Jess took her bleeding wrist. Jess closed his eyes as he whispered a healing incantation to seal the wound and send a small burst of energy into her.

Her amulet glowed, accepting Jess's essence energy, and she smiled gratefully up at him, reassuring him she was fine.

"Thank you, Angel. This will be an extremely big help should we run into any trouble." Red dropped a kiss on the top of Angel's hair before scooping up the bowl, placing a metal lid on top. "Don't sit up too late tonight, okay?"

Angel nodded. "Of course."

"Goodnight, my loves," Red said to them all before she breezed out of the room.

The men chorused a goodnight after her.

"Good job, you two." Tom placed a hand on Bowie and Angel's shoulders.

"Thanks." Bowie grinned.

"Come on, Angel, let's tuck you and the girls in. You can have an hour's worth of movie time, then sleep."

"Okay," Angel replied. She wouldn't have minded if he wanted her to sleep right now, she was that tired.

After a quick shower, she brushed her teeth and put her pyjamas on, then happily snuggled into the king-sized bed, under the soft, heavy covers between Sam and Jane. She fell asleep as soon as her head hit the pillow.

The funeral itself was a private affair, with only Rob's local farmers and the rural districts' Association of Stock Breeders attending. But the wake, as expected, was indeed packed to the rafters with townspeople and acquaintances from the surrounding districts.

The mansion held a sombre vibe, but only for a short while. Like all good country folk, you couldn't keep them down for long. They all shared entertaining stories as they celebrated Rob Black's life, and what he and his family had done for the community for hundreds of years.

If only they knew. Bowie brushed against Michael's mind.

Thank goodness they don't, Michael replied as he reached for a pastry from one of the passing trays.

Eddy and Sam stood by Max's side as Mr. Kemp placed his hand on Max's shoulder while he conveyed his sympathy and condolences. Max nodded awkwardly, not used to so much warm attention, but he allowed Mr. Kemp to do what he needed to make himself feel better.

Red and her ladies, who'd made enough food to feed an army, were making sure they refilled every tray with sweet and savoury morsels to tempt the grieving and the curious. The mourners spilled from one spacious room to the next as tea, coffee, and scotch aplenty was poured to comfort all.

Red, Bowie and Michael each wore a different face, after casting an identification spell that would fade as soon as they left the Blacks' property. Sam kept forgetting who they were as they stood huddled in a corner with a plate of food, looking like any other soul mourning a valued community member.

Brendan held his scotch as his eyes roamed the room. Something odd was lingering in the air, but he couldn't put his finger on it.

He glanced over at Max, who was deep in conversation with his teacher, and nodded absently to the young man who was asking him if he would still keep his job, now that his employer was dead. He forced himself to assure the man his job would be safe before his eyes strayed back to Max, trying to hear his conversation.

"If you need anything, Max, anything at all you just let me know, okay?" Mr. Kemp smiled warmly.

"Thanks, Mr. Kemp. I appreciate that." Max was still feeling pretty numb about the entire situation. He'd been so mad at his dad for kidnapping and hurting Angel…he still wasn't sure how he felt about any of it. One thing he did know, though, was that he wanted to get as far away from his cousin as possible.

"Let's get some fresh air," Eddy suggested, grabbing a plate of butterfly cupcakes stuffed with homemade strawberry jam and whipped cream.

Sam grabbed one off the plate and nodded. "Good idea. It's getting stuffy in here."

Brendan saw the three youths heading towards the front door. He did not want Max out of his sight, as soon as this ghastly pretence of mourning Rob was over, he wanted to take Max and get the hell out of here as soon as possible.

"Max!" he called.

The three young people stopped and turned. Samantha felt a charge of anger build with every step that Brendan took towards Max. *Why can't I just zap him?* she wondered, feeling her energy surge. *I'd only have to do it once…No one else would notice…*

Sam, stand down! Bowie commanded.

Red caught the conflicting energy, and, right on cue, followed Brendan as he approached Max.

"Max, I don't want you leaving our guests—I'm sure there are a lot of people here who would like to talk to you about your father before we head overseas tomorrow."

Max nodded unenthusiastically as Eddy's dad, Steve, walked over, placing his hand on Eddy's shoulder. "Brendan, I think these poor kids are probably needing a break from this atmosphere. Give them five minutes outside to just be kids, hey? No harm in that."

"No, I…"

"Hello, gentlemen," Red interrupted. "Would you like to try a piece of chocolate brownie, it was Rob's favourite. He requested it every time we had a function in the community." She smiled sweetly and practically shoved the plate in Brendan's face, not giving him a polite way to refuse.

Brendan frowned, not wanting to be distracted by the sweet old lady, but the scent of the brownie had him drooling. He chose a piece and, as he brought it closer towards his mouth, suddenly felt an overwhelming urge to shove his face into the entire plate full of delectable-smelling morsels.

As soon as the moist brownie crossed his lips and melted against his tastebuds, his pupils dilated. He had to force himself not to moan; if this was Rob's favourite, he understood why. But the magic ingredient didn't quite register with him just yet.

"Oh, forgive me, I forgot about the red velvet cream!" Red cried. "It goes perfectly with this. Please, come with me, it's in the kitchen." Red took off with the plate of rich brownies, and Brendan followed like a puppy. She knew once he'd gotten a mouthful of the cream, laced with Angel's blood, he would be out of action for the remainder of the day.

Now! she whispered against Michael and Bowie's minds as she walked towards the kitchen with Brendan at her heels.

The boys left through a side door, walking down the lengthy driveway lined with vehicles, to where Jess and Tom sat waiting in the parked jeep, ready for a quick getaway.

Eddy, Sam, and Max went through the front door, followed by Steve, who was carrying two bike helmets. Tom had warned Steve earlier that they were getting Max out from under his cousin's nose. Not having liked Max's dad overly much, Steve liked the cousin even less, and was happy to help get his son's best mate somewhere safe for a few hours.

Once they were outside, Sam released a deep sigh. So far, so good; they just had to make it to the jeep.

Eddy turned to Max as his dad passed him his helmet. "If you need us for anything, just call."

Max nodded and hugged Eddy before Sam put her hand in his and tugged him down the driveway.

Hearing the rev of the Harley outside, Brendan frowned and turned, getting a bad feeling. Red quickly reached for the bowl of whipped cream and thrust it under Brendan's nose.

"There you go, dunk your brownie in that, just the way Rob loved it!"

It did the trick. Just as Brendan was ready to rush out the door to check Max's whereabouts, the cream laced with Angel's blood beckoned to him, intoxicating his senses. He grabbed the bowl away from Red, whispered, "Excuse me," and dashed from the kitchen, racing upstairs to lock himself in his room and devour every morsel.

Red took the opportunity to vacate the premises, assuring her ladies that they'd done enough and it was time to go. She fled home to contact the Council and update them on the successful extraction.

Chapter Eleven

They sped down Glenormiston road, past the store and up Trufood road, and as soon as they crossed the cattle grid at the college's back entrance, the protection barrier of wildfire danced along the border of the college's grounds. It reached towards the sky, preventing any Vein from entering.

"Whoa," Max exclaimed as he looked through the jeep's back window at the wall of electric-blue flame, impressed. "What is that?"

"It's our version of an electric fence," Sam answered, relieved now that they were safely behind it. "It will paralyse any force that enters our grounds who intends to cause harm."

Max nodded, feeling safe in the knowledge that Brendan couldn't step foot onto the college grounds.

Jess pulled the jeep up into the driveway, but kept the engine going. "All of you, get inside the house, we don't want you leaving it at all. Tom and I will be back later."

"What's going on?" Bowie asked as he got out of the jeep.

"Council meeting," Tom answered.

"Okay." Michael waited for Max and Sam to get out before he shut the door, waving a hand as the jeep took off.

"Perfect timing for a bit of 'Q and A'. What do you think, Max?" Michael asked the young boy.

Max looked at Sam, who nodded. "You really need to know the truth about your stinking family."

"Sam," Bowie reprimanded.

"No, it's okay," Max shrugged the insult away. "I need to know, to understand."

Sam nodded. "All right."

The front door burst open, as Angel and Jane stepped out, grinning when they saw Max.

"It worked!" Angel sounded relieved.

"It sure did kiddo, like a charm." Bowie ruffled her hair.

They smiled at each other.

"Right, let's get some snacks and head into the lounge for Max's 'Q and A'."

Michael led the way, and between the five of them they got Max comfortable. They set up a spread consisting of cold glasses of freshly-made Lemon Balm cordial, hedgehog slice and a bowl of chips.

Max sat on the couch as he watched the surrounding activity, how they made jokes and teased one another with the ease and comfort of family. As lucky as he felt at having formed such a great friendship with Eddy over the past nine months, a little piece of his heart felt sad; it suddenly hit him how lonely he'd truly been all these years, having missed the close-knit bonds that having a family created. His father had only ever been a dictator.

Sam plonked down on the seat beside him, flashing him her pearly-whites as she handed him a slice of hedgehog.

"There you go." Michael handed them both a glass of cordial.

"Thank you," Max said shyly.

Poor kid, Michael brushed against Bowie's mind.

Yeah, it can't have been easy for him. Bowie sat on the rug opposite the couch, leaning back against a large leather pouffe, stretching his legs.

He's got the hots for Sam. Does that bother you?

Nah, Bowie returned. *Feeling's mutual by the looks.*

Sam turned and stared at Bowie, then Michael. *You know, I can hear you.*

Angel and Jane burst out laughing, having been privy to the silent conversation. Max frowned in confusion, oblivious to the private joke.

Bowie turned to Max. "One of the upsides to being a member of our family…"

"Or downsides, however you want to look at it," Sam interrupted.

"Like I was saying," Bowie continued. "One of our skills is that we can hear each other's thoughts at times, which is a great benefit in emergencies."

"And isn't, when you want to keep your thoughts to yourself," Sam scoffed.

"*Can* you keep your thoughts to yourself?" Max asked her.

"Yeah, with practice," Bowie answered, bringing Max's attention back to him.

"Fletch said I was half 'heavenly soul'. What does that even mean?"

"What *did* your father teach you about your family?" Jane raised an eyebrow as she grabbed a handful of chips, flicking a long, auburn lock over a shoulder.

Max looked at her for a moment, before answering carefully, "He told me our ancestors were incredibly powerful people who had fallen ill over time, and that they…*we* need a special type of person to help our lineage stay strong."

Michael shrugged. "Pretty accurate. Although he did forget a lot of particularly-important details."

Bowie drained his cup of cordial and pulled an apple out of the basket that Angel placed down with the other snacks before she sat behind him on the pouffe, tucking her legs up.

"Where do we start, to make this easy?" Bowie pulled out his pocket-knife and ran the sharp blade through the apple. He placed a slice into his mouth, chewing while considering what to tell Max without over-whelming him; after all, he'd just buried his father.

"Your friend, the tall skinny one?"

"Eddy." Max nodded.

"Right, Eddy. Eddy is a pure-soul, a human. Mundane, with no special gift in particular, apart from being a kind, thoughtful human. He, like many humans, has a vital role to play in sustaining the balance which keeps Mother Earth spinning on her axis."

"That doesn't make sense, though." Max frowned. "If it's the humans who have stuffed up the planet, how can their role be important? Wouldn't the earth thrive without humans?" Max sounded confused.

"Good question. Here's the answer, which pure-souls have no idea about." Bowie sat forward, eyes gleaming. "Many humans have indeed destroyed our planet over the past two-hundred-thousand years, but it is the purest of souls who help our world go 'round, the souls who go above and beyond with every breath that they take. Those who care for the planet, the animals, and other souls in need. All those who volunteer; healers, humanitarians, environmentalists, artists, the truly mindful…it is their heartbeats, their happiness, their helping hands that keep Mother Earth spinning."

Max frowned, still looking confused.

Bowie continued, "It is the purest of souls' energy, flowing from their passion, their love and light, that holds the sun's heat. This stops Mother Earth from freezing into a solid mass."

"Don't you mean carbon dioxide, produced from the forests and ocean?"

Bowie shook his head. "Without the purest of souls, even the carbon dioxide could not stop Mother Earth from freezing."

Max sat back, silent for a moment as he let Bowie's words sink in. He nodded before saying, "That is unreal."

"That's for sure." Sam grinned.

"What about my family? What do they do to help Mother Earth and the pure-souls?" He looked eager and hopeful that it was something important.

Sam shifted in her seat as she looked at Max, waiting for Bowie to answer.

"Nothing good, I'm afraid," Bowie answered reluctantly, not knowing what to say.

He sliced off another piece of apple as Angel's hand reached over his shoulder and carefully took it, avoiding his sharp blade. He dropped his head back to look at her and smiled. He was grateful to see her eyes were bright and light, fully recovered after what Max's bastard-family had done to her.

He paused for a moment, before meeting Max's eyes and continuing, "Your family, your ancestors, are a type of disease. Parasites that thrive on creating chaos; they do nothing but destroy all that is good in this world."

"Thay can't all be bad?" Max almost pleaded.

Bowie shrugged, he did not enjoy seeing the frown that flashed across the poor kid's face, and looked at Michael, wondering if it was better that he take over?

"You see, Max, your father's people, Veins, have the ability to make humans harm themselves, each other, and Mother Earth. The more pain and destruction they create in the world, the more they thrive." Michael filled his glass with cordial.

Max thought for a moment. "Like Brendan, making that man jump off the Ferris Wheel?"

"Exactly." Michael nodded.

Max looked at Sam. "After the bus accident, when everyone was frightened and hurt…There was this weird kind of energy inside me that felt so good, but then, as soon as I felt the rush, there was something that made me want to reject it." He shook his head, before finishing. "The same thing happened on the Ferris wheel."

Sam took Max's free hand and squeezed it.

"That would have been your heavenly soul reacting to the negative energy," Bowie said, passing another slice of apple over his shoulder to Angel, enjoying listening to her little crunches behind him.

"My half-heavenly soul?" Max raised an eyebrow, becoming more confused.

"Your mother, I wonder how she became involved with your father? It's a bit of a mystery." Jane raised an eyebrow.

"What exactly is a heavenly soul?" Max asked.

"All right, everyone up." Bowie sprang to his feet, clapping his hands.

He pointed at Michael, directing him to stand opposite him.

Sam stood opposite Angel, and Jane stood opposite Max.

Bowie placed his hand on his chest. "I was born of royal blood, I am an elemental-soul. I can conjure the elements, and my role is to heal and protect Mother Earth. But my most important role is to protect my soul-sibling, a heavenly soul." He nodded to Michael. "Until the day my essence calls to its equal, I am solely responsible for Michael's wellbeing."

"Like a shrink?" Max smiled.

"Yes…no, not really, not at all." Bowie shook his head.

"Next," Michael said, not wanting to confuse Max further.

Jane smiled at Max as she placed her hand on her chest. "I, too, am an elemental-soul. My heavenly soul was called to a higher purpose and, therefore, I am without a heavenly soul to protect. I go where I am bid by our Light Accords and continue to do good work as I go about my normal studies, fitting in to the mundane world."

Sam smiled at Max. "I am blood-sibling to Bowie Storm, and soul-sibling to Angel Cloud. My purpose in this life, apart from protecting

Mother Earth, is to protect Angel, until the day arrives when either her or my soul-essences are united with our soul-partner. Until that day, I would die to protect Angel."

Angel watched Max's face fall with that last piece of information.

"Fear not, Max. For although Sam would die to protect me, I would not allow her to fade. I have the ability to gift life where life is deserving, to keep the balance of good, and, as far as we know, so do you."

"You saved that sheep that day, on Mount Sugarloaf. I felt a shift in the air, a surging energy."

"That's right." Angel smiled.

Max looked confused. "I've never felt anything like that. I don't think I have any gifts."

"Max, you're young, and your father may have cloaked your abilities. But, like Sam and Angel, you have plenty of time to learn and harness your gift. We can teach you—we just have to wait for the Council to decide what is to be done with you." Michael sat back down.

"Done with him?" Sam frowned.

"Don't stress, dear sister of mine." Bowie stepped forward, placing his arm around her shoulder. "As far as we know, there has never been child born from the union between a Vein and a royal-soul. They just need to decide if Max is worth going to war over, if the Veins want him."

"War?" Max tilted his head, eyebrows drawn.

"Brendan is an ancient Vein. He will not allow us to take you without any repercussions," Jane said, reaching for her cordial.

Max had so many questions, he didn't know where to start. But he was interested in ensuring Angel's safety; if Angel being hurt also hurt Sam, he would do everything in his power to stop that from happening. "What did my cousin do to Angel? And, if I'm half Vein, will I want to hurt her too?"

They all looked at Max, realising no one had considered this possibility. Michael and Bowie exchanged a concerned look.

Sam's heart accelerated at the thought of Max wanting to hurt her soul-sibling, and then what her blood-sibling would do to Max!

*Oh my stars…*she whispered to Angel, and, subsequently, the entire room, apart from Max.

Michael raised his hands. "Let's not jump to any uncomfortable scenarios, kids. Max, do you have any other questions?"

"Only another hundred. Can you show me some of your magic?"

Bowie laughed. "We don't call it magic, mate, but sure. What do you want to see?"

"You say you conjure the elements, what good does that do?"

"Come with me." Bowie led the way to the study and walked towards the world globe. They all stood around as Bowie closed his eyes and whispered to Mother Earth, asking her to reveal her desire. The globe spun around once before stopping on inland Australia.

Bowie looked across at Max. "Whenever we use our gifts, they are only ever to benefit another soul, or our planet. So, in order for me to show you how I make it rain, for example, I may do so to benefit a drought-afflicted region only. Pay attention."

Bowie spun the globe once more. Max's eyes widened as all the continents disappeared before revealing jagged cracks that sliced deeply into the earth, running across hundreds of miles of dry, dusty soil.

Bowie reached into the globe, his hands seeming to touch the sky above the thirsty land. He closed his eyes and concentrated on his elemental powers. After several minutes of silence, the blue skies vanished to be replaced with grey rain clouds, leaking droplets that fell upon the parched land.

Bowie sighed as he pulled his hands out of the globe, looking a little tired. He smiled. "A gentle rain that will fall for a week, so as to not wash more soil away, but to drench it thoroughly."

Max shook his head. "That is so cool!"

"It really is." Bowie grinned. "Usually we portal physically to a location in need, but, as I have used the globe, the High Council would have been alerted to my action and will keep their eye on the area."

"So neat." Max grinned. "What else? Can I see what you do, Michael?"

Michael reached across and placed his hand on Bowie's chest, the other on his heart, and whispered a spell. In seconds, Bowie's energy returned.

"To heal, help, or restore my soul-sibling's energy is always a must. We rely on each other at all times."

Max nodded, saying, "You're all so lucky to have each other."

"And now you have us as well." Angel smiled, hoping to chase away the shadow that crossed his features.

"How about we take Max to the haystack?" Sam asked.

"Tom said to stay inside the house until they return from the Council meeting," Bowie answered.

"Oh, come on!" Sam cried. "We've been at a stinking funeral! We need some fresh air and sunshine." She looked at Max after feeling Angel cringe at her poor choice of words.

"Sorry, Max, I didn't mean…"

"It's okay," he cut her off, feeling awkward about his association with his family. Yet, they were still his family. He'd just buried his father, a man he didn't really know, had never been comfortable with. All he had left was a cousin he couldn't stand, and a dead mother who could be his saviour in all this mess. And a mess it was.

Michael could see the stress on Max's face and his heart went out to him. "Don't go past the haystack."

"Thank you!" Sam threw her arms around Michael's waist, hugging him hard, before turning around and grabbing Angel's and Max's hands. "Come on, Jane!" she cried happily.

Jane laughed and grabbed Angel's other hand, and they headed off for an afternoon in the sun.

Bowie sighed when they disappeared out of sight. "I wonder what the Council is going to do with him?"

Michael shook his head. "I've got a feeling they'll want to protect him."

"I hope so. For his and Sam's sake."

"Shouldn't be too long now."

"I'm going to do a perimeter check."

"Good idea. I'm going to give Beth a quick call, then I'll start on the south side."

"I think you need to evaluate your situation with her, Michael…she's only going to get hurt in the long run, when your essence finds its equal."

Michael's face fell. "I know," his response was full of anguish.

"Shit, sorry. I didn't mean to upset you." Bowie felt a rush of guilt. He hated seeing Michael upset, for any reason.

"No, you're right. Fact is, I'm crazy about this girl, and it kills me that a simple soul-partner ceremony will wipe clean any feelings I have for her." He shook his head. "What we do, it's worth all of it, every sacrifice. But sometimes…" He trailed off.

Bowie clapped him on the back. "I know, mate. I know."

"Alrighty, then, enough with the self-pity party." He forced a smile as he headed to use the kitchen phone. "I'll check on the rug-rats after this call."

Bowie saluted as the back door slammed shut. Jumping on his trail bike, he started the engine and took off to start the perimeter check.

When Brendan woke from his drug-induced frenzy, he was euphorically calm, yet starving for more of that sweet, intoxicating essence. Then the realisation dawned on him…Max was missing. Taken from right under his nose. And it was the young girl's blood essence that still danced upon his tongue; Angel's blood, throbbing deep in his veins, making him lust for more.

He roared in fury at being taken for a fool so easily. It was time to implement another plan of action before leaving the country for good...

Christmas Eve was filled with preparations for the festive day ahead. Mrs. McGoldrick helped the girls hang extra decorations on the tree and string tinsel along the staircase. Red popped over and they spent a few hours baking chocolate puddings, peppermint bark, gingerbread houses, and Christmas cookies for the girls to decorate. There were plenty of other goodies to share with neighbours and Council members who came to call.

After spending hours in the hot kitchen, Jane, Angel, and Sam headed off to join Max, Bowie, and Michael at the pool. They'd finished ensuring all the horse and cattle troughs were full and the extra summer feed distributed.

As Angel pushed the pool gate open, she saw that Patricia and Elizabeth had already been dropped off and had brought a picnic along with them.

"After all our snacking in the kitchen, I can't possibly be hungry." Jane chuckled. "But that smells like southern fried chicken."

"Why does everything that's fried taste and smell so good?" Sam agreed.

"Until it doesn't," Angel said, running full-pelt and diving into the pool, grateful when the cool arms of the water removed the cooking heat that had permeated her skin.

"Hello, young loves!" Elizabeth called happily as Jane and Sam came to peek at the picnic basket. "Please, help yourselves, there's plenty to go around."

"It's good." Michael passed a plate to Jane, who dug in with enthusiasm.

"Oh, my lord," she mumbled around a chicken thigh.

Bowie agreed as he wiped the chicken grease off his fingers onto a paper towel before jumping up and pulling Patricia with him. "Let's make the most of the inflatable before the sun melts it."

"I agree." Patricia laughed in delight as Bowie ran like the wind before climbing up the steps and hurling himself down the wet, soapy slide. He flew high off the end before making a huge splash, inches from Angel.

She dove out the way, but didn't avoid his wave as she resurfaced, spluttering in laughter as she choked on the swirling water.

"Sorry, kiddo." He chuckled before yelling out, "Watch out!" as Patricia flew towards them, screaming.

Max sat on the side of the pool in the shade of a gumtree, watching them clown about. He was feeling anxious about the decision the Council were making regarding his future. When Tom and Jess had returned from the meeting, the verdict on his situation was still unclear. The Council were searching their history records, trying to locate Max's mother's family. They were also trying to ascertain if Max may be a future threat to any heavenly soul, and whether his Vein blood would lust after a heavenly soul, when he himself was half-Heavenly.

"The jury's still out, mate. There are a few factors the Council need to consider before making their final ruling," was all Tom had said.

"You'll be okay, Max," Jess had said. "It won't be long. Until then, our home is your home."

"Hey, you." Sam smiled, interrupting his thoughts as she sat down beside him, sighing with happiness as her feet splashed into the cool water.

He smiled, liking how her yellow bathers made her look like a summer babe with her beach-blonde waves. *God, she was cute.* "Hey," he replied, grateful she couldn't read his mind.

"You can invite Eddy over, if you want?" She leaned in closer and whispered, conspirator-like, "I think Jane would like that."

They smirked at each other before chuckling.

"He is in Warrnambool with his cousin."

Sam nodded, before asking, "Wanna swim?"

"Yeah." He slid off the side and dunked under the water, smiling up at her through the ripples.

Sam followed, glad to see him looking happier. She was as worried as he was, regarding his future, and prayed the Council would let him stay here with them.

After two hours of pool fun and chillout time, Jane announced it was time to head inside and exchange gifts under the Christmas tree.

"Off you go, Michael." Elizabeth smiled prettily. "I want to talk to Angel about your gift."

"Oh, is that so?" He crossed over to her as he slung his towel over his shoulder, smiling down at her. "You know," he teased, "I can read Angel's mind, so it won't really be a surprise."

"Michael!" Angel threw a hard rubber ball at him, which missed and sailed over his shoulder. Bowie plucked it out of the air effortlessly.

"All right, you lot. Back to the house for Christmas goodies. Come on, hurry up, or else Red will hunt us down." Bowie winked at Angel before turning around.

"She's so cute, she would never." Patricia looped one arm through Bowie's, and the other through Jane's as they followed Sam and Max through the gate.

"Don't be too long." Michael grinned at Elizabeth. "Bowie wasn't lying, Red will hunt you down."

Elizabeth blew him a kiss, then, as they left, turned to Angel. "Let's talk in the water. It's so hot out here."

Angel dropped her towel and slipped back into the cool water, hanging onto the side of the pool, wondering about this gift Beth had for Michael.

"Angel, you know I really do love Michael..." As she spoke, she looked over her shoulder at the retreating bodies as they disappeared through the college grounds towards the homestead.

Angel resisted the urge to roll her eyes. *She knows I'm twelve, right?*

"And I'd never do anything intentionally to hurt him, which is why I'm sorry for doing this." Elizabeth turned her full attention toward Angel.

"Doing what?" Angel asked.

The look in Elizabeth's eyes had Angel's blood running cold. They were black, unfeeling, and pupilless; exactly like Brendan Black's when he'd attacked her.

"Elizabeth?" Angel whispered, pushing away from the edge, gliding backwards to escape the girl who was obviously not herself.

Elizabeth stood where she was, staring sightlessly at Angel.

Two things happened simultaneously that turned Angel's blood ice-cold, despite the 38-degree day.

Elizabeth's mouth dropped open, her chin hanging down to her chest like rubber as her arms elongated and stretched towards the ground before slipping into the water, reaching towards Angel.

Angel didn't have time to scream as she desperately tried to dive away from Elizabeth's malevolent hand, which darted towards her like a launched missile.

She cried in despair as Elizabeth grabbed her around her throat. She took a shallow breath before Elizabeth pulled her under the water, thrashing her about like a cat playing with a mouse.

Angel clawed at Elizabeth's fingers, which were the size of a baby's wrist, feeling as if her lungs would explode. *Michael, Sam, Bowie!* She repeated her mantra over and over again, until the last air bubble popped out of her little mouth in the shape of an o, then her world went dark.

Michael shook his head, certain that he'd felt something in that moment as Red passed him a cup of punch. "Thanks Red," he smiled. *Angel?* He waited.

Bowie stood at the same time Sam did, and they stared at each other. "Can you feel that?" he asked her. She nodded.

"Feel what?" Patricia asked.

"What is it?" Red frowned.

Tom stood wearing a worried expression. "Angel, she's gone."

"Gone off the property? She can't have, the barrier…" Red glanced at Patricia and Mrs. McGoldrick, knowing she couldn't finish that sentence.

Tom, Michael, Bowie and Jess bolted out the front door and towards the swimming pool with Jane, Red, Patricia and Sam on their heels.

Mrs. McGoldrick waited by the front door, not up for running in this heat, knowing Angel would be all right with her family coming to her aid.

As Bowie sprinted around the corner, throwing the pool gate open, his heart lurched in his throat as the sight before him stole his breath.

Elizabeth was leaning over Angel's limp body, crying her eyes out. She turned when she heard them approach. "I don't know what happened!" she cried. "I turned my back on her for a second, and when I turned around again, she was on the bottom of the pool. I pulled her out, but she hasn't woken up! Michael?"

Michael placed a hand on Elizabeth's shoulder as Bowie fell to his knees beside Angel. He placed his cheek against her nose and mouth, watching for any movement over her bubble-gum-pink bathers. He moved to cradle the back of her head, spying the marks around her throat. Frowning, he leant closer, trying to catch the scent of those fingerprints.

Get Elizabeth and Patricia home, now, he pushed towards Tom. Aloud he said, "I've got a pulse, she's okay."

"Oh, thank goodness," Patricia said, patting Bowie on the back.

"Patty, Beth, let me take you girls home. I think we need a quiet one, to sort Angel out."

"Of course. I'm so glad she's okay." Patricia sighed. "Come on, Beth."

"What about the presents?' Elizabeth asked sadly.

"Another time, dear," Red said, her voice kind, but firm.

Elizabeth hugged Michael. "I'm so sorry, Michael. I should have been watching her more carefully."

He forced a kind smile, hiding his confusion, desperately wanting to hear what Bowie had to say. But he replied, "It's okay, I'll call you tomorrow. Thanks, Tom."

Tom nodded as he led the girls to Jess's jeep, to take them into Terang.

Once they were out of sight, Jess placed his hands against Angel's limp body and whispered a healing incantation.

Angel could feel Jess's energy essence swirl within her, making her heart beat strongly. She could feel Sam and Bowie, Red and Jane, all sending her positive, healing thoughts.

Max stood to the side.

Angel opened her eyes; her body trembled involuntarily. She was furious.

"Angel?" Sam bent down and took her hand.

Sam, I can't talk...my throat.

Bowie scooped her up. "Come on, let's get you inside, out of the sun."

It's going to be okay, Angel, Red and I will heal you. Michael brushed the thoughts against her mind. *Questions later. For now, healing.*

Yes, Michael.

Bowie shook his head, biting his tongue, preventing the thoughts swirling around his head from being heard.

Inside, he placed Angel on the window seat overlooking the rose garden, which was in full bloom, as Michael and Red placed their hands on her body, feeling for injuries. Jess asked Mrs. McGoldrick to grab an icy-pole.

Sam paced before Jane put her arm around her, calming her. "It's going to be okay, look."

They turned to see the bruises on Angel's throat lift and vanish, and, within moments, she threw the pool water up into a waiting bucket held by Jess.

Mrs. McGoldrick hurried in, her look of concern turning to one of relief as she passed Angel a homemade lemon and honey icy pole. "For your throat, dear."

"Thank you." Angel smiled.

Mrs. McGoldrick stroked Angel's wet hair before turning around and heading back to the kitchen to make herself a pot of tea to drink in the rose garden. She took an extra cup, hoping Red would follow her out so they could discuss the final Christmas Eve party preparations.

"Are you okay, love?" Red asked.

Angel nodded, kissing Red's cheek.

"Right, then. You tell Jess all about it, and we'll go from there." Red nodded before leaving the room to join Mrs. McGoldrick.

Sam popped a dry towel around Angel's shoulders and sat next to her.

Jess stood to the side, waiting. *Poor little kid looks like a ragdoll.* He shared the silent thought with Bowie, who agreed. Her bright blue eyes seemed too large for her head.

"When you're ready, Angel."

She nodded, sucking on the icy pole for a few seconds longer before starting.

"It was Elizabeth, but it wasn't *Elizabeth*, her eyes were all black, like a shark's. Like Brendan's and Max's dad, when they did what they did to me." She looked apologetically at Max before continuing.

"Her arms stretched over twelve feet, and her hands grew big enough to wrap around my waist, let alone my throat." She shook her head, looking at Michael. "It wasn't Elizabeth."

Michael paced back and forth, looking at Bowie, then Jess.

Jess folded his arms. "She was a conduit."

"A what?" Sam asked.

"She was being used to create harm—a conduit, a medium."

"My cousin?" Max sounded ashamed. He looked at Angel. "I'm so sorry, Angel."

"Max, it isn't your fault. Please don't feel guilty."

"But I do. He's hurting you because of your blood, because you helped me escape."

"Yes, but you helped me escape, too, remember?"

Max thought for a moment. "If my cousin wants me, I should just go to him."

"*No!*" Sam cried. "You can't, Max, he is pure evil!"

Angel sucked on the healing icy pole, grateful as the bursts of lemon and honey soothed her throat, watching Sam and Max stare at each other.

"Look," Bowie sighed, sensing Michael's fury. After all, his conduit girlfriend had just tried to kill his blood-sibling. "We all just need to chill out a bit. Angel's all right, aren't you, kiddo?"

"Yes," she nodded, knowing he wanted her to help calm everyone's emotions. She closed her eyes briefly and felt her amulet glow as she thought loving, calm intentions towards all in the room. She frowned. Michael was blocking her. And he was blocking himself.

Bowie? She sent her thought directly to him, shielding herself as best she could from the others. Catching Michael's gaze, she knew he'd heard her.

"What's wrong?" she blurted, staring at her blood-sibling.

Michael ran his hands through his hair. "Nothing," he replied shortly, his body language betraying his response.

"It doesn't look like nothing." Angel tried again, worried about his nervous energy.

"Leave it, Angel," Michael snapped uncharacteristically.

Bowie turned his full attention on Michael now, sensing what had alarmed Angel. Michael was doing something he'd never done before, even when Bowie wished he *had* done it, during those times he'd been intimate with Elizabeth. He was shielding his thoughts.

"Michael, what are you up to?"

Michael shook his head and forced a calm he did not feel.

He'd just seen his blood-sibling close to death because his girlfriend had inflicted physical harm beyond her strength, no thanks to a filthy Vein who was right under their noses.

Jess, too, focused on Michael. "Michael?"

"Look, I'm okay, seriously. It's just…seeing Angel hurt by Elizabeth's own hands due to being manipulated so invasively…" He shrugged. "I just need a few minutes to calm down. That's all."

Jess nodded. "That's understandable. I'm going to chat to Red; we'll have to call a Council meeting tonight." He turned to Max. "No doubt we will soon have more information regarding what is best for you, Max."

Max nodded. "Okay."

"You know what? It's Christmas Eve!" Jane cried, trying to lighten the mood. "Let's all get our festive vibe back on, shall we?"

Jess smiled. "Great idea. After the Council meeting we will have a house full of hungry guests, so let's get organised."

Sam tugged Angel off the couch. "We'll help Mrs. McGoldrick set up the parlour before we get changed."

Michael ruffled Angel's hair as he smiled down at her. "Glad you're okay."

"I *am* okay, Michael. You don't need to worry." She knew he was still shielding his thoughts, but understood why he might need to.

He bent down and hugged her tightly. She wound her arms around his neck, squeezing him back.

Bowie and Sam shared a smile before he turned to Max. "Do you want to hang with the girls, or take a spin on the bikes?"

"A spin sounds great."

"Great. Girls, we'll see you in a couple of hours."

"Yep, have fun!" Sam called as she tugged Jane and Angel towards the parlour. Red and Mrs. McGoldrick had finished their tea, and gave multiple orders during the next two hours as they prepared for the Christmas Eve celebrations later that night.

Chapter Twelve

Christmas cheer masked the foreboding atmosphere as the Council members celebrated the evening, along with their families. They pushed their concerns of Brendan Black's deeds, and the growing force of Veins, to the side for a few hours. Jane, Max, Angel and Sam were mingling with the Council members' kids, all sharing stories of their year as they ate themselves near-sick on the sumptuous Christmas Eve feast.

After an enjoyable dessert, the High Council handed out small presents, and Angel frowned, wondering why Bowie and Samantha received nothing.

Sam smiled at Angel, hearing her thoughts. "It's okay, Angel. Who needs presents anyway?"

Bowie smiled knowingly at Michael, who smiled back genuinely for the first time since they'd seen Angel and Elizabeth at the pool.

The room fell silent as two figures stepped through the wide, double-doors of the parlour.

"As if we would ever forget you, darling Samantha." A gentle breeze of a voice rang out.

Sam turned with sheer glee at the sound of her mother's voice and screamed in delight as she ran like the wind into her mother's waiting arms.

Bowie was at his father's side in two strides, then, after shaking his hand enthusiastically, hugged him long and hard.

Sam's delight turned to tears and her mother, too, wept in happiness before turning to embrace her son. "How handsome you've grown, my darling boy," she whispered.

Michael walked over to Angel and sat beside her on the couch. He sensed both her joy that Sam and Bowie's parents had returned, and her sadness that she would never have this moment with their parents again. It made him slightly regretful about the decision he'd made, many hours ago. But he couldn't—no, he *would* not alter his course.

Angel looked up at him, sensing a dark cloud touch her mind ever so briefly.

She looked across at Bowie, who met her gaze. He'd felt it too.

It thrilled Johanna and Crow Storm to be with their children once more. They hugged them tight, before their eyes met those of the children whom theirs were born to protect, children who'd lost their parents. Johanna rubbed Bowie's arm before she stepped forward and opened her arms wide. "Michael, Angel, it's so nice to see you both."

Angel, who'd always considered Johanna and Crow to be her aunt and uncle, happily rushed into Johanna's open arms, and pushed her face into her Tweed-scented chest.

Michael and Crow embraced as Crow whispered words of sympathy regarding their parents.

"Thank you, Uncle Crow." Michael smiled before reaching towards Johanna. "Aunty, it is so wonderful to see you."

"As it is you, Michael." She kissed his cheek.

"Well, we've got something for the four of you." Crow smiled as the party atmosphere and noise resumed around them. "Come." He turned and headed towards the lounge, where the enormous Christmas tree stood.

They all followed him and waited as he retrieved four small packages then handed them one each. "Thank you." Angel smiled up at Crow as he placed the gift into her small hand.

He looked down at her for a while longer before turning to his son. "Here you go, my boy."

Bowie grinned, he loved hearing his father call him 'my boy.' It hit him hard, in that moment, just how much he had missed his father. He blinked tears back and forced a cheerful smile as he met his dad's gaze. "Thanks, Dad," he said, being mindful of the moment.

Crow smiled. "You're welcome. Now, come on, all of you open them up!" he cried enthusiastically, grinning at his soul-partner.

Johanna sat on the arm of a chair as she watched each of the children rip open the paper to find a small, velvet box inside. They each paused for a moment before flipping the lids open to gaze in astonishment at what lay inside. What first appeared to be an antique, glass marble, suddenly become so much more under closer inspection.

Bowie and Michael each picked up the black, leather wristbands. They had intricate patterns pressed into the leather where the half-marble sat perfectly in the centre, with a silver frame holding it in place.

The girls pulled their white-gold chains out of their boxes to hold up a complete, round marble that hung heavily, mesmerising them as they looked closer. Beneath the glass sat Mother Earth, her oceans swelling, clouds dancing in the sky so blue, the wind, its partner.

All four gasped in surprise as they watched the movement beneath their glass gifts' surfaces, before meeting their elders' eyes.

Crow smiled. "These gifts came from Mother Earth herself, delivered to the Light Accords via the Angels above, created especially for you." He paused, smiling at each of them in turn, before adding softly. "Our Soul Keepers of Glenormiston South."

Johanna beamed at them. "We are so proud of you. All of you." Her gaze met Michael and Angel's. Michael rubbed Angel's back, sensing her becoming overwhelmed with the love being gifted to them.

Johanna rose and moved towards Angel and Samantha, placing the chains around each of the girls' necks. The marble hung close to their hearts and sent a small surge of energy around them.

"Did you feel that?" Sam gasped, looking at Angel.

Angel nodded. "What was that?" She turned to Johanna.

"That is Mother Earth's essence. She is letting you know that she appreciates all that you do for the pure-souls and all that you do for her." Johanna smiled. "May you keep the souls safe."

"With every breath that we take," the girls whispered.

Crow took Bowie's leather strap and placed it around his wrist before turning to Michael and doing the same. They watched in fascination as the leather strap bound itself closed, with no clasp needed to hold it steadfast around their wrists.

"That's neat." Bowie grinned.

Michael agreed, as they both felt a burst of energy tingle into their pulse point and travel along their arms, towards their hearts.

"It's a gift from Uriel and the Light Accords. May you keep the souls safe."

"With every breath that we take," the boys replied.

"These are the first of their kind, and they're being gifted to you after the tragedy that befell your parents." Crow looked at Michael, then Angel, before continuing, "If ever you find yourself in peril, and your soul-sibling is not by your side to help you, then your charm here will keep your heart beating until your soul-sibling arrives."

"It is a wonderful gift." Sam smiled at Angel. "Although not necessary, really. We'd never leave each other's side in a dire situation, would we, Angel?"

"No. Never."

"Which is fabulous to hear, my darling girl." Crow smiled at his daughter. "This is a gift for the unseen, the unexpected."

Bowie nodded, knocking into Michael's shoulder. "Like Sam, I don't plan on ever letting this guy out of my sight when danger is nearby."

"Speaking of danger, if we don't join the festivities before the clock strikes midnight, we'll be in trouble." Johanna took Crow's arm as she looked down at Samantha.

"Samantha, would you like to introduce us to your new friend?"

"Max? Yeah, sure." Sam beamed as she led the way for her parents to follow.

"How about a cup of punch?" Michael asked Bowie.

"Sounds like a plan. You coming, Angel?" Bowie watched as Angel sat on a chair, holding up her marble Mother Earth so she could stare into her moving globe.

"In a minute."

"You all right, kiddo?" Bowie paused, sensing her melancholy vibe.

Angel sighed. "I am all right, I'm just going to enjoy some quiet for a minute." She looked up into his warm, amber eyes.

Michael moved towards her and said, "Come here."

She stood as he reached for her and allowed him to hold her close and tight for a minute before wiggling out of his arms.

He smiled down at her. "I love you. You do know that don't you?"

She looked up into his eyes, which sparkled under the lights of the Christmas tree. "Of course. I love you, too." She tried to touch his mind, to see where his thoughts were at, but he was still shielding them.

"Hey," he said, his voice soft. "Maybe I'm just trying to hide your Christmas present from you?" He knew she was concerned and curious as to why he was guarding his thoughts, and knew that Bowie was, too, which is why he'd suggested a glass of punch.

She smiled up at him and said, "Sure." She sat back down and pulled the soft blanket across her legs as she picked up the heavy glass ball, to stare into the magic of it.

Michael clapped Bowie on the back. "Come on, let's get that drink."

"Yeah, sure." Bowie looked over his shoulder at Angel one final time before following Michael out of the room and back to the festivities.

Entering the crowded room, Michael pointed to Andrew Light and said to Bowie, "Why don't you catch up with Andrew? I'll go get our drinks."

Bowie nodded, heading over to chat with Andrew, who, as always, held a captive audience with his vivid storytelling.

Michael arrived a few minutes later, and, as Andrew was still deep into re-enacting his latest mission, silently handed Bowie his drink, who nodded his thanks.

Bowie took a mouthful, expecting the usual kids' flavoured punch, and raised an eyebrow as the delicious flavour of the adult punch slid down his throat. He raised an eyebrow at Michael, who grinned, and they both drained their cups.

"Another?" Michael grabbed Bowie's empty cup.

"You don't have to ask me twice," Bowie said enthusiastically.

Michael disappeared to refill their cups, and returned quickly, handing Bowie a full cup.

"By the Angels, that's good." Bowie chuckled as he downed the second as fast as the first.

"Yeah, it's got all the right stuff to give you a nice little buzz. Another?" Michael offered.

Bowie grinned. "Sure." He passed Michael his cup and walked over to lean against the wall, watching his soul-sibling mingle through the crowd to get them a refill.

An hour from midnight, the party was in full swing, without looking like it was even close to slowing down.

Bowie hiccupped and frowned, thinking those last two drinks might have been more than enough.

Michael returned, grinning, and pushed another cup into Bowie's hand.

"Gee, mate, I don't know...it's strong."

"I think you're tired is all. We'll finish this, then head up to bed." Michael held his cup to his lips as if enjoying more punch.

Bowie looked around the room, which seemed to tilt, enjoying having his senses muddled for once.

Fletch walked by. "You boys aren't drinking the adult punch, are you?"

"Us? No way, sir, Fletch, sir," Bowie saluted before cracking up at himself, spilling some of the punch down his shirt.

Michael inwardly rolled his eyes. He knew he should have steered Bowie upstairs to their rooms earlier, but he'd thought one more cup should do the trick for what he'd planned.

Fletch stopped and turned back to them. "Underage drinking. Both of you grab a bottle of water and go walk it off before bed. Now."

"Yes, sir." Michael grabbed Bowie's arm and led him into the kitchen. Taking two bottles of water from the fridge, he led Bowie out into the warm, summer night.

"Well, guess it could have been worse." Bowie slung an arm around Michael's shoulder and hiccupped again.

"Yeah, it could have." Michael turned Bowie along the winding driveway as the stars twinkled brightly above. Seriously, Fletch sending them out for a midnight walk to sober up could not have been more perfect if he'd planned it himself.

"What's that?" Bowie asked.

"What?"

"That first glimmer of a positive thought I've felt from you all day, shielded as it may be."

Michael smirked, wishing he didn't have to betray his soul-sibling like he was about to.

"Well, it *is* Christmas Eve, so I thought I'd get with the program."

"About time," Bowie snorted as they turned up towards the stables. "Yeah," he sighed, "a little nap in there sounds good." He stumbled, trying to stay upright.

The combination of the punch and the little something extra Michael had added to Bowie's drink made him pass out before they reached the stable doors.

Michael swallowed the lump of regret that climbed up his throat as he struggled with Bowie's lanky form, finally getting him up over his shoulder and into the stables. Crossing over to a few bales of hay stacked in the corner, he placed Bowie down as gently as he could, sitting him with his back against the bales. It took him a few minutes to search for some rope to tie Bowie's wrists together, then his ankles, before standing back, considering his next move. It was almost a relief to not have to concentrate on shielding his thoughts now that Bowie was out of it.

This was his one chance to get to Brendan Black. To get to him and take him out. His plan: get to the portal and reach the High Council's weapons hall, then make his way to the Blacks' mansion and end the ancient Vein.

He refused to let Brendan hurt or use anyone he loved ever again. It was his duty to protect Angel, and he'd make sure Bowie was here to protect them all while he was off taking care of business. He released a frustrated groan, hands clasped tightly behind his neck as he strode to the window, peering into the darkness as an owl screeched. It was time to make his move.

"Michael," Bowie groaned groggily, hearing every thought that Michael had just had.

Michael turned, surprised Bowie was awake, although he shouldn't have been. He didn't know what to say, so said nothing.

Bowie felt a flare of panic at the look on Michael's face, and fear ran down his spine—fear for Michael. "You cannot go, it's suicide!" He yelled, struggling against the restraints.

"I'm sorry, I truly am. But I can't let him use the people I love to hurt Angel! He got to Elizabeth so easily, right under our noses." He clenched his fists in frustration, pushing them against his eyes for a second, taking a deep breath before looking at Bowie.

"I will not allow him the opportunity to try that again."

"Untie me, take me with you! I'll protect you, and I'll protect her! Let's do this together. Please, I'm *begging* you. *Don't* do this." Bowie focused his energy on fire to burn the ropes off, but frowned when nothing happened.

He glared at his soul-sibling.

Michael shrugged apologetically. He'd laced Bowie's drink with a binding herb, preventing him, momentarily, from using his gifts.

He knelt beside Bowie and placed his hand on his shoulder, squeezing it lightly. "I'm sorry, you're too valuable. I can't put you in harm's way. I won't."

"Bloody hell, Michael! It's my *job* to protect you!" Bowie's voice broke in frustration and fear. It was his sole purpose in this life to protect the royal Soul Keepers of Glenormiston South, and his number one priority was to protect Michael, at all costs. But how could he do that when the one he was trying to protect had outwitted him, had taken matters into his own hands?

"You'll take care of her for me, won't you?" Michael asked, regret sliding along his skin like an uncomfortably-tight sweater. This could be the last time he would ever speak to Bowie Storm again. The one elemental-soul who'd protected him, protected all their family, with no thought for his own safety. Always.

Bowie stopped struggling as he looked up at Michael. Anguish filled his soul as he read the finality of Michael's decision in his eyes.

He tried one last time, his voice trembling. "It doesn't have to be this way."

"Yes, it does. Now, promise me you'll always look after her?" Michael implored.

"You know I will."

They stared at each other before Michael placed his hand on Bowie's head and whispered, "Goodbye, brother. I'll see you in the next dimension."

"Michael, wait!" Bowie cried as Michael sprang to his feet and vanished out the door, leaving him feeling shattered and alone in the world.

Hours passed as Bowie struggled with the ropes, held fast by Michael's binding incantation. Feeling devastated, he fell back against the hay and cursed in frustration. He closed his eyes and, unwillingly, fell into an exhausted sleep.

Dawn greeted him as it peeked through the window, kissing him awake, and, with that, he whispered fire along the rope and stood, a little unsteadily at first. The blood in his body flowed and pumped, all traces of the herbs blocking his essence now gone.

He stepped out into the crisp morning air and whispered to the wind. As it flowed around him, giving him a burst of refreshing energy, he looked toward the homestead before turning and jogging down the road. Over the cattle grid he went, past Red's little house and straight towards Quicks' paddock and the portal. Diving into the wild wind as it whipped him about, he thought of one place and one place only: Blacks' mansion.

He stepped through the front door, immediately sensing the house was empty. An odd odour permeated the air. He sensed Michael had been here, but not for many hours. Bowie searched the house, out-sheds, stables, and the farmers' cottages…there was no trace of Michael, or Brendan Black. He stood as the sun kissed Glenormiston South, closed his eyes, and pushed one clear, direct thought to Michael Cloud. *Where are you?*

He waited, hopeful. *Please, Michael, hear me. Please.*

He could have wept. There was nothing. Just emptiness. *My god, how can I go home without him?* He felt numb. Grief rose within him, wanting to consume him.

It was Christmas morning, Angel's first without her parents. Now, Michael was gone. He could have cried, but held back the choking sob.

It was time to go in and face the music. And the band would not be playing a soothing tune.

"Oh my God, this is the best thing I've ever tasted," Jane moaned around her Aunty Red's warm cream puff filled with fresh whipped cream and strawberries dipped in chocolate sauce.

Red laughed. "You say that every year, dear." She glanced out her large kitchen window where the fuchsias dripped with colour at this time of year, filling her garden with the comforting hum of honeybees.

"Aunty Red?"

"Mm, yes, dear?"

"Why is Bowie standing in the backyard looking like the world is about to implode?"

Red turned from her bright green splashback and walked into her little backroom to see Bowie Storm standing in the middle of her yard, looking lost and forlorn.

"Why, I don't know, dear Jane. But we are about to find out," she said, walking outside. Stepping onto the lawn, she reached Bowie and saw traces of dried tears. Her heart thudded uncomfortably as she immediately sensed that something grave was at hand.

"What is it, Bowie?" She placed a hand on his arm as he turned glowing, amber eyes in her direction.

"I'm sorry, Red…I need to call a Council meeting."

"Now, dear?"

"Right now." He swallowed, forcing himself not to break down when her perfect, intelligent blue eyes filled with sympathy and concern.

"Okay, let's go inside."

She led him into the house and said to Jane. "Dear, jump on the phone and call the homestead, please."

Jane shoved the last bite of cream puff into her mouth as she grabbed the phone off its cradle. Like Red's carpet tiles, the phone belonged in the '80s, but Red loved the nostalgia behind it. Jane pulled the cord around into Red's room so she could speak privately without Bowie hearing.

"Merry Christmas, darling girls!" Johanna breezed into the opulent room where the twelve-foot-tall Christmas tree stood in all its glory. Sunlight streamed through the open windows; the Christmas ornaments glistened like a sea of jewels.

Angel and Samantha had been up for over two hours; they had fed the ponies and chickens, collected the eggs, showered, and put on their Christmas dresses. They'd piled up a plate of biscuits and cakes, fruit, and made a pot of tea, just the way Johanna liked it. They'd also set up the table in the Christmas room.

Johanna smiled as she walked over to the girls, hugging them both and smothering them in kisses before pouring a cup of tea.

"Well, this looks delicious." Crow walked in with the paper tucked under his arm and scooped Sam up. He swung her in a circle before dropping a kiss onto her hair and placing her down.

"Whoa, Dad," she said, giggling and dizzy.

Angel laughed as she steadied her friend.

Crow smiled down at Angel before bending to offer her his cheek, which she kissed. "Merry Christmas, Uncle Crow."

"Merry Christmas, darling."

Johanna passed him a black tea, and they went to sit near the open window, enjoying the relaxed atmosphere of the morning.

"If only every day could start like this." He grinned at his wife.

"I agree." She smiled, selecting a Christmas cookie to dunk into her tea. "Girls, why don't you go up and wake the boys?"

"Oh, let them sleep a while longer. Teenage boys need their rest to do all that growing, and I'm sure young Max needs to recover from his first Council party," Crow said good-naturedly as he picked up a piece of melon.

Angel and Sam shared a smile, not wanting to add what they thought of teenage boys, especially their brothers, as the hallway phone rang.

"That will be Red saying what time she and Jane will be arriving." Johanna went to place her teacup down.

"I'll get it!" Angel ran to the phone, snatching it up, and was delighted to hear Jane's voice.

"Angel, I need to speak to Uncle Crow, right now."

"Oh, okay, hang on a sec." Angel placed the phone on the hall table and went back into the room. "Uncle Crow, Jane needs to speak with you right now."

Crow smiled as he got up, and carried his cup with him into the hall-way. "Hello young Jane, what's happening?"

Johanna smiled at the girls as they waited to see what the outcome of the phone call was. Silence greeted them before an ashen-looking Crow entered the room.

Johanna stood immediately. "Crow?"

"We have to go to the Gatekeeper's immediately, a Council meeting has been called." His eyes shifted to Angel.

"Oh, really? It's Christmas morning." Sam plonked down onto a chair as she reached for another biscuit.

"Samantha, I need you and Angel to stay here, and I mean that. Do not leave this house, Jane will be arriving shortly. Tom and Jess will meet us at the Gatekeeper's." Crow placed his cup on the side table.

"Should I wake the boys?" Angel asked, an uncomfortable tingle travelling along her spine.

"No, dear heart." He didn't know what else to say to her. Not yet.

"Crow, let's go." Johanna bent and quickly kissed both the girls before heading out the door, Crow one step behind.

As the front door closed, the girls looked at each other.

"Well, what do you think that was all about?" Sam said, plucking up a handful of cherries to eat with her biscuit.

"I'm sure we are going to find out soon enough."

"Well, at least we have the house to ourselves for a bit, and, with Jane coming, I think we can blast some tunes without hearing anyone groaning about our choice of music."

Angel grinned. "Let's do it then."

The Council remained icily silent for several minutes after Bowie finished retelling his story. He ran his hand through his hair before placing it on his hip, wondering what his punishment would be for failing to protect his soul-sibling.

Crow swallowed in frustration for his son. Despite his age, he'd always taken his responsibilities very seriously when it came to protecting Michael Cloud.

Fletch broke the silence. "Jess Callum informed us of the tactic that Brendan Black used in manipulating the pure-soul, Elizabeth Kavanagh, to injure Angel Cloud. We did send three of our most experienced Vein hunters to the Blacks' mansion after that incident…They did not return. We still have several of our members trying to locate them as we speak." Fletch turned to Bowie.

"Young man, I do believe that Michael Cloud illegally drugged you, suppressing the use of your gifts. And I do blame myself somewhat; I did catch a scent of something untoward in your cup last night, but, unfortunately, I assumed it was the mixing of the alcohol with the children's punch."

"What do I do about Michael?" Bowie tried not to yell. All this talk seemed insignificant considering what could be happening to Michael right at that moment. Like Angel, he possessed a heart that beat pure, strengthened by a powerful amulet. If it fell into the hands of a Vein, it would be catastrophic to the world around them.

All eyes turned to the handsome, frustrated seventeen-year-old.

Johanna broke through the circle of souls around Bowie and stood beside her son, placing her hand lovingly on his arm.

"Johanna?" Fletch raised an eyebrow.

"I need to address the Council. I feel that my son is the most suitable candidate to search for Michael Cloud, and should be given the honour to do so."

"I agree," Vicki Light called, as Red, Tom, and Jess, along with several other Council members agreed.

Johanna knew Bowie would never rest until he'd served his duty in searching for and protecting Michael. She didn't want to think about what he might do if this permission wasn't granted.

"Yes, I do believe you are correct, Johanna. Bowie Storm, what do you say?"

"I will not rest until my soul-sibling is safely returned to us. I will not stop searching for him, or die trying. This, I swear." With those words, Bowie felt a heavy, unseen weight fall around his shoulders. They were the arms of regret; arms that would weigh him down in times of doubt and disbelief. These unseeing arms had fingers that would pinch, and pinch deeply, until he fulfilled his oath. If Michael Cloud was dead, then the burden of those pinching, punishing fingers would forever be Bowie's to bear.

Concern filled Crow for his son. He was young enough to think the oath he'd just made would be easy to endure, because of his love for his soul-sibling. But the heaviness he was feeling now on his young, lean shoulders would feel like a boulder within a year. How long would it take him to find Michael? His eyes met Johanna's, and the look of grief on her face filled his heart with sadness.

"Bowie Storm, you were gifted with a high power many months ago by the grace of Uriel and above. I can assure you, those powers will be fully activated when your mission begins. Which is immediately."

Bowie looked into his mother's eyes. "Mum, please say goodbye to Sam for me. And tell Angel that I'm so sorry. Tell her I will not return until I find Michael."

Johanna turned to her son and wrapped her arms around him. "Of course, darling. You can do this, Bowie, I know you can. Michael will be okay, and you will bring him home to us."

"I will. Of that, I have no doubt." Bowie nodded as his father approached, followed by Red, Tom and Jess. Looking at his soul-trainers, he said, "Keep the girls safe 'til we return."

Tom hugged him hard. "You know we will, mate."

Jess lightly punched him on the arm. "Now, it's these sorts of oaths that separate the real men from the boys." He grinned light-heartedly, trying to send Bowie off without too much doom and gloom.

Bowie forced a smile. "Thanks, Jess."

Vicki Light stepped forward and handed Bowie a small, black backpack. He took it, hesitating as Fletch called down from the other end of the hall, "That contains everything you need to portal from one country to the next on your search."

Bowie nodded his thanks before turning to his parents. "Mum, Dad...I'm sorry if I've let you down."

"Son," Crow shook his head, "That could, and will, never happen." Crow hugged Bowie to him one last time. Johanna held in tears of fear and kissed her son's cheek.

"Goodbye, my love," she whispered. "My baby boy."

Bowie detected his mother was close to tears and cupped her face. "Mum, I love you, and I need you to believe I can do this, that I am going to be fine as I do it. Please, Mum," he almost begged her. He needed her to believe in him.

"Always," she whispered fiercely, and smiled brilliantly up at him.

"May you keep the souls safe," Fletch called as the Council bowed to Bowie.

"With every breath that I take." Bowie returned a bow before turning briskly, leaving the Council members behind him, along with those he loved.

Once the double-arched doorway closed behind him, he stood in Red's little back room and paused for one moment, before heading off. He jogged through her back gate and beyond to the Quicks' paddock.

Bowie stopped before the five giant trees and shrugged into the backpack, tightening the strap around his waist. He glanced behind him towards the college grounds, imagining Sam and Angel waiting for Christmas day to begin once their family returned.

Filled with a multitude of diverse emotions, he took a deep breath to clear his heart. Now wasn't the time to be consumed with regrets and 'what ifs.' He pushed one loving thought towards each of the girls before stepping into the electric-blue wild wind, thinking only then of Michael.

Chapter Thirteen

I love you, kiddo. Forgive me. Angel turned to the voice that whispered in her mind, thinking he was behind her. She frowned. "Bowie?"

Sam turned to Angel as Bowie's voice whispered to her, *I'll be back, Sam. I promise you.*

"Angel?"

"Yeah, I heard it, too."

"What's going on?"

Angel shook her head. "I wish I knew."

Jane walked into the room carrying a hot plate piled with maple syrup-coated pancakes. Max, who'd woken twenty minutes ago, followed with a plate of crispy bacon and a bowl of whipped cream, Moonie at his heels.

"Oh, now you are talking!" Sam said, easily distracted. It was Christmas, after all.

Angel pushed the niggling feeling aside and went to the side table, breaking off a piece of bacon to drop down to her favourite kitten, stroking his silky fur for a moment as his grateful purr vibrated through the air. Grabbing the serving utensils, she began to pile the steaming food on plates for everyone. Once they were served, they took their feast to the outside picnic table overlooking the sweeping lawns and ornate gardens before hungrily digging in.

"Oh my god...delish!" Sam grinned, watching as maple syrup dripped down Max's chin.

His green eyes sparkled as he smirked back at her, wiping the sticky trail off.

They heard Tom, Jess, and Samantha's parents walk through the house before joining them in the garden.

"Now that looks good," Crow burst out enthusiastically. "Let's grab a plate and join our young people here. Come on, now." He may as well have physically forced them all back into the house as he ushered them hastily inside, calling over his shoulder, "Jane, Red will be here shortly."

"Okay," she called, before shovelling in more pancakes with crispy bacon.

Johanna turned to Crow once they'd entered the parlour, as Tom and Jess began filling their plates.

"They deserve a decent brunch, love. Let them fill their bellies and have an hour of fun before we break the news to them," he said before she could speak.

Her heart melted, as it often did with her husband's kindness. "Of course." She smiled through her tears as he bent to brush them away with his lips.

"Come now, love." He smiled, squeezing her hands gently, knowing her concern for their son.

She nodded as Tom handed her a plate. "Thank you, Tom."

"You're welcome." He grabbed a tray of cups, filled a fresh teapot, and followed Jess out into the garden.

Brunch was a bright affair, although when the girls asked where their lazy brothers were, they were diverted into a fun Christmas treasure hunt that entertained them for two hours. They returned, happily exhausted, with a bounty of Christmas goodies to share with everyone, including treats for the cats and ponies.

"I think it's time for a swim," Angel said to Jane, wiping her sweaty brow.

"Oh, yeah, I'm impressed the slide hasn't melted yet!" Jane ran to her swim bag to grab her bathers.

"You mean before *we* melt." Sam grinned at Max. "You coming?"

"Definitely."

"Jane, Max, can you please go on ahead? We need to speak to the girls for just a moment," Crow said as he leant against the doorway.

Sam looked up at her father as Angel went to grab them all an icy-pole.

"Sure, no problem. Come on, Max." Jane headed towards the back door with Max, collecting an icy-pole off of Angel as she did. "See you soon," she said softly.

Angel walked by Uncle Crow, who was still leaning in the doorway, and handed Sam an icy-pole before she sat on the couch. Sam plonked on the couch beside her, slurping noisily on her icy treat.

Johanna stood near the Christmas tree as Jess and Tom sat on the couch opposite Sam and Angel.

Angel immediately lowered her icy-pole and waited for the news. It must be bad, for everybody to be milling around with such serious faces on Christmas day.

Sam caught on to Angel's vibe and lowered her icy-pole. "What's happened?"

Johanna looked across at Crow, who pushed himself away from the doorway and crossed over to join her, placing his arm around her shoulders.

"We have some news that will be upsetting, but please know that everything is going to be all right."

The girls looked at each other before their solemn faces returned to Crow.

Crow wasn't sure where to start. With perfect timing as always, Red stepped into the room and walked across to the window seat, sitting carefully as she was holding a small glass of red wine.

After taking an appreciative mouthful of the 'Brown Brothers' red that she liked to partake in at Christmas time, she informed the girls about Michael drugging Bowie to prevent him using his gifts, and everything that had followed thereafter.

The girls sat in silence after Red had finished. Jess stood to remove their melting, dripping icy-poles and deposit them into the bin before standing near Tom, waiting.

"Where's Bowie now?" Sam asked, worried.

"We don't know, sweetheart," Johanna answered as she crossed to her daughter and sat beside her, putting her arm around her shoulders.

She looked at Angel, who was sitting silently, squeezing her sticky fingers together. "Angel?"

Angel looked at Johanna, her eyes filled with tears. "We don't know where Michael went, so how will Bowie know where to find him?"

Crow nodded. "That's a good question, Angel. You understand that Michael and Bowie have powers unlike most royal-souls their age?"

Angel nodded, meeting his eyes.

His heart broke a fraction as a fat tear fell from Angel's lashes. He took a deep breath to steady his voice before replying calmly, "Wherever Michael may be, his essence will call to Bowie's. Eventually, no matter how much time may pass, each of the boys will be searching for the other."

"But Dad," Sam cried, "what if something really bad happens to one of them? How could they hear, feel, or help each other then?"

Crow sighed as he looked over the girls' heads and into his wife's worried eyes.

"Girls," Johanna said, reaching around Samantha to rub Angel's back, "I know you have many questions, and we will be here to answer them, I promise you. We, and the Council, would not have allowed Bowie to proceed with this mission if there was no chance of it being a success."

Crow nodded. "Bowie is resourceful, and determined to succeed in his mission."

"But that's just it, Dad! Bowie won't ever return if he doesn't find Michael!" Sam cried in despair.

Crow sighed deeply, wanting to comfort his small daughter. He forced a smile and said, "Samantha, you trust your brother, don't you?"

She was quiet for a second before she nodded.

"Then, please, try not to worry. It's Christmas day. Go, swim with your friends, everything will be all right."

Sam frowned, turning away from Crow to look at Johanna questioningly.

"It will be all right, darling, I promise." She smiled softly, stroking a hand over Sam's blonde curls.

Sam hugged her mother, before reaching across and grabbing Angel's hand, pulling her up off the couch. "Come on, Angel, let's get our bathers on."

Angel numbly allowed Sam to drag her from the room and upstairs, thinking about Michael and all the horrible things Max's uncle may have done to him. Neither of the girls spoke until they reached Angel's doorway.

"Sam?"

"Yes?"

"I don't feel like a swim right now. I think I need to be alone for a little while. Is that okay?"

Sam swallowed her tears, filled with sympathy for her friend, and forced a smile.

"Of course it is." She wrapped her arms around her friend's shaking shoulders as Angel cried softly.

"I'm so sorry that Bowie didn't protect Michael. Just know, that I will always protect you, no matter what. I promise."

Angel hugged her back tightly, sniffing. "It wasn't Bowie's fault, Sam. Michael drugged him..."

"Yeah...still," Sam smiled a watery smile at Angel, "even if you drugged me and broke my legs, I'd still be there to protect you."

Angel laughed through her tears. "Oh, Sam. Don't you know that I'd never do anything to hurt you? And I want to protect you, too."

"We should have been born before our brothers, we could have taught them a thing or two."

Angel nodded in agreement.

"Won't you come swimming?" she asked. "You might feel better?"

Angel shook her head. "I just need a little bit of quiet time."

"Okay. Well, as it's Christmas Day, and the time for giving, I will give you just a *little* bit of quiet time."

"You are so generous, thank you." Angel smirked as Sam walked backwards to her room to get her bathers.

Angel sighed, closing her bedroom door before walking across to her window and, opening it wide, crept out onto the roof, shaded by ghost gums. She couldn't walk into Michael's bedroom just now, knowing his scent and his absence would overwhelm her. Instead, she sat under his eave and looked out across Glenormiston's perfectly-blue sky.

Alone, with no one to hear, she allowed her twelve-year-old tears to flow with worry for her brother. She grieved for him and their parents on what should have been a joyous day.

Then she dropped her head against her drawn-up knees and cried for Bowie, too, knowing how much he would blame himself for not being by Michael's side in his time of need.

She was cross with her brother.

He may have been trying to protect Bowie, but, in doing so, had doomed them both to unimaginable pain. The kind only a royal-soul forced to separate from his soul-sibling would know.

Angel jumped with fright as something furry brushed against her bare leg, startling her momentarily. She laughed as the sweet black-and-white face gazed up at her, meowing, huge green eyes imploring her to be happy.

"Hey, Moonie." She whispered through her tears. Scooping him up, she remembered the day she had saved him, when Bowie had given her the first lesson regarding her gifts.

She'd hated him that day, and on the many days that had followed, when he'd inflicted pain on pure-souls, and her, so she could gain a better understanding of her gifts and her role.

Angel rubbed her face against Moonie's soft fur as the creature purred, curling itself into a ball on her lap, ready for an afternoon sleep. His purrs were a comforting sound, and she dropped her head against the stone wall under Michael's window, closing her eyes.

The breeze carried the horses' whinnying from across the paddocks, mingling with the screams of delight and laughter of her friends. It all seemed so perfect. Almost as if two giant chunks of her life weren't missing…

Chapter Fourteen

Bowie

Time ticked by faster than one could imagine as Bowie travelled through one portal to the next, one city after another, one continent blurring into the next as he picked up traces of Michael's soul-essence, which called to his. It soon became an exhausting, blurry quest of misery.

From each crowded city that fell, darkness spilled and spread into surrounding country areas, poisoned by Vein activity, which seemed to grow in strength and numbers. Everywhere, pure-souls were being influenced to use their positions to create the most destructive bedlam toward each other, and to Mother Earth.

He connected with other royal-souls along the way when he heard their calls for help and, true to his role, would aid all he could when help was needed. Every pure-soul he saved, every action he took to heal Mother Earth, slowed down his quest.

There were times when he'd feel his essence light up as it searched, reaching for Michael, almost making the connection…before, once again, all traces would disappear. Michael was being cloaked, but

Bowie was getting closer with every day, week, month, and year that passed.

And for every month that passed without success, the weight of his oath grew heavier on his shoulders. There were times he'd feel himself leaning against a wall or a tree, the burden pushing him down, and he'd have to remind himself that he could, in fact, bear it and stand straight.

There was no doubt it was getting harder to do so; the unseen fingers bit cruelly into his shoulders, only making him more determined to succeed.

As he aged and travelled, assisting the royal-souls, his gifts became so powerful that they asked him to take the lead in dire situations. He put out monstrous fires deliberately lit by a pure-soul whose mind had been poisoned. He influenced plant growth in the Amazon and poured his energy into freezing gigantic icebergs that were melting too fast. Assisting in the production of healthy harvests and community gardens that spread far and wide to feed the homeless and struggling, he filled dams and dried riverbeds with rain, and quenched drought-stricken areas, forcing nature to grow and flourish, with more healing rains to come.

As hard as he and the other royal-souls worked, something truly evil was at play. The earth seemed to fall into chaos and despair no matter how hard they worked to stay on top of the destruction.

On his twenty-fourth birthday, he'd just arrived in the city sinking into the Adriatic Sea when his essence glowed brightly. His breath caught…this was the strongest pull he'd felt yet. He could feel Michael close by. Perhaps it was because it was their birthday? He didn't know for sure, but he assumed that was helping.

He headed towards the pull of energy, navigating his way down a labyrinth of alleyways, crossing bridges and waterways. Bowie kept to the shadows, whispering to the wind to assist him, calling out to Michael's essence.

He stepped towards the entrance of a villa, the weight of his oath almost making him stumble into the canal. Bowie righted himself, cursing under his breath. He could hear voices in the front room as he slipped through the open doorway of the abandoned building that seemed to float on the water.

The Veins' laughter slid greasily over his skin. He sensed they were young, and disgruntled at having to guard the royal-soul while their brethren were out plotting and spreading their disease of discord. As they carried on with their drinking, grumbling, and card game, he skilfully crept by undetected.

Along the hallway, he turned down a flight of stairs soaked with water. The scent was dank, and a chill hung in the air. The pull was getting stronger, and his heart was beating furiously in his chest. *This is it!* Entering the pitch-black chamber, he whispered, "*Light,*" and waved his hand as an amber ball of light glowed in his palm. He cast it above, lighting the chamber, and his heart froze.

Michael lay on a tomb-like slab of marble surrounded by water. He was pale, thin, and fading. Long Vein-like tubes were attached to his chest, connected to glass pods that hung from thick beams in the ceiling. They looked like giant lightbulbs, each one filling with blood from Michael's body. His amulet powered his heart, kept it beating to keep him alive, producing more blood.

Bowie noticed that the marble from Mother Earth, clasped in Michael's wristband, was almost black, but still held a tiny glow of life within it. Just.

He whispered, "*Shield,*" and flung one hand towards Michael's chest, protecting him. Then he whipped his other hand toward the leech-like tubes, whispering, "*Fire,*" and shooting a deadly inferno towards them, burning them to a crisp in seconds.

The glass bulbs looked like they would explode and shatter all over them. Bowie called for ice and froze them in an instant, the weight sending them falling towards the water below. He calmly summoned the wind to catch them, before easing them delicately into the water, without making so much as a splash.

The Veins' laughter above the stairs trickled down. So too, did one set of footsteps.

"Luigi, don't go feasting on your own. Wait for us."

"You know we are not supposed to eat from it, Steven. Brendan will kill us."

"Oh, ease up, Richardo. Brendan won't notice if we've taken a small bite or two."

Bowie cursed under his breath, then lay his hands on Michael's chest, forcing a natural flow of energy through his fingertips and palms, shooting a lightning bolt of energy into Michael.

He closed his eyes and whispered desperately to Mother Earth, hoping the energy from his bracelet would gift Michael with a boost. It was the first time he'd ever wished to have been born a Heavenly soul, and not an Elemental.

The footsteps grew closer as Michael's eyelids fluttered open.

"Bowie, thank the Angels," he whispered, a smile lighting up the dark grooves beneath his baby-blues.

Bowie grinned. "You know, I'm going to kick your arse hard when you're in better shape, mate."

"I look forward to it."

"Good, now hold that thought." Bowie leapt onto the marble slab with Michael as he spun toward the arrivals, who were now hip deep in the water.

"What the hell!" Richardo yelled as Luigi and Steven rushed in behind him.

"I've got this!" Steven yelled out gleefully as he thrust his wrists in Bowie's direction, sending several long, bloody veins towards Bowie, their razor-sharp ends getting closer by the second.

"Any time now, mate," Michael suggested weakly.

"All in good time," Bowie said good-naturedly, feeling the happiest he had in an awfully long time. He briskly made a circle with one hand and whispered to the water, which flew up and surrounded the three Veins. Making a fist, he thrust it hard towards them. Then he opened his palm, sending an amplified lightning bolt towards them, electrifying them in seconds. The sizzling sound was brilliant.

The stench of burnt Veins, not so much.

Once they fell face-first into the water, scorched beyond recognition, Bowie dropped his hands and turned to Michael. "Ready to go home?"

"Like you wouldn't believe." He weakly reached up, and, as Bowie grabbed his wrist, pulling him upwards and throwing him over his shoulder, Michael passed out from the combined loss of blood and essence, and utter fatigue.

"It's okay, mate, I've got you now." Bowie's relief had no name. The weight of Michael across his shoulders was a weight he would carry every day, if he must, if it meant knowing his soul-sibling was safe.

He was worried about Michael's state, but he knew that, once they were home, he would receive the best care. Now to just get to the portal without running into any complications.

It wasn't until he was making his way through the building and out towards the alleyway that he realised the burden of his oath was no longer crushing him with its impending weight. The biting fingers that had been digging into his flesh and bones for the past seven years, bruising him even now, had lifted.

Thank goodness for small mercies. He continued along the alleyway before turning towards a narrow canal where he'd left the gondola tied to a small jetty.

Bowie lay Michael along the seat and covered him with a blanket. Untying the gondola, he grabbed the push pole, and whispered to the wind to propel them swiftly along in the direction of the portal. Once they arrived, he felt a nervous energy wash over him.

It had been seven years since he'd seen his parents, his sister...Angel. He wondered how she'd handled the absence of her blood-sibling? The girls would be nineteen now; he wouldn't recognise them from the cute little kids they'd been. He wondered how much had changed as the wind pushed them gently against the side of the ancient building in the middle of the sea. Bowie asked the wind to cease, then secured the raft before scooping Michael up in his arms and shifting him onto his shoulder.

They entered the decrepit-looking building, Bowie stepping into the rounded tower where the electric-blue wild wind danced, waiting to embrace him. He stepped closer, gripping Michael, and whispered, "Glenormiston South."

Michael groaned as the wild wind slapped at him.

"It's okay, mate, we're nearly there, we're nearly home. Just hang on a little longer." Bowie stepped into the wild wind. Within a second, it swept them up in a storm of light, one that felt like it was tugging them in a million directions as it flew them to the place for which their souls both longed.

Chapter Fifteen

S am's lips parted under the soft, yet firm, mouth kissing her to dizzying heights. His aftershave wrapped around her like his strong arms, holding her flush against him as he kissed her. He ran his hand down the length of her blonde curls, grabbing a handful before tugging her head back so he could look into her amber eyes, filled with desire.

Her lips, glossy and pink, turned up as she asked him. "Why have you stopped?"

"Because your sister is walking this way." Max grinned.

They turned to watch Angel approach. Despite the frown on her face, she was beautiful as she marched towards them.

Baby-blue eyes glowed in a face that suited her name, framed by a mass of silky blonde hair that fell down her back. Her skin was smooth and creamy, her figure, clad in blue jeans and a black turtleneck, was athletic and strong, thanks to her genes and Eddy's martial arts lessons. He'd been holding them in the college's wellbeing building for the past two years on weekends and school holidays

They'd all graduated from their high school, Terang College, the year before and were well into their first year at the Agricultural College, which was thriving and operating at full capacity.

Over the past seven years, they'd filled the Holistic Horticulture courses to the brim. The pure-souls had finally caught on to the use of farming techniques that didn't deplete and poison the soil, still enabling them to make a profitable living and help heal the earth.

Samantha and Max had signed up for this course, and Tom was one of their lecturers.

Eddy worked part-time in the Wellbeing Hub, where he taught Karate, and studied psychology.

Angel worked part-time with Jess in the Agricultural department, where she was studying to be a Veterinary physician. Elizabeth also worked in the Agricultural department.

Not long after the girls had graduated, Sam and Bowie's parents left to resume their Soul Keeper duties on the High Council, travelling the globe and healing all they could.

Since Brendan had taken Michael, three more heavenly souls had disappeared from around the globe. And with their extracted soul-essence, which the Veins used for destruction, Mother Earth and her pure-souls were affected. No matter how hard the royal-souls continued battling against the Veins' mayhem, the rise of ugliness and death prevailed.

"Eddy should be here any second," Angel said as she reached them.

"Why so serious? We've just had a fun-filled fortnight away; you should be chillaxed, not wearing that frown, as pretty as you wear it." Sam reached out and smoothed the frown line between Angel's brows, making her laugh.

"Sorry, I didn't realise I was frowning." Angel forced a smile for Sam as a voice called from behind.

"Wait up, girl!" Gary, a friend of Eddy and Max's, called out.

They'd just left the bus from Halls Gap, where they'd spent two weeks hiking and healing with another group of college students from Bendigo. Most, like Gary, were pure-souls, but there were two others who were elemental-souls. When they'd had the chance to slip off with them, uninterrupted, for an hour, they had all shared their growing concerns with the negative disturbances affecting country Victoria.

This time of year, midwinter, Halls Gap and most of the Western District, were as green as a tree frog. But, eerily, this year, and the one before it, the earth had remained dry, no matter how much rain fell, and Mother Earth was thirsty.

Because the college was on the Soul Keepers' hallowed grounds, it was always green, even in the summer months. That was because of the elemental-souls pouring moisture into the lush landscape, where the Veins poisonous influence could not reach.

On top of the erratic weather patterns, there was an increasingly-high number of mass murders and suicides, with both of their hometowns being severely affected.

Something had to give, and soon.

"Hey, where d'you go, girl?" Gary caught up to Angel, clutching four hotdogs he'd grabbed from the corner milk bar while they waited for Eddy to give them a lift back to the college.

Sam hid her snicker as she saw Angel roll her eyes. Max couldn't help himself and chuckled at Angel's annoyance. She'd told Gary at least five times in the past fourteen days, let alone over the past seven months that they'd studied together, that she did not eat meat.

She hid her groan as he passed Sam and Max a hotdog before holding one out to her.

Angel folded her arms and stared unblinkingly at him, silently begging Eddy to hurry up.

"Not hungry?" Gary asked, causing Sam to burst out laughing.

"Christ, Gary, Angel doesn't eat meat, remember?"

"Oh, yeah. Sorry. Although, technically, a hotdog isn't really meat, you know?"

"Gary, you're not doing yourself any favours, mate." Max said as Angel turned away, sighing in relief as Eddy honked his car horn, pulling up to the curb.

She scooped up her backpack as the others grabbed their gear and piled into Eddy's brown, beaten-up station wagon.

Angel dropped a kiss on Eddy's cheek as she jumped into the seat beside him. "It's good to see you, Eddy."

He beamed at her. "You, too." He nodded at the others as they climbed into the back.

"Has it been boring without us, Eddy?" Sam asked, snuggling against Max, who wrapped his arm around her.

"Of course," Eddy said, grinning at Sam in the review mirror, before turning up Terang-Mortlake Road, heading towards Noorat. "Boring as. Although, things did get pretty interesting the day after you left—had a couple of surprise visitors rock up."

He cringed inwardly, knowing he wasn't supposed to say anything, so quickly changed the subject, and chatted briefly about the animals and vaguely about the two new counsellors who were heading-up the well-being team. One would see clients from around the district, whilst the other would liaison with Camperdown and Warrnambool's Headscope.

"Oh, maybe one of them will grab our young Angel's eye here, mm?" Sam reached across to the front seat to tug lightly on Angel's ponytail.

She turned around in the seat and flashed Sam a smile. "Who's got the time?"

"Pfft, who indeed," Sam sighed, looking up into Max's green eyes. They'd intensified in colour in the last seven years. His cuteness as a twelve-year-old had always captured Sam's heart. But as a nineteen-year-old, Maxwell Black had morphed, as far as Sam was concerned, into a downright sexy individual whom she had a hard time keeping her hands off.

Angel turned around, seeing the frown on Gary's face at the talk of there possibly being someone who might catch her eye.

Eddy drove past their old primary school and turned down Glenormiston Road.

Max grew quiet, as he always did when they drove by Blacks' mansion. Sam patted his thigh, sensing his unease, and he rewarded her with a calming smile.

He'd been so relieved the day the High Council had placed him in the caring hands of Tom and Jess. They'd allowed him to grow up at the college with Sam and Angel, to develop his half-Heavenly gifts.

It hadn't been easy; he'd felt the disturbing, dark pull of his cousin calling to him. And lately his dreams were filled with a darkness that, he was ashamed to admit, filled him with pulsating pleasure.

"Here we go." Eddy turned the car onto Trufood Road, and up towards the back entrance of the college, hooning over the cattle grid.

There were students attending the horses, tidying up loose ends before getting ready for the last term of the year, which started tomorrow.

Finally, pulling up in front of the homestead, Eddy kept the engine running as they got out, thanking him for the lift.

Garry sat in the back, as he and Eddy would go to park in the student car park then head off to the campus dormitories.

"Thanks so much, Eddy." Angel smiled.

"You're welcome. See ya."

"You'll see me in class tomorrow, Angel!" Gary called.

Angel raised a hand as she walked towards the front door, mumbling, "Unfortunately I will," causing Sam to laugh her head off.

Max carried Sam's bags as they followed Angel into the house.

Tom met them in the foyer. "Good trip, gang?"

Angel hugged him hello. "It was. Despite gathering some disturbing intel from our Bendigo clan."

"Yes, we've received a call. We've a Council meeting with them tonight."

"Do we need to attend?" Sam asked as Max shook Tom's hand hello.

"No, it's for High Council members only, in Bendigo. Angel, I should warn you, your thirteen will be selected in the next month."

Angel froze on the stairs. Turning, she looked down at Tom. "But it's not time?"

"I know, pet, but it's close to the time." He looked up at her, wanting to tell her the other news, but he had been asked not to just yet.

"Where's Jess?" Sam asked, following Max to their room.

"There's a mare in labour, he's been with her for the past three hours."

"I'll go and help." Angel went to turn down the stairs when Tom stopped her.

"She's okay. Red is with him, they've got it covered. Just go up and unpack, enjoy your last few hours of freedom; next term is going to be a busy one. Mrs. McGoldrick has made a fresh garden lasagne just for you."

"Oh, yum, she is an angel. Thanks, Tom." Angel headed up the remainder of the stairs and along the landing before turning down the hallway to her room.

Sam and Max's door closed with a bang before laughter and kissing sounds emitted from within.

Angel chuckled as she shook her head and walked into her room, closing the door behind her. She opened her window, smiling when Moonie leapt up onto the sill before flopping onto the window seat, kneading a cushion as he purred away.

Angel stroked his silky fur before dropping a kiss onto his soft head, grabbed a towel, and left for a long soak in the tub. She needed to wash away a fortnight's worth of dust that the bush shower hadn't really removed.

On their return from the Council meeting in Bendigo, Tom and Jess went to the Gatekeeper's cottage, entering through the front door. In the room opposite Red's bedroom, Michael lay on pristine white sheets in a spotlessly-clean room that looked more like the inside of a crystal sphere than a bedroom. It should have been chilly, but the temperature was perfect for healing.

Michael had lain limp and drained since returning through the portal two weeks ago, and Fletch, Jess and Red had all been working on him, trying to revive his energy essence. Even the combination of Bowie's and Michael's globes did little to reduce the poison that still circulated inside his heart.

His amulet, although strong, had been violated and subjected to too many years of abuse. They sensed that there was something preventing his amulet from fully healing his abused heart and body, but, as of yet, could not detect it.

Bowie stood against the far wall, his arms folded. He'd barely left Michael's side, except for when Red persuaded him to take a quick shower once a day.

"Any change?" Jess asked as he clapped Bowie on the shoulder before walking over to Michael's bedside.

Bowie shook his head.

"Bowie…" Tom turned to look at the young man, amazed at how *together* he was, even after all he'd endured whilst he'd been away on his quest to find his soul-sibling; he was beyond proud. "You need to go and see Samantha, it's time to let her know you're back, and to let Angel know that Michael is all right."

Bowie raised tired, amber eyes to his soul-trainer and shook his head. "Tom, I am not leaving his side. Not for anything."

Tom nodded his head. "Okay, then the girls will come here."

"No," Bowie said abruptly. "I don't want Angel seeing Michael this way."

Jess sighed as he turned to face his soul-sibling and soul-student.

"Let's leave it for tonight, fellas. We'll see if we can sort this out tomorrow. But Tom's right, Bowie, the girls need to know. They've missed you both dreadfully all these years."

Bowie ran a hand frustratedly through his dark-blonde hair before folding his arms again, shrugging a shoulder. "Yeah, okay. Fine."

Red walked into the room with a tall, beautiful, auburn-haired twenty-year-old.

Bowie smiled at Red before his gaze rested on the striking girl. It took him a full minute to realise who it was. "Jane? Haven't you grown up!"

Jane laughed as she crossed over to Bowie and threw her arms around his neck. "Funny how that happens, so have you." *Nicely.* She didn't shield her thoughts, making him smile.

"How have you been?" he asked as she stepped back.

"Very well, thanks. Busy battling the demons."

Bowie nodded as he followed her gaze to Michael.

"As have you," she added quietly.

"We do what we must."

"Yes, we do. I think we'll need Angel's help to ease the toxicity in Michael's soul-essence," Jane said to her aunt.

"No." Bowie looked at Jane.

"Actually, my dear boy, we must," Red said firmly.

"We have had several High Council members work on him, to no avail. Do you really think Angel can help him on her own?"

He didn't mean to sound dismissive of Angel's skills. But it concerned him how she would react when she saw her blood-sibling in such a poor state of health for the first time in seven years. And he still carried such guilt that he hadn't been able to protect Michael from Brendan Black.

"Bowie, it is all going to be fine. Angel isn't the little twelve-year-old you left behind. Trust that she can handle this."

Bowie looked at Tom, then Jess. They both offered him a smile.

"She'll be fine, mate," Jess assured him, seeing the worry in his deep, amber eyes. The cool kid that had left them had grown into a good-look-ing man.

"Okay. I guess I don't have much of a choice, do I? Not if it means Angel can actually help Michael."

"Exactly." Jane crossed over to Michael and lay a hand against his chest. "It's times like these, Aunty, I wish I'd been born Heavenly."

Red placed her hand on Jane's shoulder as they looked down at Michael, lying still, as if death were already upon him.

"You do just fine as you are, my dear. And it isn't Michael's time. I can feel it." She placed her hand on top of Jane's and whispered love into Michael's heart, hoping he could feel it.

Chapter Sixteen

The first day back was always gruelling, especially after a fort-night off, with days filled with nothing but relaxing activities and casual study. But this day was extra tiresome because several of Angel's fellow students were sporting hangovers from making the most of their last day of the holidays the day before.

They'd treated a cow with an abscess the size of a human's head. This had caused a few of the hungover individuals to vomit, once they'd released the foul smelling, septic fluid. Angel felt queasy herself, on top of feeling the pure-souls' pain and sickness, but focused her energy on easing both the cow's and the students' physical symptoms.

Jess touched her lightly on the back as he walked past, letting her know he appreciated her efforts. He was grateful he could wave them all off to their next class, which was two hours of theory. This only added to Angel's exhaustion.

After lunch, they checked on the baby foal and its mother before heading into Terang's veterinary clinic to watch two surgeries. By the time the bus dropped them back to the college, Angel felt as if she'd completed a week's worth of classes, not a single day.

Feeling relieved to walk in the front door of the homestead, she took a deep breath and embraced the calming energy of home that revitalised her. Her mouth watered as delicious aromas flooded her senses.

She headed down to the kitchen, stomach rumbling, wondering what Mrs. McGoldrick was cooking, and froze at the sight of the stranger standing at the stove, his back to her.

He was tall, with broad, strong shoulders. Faded jeans hugged long legs and a narrow waist as they sat low on his hips. His back muscles seemed to ripple under his black t-shirt as he stirred the contents of the saucepan. His scent was as divine as whatever he was making, and she was dying to see if his face matched the rest of him.

Hearing her thoughts, he hid the smile in his voice. "Would you like a taste, Angel?"

His voice caressed her, and her mouth went dry.

He left the spoon in the saucepan as he turned, grabbing a tea towel to wipe his hands on. As soon as his glowing, amber eyes met her baby-blues, it was his turn to have his mouth go dry. *My God, but she has grown up to be one hell of a sexy...* He slammed the shield over his thoughts as soon as he saw the corner of her lips turn up.

"Hello, Bowie." It was clear she was shielding her thoughts now, too.

"Oh, good. You're back." Sam breezed in behind Angel, giving her a hug. "Look who's come home, finally." She grinned at Bowie. Turning to Angel, she said, "I nearly had a heart attack when I got home earlier to find Mr. Tall-and-unusual standing in the kitchen."

Angel couldn't take her eyes off Bowie's face. Thick, silky, dark-blonde hair falling into amber eyes that were framed with perfectly-shaped eyebrows. His lips, full, with the hint of a smile. Strong cheekbones, but not too angular.

But there was something else, something that no one else could see, but Angel could. There was pain etched behind the glow of his glorious eyes, a weight that may have been physically lifted, but still remained, gripping his soul tightly.

"Am I not going to get a hug hello, kiddo?"

He grinned at her as he stepped around the butcher's block and towards her, dropping the tea towel.

"I'll take another one." Sam hugged him hard, which he returned, dropping a kiss on the top of her head.

"It's so good just to feel you," She murmured against his chest.

Can't wait.

Sam grinned as she turned around, letting Angel know she'd heard her thought.

Bowie stepped closer and slid his arms around Angel's shoulders as he looked down at her. Her eyes sparkled like aquamarine gemstones, and her hair brushed silkily against the back of his hands. Stardust freckles scattered lightly over her nose and cheeks. He felt the ridiculous urge to kiss each one of them.

By the Angels, get a grip and just hug her already!

As he drew her against him, her arms wound about his waist, feeling every firm muscle, his scent overpowering her senses as her cheek pressed against his chest. She could hear his beating heart thumping as quickly as hers seemed to be, as his breath tickled the top of her hair. She breathed him in, deep and slow, savouring his scent.

Electricity hummed between them, making Bowie frown, which he twisted into a casual smile. "It's so good to see you both," he said before holding Angel away from him. Feeling his body stir, he quickly turned back to the stove, saying, "Better get that sauce."

He shielded his mind solidly, wondering what the hell was going on. Why was he was reacting to Angel like an out-of-control teenager? Yeah, okay, she was sublimely stunning on every level, but he'd never felt like this with anyone before. Over the past seven years he'd seen and worked alongside plenty of beautiful women, and had taken comfort with a few of them, who had been equally happy in returning his affections.

Angel's thoughts were all over the place as she looked at Sam, wondering if she'd felt the strange vibe in the air.

By the look on her face, she had. Thank god Max suddenly walked in the kitchen, followed by Tom, preventing her from saying anything about it.

"Good, you've all reconnected then?" Tom walked to the fridge to grab the half-eaten sandwich that he hadn't finished at lunch time.

"Oh, yeah, you could say that." Sam smirked as she planted a kiss against Max's lips. "Mm, yummy," she whispered against them before kissing him again.

Bowie raised an eyebrow. "How long has this been going on?"

Sam burst out laughing. "Oh, dear brother. I'm not twelve anymore, and, yes, we share a room, and, yes I am no longer a…"

Max squeezed her hand, trying to get her to shut up as heat flooded his cheeks.

"I think he gets it, thanks, Sam," Tom interrupted. Bowie was grateful he had.

"Where's Michael?" Angel asked.

Bowie turned from the stove as Sam stepped towards Angel, placing her hand on her arm.

"He's safe, Angel. He's home."

Angel spun around to run upstairs to Michael's room when Bowie's voice stopped her.

"Angel, wait."

She turned, meeting his eyes, which were now filled with concern. "He's at Red's, in the healing room."

"What's wrong with him? What happened?" She frowned, feeling a sense of dread fill her.

Tom nodded. "There's a lot to discuss. But, for now, I need you to sit in the healing garden."

"Right now, when my brother's finally home, you want me to go sit in the healing garden?" She sounded exasperated.

"It's *because* Michael is home that I need you to sit in the healing garden, Angel. He needs the pure energy from both his blood- and soul-sibling." Tom crossed over to her and put his arm around her shoulder, steering her towards the back door. "He is not in a good way, pet. You've had a big day, and we need you calm, centred, and charged. Can you do that for him?"

"Of course," she replied. Bowie detected both defeat and heat in her answer.

"Bowie?" Tom nodded to Bowie.

"Yep, I've got this."

Sam called from behind her, "I'll be right here if you need me."

"Thanks," Angel called softly as she walked out into the lush, sweet-scented garden.

"I've got the sauce covered, Bowie," Max said, walking over to stir the pot.

"Righto." Bowie nodded to Max, meeting Sam's eyes and thinking they needed to have a conversation.

Sam raised an eyebrow, hearing his thoughts, and waved her hand for him to follow Tom outside, which he did.

"Angel, absorb all the energy Bowie gifts you with. Jess told me about the animals today, even the hungover, ill ones. So you do need a boost. Michael isn't going anywhere; he's home and safe, and we will all do our part to restore him to full health. This is your part, okay?"

"Yes, Tom."

He looked at Bowie. "I'll leave you to it. Once you're done, bring Angel to Red's. We'll meet you there."

"Yep, no worries." Bowie sat amongst the damp, happy faces of the chamomile patch.

Tom left, leaving Angel standing and looking down at the man who was no stranger, yet did strange things to her.

Bowie tilted his head back to look up at her, standing there hesitantly, and held a hand up for her to take. "Angel?"

She hesitated for a second before taking his hand. She allowed him to tug her down to sit cross-legged across from him, their knees touching.

It's just Bowie—stop looking at him like that. She took a deep breath as she met his eyes. Her heartbeat accelerated. *What the hell?*

Bowie Storm had grown into a thing of rare, male beauty, and it was doing things to her insides…complex things she didn't have time to work out.

He frowned slightly, feeling it too. They needed to concentrate, for Michael. "You need to open yourself up to me completely for this to work, Angel. You know the drill." He placed his hands, resting palms-up, on his knees.

She swallowed, nodding, wondering how she could stop her descriptive thoughts, being so close to him. His scent, those eyes… *Angels above, help me,* she begged. When her fingers slid over the flesh of his palm, her palm fitting into the centre of his, they were both slammed with a current of energy, making them gasp out loud.

He sensed she was about to pull away, and closed his fingers around her hand, shaking his head once. "We need to use this energy, don't be afraid."

She nodded, meeting his beautiful, amber eyes that seemed to have flames flickering beneath the surface.

He took a deep breath and whispered to Mother Earth, feeling the wind pick up around them in the garden. It embraced them, enclosing them in a circle before it turned into a ball of fire; not burning them, but sending a hot force of energy through them.

Angel's eyes remained unblinkingly on Bowie's as he continued to silently call on his Elemental gifts to recharge and embrace this heavenly soul before him.

A gentle rain fell, soaking them in an instant.

Angel closed her eyes and tilted her face up to the cleansing shower, feeling it wash away all the stress from her day. It filled her with an overpowering sense of energy as the ground beneath her, and the zillion microorganisms of the earth's creatures' energy, flowed up within her before lowering back into Mother Earth.

Angel sighed, feeling at peace as she opened her eyes to find Bowie smiling across at her as his thumb lightly caressed the back of her hand. The warm wind dried them in an instant.

"Last part." He stood, tugging her to her feet, and placed the flat of his palm against her chest. His other arm slowly circled around her back, holding her steady.

Her breath caught, and she thanked the stars for her ability to shield her thoughts as she drew closer to him, his large, warm hand against the beating of her heart.

"Ready, kiddo?" He looked down into the depths of her eyes, shining brightly with Mother Earth's gifts, and something else he forced himself not to think about. She was his soul-sibling's kid sister—hell, almost *his* kid sister. He forced himself to focus solely on the next task at hand.

She nodded, thinking she was ready, but when he closed his eyes and focused on sending his Elemental energy straight into her beating heart, her amulet sparked unlike anything she'd ever felt, taking her breath away. It continued to send a pleasant, overwhelming wave throughout her entire body, making her see stars before the wave of energy knocked her off her feet.

Bowie felt the unusual peak of energy slam into her and caught her as she fell. He swooped her into his arms and whispered the elements away.

Angel rubbed a palm against her chest, which pulsated as she looked up into Bowie's eyes, which, even now, swirled with amber flames. She could read the confusion in them.

"Bowie, what was that?" she asked breathlessly. It all felt so familiar being with him again, yet pleasantly unfamiliar too.

"I don't know. I've done it to Michael before and have never felt that intensity. It must be your gifts peaking, as you're close to your coming-of-age ceremony." His eyes dropped to her pretty, pink lips before meeting her eyes.

They were both shielding their thoughts, but their tell-tale gaze spoke volumes. "You good to stand?"

"Yeah." She wiggled out of his arms and reluctantly stepped away from his warm, firm body.

He stared at her unblinkingly for a few moments, before saying, "Let's go, then."

It was a pleasure to watch him turn and walk towards the driveway; his silky hair danced in the breeze, carrying his scent back to her, making her mouth water for a taste.

Get a grip, girl, she hissed as she followed him around to the car. *It's time to focus on Michael,* she chastised herself, and she was grateful that the short trip to Red's house was a silent one.

Jane greeted them at the front door and hugged Angel before leading them into the healing room.

It shocked Angel to see her blood-sibling lay so still and pale. Her despair brought tears of fear to her eyes as she rushed to his side.

"Michael," she whispered, urgency in her words. "Michael, can you hear me?" Her tears fell onto his face, which she quickly brushed away, when his hand raised to catch her wrist.

"Angel..." He opened his eyes. Their usual bright blue was gone, replaced with a dull, murky grey. "My little Angel," he whispered again, forcing a smile through the pain consuming him.

She bent and rested her forehead against his pale and cold one as her tears continued to fall. "Where have you been all this time, Michael? What's happened to you?"

A warm hand rubbed her back. "Time for questions later, my dear," Red ordered. "It's time for you and Bowie to see if you can fully restore Michael's health."

Angel turned to Red, who nodded gravely.

"He has been with us these past two weeks while you were away. The High Council have been unable to aid him." She didn't want to add that Angel and Bowie were Michael's last hope; he was fading quickly.

Angel looked across at Bowie, who was leaning, arms folded, against the far crystal wall. Spheres of light flowed along one curved wall to the next in a constant hum of energy.

Jane, Tom, and Jess stood in the doorway. "We're going to the hall with the other Council members to pray for Michael. Just holler if you need us." Tom nodded to Angel and Bowie.

"They'll be just fine, won't you, dears?" Red smiled at them before whispering, "May you keep this precious soul safe."

To which they replied, "With every breath that we take."

Red nodded before leaving the room. As she stepped through the doorway, crystals formed, sealing them in the bright room that swirled with healing energy.

Angel met Bowie's grim expression before looking down at Michael.

He smiled weakly up at them. His eyes, which were not *his* eyes, were freaking Angel out slightly.

"Just breathe, Angel, you've got this." He whispered, reaching for her hand.

She clasped her fingers around his, wiping her eyes dry as she nodded. She would bleed every ounce of energy she possessed into her blood-sibling. She'd do whatever it took to keep Michael's heart beating.

"I'm going to get you strong, Michael. I promise."

"Yeah, and as soon as that happens, I owe you an arse-kicking," Bowie said without a hint of a joke.

Michael attempted to laugh, but his chest rattled like an engine that needed oiling.

"Okay, let's begin," Bowie nodded to Angel.

She placed her palm against Michael's chest, her other over her heart. Bowie placed his palm on top of Angel's, his other against Michael's chest.

Taking a deep breath together, Bowie called on the crystal elements to strengthen his soul-sibling as Angel tuned into the powerful energy swirling within her, gifted from Bowie.

Angel felt a dark energy within Michael immediately, swirling in his blood, searching for something else as it wrapped around his weakened heart.

His amulet felt unclean, unable to power his heart and restore his essence.

Bowie could feel the power of Angel's energy flowing through her and into Michael, through the contact with her skin.

Although he'd placed his hands on Michael before, attempting to heal him with Tom, Red, and Jess, this moment was unlike any of those.

The room pulsated with every thrust of energy Angel sparked into Michael's chest; it was electrifying. They worked tirelessly for three hours, and with each minute that ticked by, Michael's heart seemed to cleanse itself of the wicked intruder that leaked into his essence via the Veins' intrusion. His amulet started shining within his chest, and as it poured its ethereal energy into his beating heart, it sparked his soul-essence to shine.

A burst of energy flowed up from Michael's chest and through Angel's palm before knocking her backwards, forcing her off her feet. The walls beamed and the spheres of clear light burst into a rainbow of colours, lighting the room up like a Christmas tree.

Bowie quickly crossed to other side of the room and reached out a hand to Angel. "You okay, kiddo?"

"Yes, I think so. Thanks," she said as he pulled her to her feet, before they both went back to Michael's side.

They felt enormous relief as they looked down into Michael's eyes. The grey murk was gone, and his bright blue eyes smiled up at them. His handsome face was filled with healthy colour, and his body appeared muscular and fit.

He sat up. A burst of laughter escaped his lips before turning to tears. Tears of fright for what had passed, for years of torment and pain. Tears of guilt and regret for what he'd put himself and Bowie through, for wasted years. Tears of relief to be well and home again.

He reached out to them and embraced them fiercely, overwhelmed as a flood of emotions swept through him.

Michael kissed the top of Angel's head before looking his soul-sibling in the eye. "I'm so sorry, Bowie, for everything that I've put you through."

Bowie shook his head, not knowing where to start. "I want to kick your arse so hard. But I'm so happy to see you restored to you again that I don't think I have the heart to hurt you." He smiled.

Michael laughed, the sound lighting up the room before he turned his eyes back to Angel.

"Not so little now, little sister," he said.

She smiled at him. "Well, it has been seven years."

"Indeed, it has." He took her hand. "I'm so sorry, Angel. I left to protect you, protect those I loved, and it kinda backfired."

"Yes, it did, Michael Cloud." A voice called from the doorway, and they all turned. A furious-looking Fletch stood there with three other High Council members they'd not met before.

The feeling of joy evaporated from the room as they stepped in.

"Now that your health has been restored, Michael, you are being summoned to speak to the board about your actions. Drugging your soul-sibling and putting your precious life in grave danger."

"Now?" Angel shook her head. "I've only just gotten my brother back after seven years, surely an inquiry can wait?"

Four sets of unimpressed eyes pinned her in place. She swallowed, almost wishing she hadn't said a thing.

"Young Angel Cloud, Bowie Storm is to accompany you to the homestead. You shall stay there, and we will send Michael home once we have finished asking him the questions we need to in order to eliminate our enemy. If that pleases you?"

Angel looked at Michael, who had placed a hand on her shoulder. "It's okay. Go home, rest. I'll see you soon enough."

She nodded as he put his arms around her. Holding her close, he whispered, "I've missed you."

She pushed her face into his chest, loving that his arms were around her at last. Arms that felt so strong, so capable. Her brother was finally home. She couldn't answer, not trusting her voice not to break, so she nodded instead, that she'd missed him, too.

"Okay, let's go." Bowie reached out and took Angel's upper arm, pulling her to his side.

She allowed it, feeling fatigued. The four men in the doorway moved aside so they could pass.

Fletch looked down at her as they walked by. "I, and all the royal-souls, thank you both for your efforts."

"Sure, it was our pleasure," Bowie said dryly before looking over his shoulder and winking at Michael. He led Angel down Red's corridor and out the front door, and as they approached the car, he felt her lean heavily against him. Looking down, he saw how pale she was. Her eyes rolled into the back of her skull and he caught her as she passed out.

Fatigued to the max. He placed her in the back seat; she needed several hours of solid, healing sleep.

Once he got her home and up into her bed, he whispered to the wind, guiding a gentle, loving breeze to kiss her from head to toe, wishing it were his lips caressing her flesh instead.

"Oh my god, do I need to hose you down?" Sam called from the doorway, hearing Bowie loud and clear.

He waved his fingers in the window's direction, and the breeze left. "Funny." He looked at his blood-sibling.

She grinned. "Yeah, it kinda is, actually." She walked over to Angel and pulled the covers up to her chin. Running a hand over her hair, she turned to Bowie. "Sorry, Max and I burnt your sauce, we had…an emergency."

Bowie didn't want to think about what sort of 'emergency', but he let her get away with the white lie.

"Jane called. She's coming over with pizza." Sam hoped that would satisfy him.

Bowie's stomach automatically rumbled. "Good."

"So, Michael's all healed now? I'm glad."

Bowie nodded as he looked down at Angel. "Yeah, thank the stars."

"I'd say, 'thanks to you and Angel.'"

Bowie nodded. "Like I said, thank the stars."

They grinned at each other as Max called from downstairs, "Sam, does Bowie want a beer?"

"No, Bowie doesn't, thanks!" Bowie called out, looking at Sam. "So, cute little Max isn't so cute and little anymore?"

"Oh my god, I know! He's delicious, isn't he?" Sam squealed.

"Oh, yeah." Bowie fanned a hand in front of his face. "He is sooo juicy." He stopped the fun and games suddenly and looked down at her. "What's going to happen, Sam, when you come of age and your soul-essence calls to another?"

Sam's face fell. "I don't want to think about that right now, Bowie. I love Max."

"I can see that. But you know that when your soul-partner's essence calls to you, any feelings you have for Max will be wiped clean automatically. Where is that going to leave the poor guy?"

"Oh my god, Bowie…stop! I've just gotten you back. I think that's big enough to deal with at the present moment, don't you?"

Bowie sighed, hating to see the frown replace the sunny smile on his little sister's face. "Yeah, you're right. 'Seize the day', and all that jazz. Maybe I will have that beer with Max after all."

"Pizza's here," Jane called up from the foyer as Max let her in.

"Okay, my brother. Let's have a fun night and catch up, all right?"

He sent one last, lingering look back at Angel, who was sleeping soundly, before he walked towards Sam and slung his arm around her shoulder. "That we can do." They walked out the door and downstairs, each looking forward to catching up on what the other had been up to during the past seven years.

Chapter Seventeen

Max tossed and turned, disturbed by the visions assaulting him. This dream was more powerful than any other he'd experienced. His body pulsated in delighted anticipation of not only absorbing a heavenly soul's pain and fear, but consuming her blood-essence. He envisioned opening himself up, allowing his veins to slither from his flesh to deeply penetrate hers, to absorb and taste every delicious, sweet drop until she was nothing but a dried husk…Nothing but dust…

He bolted up in bed, his breath escaping in an angry *whoosh* as he ran a shaking hand through his dark hair.

What the hell was that?

"Bad dream?" Sam asked sleepily, placing a hand on his back, which was slick with sweat.

He sat rigid, terrified to turn to her, to touch her, as the vile hunger to taste, to harm, still pulsated within him. He did not want to hurt her.

"Babe, what's wrong?" Normally he would have turned to her by now, kissed her back to sleep, amongst other sweet things, but he sat unmoving, his breathing heavy.

"Maxwell?" She waited, as cold fingers of concern crept along her spine.

"I'm all right." He forced himself to sound calm, taking a deep breath to steady his next words. "Bad dream. I'm going to go run it off." He turned to her and brushed a quick, chaste kiss across her lips. "Go back to sleep, baby, I'm fine."

"Are you?" she raised an eyebrow.

He forced a smile as he sprang to his feet, pulling on his trackpants and shoving his feet into his sneakers. "Yeah." He reached for his t-shirt, pulling it over his head as he crossed towards the door. "I'll see you soon."

Sam frowned as he left, closing the door behind him. She'd sensed his dreams becoming darker the older he grew and knew that he struggled with the instincts in his DNA. But he fought against them and won; the heavenly soul within him won the battle every time the darkness loomed. She was proud of him and his accomplishments. The pull he felt whenever Brendan called to him was difficult to ignore, she knew.

Sighing, she rolled over and shoved her face into her pillow, hoping Max would run his demons off as she focused on getting back to sleep.

Angel

As Angel slept, a foreboding shadow crept closer in her dreams. Icy fingers stroked across her bare flesh as a draught of air sent a foul stench in her direction. She held her breath, preventing more of the revolting odour from permeating her senses, her soul.

Something was wrong.

She tossed in her blankets, praying she'd wake and escape the dream before it turned into a nightmare as she turned to run from the oppressive feeling that was drawing closer. The warm, soft blankets transformed into a hard brick pavement, made ice-cold by night's kiss. Something was pinning her down, she couldn't move. It was then that she realised she wasn't asleep…she wasn't dreaming…she was outside, and it was cold and dark…

This was real.

She stopped struggling and froze in shock as a shadow loomed closer, reaching towards her and casting a black ring of pain around her, preventing her escape. She cried in fright when the darkness encased her in its tomb-like prison. She couldn't remain still for long; the pain inside her was building to an intolerable level. She screamed out in frustration as her eyes met the unblinking stare of her friend, Maxwell Black.

Sam! She pushed hard towards her soul-sibling. *Sam, there's something wrong with Max. Please help me…please hear me!* She forced her thought through the shield, before she cried out to Max, "Stop, Max! *Please* stop!"

He stared at her through black, pupilless eyes before opening his arms wide, his veins protruding from his flesh, sliding towards her, thirsty for her essence.

She willed her body to escape the dark ring as the veins slid through it, willed her mind to calm, but terror won out as the veins stroked her flesh, searching for an entrance. Her eyes watered as each miniscule mouth with razor-sharp teeth bit into her flesh, inflicting unimaginable pain, before pushing their tiny jaws inside her body. The darkness inside her grew to an excruciating level as it rose to meet Max's intruding veins. A scream of fury escaped her lips.

Was this the same unbearable pain that Michael had suffered for all those years? The violation? She'd sensed a disturbing flow of dark energy enter her the moment the healing spell was complete, relieving Michael from the torture within. She didn't understand what it was at the time. Now it was clear; it was the residual poison from the Veins that swirled within her now.

She focused on her heart as she whispered to the Angels above, hoping Max's black ring would not prevent her call for help. Tears rolled down her face as she tried once more to reach Max's heavenly soul.

"Max! *Please,* Max…stop! You have the ability to *stop!*" she screamed in terror, as the evil residue inside her connected to Max's veins, inducing utter agony within her. Max's ruby, the one he always wore around his neck, pulsated before sending an electric red haze over them both, almost blinding Angel.

What happened next made her weep with relief.

Sam came running out of nowhere, like a bat out of hell, and thrust her open palm in Max's direction, sending a lightning bolt straight into his chest.

He flew back ten feet, landing with a thump on the moonlit lawn, his veins extracting from Angel's body and returning to his flesh.

The black veil around Angel vanished. She lay stunned and weakened before rolling onto her side as Sam walked by her. "Are you okay?" She looked both concerned for her soul-sibling and furious simultaneously.

Angel nodded, taking a shaky breath as she watched Sam continue towards Max's body, which was still lying on the ground.

He moaned as he rolled over.

Thank the stars, he's not dead. Sam's thoughts brushed against Angel's mind.

Angel knew her soul-sibling would not have coped if she had killed the man she was in love with, despite his uncharacteristic actions.

"What's happened?" Max, clearly stunned, rubbed at the burnt hole in his t-shirt, his chest feeling as though it was on fire. He looked up at Sam, then across at Angel as she shakily pushed herself to her feet, looking pale and drained of energy.

"What the hell do you *think* has happened, Maxwell?" Sam shouted, hands on hips, as she glared down at him.

"Shh, Sam." Angel quickly crossed over to her soul-sibling, placing a comforting hand on her arm as she looked towards the dormitories. "We don't want to wake anyone."

Max sat up on the damp grass, looking up at the girls. "I was jogging, that's it. I don't remember anything after the fifth lap of the dorms."

"So, you don't remember violating my soul-sibling? A heavenly soul that the other half of *your* soul just happens to find irresistible?"

"What?" Max paled, looking devastated. "Angel, please tell me I didn't?" He jumped to his feet and took a step towards Angel, regret filling his handsome features, his green eyes full of sorrow as he shook his head.

Sam stood in front of Angel. "Oh, no you don't, buddy. Not one step closer, or I will gladly zap you again."

Max shook his head. "Sam, please! I don't understand what's happening here, but if you actually believe that I could hurt Angel…" He looked grief-stricken as he looked at Sam, then Angel.

Angel felt his despair and her soul-sibling's fury. She brushed both of them with the grace of calm, hoping to put Sam's fire out.

Sam turned to look at her over her shoulder. "I don't want my 'mad' to be calmed just yet, if you feel me?"

"Oh, I feel you. But look where we are, Sam. If someone decides to go for a night stroll, we'll have some explaining to do."

"I think somebody already *does* have some explaining to do. Right now." Sam turned her blazing eyes back to Max, who actually cringed.

"Samantha." He spoke calmly. "I'm telling you, I don't remember hurting Angel. I would never do that!"

Angel walked around Sam, grabbed the leather strap around Max's neck, and tried to pull it off. The leather would not break.

Max frowned down at her as he said, "What do you want with my mother's ruby, Angel?"

She shook her head, stepping back. "That was glowing, as if it was on fire, when you were…well, to put it bluntly—sucking my essence from me."

Max cringed again. "Jesus, Angel! I'm sorry, I truly am...I don't recall a thing. Are you okay?"

"I'll be fine. I think whatever I've absorbed from Michael, and whatever is in your ruby, cast a spell over you, Max." Angel looked at Sam. "Can you get this off of him?"

"Not here. Let's go to my room."

The three hurried back towards the homestead and slipped into the darkened foyer, about to creep upstairs, when a light fell over them from above. They looked up toward the dark landing and saw Bowie leaning over the railing, watching them.

"And what would you three be doing out and about after three o'clock in the morning, pray tell?"

As furious as Sam was with Max right in this moment, he was also the love of her life, and, aside from Angel, had been her best friend for the past seven years. She felt an overwhelming need to protect him from her brother, let alone from the Council, despite what he'd done; after all, he had done it 'unknowingly', or so it seemed. "Sometimes, Bowie, when people can't sleep, they go for a run. That's what we were doing."

Bowie took in Max's running gear, then Sam's oversized t-shirt, before his gaze drifted to Angel in her green, short-sleeved shirt and matching pyjama shorts, her feet bare. He raised an eyebrow. "Is that so?"

Angel felt Sam's plea to keep Max's secret safe, so said, "Actually, I just ducked out to find Moonie, I sleep better with him."

"Couldn't find him, then?" Bowie didn't see the cat anywhere.

Angel shook her head, feeling somewhat more naked the longer Bowie looked her up and down with his smouldering, sleepy amber eyes.

Sam could feel Angel's energy and interrupted Bowie's interrogation. "Well, this has been super swell, but we've got an early class, so..." She headed up the stairs towards Bowie, with Max two steps behind.

Angel walked behind them as Sam called out, "See you in the morning," before she quickly closed her and Max away in their room.

Bowie watched Angel's pale face as she went to walk by him and felt her low energy. He grabbed her by the upper arm, halting her in her tracks. "What's happened?"

She opened her mouth to tell him, 'Nothing' when he bent closer.

"Don't lie to me." His voice was cool, his breath sweet.

She looked into his eyes as he stared down at her, as though he could read her mind. Her heart thumped. She made sure her shield was protecting her thoughts, but not before she felt Sam brush against her mind.

Distract him, Angel…do whatever it takes.

"Well?" Bowie said, his thumb caressing the inside of her arm automatically, almost mesmerised by the softness of her flesh. Electricity once again hummed between their bodies.

Angel watched his mouth shape the words, his lips, so close, his scent overpowering her senses, and she did the only thing she could think of in that moment. The only thing she wanted to do. She stood on her tiptoes, and slid her lips across his, shocking them both.

He paused, wanting to step back, but her lips, so soft and alluring, made him want another quick taste. He leant into the kiss, his hand, which had been holding her arm, now sliding around her waist, bringing her soft body flush up against his as he deepened the kiss to electrifying depths. It was like sipping nectar straight from a flower's cup.

She gasped, her body filling with a pleasant tingle when he pulled her against him. When their tongues danced together, a radiant rainbow lit the darkened landing area.

Angel leapt back, momentarily startled by the colourful light that soon dissipated as they broke contact.

She met Bowie's eyes, which were frowning ever so slightly.

"Interesting," he whispered.

"Goodnight," Angel said, then sprang around him, making it to her room in record time before she slammed the door behind her, hearing Bowie's low chuckle.

"Ah, fun times," he said to himself as he turned the downstairs light off, before heading to his room. He knew he needed a decent sleep before his role as student counsellor began the following morning, but, after that moment with Angel, he didn't think it was possible. After three hours of tossing and turning, he proved himself right before falling into a deep sleep an hour before his alarm went off.

The following morning, Angel tried to make it downstairs early enough to avoid Bowie in the breakfast room, only to walk in and see him engaged in a lively conversation with Mrs. McGoldrick.

"Good morning, dear." The always-kind lady beamed at her.

Bowie turned to Angel and smiled at her over his coffee cup. "Morning, Angel."

She smiled at Mrs. McGoldrick, avoiding Bowie's gaze as she replied, "Good morning," and headed over to help herself to some scrambled eggs.

"Sleep well, did we?" Bowie's voice held a sweet note to it as she looked over at him, sitting at the table, filtered with sunlight.

"Better than you, by the looks of it." She couldn't help the grin that broke across her face, which, unbeknownst to her, made her look irresistible, with the sunlight falling across her golden mane like a halo.

"Mm," was all he said, looking at her lips as Max, Sam, Tom and Jess walked in the room.

"Everyone's up bright and early today. Good," Tom said, pouring a coffee. "Mrs. McGoldrick, can you please run into Terang and pick up the bakery order for the canteen today?"

"Of course, dear. I was hoping to have a spot of tea with Edna Royal in town this morning," she said, smiling. "I'll do that now then, shall I?"

She was used to Tom or Jess sending her off on errands so they could discuss private matters. She'd never questioned why, as she was always happy to accommodate her employers, wonderful as they were.

"Thanks, Jean," Jess smiled fondly as she removed her apron and headed out the room.

"Have a great day, dears. I'll see you all later."

"Bye," they chorused.

As everyone filled plates or bowls and gathered around the table, they waited for the noise of Mrs. McGoldrick's car engine to fade as it headed down the driveway and into Terang.

"Right. Aside from classes today, we need to focus on pouring some goodness back into the soils around Victoria. We still cannot stop the dry, it appears to be spreading. We have Bendigo, Hamilton, and Gippsland heading up a team of Elementals who'll pour energy in, as a combined group effort, at two p.m. Bowie, Sam, I'll need both of you to meet me here on time, please." Tom buttered some toast before smearing it with fig jam.

"I don't understand why we can't stop these bloody Veins from permeating and poisoning the soils?" Sam sounded frustrated as she plonked down in a seat, filling up a bowl with cornflakes.

"We may have Michael back, but the other heavenly souls who were taken are obviously being drained and used for their essence-energy," Jess said around a mouthful of eggs.

"And," Red breezed into the room like she was already aware of the conversation, "a powerful soul was tapped into last night. We don't know who, or how, but their essence has added to the Veins' strength." She poured herself a milky tea. "The Council have been notified of several earthquakes that have hit around the globe in areas that have never been impacted before, setting off electrical fires and tsunamis. This is looking to be a global catastrophe."

Angel and Sam slammed shields on their thoughts as they exchanged a worried look with Max before averting their eyes from each other, busying their hands with finishing their breakfasts.

"That doesn't sound good at all, Red." Bowie poured an orange juice as he checked the time.

"No, it is definitely not good, which is why the Council have pushed forward your coming-of-age ceremony, Angel. Once your partner's soul-essence boosts your gifts, we will have a chance to finally put an end to our world dying, and stop the pure-souls turning on one another."

All eyes went to Angel as she froze, looking at Red. "When?"

"A week from today, when the moon is full. Yours too, Samantha."

"What? No!" Sam cried, not wanting to lose Max. The thought of her essence calling to another, and losing the love she felt for Max, was overwhelming. Her eyes met Bowie's, filled with tears. "Do I have to? Do I absolutely have to do this?"

"I'm afraid so." Bowie shrugged, not happy to see his sister upset. Also, strangely, not happy with the thought of having to see Angel hook-up with some unknown random that would come into all of their lives.

Angel was thinking the same thing. She didn't want to lose her connection with Sam, to have her replaced by some other elemental-soul she didn't know. To have him come into her life, disrupt her routine, her way of doing things…What if he was a bossy old geezer?

Oh my stars, Sam.

"I know, Angel," Sam said aloud.

They exchanged a pitiful look, knowing they'd no choice in the matter. This is the way things were done; the way they'd always been done.

"How do we track this source, the one that was used last night, Red?" Jess asked.

Red shook her head. "It was activated before three this morning. The Council were trying to track it, but lost the connection." she sighed. "Strange, it just totally disappeared off the radar. Fletch is going to do a locator spell tomorrow night, when the stars align. That way, we can locate this evil, then destroy it and whomever wields it."

Sam tried to act normal as she finished her juice. She knew Red was talking about Max's ruby, which she'd removed from his neck as soon as she and Max had closed themselves off in their bedroom. And if the power of the stars aligning could assist Fletch from not only locating the ruby, but Max, too…Sam cringed. She knew there was nothing she could do to save him once the Council discovered his vile abuse against Angel.

She abruptly pushed herself away from the table, almost in a panic, as she forced out a loud, "Gotta go, don't want to be late for class! Come on, Max, Eddy will be waiting," then shot out of the room.

"Good point." Bowie checked his watch again as he pushed up from the table. "Don't want to be late for my first session. Red, if there is anything I can do to help the Council locate this thing, let me know."

"Thanks, dear." She smiled at him.

"See you at two, Tom." He looked at Angel. "Have a good day, kiddo, stay out of trouble." He grinned, watching as a pretty flush swept across her cheeks, before heading out.

Angel pushed her hair behind her shoulders as she gathered up the dirty dishes to do a wash for Mrs. McGoldrick, missing the look Tom and Jess exchanged.

She worried about the earthquakes as she headed into the kitchen. About the soil and Mother Earth's future, even though she knew the Elementals would do everything they could to heal her. What was niggling her especially was the possibility of Max being prosecuted for something he couldn't recall doing, however horrific it had been. Sam would suffer terribly if anything were to happen to Max, and she would not see her soul-sibling destroyed by his death. Even if Sam's essence called to another, at least Max would still be alive, and would remain in their lives. Hell, she loved Max, too, he was like a brother, despite him invading her body last night.

She washed the dishes and threw a tea towel over them before heading up to grab her books. Her mind whirled with a million questions, and, seeking the answers to them all, she headed off for what she hoped would be a productive day of classes.

Michael spent a long night, and much of the following morning, with the Council. He answered every question, shared every minute piece of information that could possibly benefit the Soul Keepers in helping to eliminate the threat to all the pure-souls and Mother Earth.

He'd headed to the homestead after nine a.m. and had walked into an empty house, as everyone had already gone about their day. He stood in the foyer for the first time in seven years and took a deep, appreciative breath. Because of Bowie, he was home. He was alive and well because of Bowie and Angel.

He walked through the homestead, taking in every inch, absorbing its presence. Michael was excited to start his new position the following day as counsellor to the students at the college, and with the Headscope teams in Camperdown and Warrnambool. He needed this day to catch up on sleep and get his bearings, wondering when he'd see Elizabeth again, and if her heart was still available.

Chapter Eighteen

"Angel, what are we going to do?" Sam whispered.

"We'll figure something out," Angel replied quietly, as the family cleaned the dinner dishes up. Tom and Jess had just left, heading back to their overseers' cottage.

They'd each had a full day of classes, teaching, counselling, and healing. Tom, Bowie and Sam had joined their energy, through the world globe, with the other Victorian elemental-souls and had increased the moisture levels throughout the region's depleted soils. For the moment, thankfully, the land was retaining the moisture.

Angel had brushed three individuals' minds during the day who were crippled with suicidal thoughts. None of them had ever portrayed such depressive thoughts over the past seven months she'd known them; she sensed that a Vein had manipulated their thoughts. Chaos seemed to be growing all around them.

"I'll wash up," Michael said as Max was about to fill the sink.

"Hold the phone. Do you feel okay?" Sam chuckled. "Someone offering to wash up? I am so glad you are back home."

Michael grinned at her. "So am I."

Bowie perched on the butcher's block and opened his pocketknife. He retrieved a crisp, green apple, slid the razor-sharp blade through its flesh, and cut off a slice as he watched the action around the kitchen.

Max filled the kettle and put it on top of the old stove to boil while Angel opened the fridge to grab the lemon cheesecake for dessert.

"Does anyone want something sweet?" Angel asked the room as she swept the knife through the cheesy filling.

Bowie leant close, his amber eyes glowing as he answered in a low tone. "Yes, please."

She lifted her eyes and forced herself not to get giddy as his handsome face stared intently at hers, a mere inch away. They both thought of the kiss the night before, the one that had kept them individually awake for hours…

She moved back a fraction and pushed a slice towards him. "There you go."

Sam snickered as she reached to pull out the teacups, wanting to say something snide to her blood-sibling, but not wanting to embarrass Angel.

Thank you, Angel brushed against Sam's mind, knowing Sam would have loved to knock the grin off Bowie's handsome face.

"How was your first day at work?" Max asked Bowie as the kettle rang out.

"Great, actually." He used a slice of apple to scoop up the cheesecake. "And I had lunch with a lovely old friend." He looked pointedly at Michael.

It took Michael a moment to realise Bowie was addressing him; the room had fallen silent, apart from him sloshing around in the sink. He turned his head to see Bowie looking at him.

"Go on, then, out with it," Michael said.

"Your pretty ex-, Elizabeth."

Michael stopped what he was doing and turned, reaching for a tea-towel. "You've seen her, talked with her?"

"Well, we didn't eat our sandwiches like a pair of mutes. Yes, we talked, and she is expecting a visit from you tonight."

"Bowie, you've been home for hours, we've sat through a meal, and you're only just telling me this *now*?"

"All in good time, my friend." Bowie slid off the butcher's block and patted Michael on the back as he placed the dirty plate in the sink. "She lives opposite the cemetery now, up on the hill."

"In the yellow cottage?"

"Yep. Car keys are on the hall stand." Bowie grinned.

Michael looked around the room. "Is everyone okay with me going for the night? I think Beth and I have a lot of catching up to do."

Angel turned to her blood-sibling. "Michael, you've been through seven years of hell, you don't need our permission to leave for the night."

Michael crossed over to her and wrapped his arms around her. "I haven't asked you how you've been feeling since you…you know, fixed me up?"

"Let's see if honesty spills from those precious lips now." Bowie spoke in a low volume as he leant back against the sink, folding his arms, eyes watchful as he stared at Angel, who flushed before meeting Michael's eyes.

Sam froze for a second, wondering what Bowie was implying. *Hadn't they shielded their thoughts enough last night or this morning?*

Max put the filled teacups on the butcher's block for anyone to take and Sam quickly grabbed one, thrusting it towards her brother, hoping to distract him from his train of thought.

"Tea?"

He gazed down at her, seeing a flicker of panic filter across her petite face. *What is she up to?* "Yeah, thanks." He took the tea from her, taking a mouthful.

"What do you mean, Bowie?" Michael turned towards his soul-sibling.

Sam and Angel exchanged a panicked look as Max put his arm around Sam, hoping to calm her jittery nerves so as to not give them away. He was nervous as hell himself at the prospect of either of the brothers learning what had taken place last night.

Bowie didn't want to prevent Michael from spending time with Elizabeth. The Angels knew he'd earned some time to himself after all he'd endured. So, he altered his truth. "Angel wasn't feeling well last night, and I believe she is still exhausted from our healing efforts. That's all I meant." Bowie shrugged casually, avoiding Michael's eyes as he drained his tea. He placed the cup in the sink, taking over the washing duty from Michael. He'd bide his time.

"Oh." Michael looked at Angel. "How are you feeling now, though, for real?"

Angel forced a smile, feeling Sam's energy and worry for Max. "I am totally fine, promise." Her baby-blues shone up into his.

"I'm glad." He rubbed her shoulder. "If you need a boost, go sit in the healing garden, okay?"

"Of course."

"Just make sure you are not outside after midnight; Tom said the boundary protection spell has been blurred with the dark energy, so no breaking curfew. You need to be inside the homestead for full protection, got it?"

Angel nodded.

"Especially this close to your soul-essence ceremony," he said.

"Ugh, please do not remind us." Sam shoved the jug of milk back in the fridge and slammed the door.

Michael reached across and ran a hand down her shoulder-length blonde curls. "Sorry, love."

Sam caught his hand and squeezed it. "Not your fault, I'm just not ready to commit to someone I don't love." She looked sadly at Max.

"You do know, don't you, that whoever your essence chooses, you have already been in love with this soul since before you were born?" Michael tried to comfort her with a history lesson. "Once the words have been shared, your essence, and his or hers, will automatically bond you, and your love will be one of the most powerful gifts that will help heal our world."

"Yeah, I know all that, Michael, and thanks for the pep talk. But that doesn't change how I feel about Max right now, in this moment, and in every moment we've shared for the past seven years. I don't want to lose that."

All eyes, filled with sympathy, gravitated towards Max, who remained silent as he sipped from his teacup.

Michael nodded. "I get it, and I completely empathise with you both. The years I've been away have prevented my…" he looked across at Bowie, "*our* soul-essence ceremonies, and, to be honest, I don't want anything to take away what I feel for Elizabeth. Even after all these years away, I love her still."

"Which is why you shouldn't waste another second here with us. Off you go," Bowie said as he stirred the bubbles in the sink, wanting Michael gone so he could pounce on the three deceivers.

Michael dropped a kiss on the top of Sam's, then Angel's, head before smiling at Max and saying, "Thanks, Bowie. I'll see you all in the morning for breakfast."

"Nice and early, counsellor," Bowie said as Michael headed toward the door.

"Will do." Michael saluted the air before snapping up the car keys and heading out the front door.

Max, Angel, and Sam exchanged a long look, happy that one of their elders was gone, and turned to leave the room so they could have a quick meeting about Max's ruby upstairs.

"I'll see you all in the lounge in three minutes, sharp," Bowie said, his back still turned to them, hands in the warm bubbles.

"Oh, I need an early night. I've got, um, a test-thingy first thing," Sam blurted.

"I've got to assist at an early surgery in Cobden." Angel cringed at the lie.

Max, insightfully, remained silent.

"Two minutes, with nothing on your tongues but the truth," he said in a tone that made the air feel icy.

The three exchanged another look. "Fine," Sam spat, before marching towards the door, Max on her heels.

Angel stood, wanting to gauge where Bowie's thoughts were at, and what was possibly about to go down. She bit her lip, and tentatively reached out towards his mind, hoping to grab some intel to forewarn her friends with.

"Are you really going to try that?" Bowie turned, pinning her in place with smouldering eyes, an eyebrow raised in question.

She swallowed. "Well… actually, I wasn't, really…"

"Cut it out, Angel, lying really doesn't suit you."

She bit her lip, thinking of a response, but he was in front of her before she could blink. She stopped her surprised squeal from escaping her lips as his body moved closer. Angel tilted her head back to look up at him, her breath catching in her throat. Damn him for being so gorgeous! She didn't know if the electric charge in the surrounding air was happening in her imagination alone.

It wasn't. Bowie frowned, he'd felt it, too.

They stood, lost in each other's eyes, each of their thoughts a labyrinth of questions, to which neither could find the answers. Yet, even whilst deep in their own thoughts, their bodies automatically moved closer to the other's, the air pulsating thickly around them, making it difficult to breathe. As they each drew in a deep breath, it filled them with the other's scent. It overpowered them in the most delightful of ways, making their heads spin, making them want to drink that scent in…consume it all…

Bowie bent closer, his eyes ablaze with desire, and his lips were about to brush hers when Sam yelled, "Time's up!"

They jerked apart as Bowie whispered, "Well, I'll be damned."

"You probably will be, if we don't get an early night." Angel stepped away from him, turning to the door.

He grabbed her and, despite the speed, brought her back towards him gently, sliding his large hands around her waist, moving her against him. As his head bent towards hers, he brushed against her mind. *Ceremony be damned, too. I want one more taste before you're another's...*

She had to agree. Right or wrong, the feel of his body against hers was overwhelmingly delicious. Sparks of fire ignited along her flesh at the thought of his lips capturing hers; it had her insides melting, and her pulse points racing.

He closed the distance. His lips glided over hers, softly at first, then drinking her in like he was dehydrated, before angling his head. He parted her sweet lips, swallowing her moan of pleasure, deepening the kiss that sparked an inferno of lust within them.

Angel's hands cupped his jaw. She wished she could climb into his mouth and absorb his essence. *Where did that thought come from? Forget it, concentrate.* She slid her tongue over his, feeling overwhelmed with the intense sensations. She could not stop the soft cry of pleasure that escaped her lips.

The erotic sound made him see stars, and he pulled her harder against him, his groin throbbing for release as he sucked on her tongue.

"Ahem," Max muttered awkwardly from behind them.

They didn't immediately bolt apart, but lingered on one, final kiss before Angel stepped back, Bowie's hands still on her hips. They stared at each other, breathing heavily, heartbeats steadying, before Bowie shook his head, releasing her.

"Right, um..." He ran his hand through his hair, clearly distracted. "Off you both go, I'll be there in a second." He spun away, wanting to hide the bulge in his jeans.

As Angel and Max headed towards the lounge, Max whispered, "Was that your plan to distract him again?"

"No," she whispered back. "I don't know what the hell that was." She shook her head as she walked into the room and joined Sam on the couch. They faced the blazing flames, which sent odd shapes around the room as they danced in the grate. The nights were especially chilly this time of year.

"Good job," Sam patted her leg. "We've got this. Don't anyone panic, keep it together, okay?"

Max and Angel nodded, both nervous about what Bowie might have to say.

He strolled into the room, not looking at Angel, worried it might make his maleness react. "Okay, here's the situation..." He walked towards the desk and turned to lean against it, folding his arms. "Something happened between the three of you last night, and it has affected Angel's energy levels."

"No, that was due to helping Michael..."

He held up his hand, stopping Angel as he pinned her with his gaze. "I said no lies."

The room fell silent. Angel shifted uncomfortably.

"Bowie," Sam tried. "I don't know if you've noticed, but we are not twelve anymore."

He almost laughed as he took his eyes off Angel's lovely face before looking at his sister. "Oh, I've noticed. Thanks for that."

"And, we have been looking after ourselves well enough, without your guidance or odd questions, for the past seven years, and..."

"That may be so, Samantha," Bowie cut in firmly, his voice dropping. "But you are also aware of our rules. Your elders, namely, me, are in charge of you in every way, until you come of age and meet your soul-partner."

Sam squirmed a fraction, feeling the energy in the air spark with his temper. He was close to losing his patience.

"I have returned, am of age, and am now within my full authority to ask you any question and demand an honest answer." His tone filled with frustration at having to defend himself.

Sam raised an eyebrow, thinking of a clever comeback, but was too nervous to say it.

It's okay, Sam, let him get it out of his system. Angel brushed against Sam's thoughts, hoping to calm her soul-sibling.

Bowie looked at her, unblinking. "Oh, I plan to get it out of my system, thanks, Angel."

They stared at each other for a moment, and she cringed, thinking she'd shielded herself well enough from him.

Obviously not.

She tried not to think about anything at all and, instead, pictured a bowl full of cherries; red, shiny, glistening, juicy cherries. As sweet and delicious as Bowie's lips...

He grinned instantly. He couldn't help himself as he watched her flush.

By the Angels! Angel looked at Sam, frustrated.

"Well, this is fun and all, but..." Sam trailed off.

Bowie shook his head, trying to focus on the matter at hand. "Enough. Let's just cut to the chase. I want some straight answers so we can sort this out."

"Sort what out, Bowie?" Max asked as politely as he could.

Bowie turned his intense, amber eyes onto the young, half-Vein, half heavenly soul.

Max wished he hadn't asked.

"You three, the energy last night, Angel's energy on the staircase...I've seen that kind of depletion before. I spent half the night trying to figure it out. I didn't want to discuss it this morning, but after Red mentioned the details about how a powerful soul had been tapped into, it all fell into place. So, I will ask you one, final time. What happened last night?"

The three remained silent. Angel and Sam exchanged a look before glancing at Max, who stood and began pacing.

Bowie waited impatiently, thinking, *at least we're getting somewhere now.*

It was a few minutes before Max turned to face Bowie.

"For months now, I've been having shocking nightmares that fill me with an insatiable hunger. For what, though, I've had no idea." He swallowed, looking down at Sam.

They both recalled the nights when he'd woken after his terrible dreams, only to find themselves tangled in each other's arms, lost for hours in lustful pleasure afterwards.

"Anyway," Max cleared his throat, "last night, something was different...I had a dream that I was absorbing Angel's essence, and I was terrified when I woke because it was the strongest pull I'd ever felt to wanting to actually hurt anyone." He looked down at Angel. "I'm so sorry."

"It's okay Max, you weren't in control."

"Continue, Max." Bowie didn't want to cut Angel off, but he was getting a bad feeling about what was coming next, and he wanted to hear it now.

"Well, I thought I'd go for a run, that part wasn't a lie. I'd done a few laps, then, before I knew it, Sam was hitting me with a bolt of lightning, and I was flat on my back."

"*What?*" Bowie looked at his blood-sibling.

"Just you wait until you hear the rest," Sam defended herself.

"Come on, then." Bowie was losing his patience.

"Angel, I guess you should take over story-time." Sam got up from the couch and went to make them all another tea.

Bowie turned to Angel, waiting.

She looked up at him from her seat on the couch. "To be honest, I don't know how I got outside. I was asleep, and then I was out between the dormitories, pinned to the ground. I couldn't get up. Then Max cast a black ring around me, and I could feel something within me, reaching towards him…something cold and evil. It made me ill." She ran her hands up and down her arms, as if to ward off the horrid, intrusive memory.

The fire flared, sending heat around the room as Bowie whispered to the flame, moving his fingers in the fireplace's direction.

Neat, Max thought.

Bowie met Max's eyes for a moment, before turning back to Angel. "Go on, kid—Angel." Somehow, after the lip-locks they'd shared, calling her *kiddo* just didn't seem right anymore.

She looked up at him. "Max wasn't *Max*, his eyes were black pits. I couldn't reach him in any way, and then…well, he sent his veins into my flesh and started absorbing my essence. But something wasn't right within me, either. I felt it the moment we healed Michael." She shook her head, trying to make sense of it all. "It was like, something left him and entered me, and Max absorbed it, I think?" She sounded frustrated and confused.

Bowie was exasperated. "Why the *hell* didn't you tell me what you'd felt after we healed Michael, Angel?"

"I don't know!" She stood and echoed Max's earlier movements as she paced. "It was a shock, seeing you and Michael after all these years, and I thought it might have just been *that*, or fatigue, or something!"

She turned to face him, holding her hands up questioningly before dropping them again as Max rubbed her back.

Sam walked in with a tray filled with cups of tea and slices of the cheesecake. She passed a cup to Max, then sat on the couch and spooned up a delicious mouthful of the creamy filling.

"There's something else," Max said before he took a sip of tea.

All eyes went to him.

"Every time I've woken from a disturbing dream, my ruby has been glowing.

"It was so bright last night," Angel added, "that it was almost blinding."

"Your mother's necklace?" Bowie asked. "You're not wearing it, where is it?"

"In my room." Sam scooped up her last piece of cheesecake. "I've shielded it."

"Go get it."

"No. I can keep it safe, Bowie,"

"Sam!" He turned to face her fully. "Go and get it now."

"*No,* I need to protect Max from the Council! If they know what he did to Angel, he'll be punished, or killed! Please, Bowie…" Sam stood and crossed over to her blood-sibling.

Bowie hated seeing fear fill his sister's eyes; hated seeing her beg anyone, let alone himself.

She grabbed his hands, eyes glistening with tears. "Bowie, I can't let them hurt him," she whispered. "I can't."

Angel looked across at Max, who appeared to be in as much turmoil as Sam was herself. Not because he was worried about his own life, but because he loved her so much that he couldn't bear to see her in pain. *That's pure love.*

"Look, Sam, *I* can shield it. If it is found anywhere near Max, and they put one and two together, there'll be nothing I can do to protect him. Go get it, then I'll lock it in my office. I'll cast a protection spell so it will be safe, I promise. Safe until I can figure out what to do about this entire mess, anyway."

"Really, you'll help us?" Sam's tears of relief ran down her rounded cheeks.

He pulled her into his arms and cradled her head against his chest. It felt good to hold her, to comfort her. He'd missed his little sister whilst he'd been off searching for Michael.

"Of course…even though it may go against my better judgement. What are big brothers for?"

"Oh, Bowie! Thank you, *thank you*!" she cried happily. "If anything were to happen to Max, I don't think I could survive that." She reached up and dropped a noisy kiss of appreciation against his cheek before turning to Max and throwing her arms around his neck.

He held her close, his calm green eyes meeting Bowie's amber pools of fire. He knew Bowie had more questions, and he'd answer them all night if he had to.

"Bowie?" Angel asked. "What will the Council do to you, if they know you've concealed this from them?"

Of course she would be considering things more carefully…

All eyes turned to her before returning to him.

"Well, I'll get my arse kicked for sure, big time," Bowie replied coolly.

"No, seriously, what could happen?" Sam didn't want either man to be punished and needed this answer to help calm her nerves.

Bowie reached for a cup and took a long mouthful. How truthful could he be without making this situation more stressful?

"Truth," Angel said, guessing his thoughts.

He raised an eyebrow, meeting her gaze. "To put it simply, it wouldn't end well. Let's face it, Max may well be half-Heavenly, but it was his evil half that committed the crime. Sorry, Max," he added as he saw Max cringe uncomfortably.

"No, please…you're right." Max shrugged, ashamed.

"It was Max's unsavoury genes that consumed part of your essence, Angel. That is punishable by death."

"It's bullshit." Sam shook her head. "It had to have been the ruby that was making Max do it."

Max, shook his head; after last night, he'd nothing to say to defend himself.

"But what happens to you, Bowie, if you are found with the ruby, and it becomes known that you have protected our supposed-enemy? Sorry, Max." Angel hoped a real answer would emerge this time.

"I will be sent to the High Council, where I'll be shocked by my

Elemental brethren until my heart stops, then I'll be revived by my soul-sibling. And then the process will be repeated as many times as necessary until the Council are satisfied with my punishment."

Their gasps filled the room.

"That is barbaric!" Sam cried.

"So is the crime." Bowie shrugged, turning to Sam. "How would you feel if it were any other Vein who had violated Angel?"

Sam was silent as she absorbed his words. She looked across at her soul-sibling. "I'd want them dead," she whispered.

"Exactly. And that is how the Council will feel, hence the punishment for betrayal."

"I can't allow you to put yourself in harm's way for me, Bowie." Max shook his head.

"I'm sorry, but yes, he can." Sam looked between her two men. "Because we are not going to get caught with the ruby in our possession."

What are you thinking, Sam? Angel could feel Sam shielding a growing thought.

Sam shook her head once at Angel. *Just wait.*

"I've just had an idea," Max said as he placed his cup on the tray. "Brendan gave me the ruby, he said it was my mother's. But what if it's always been a Vein's tool? A way to use me?"

"It certainly has the power to manipulate you," Angel added. "You would never have hurt me otherwise."

Max turned to Angel. "What if, now that you are getting close to your ceremony, coming closer to your full powers, Brendan's trying to get to you?"

"That's an interesting question, Max, and one we will investigate. But first, Sam, can you *please* get me the ruby?" Bowie said, tired of asking for it.

Sam nodded and dashed out of the room, racing upstairs to retrieve it.

Bowie sighed internally as he looked across at Angel. She sat, leaning back into the cushions, knees drawn, arms wrapped around them, watching Max thoughtfully.

Watching her sitting there, wearing a concerned expression across her beautiful face as she worried for Max, did things to him. Made him think about all the things he wanted to do to her. And he'd no right thinking about those things this close to her ceremony, only one short week away. How cruel the timing of it all was…Sam ran back into the room, interrupting his thoughts.

"Here it is," she said, holding out the ruby.

He took it, nodding his thanks. "I'll go shield it in the office. Max, when I get back, I've got a few questions to ask you about Brendan and these dreams you've been having."

"Yeah, sure. No problem." Max nodded.

Bowie looked at the girls. "Why don't you two go up to bed?"

Angel nodded, as Sam crossed over to kiss Bowie's cheek. "I really appreciate what you're doing."

He looked down at her. "No worries. But from now on, no more secrets. Got it?"

"Sure." Sam nodded.

"Have *you*?" Bowie looked across at Angel.

"Yes," she replied, offended that he'd asked.

"Good. Goodnight then."

He strode briskly from the room, wearing his jeans better than anyone had a right to.

Angel rolled her eyes at herself as she got off the couch. "'night, Max," she called, heading towards the door.

"'night, Angel."

Sam kissed Max. "I'll see you soon."

"We'll see." He gave her a small smile and she raised an eyebrow at his cryptic reply. "As in, we'll see if it's soon…I think Bowie has a lot of questions."

"No doubt."

"Your brother slightly terrifies me."

Sam chuckled as she ran a hand over his night stubble, that sat so well over his chiselled jawline. "You'll be fine. Look what he's doing for you."

"Doing for *you*, you mean."

"Doing for us." Sam kissed him briefly. "Like I said, I'll see you soon." She flashed him a radiant smile before heading up the stairs and knocking on Angel's door, opening it, and stepping inside.

"I have a plan."

"Me, too. Shut the door."

Chapter Nineteen

Angel cursed herself for not thinking to wear shoes as the gravel bit into the soles of her feet. She ran along the road, hoping to get to Quicks' paddock and the portal before he caught up to her. She patted the pocket of her thin nightrobe, making sure the ruby was still inside.

Angel and Sam had thrown a few ideas around about how to protect both Max and Bowie, before Sam volunteered Angel to break into Bowie's office, then locate and steal the ruby. They waited until Bowie finished interrogating Max, which lasted until well after midnight, then waited another hour after that, just to be sure that he was asleep. Sam promised to keep watch and let Angel know if Bowie woke.

Angel's mission: get the ruby, then get to the portal and make her way to the Blacks' abandoned mansion to conceal it somewhere that would lead the Council to believe it had been Brendan Black who had created the evil energy surge. Therefore keeping Bowie free from any involvement, keeping Max alive, and allowing Sam's heart to continue beating with joy.

A horse whinnied as she ran past the stables, praying the crescent moon would stay behind the clouds for just a few minutes longer. Looking over her shoulder, her heartbeat accelerated...the dark figure was gaining on her.

Sam! She cried to her soul-sibling, waiting.

Shit, Angel, I'm sorry! I fell asleep, Bowie's gone.

Yeah, he is, and he's about to catch up to me. I won't make it to the portal!

Oh, no Angel, you can't let him get you! Hide somewhere...I'll find you!

Angel ran past the conservation building, pumping her legs as fast as they could carry her to the hay shed; she'd lose him in the dark fortress of hay bales. She brushed the direction of the Gatekeeper's cottage against Bowie's mind, hoping that she blended in well enough amongst the shadows as she sprinted for the hay shed.

Angel darted into the immense shed, reaching along the wall of hay in the darkness, searching for an area to climb up. When she found a handhold, she scrambled up the bales, ignoring the rough needles of straw that jabbed against her hands and scratched her bare legs on the climb. She found a space where a rectangle bale had been removed for airing and stuffed herself inside the gap, trying to quieten her unsteady breathing. It stopped in a second, as Bowie's voice filled the hay shed.

"I know you're in here, Angel. Just come out and save us both the trouble, would you?" His voice dripped with impatience. He knew he couldn't risk sparking a light amongst the thousands of dry bales without creating an inferno. "Last chance, Angel."

No reply. He cursed and began the search.

Angel clenched her fist. How was he not out of breath? She bit her lip, debating what to do, hoping he would give up and go away. Her legs were itching where the hay scratched her. Nothing a hot shower wouldn't fix.

"Angel?"

She froze; his voice was coming from right in front of her. She pushed herself back as far as she could, felt the rough needles jab into her back, and squealed involuntarily as a large, cold hand placed itself on her chest.

"Gotcha!" His voice was smug, with no hint of apology about where his hand was placed.

"Do you mind?" She hissed, slapping his hand away before he grabbed her upper arm and jerked her out of her hiding place.

"Not at all." He sounded both confident and fed up.

He pulled her behind him as they stumbled their way down the haystack. Angel reached into her pocket and dropped the ruby into the loose hay, where it would be easy enough for her to find later, as they reached the ground.

He swung her around to face him before releasing her. "What have you got to say for yourself, breaking curfew after everything we talked about?"

Even with the shadows dancing around them, she could see the irritation on his face.

"Not a lot." She tried for a casual shrug and cursed herself as his beautiful, amber eyes seemed to penetrate her secrets.

"Angel, cut it out, I know you have it. Where is it?" He clipped out each word in frustration.

She honestly didn't know how to play this one out. She hated games, but Sam's desperate pleas to keep both Max and Bowie safe clawed at her soft heart.

But, then again, as Bowie had pointed out earlier, he was her elder, and the thought of disobeying him upset her as much as the thought of him and Max being punished. Almost. Dilemmas surrounded her.

Sam? She pushed towards her soul-sibling, riddled with guilt and uncertainty.

I'm coming. Just get him mad…he won't be expecting that, it'll throw him.

I can't!

Yes, you can. What if the Council finds it in his possession, Angel? It will be his life, and Max's on the line. Please!

She took an internal deep breath, apologising to the angels for what she was about to do.

"Listen here, Bowie, we've been handling things just fine without you, while you were off on your quest. Which you wouldn't have needed to go on in the first place, by the way, if you'd done your job properly and protected Michael!" She stepped forward, jabbing a finger sharply against his chest for impact.

Nice one! Sam cheered, getting closer.

The look on his face stopped her from hurling another insult his way.

She felt like a criminal, knowing he prided himself on his loyalty and honouring his role. One more insult would cut him deeply. Standing here alone with him, and only the Man in the Moon as their witness, she knew she wasn't brave enough to say one more word.

He took one menacing step forward. "I'll pretend you didn't just say that. Now…where is it?" Cold steel laced his voice.

She stepped back, wrapping her arms around herself as she shook her head. "I don't have it." Well…technically, she wasn't lying.

He groaned, frustrated, running his fingers through his hair before placing his hands on his hips. "Last chance. Hand it over now, or you are going to be in a world of pain."

"Are you threating me?" She tilted her head, wondering how serious he was. She didn't think he would actually do anything to hurt her.

"Yes. Be smart and take it as a clear, direct threat. Hand. It. Over." He looked at her, unimpressed.

Angel could hear it in his voice: The build-up. The danger.

Angel, don't give it to him, you can't!

Hurry up, Sam!

Bowie stared at her, unblinking. "Now."

Don't do it, Angel! I'm almost there!

She stepped closer and whispered, "Or what?"

Big mistake. Huge.

Before she knew it, a white light burst from his outstretched palm, and he sent a small force slamming through her body like a warm shock wave. Pleasant for a second, but then fiery pain built within her.

She gasped, knowing it would have hurt more if he'd intended it to. "Bowie, please!" she cried, shocked.

By the look on his face, he was about to take his punishment to the next level; his eyes were ablaze with amber fire.

"What the *bloody hell* are you doing, Bowie?" Sam screamed from behind them.

Finally! Angel cried.

Sorry about that…didn't think my psycho brother here would actually *zap you!* Disbelief laced Sam's words.

Bowie dropped his hand cutting off the pain he was using to torture Angel, but his steely gaze held her in place. She wrapped her arms around herself, frowning as the pain sent residual shock throughout her system. They stared unhappily at each other.

The slap on his arm made him turn his blazing gaze towards his sister, releasing Angel from his invisible prison.

"By the Angels, Samantha! What do you think you two are *doing?*" He sounded furious, and his use of her whole first name let her know how displeased he was.

Sam was bristling with anger. She couldn't believe Bowie had just zapped Angel! At least he didn't have the ruby. She ignored his question and asked Angel instead, "Are you okay?"

Angel nodded, still shocked that Bowie had zapped her.

"Samantha, what are you up to?" he repeated, bristling with anger.

"We aren't up to anything. When I noticed Angel was not in her bed, I thought I'd look for her, only to find my brother performing a punishing act on her. Like, *what* the actual hell?"

"Well, little sister, if neither of you had taken what wasn't yours to take, we wouldn't be here in the first place."

"I haven't taken anything."

"Are you seriously going to just lie straight to my face, regardless of the consequences?"

Bowie's handsome face turned towards Sam causing his hair to fall across his eyes.

Angel felt both pride and fear for her soul-sibling, standing strong as she faced her brother. Sam stood, fists clenched by her sides as she shook her head, causing her hair to brush her shoulders while she returned her brother's glare. Angel spotted the tell-tale sign of a nerve ticking near Sam's jaw. She was nervous, just as Angel was. And rightly so.

"Where is it, Samantha?" He watched her swallow nervously. He was growing tired, standing out in the cold morning light, hoping he'd get some sort of answer soon.

"Last chance," he said.

"I can't."

"You have to."

"I'm trying to keep you safe!" she yelled in frustration.

"God damn it, Samantha! I don't need you or anyone else trying to keep me safe." His eyes blazed between Sam and Angel, fists clenching and unclenching in fury. He was referring to Michael trying to keep him safe when he went after Brendan Black. *And look how that ended…*

Sam looked anxiously at Angel. "I don't know what to do!" she cried out in confusion.

Bowie watched Angel out the corner of his eye as she briskly rubbed her arms. Her hair lay in a plait down her back, and the wind tugged playfully with the loose strands, sending them to caress her cheeks. His eyes returned to his sister's. "I'll tell you what you are going to do, give me the damn ruby, so we can all get some sleep before a busy day starts in a few hours!"

Sam considered his words.

Angel felt a warmth spread over her, chasing the icy fingers of dawn away from her flesh. She noticed Bowie's fingertips flicking an amber glow towards her, warming her. She flushed at his wanting to comfort her after he'd just shocked her with a pulse of lightning; he'd always been such an enigmatic soul.

Angel shook her head. "Why don't you just take Sam back to the house, and let me do what I have to do?"

"I am not going to knowingly put you, or Samantha, in a dangerous position this close to your ceremony."

"Can't you just trust us?"

He sighed as he turned away from Sam to focus entirely on Angel's face. "It's not about trust, baby, it's about my duty to you, to Michael."

He called me 'baby'! Angel flushed in delight.

Get a grip, my friend. Duty or not, I cannot have my brother in danger. What are we going to do?

Bowie and Angel did not break eye contact as Angel pushed her next thought to Sam.

Can you zap him? Hold him here long enough to let me get away?

You seriously want me to do that?

Why not?

Sam considered for a split second. *That is actually a bloody good idea. You'll have to run like the wind.* Sam was hopeful at last.

I will.

Are you ready?

Yes. Are you?

We are about to find out. Sam took a deep, quiet breath, meeting Angel's gaze. *Good luck to us both. Now!*

You could lose yourself in those baby-blues… Bowie stared into Angel's eyes, wondering what she was up to, since she was shielding her thoughts. Then a shock wave of energy flooded his system, immobilising him.

"Sam?" he groaned in astonished agony.

"I'm sorry, Bowie!" Sam cried. "Run, Angel—*run!*" she screamed at her soul-sibling as she continued shocking her blood-sibling.

Angel dropped to her hands and knees and felt about the loose hay. Her hands closed on the object that had caused them all so much grief over the last twenty-four hours. Then she turned on her heel and fled.

"*Angel!*" Bowie roared after her, pain filtering through his voice.

She ignored him with great effort. She sprinted out of the hay shed area, across the paddock and towards the road leading out of the college, over the cattle grid, past the Gatekeeper's cottage, and towards Quicks' paddock.

Please run fast, Angel! Bowie's fighting me...I can't hold him much longer.

It's okay, Sam, I'm almost there. And within minutes, she was entering the electric-blue wild wind that tore the band from her plait and sent her hair flying in every direction. It whisked her through the portal, and she flew through to the Blacks' mansion in seconds. She landed on shaky feet, reaching for the trunk of a tree to steady herself as she took a deep breath.

"I'll never get used to that," she whispered to the Man in the Moon before racing towards the mansion that loomed before her, growing larger with every hurried step. She needed to plant the ruby and get back to the homestead, praying Bowie would not be too hard on Sam, terrified that they were both treading new ground, crossing a major line. The only upside to this situation was that Bowie couldn't report them to the Council without incriminating himself or Max, and he'd already given his word. So, there was that.

She approached the front door, felt the energy of the mansion, and sensed it was empty. The door was unlocked, and as she pushed it open, the sound of the old hinges creaking reminded her of a horror movie.

"Not far off it," she whispered, heading towards the room she'd been held captive in many years before. She rushed towards Rob's office and over to his desk, then threw the ruby towards the back of the top drawer before slamming it shut. Then she raced back to the door and outside. The ruby was where it belonged, and Max and Bowie would be safe from the Council's punishment.

She breathed a sigh of relief once she was off the Blacks' property and walking along Glenormiston Road, heading back towards the college. Her poor, bruised feet were throbbing, and she was bone-tired. She wrapped her arms around herself and contemplated taking the day off from classes. The approaching sound of a car startled her as its high beams flashed from behind. She leapt off the road and spun around as the horn honked rudely.

Heart in her throat, she held her hands up to block the high beams and tried to see who the mad driver was. Her startled heartbeat transitioned into an uncomfortable rhythm as her eyes met her blood-sibling's.

Michael looked at his younger sister. A rage filled him, one he didn't know he possessed. And that was saying something, considering what he'd been through over the past seven years.

"Michael?" she sounded nervous even to her own ears.

"Get in the car, Angel," he replied stonily.

She hesitantly opened the passenger side door and got into the car. Michael slammed his foot down on the accelerator before she'd even closed the door.

"Michael!" she gasped.

He shook his head once, not responding as he speed down the road towards the front entrance of the college. Silence reigned as they sped through the gate, past the overseer's cottage, and up their winding driveway.

He'd spent hours trying to convince Elizabeth that he'd been away for the past several years on family business, and had not intended to make her feel abandoned. She was only just warming up to the idea that they could have a future together when Bowie called for him. And on the eight-minute drive from Terang to Noorat, Bowie had filled him in on as much as he could. He couldn't believe his luck, seeing Angel walking along the main road as he headed home.

He turned the car into a parking space, slammed on the brakes, and turned off the engine. They stared in silence at the front door, which was wide open, Bowie's silhouette outlined in the entrance as he stood, hands in his pockets. He shot Angel a death stare before turning and disappearing inside the house.

"When we go inside, I suggest you think about every, single word that comes out of your mouth, Angel. Because I have never heard Bowie so pissed off in all my life…I don't even know if I can control him. So, I am warning you, think before you speak. Understood?"

She didn't know what to say, because in all her life, Michael had never spoken to her in the way he had right now, either. Disappointment and judgement filled his tone. She nodded before pushing open the car door, cringing as her bruised feet hit the gravel. She didn't want to stand on them, but knew she didn't have a choice.

Angel tried not to hobble as she stepped out of the car and walked inside.

"In here." Bowie's cool voice washed over her as soon as she stepped inside the foyer.

The front door closed firmly behind her as Michael pulled it shut. She could feel the heat of his anger at her back, and if she weren't so nervous herself, she'd be pissed off at the way the boys were handling this situation. Okay, no longer *boys*, and their elders to boot, but still!

Both she and Sam deserved whatever was coming to them, but this was all new. Sam had zapped Bowie, and that was a no-no. But Bowie had also zapped *her*, and that was a double no-no. So, where did that leave them all?

"Come on, Angel. Standing here isn't going to make this situation go away."

She looked over her shoulder at Michael and saw a scowl etched across her brother's tired face as he looked at the floor, not meeting her eyes.

"I'm sorry, Michael, I am. We were just trying to help."

His eyes remained downcast. "Let's just get this over with, shall we?"

She walked towards the lounge, unaware that she was leaving a trail of bloody footprints on the floorboards.

Michael winced in empathy as he followed her. When she stepped into the lounge, he diverted to the kitchen to get a bucket of warm water and some healing herbs to soothe her feet. He may have been as mad as hell at her and Sam, but he didn't like the thought of her physically suffering. Which, knowing what was to come because of their insolence, angered him further.

When Angel stepped into the lounge, her heart felt a wave of pity for her soul-sibling, who was sitting on the couch in tears. Sam rushed towards her and threw her arms around her, still crying.

"Are you all right, Sam?" Angel asked, not daring to look in Bowie's direction. She could feel his presence though. Every breath of air she took was charged with his temper, making it almost painful to breathe.

Sam nodded before releasing Angel. She wiped the back of her hand over her eyes and walked back to the couch; she didn't want to tell Angel what happened after she'd left through the portal. Her defences had weakened against Bowie's, and once he'd been released from her immobilisation spell, all hell had broken loose. In the calmest, freakiest way she could ever have imagined.

Bowie eyes had filled with flames, he was that wild. Each fingertip, pointed stiffly at the ground in anger, had lightning shooting out, striking the earth at his feet, scorching it in a black blaze as he'd stared at her, furious at the girls' betrayal.

Sam had cast a dampening spell over him, all the while crying, "I'm sorry, Bowie…truly I am! I'm doing this for you! *Please* forgive me!"

After the chill had dulled the flames in his eyes, and his energy had stopped charging the ground, he'd waited for her to fall to her knees. She'd gifted the ground with a healing spell and water, before he'd grabbed her arm and silently dragged her back to the homestead.

Once they were inside, Bowie had slammed the front door, and his rage had emitted a sound like thunder inside the house. Max had started to run downstairs, to see what was going on, when Bowie had turned blazing eyes toward him, saying in a dangerous tone, "Max, if you would please stay upstairs, we have a family matter that needs attending."

Max had looked at Sam, who'd nervously met his eyes, whilst giving him a quick nod of her head. Bowie, catching it, walked over to her and whispered harshly, "It isn't your permission that's needed, little sister."

She'd glared up at him, but the look on his face had stopped any comment about to cross her lips. Max had used a calm voice and said, "Goodnight, then," before returning to their room, closing the door behind him.

Then, whilst Bowie and Sam had stood in the loungeroom, Bowie had done nothing but glare silently at her until they'd heard Michael's car arrive. The sense of relief that Angel had returned from the Blacks' mansion unharmed, and that the ruby was away from Max and Bowie, meant everything to Sam. Any punishment that the brothers wanted to dish out was fine with her, as long as her love and blood-sibling were safe.

Angel caught Sam's message loud and clear. And that's why they'd done it; to keep their loved ones safe. End of story. She found the courage to meet Bowie's eyes. But the displeased look on his face as he glared at her knocked the wind out of her.

"Why don't you take a seat, Angel? Your feet must be hurting." He folded his arms, wishing, unpleasantly, that more than just her feet were hurting at this moment.

"I'm fine," she replied stubbornly.

"No, you're not." Michael walked into the room carrying the bucket. "Sit down."

Angel didn't want to argue with her blood-sibling after the talk he'd just given her in the car. She hobbled over to a seat and sat, almost crying in relief at taking her weight off her poor, abused feet.

Michael placed her feet in the bucket.

"Thank you," she said, not meeting his eyes.

"What have you got to say for yourselves?" Michael looked first at Angel, then at Sam, mirroring Bowie's stance. He could feel that his soul-sibling's temper was boiling and knew he needed to calm himself down in order to calm Bowie. But for the life of him, right in this moment, he wanted both of the girls to feel their fury.

The girls were silent as they exchanged an uneasy look.

"I think it's fair to say that we were only thinking of keeping Bowie and Max safe." Angel began, sensing Sam's nerves. "That's all." Angel kept her eyes on the pretty, blue herbs floating around in the warm water.

"That's all?" Michael let out a pained laugh, looking at Bowie. "That's *all*?" He turned his eyes back to Angel. "You have both gone against your elders' advice. Not only did you break curfew, but you, Sam, used your gifts to shock your own kind." He turned to Angel. "And you, breaking into Bowie's office while he slept to steal the ruby that he was going to shield to, subsequently, shield Max and protect his life. What were you thinking?"

Angel could still not bring herself to meet Michael's eyes as she answered, "We were trying to protect Bowie from higher punishment."

"Do you take me for a fool, Angel?" Bowie asked, demanding she look at him with that question.

She lifted her remorseful eyes and met his angry gaze. She shook her head once, wishing he didn't wear angry so well. But he did. He wore every expression deliciously well.

"Are you sure about that?" His voice held a note of steel.

She frowned, uneasy, wondering what he was getting at.

"What about you, little sister? Do you think I'm a fool?"

"*No!*" Sam cried. "Of course not!"

"Mm, that's funny. Because the two of you have certainly made me feel foolish. Even after everything we talked about last night, you still go and concoct a plan behind my back, which, I can guarantee, has now jeopardised all of your good intentions. So, bravo, ladies…bravo." He clapped his hands three times before tucking fists of fury under his armpits.

Sam frowned, looking at Angel before glancing up at her brother. "What are you talking about?" she asked tentatively.

Bowie shook his head, frustrated, as he raised an eyebrow at Michael. "They want to play with the big kids, but didn't care enough to learn all of the rules first. Would you like to fill them in?"

Michael let out a breath, releasing his anger at what the girls had done. He'd have to reserve his energy for what was coming. He looked down at Angel, asking, "Where did you go when you went through the portal?"

Angel looked at Sam as Bowie hissed, "You don't want to avoid the question, Angel."

She met Bowie's furious glare as she answered Michael. "The Blacks' mansion."

"And what happens when any heavenly- or elemental-soul passes through the portal?"

She paused as she considered her answer, looking down at her feet in the cooling water. And then the realisation of what she'd done dawned on her. The colour drained from her face as she lifted eyes filled with tears of remorse towards Bowie.

"Ah, Michael, I think one of our siblings is starting to see the light." Bowie unfolded his arms as he crossed over to Angel. He stood above her for a moment before kneeling to look up into her lovely face, where a crystal-clear tear stuck to her long lashes.

"What's going on?" Sam asked, her voice filled with worry.

"Oh, no…" Angel whispered, looking into Bowie's liquid-amber pools.

He nodded. "Oh, yes."

"I'm so sorry, Bowie." She felt sick as her heart beat uncomfortably.

"What the *hell* is going on?" Sam shot to her feet, arms ramrodded to her sides by the unknown fear.

Michael looked across at Sam. "When Angel crossed through the portal with the ruby, it activated a signal that the High Council detected. They are now aware that Angel was in possession of it. Someone from the Council will arrive here soon enough."

The blood drained from Sam's face, and she stumbled in fear. Bowie got to his feet, catching her arm. As angry as he was with them both, he didn't want to see either of them in distress or pain. Not deep down in his soul.

"Bowie, no…please tell me it isn't so?" Sam whispered, tears falling down her face. "What will we do?"

"It's simple." Angel stood, gasping as the soles of her bruised feet protested.

"You can heal her now, Michael." Bowie nodded toward Angel's feet; he felt she'd suffered enough.

As Angel sat back down, Michael lifted her feet out of the water and rested them on his raised knee. He placed his palm over the bottom of her small feet and whispered a healing spell. In moments, the cuts and bruises on her flesh healed. When he finished, he ran a hand over them before removing the bucket so she could place her feet down on the plush rug.

"Thank you, Michael," she whispered, finally meeting his eyes.

He looked down at her. "You're welcome, despite it all." He walked out of the room to pour the contents out into the back garden before returning a few minutes later.

Bowie still had his arm around Sam as he looked across at Angel. "Now, as you were saying, what's simple?"

"When the High Council come, I'll say that I was attacked by an unknown entity, that Sam came along and saved me, and that the ruby was left behind. I'll tell them that I was returning it to the Blacks' mansion in hopes of finding out any information regarding Vein activity."

"So, you'll lie?" Bowie raised an eyebrow.

"Yes." She met his gaze steadily. "If it means saving you and Max, I will lie."

"To Red, Fletch, Tom, and Jess?" Bowie released Sam, who shakily sat back down, rubbing her hands over her face.

Angel faltered, not wanting to lie to anybody. But she could not...no, *would* not see Max put to death for something he'd had no control over. And would not have Bowie killed, only to be revived and killed again, as part of his punishment in not reporting Max's crime.

"Angel, you know you cannot lie, don't you?" Bowie reiterated.

Angel raised her face to his, tears lining her lashes, but not one fell as her look of regret went from Bowie to Sam. "We'd lost you and Michael for seven years, we were just trying to protect you."

"Yeah, we know. And now we will have to face the consequences of your failed protection."

Bowie didn't mean for it to sound like an accusation. Angel flinched at his words.

Now she knew why Michael had been so furious. He would have to heal his soul-sibling, only to be forced to watch Bowie's heart be stopped in the most excruciating way, then perform a healing spell again, over, and over, until the Council was satisfied with his punishment for betrayal.

"What about Sam and me?" Angel asked.

"What about it?" Bowie asked, looking down at her.

"Won't we be punished, too? After all, we concealed the truth about Max."

"Yeah, we will just take the blame, they don't even have to know that you're involved, Bowie. I need to get Max out of here. I'll take him through the portal, hide him overseas," Sam said, jumping to her feet.

Michael and Bowie exchanged a sombre look before Michael addressed Sam. "You're not getting it, sweety. The Council already know everything."

An unsettling quiet filled the room.

"Everything?" Sam finally choked out.

"Why do you think I was so pissed, Samantha? My plan was perfect. And you and dear Angel here completely stuffed it up."

"How do they know *everything*?" Angel asked, feeling defeated.

"Because Fletch has been listening to this entire conversation." Bowie pointed across to the desk, and there, standing in the centre of the globe, was a figure dressed all in black, with a scowl to match. As soon as the girls' eyes connected with Fletch's, he waved a hand, and vanished.

Sam stared at Bowie, then met Angel's eyes. "This is all my fault," she whispered.

"No, Sam. No." Angel crossed to her friend and put her arm around her shoulder. "I'm just as much to blame."

"And you will be, both of you. Blamed. Punished..." Bowie folded his arms again, so frustrated by their interference.

"I think, for now, we all need to get some sleep, before the Council arrives. If either of you even *try* to step foot out of this house, I can promise you, you will not like the consequences."

Michael looked at the girls with their arms around each other.

Sam nodded. "Sure."

"Off you go, then." Bowie nodded toward their rooms upstairs.

The girls said goodnight as they walked from the room. They reached Angel's doorway first. She pushed it open before turning to Sam.

"So much for bright ideas, hey?"

"I cannot even believe the shit-show that we have caused." Sam hid a yawn.

Angel rubbed her shoulder. "Let's get a bit of sleep, or else we won't be able to put up a good defence."

"Yeah, all right. Sleep tight, Angel."

"You too, Sam."

Angel closed the door and fell face-first into her pillow, letting tears of fear for the unknown punishment fall. And they fell harder as she imagined Bowie being tortured repeatedly. And Max?

Oh my stars, she thought. *It really couldn't get any worse.*

A soft purring began behind her as Moonie headbutted the back of her head.

She rolled over and collected the soft, furry body into her arms, pushing her face into the critter's neck as she whispered, "Oh, Moonie…how can I stand by and watch Bowie suffer? Please, give me the strength for what's to come."

The cat looked at her with large, green, all-knowing eyes before he reached out a padded paw and tapped her on the nose. Angel was asleep in a second.

Chapter Twenty

Max

Max had stood at the top of the landing for several minutes after Michael and Angel returned. He'd crept downstairs to listen, ready to defend the girls if needed. The longer he'd stood and listened, the more his blood had chilled in his veins. He knew he only had one option to spare Sam any further pain. It might break her heart, but at least it wouldn't kill her, and he knew if she saw him put to death, that would certainly be the case.

Yes, what he'd done to Angel, a heavenly soul, was punishable by death. But he was also part heavenly soul, and if he could somehow be of use in bringing about the Veins' downfall, maybe he could earn a pardon? It was worth a shot.

He could feel the pull of the ruby and knew if he got his hands on it, he could execute his plan. It was time to leave. Time to put things right.

Sam

When Sam walked into their room, she felt his absence immediately. "Max?" she whispered, praying her feelings were wrong, but praying they were right at the same time. She curled up on his side of the bed, wrapping the blanket around her, breathing in his scent. She pushed her face into his pillow. There was a crinkling sound as a stiff piece of paper met with her face. Flicking on the bedside lamp, she read his note.

'I love you, Sam. You are my everything. Tell Bowie I'm sorry. I'll be back when the time is right. I'm going to make everything right—I promise. Always yours – Maxwell. xx'

She turned the light off and curled back up into a ball, holding the note to her chest. "I love you, Max. Be safe," she whispered, praying he'd hear it in the wind.

Bowie

Bowie stood staring into the flames after Michael had gone up to catch some sleep. He himself, didn't see the point in following, his nervous system was going into overdrive thinking about the punishment to come, worried about the punishment for the girls. And how could he stand by and watch Sam's heart break, when Max was put to death? The punishment might fit the crime, but surely the Council would be lenient? After all, Max was half heavenly soul, and had been unaware of the act he'd been performing at the time.

He ran his hands over his face as he knelt at the grate to poke at the smouldering logs. The ache in his shoulders had returned with the stress of the past several hours. The bony fingers of pain were squeezing tighter. He lay on his back, grateful for the thick rug as he turned his face towards the orange glow of embers and flame. His thoughts wandered to Angel. Beautiful, sweet Angel, whose taste would not leave him. Her scent still lingered in the room.

He put his hands behind his head and stared up at the rosette on the ceiling, wondering how he'd feel once she was connected with her soul-partner in a week's time. He squeezed his eyes shut, not wanting to think about her in another's arms. Seriously, if he could convince the Council of a worse punishment than his heart being shocked to death, then it would be to see Angel with another man for the rest of his days. He sighed as he opened his eyes. He watched the sun rise higher, wondering what hell this day would bring.

Angel woke after a restless three hours of sleep and ran the shower hot enough to scald her skin. After blow-drying her hair, she heard the commotion downstairs and ducked into her room, closing the door. Sam was sitting on her bed, dressed already, patting Moonie as she waited for Angel. They each looked as exhausted as the other.

"Guess we're not heading into class today?" Sam said as Angel pulled on jeans and yanked soft socks onto her feet before shoving them into knee-high boots.

"Hope not. I couldn't concentrate if you paid me. How's Max?" Angel pulled on a snug-fitting, long-sleeved black top, leaving her hair to dance silkily past her shoulders, before dashing on a squirt of her mother's perfume.

Sam looked at Angel, not wanting to say it aloud.

Angel felt Sam's hesitancy. "What is it?"

He's gone. He says he's going to make things right before he comes back.

Angel nodded, letting Sam know she'd heard her loud and clear. "That could help his position, you know?" She pulled her marble necklace over her head as she looked at Sam.

"Maybe?" Sam whispered as a sharp knock sounded at the door.

Angel pulled the door open to see Bowie leaning against the door frame. She looked up into his eyes as he looked solemnly down into hers.

Even tired, she's beautiful.

Exhaustion just adds to his male beauty.

Neither of them meant to think aloud. He raised an eyebrow as he looked down at her.

"Beauty?" His tired voice sent shivers across her flesh.

Angel shrugged, not able to look away from his eyes, exhausted, yet smouldering all the same.

"Oh my God, you two." Sam got off the bed and strolled towards the door. "You're just torturing yourselves. Six days and counting until Angel's essence says, 'I do' to some other geezer." Sam patted Bowie on the arm as she headed to the staircase. "See you down there."

Angel could hear the tension in Sam's voice. "Right behind you," she called, pushing a calming intention towards her soul-sibling before looking back up at Bowie, who hadn't moved an inch.

"What are we doing?" She wanted to run her fingers along his jaw-line, push his silky fringe out of his eyes to see them more clearly. His aftershave begged her to move closer; he made her mouth water.

He leant closer, breathing her in. Her hair was like a halo against her dark top, moulded to every tantalising inch of her athletic figure. Her jeans highlighted strong, firm thighs. He pulled his eyes away from her body to meet her eyes, which were, despite very little sleep, sparkling jewels.

"I honestly have no idea, baby," he whispered, reaching out to cup her chin, lifting it as he stepped against her.

Her heart melted as her breath caught in anticipation. His lips swept down to capture hers in a deep kiss that pulled at every muscle in her stomach, setting her essence on fire. She reached up, pushing her fingers through his hair before cupping the back of his neck, bringing him as close to her as she could get.

"Bowie, Angel, get down here now, please," Tom called calmly from downstairs.

They stopped the kiss, yet their lips remained touching, eyes on each other. Angel parted her lips and kissed him again, running the tip of her tongue along his bottom lip, wanting just one more taste.

He moaned before angling his head, taking her tongue into his warm mouth, sucking on it until they were both reeling.

"Bowie?" Tom tried again.

Bowie broke the kiss and took a deep breath so he could answer. "Coming."

He looked down at her, pressing his lips against her ear making her shiver as he whispered, "I wish we were."

She tingled all over with that statement as Bowie stepped back, allowing her to walk by him. She spotted the bulge in the front of his jeans and flushed as she looked up to meet his gaze.

"Tell Tom I'm right behind you. I just…need a moment."

She nodded, understanding. "Sure."

As she headed to the top of the stairs, he called, "Don't think I'm not still mad at you, either."

She looked over her shoulder at him as she took the first step down. "Okay," she replied as she continued the rest of the way down.

When she reached the breakfast room, she was surprised to see only Fletch, Red, Tom, and Jess. Mrs. McGoldrick was pouring cups of tea and coffee and had served hot muffins with fluffy eggs and bacon.

Angel took a plain egg muffin, since Mrs. McGoldrick had gone to such effort, but didn't know if she could eat any of it.

"Good morning, Mrs. McGoldrick." Angel kissed her soft cheek before moving on to Red.

"Good morning, dear," Both Red and Mrs. McGoldrick chimed as Angel grabbed a cup of tea and sat with her muffin.

Fletch looked down at the tired-looking girl. "Morning, Angel," he said.

She looked hesitantly across at Fletch, not knowing whether to apologise for all he'd heard last night or not. She went with a simple, "Morning."

Tom rubbed her arm as he sat beside her. "How are you, pet?"

"Nervous," she whispered as Jess smiled across at her from his seat.

Tom sighed. "I can imagine."

Bowie walked in the room. "Morning, all." He forced a cheerful tone he was not feeling as he reached for the coffee pot.

He was greeted with silence before Red forced a smile. "Morning, dear boy."

Bowie met her eyes before glancing at Michael. They both knew that 'dear boy,' coming from Red, meant she felt for their situation.

"Mrs. McGoldrick..." Tom smiled.

"Yes, Mr. Liam," she returned his smile, knowing she was about to be asked to pop into town.

"Can you grab the canteen order from the bakery this morning?"

"Of course, I'll get right on it. Have a good day, everyone." She smiled before she breezed out of the room and down the hallway towards the front door.

Once the noise of her car engine had faded, all eyes went to Fletch.

He stood by the buffet table, coffee in hand. "We have an unfortunate situation on our hands, do we not?"

"We do indeed," Tom agreed, looking at Bowie, then the girls.

"And where is Maxwell Black?"

"He's gone." Sam replied calmly before taking a mouthful of her muffin.

"Gone?" Fletch's disapproval was evident.

Sam pulled the note out of her pocket and slapped it down on the table, then continued eating her muffin.

You are so cool. Angel brushed against Sam's mind. Sam gave her a quick smile and a wink.

Jess picked up the note and read it aloud. "'I love you Sam. You are my everything. Tell Bowie I'm sorry. I'll be back when the time is right. I'm going to make everything right—I promise. Always yours – Maxwell.'"

"Well, that is one less bit of unpleasantry that we need to deal with today, isn't it?" Red sounded relieved.

"That's one way of putting it," Michael agreed.

"For the time being, Maxwell Black's future will be in the hands of the Light Accords, and he may be prosecuted as our enemy." Fletch said.

"NO!" Sam cried, slamming her fist on the tabletop. "He's trying to fix this!"

"That is ridiculous!" Angel couldn't stop herself.

"I beg your pardon, Miss Cloud?" Fletch put his coffee cup down as he stared at her in disbelief.

"Do you want the facts or not? Because if you want to know what *actually* happened, you'd wait to hear everything before you started handing punishments out."

"Angel…" Michael warned.

"No." Fletch held a hand out to Michael, "It's okay. I'll hear what Miss Cloud has to say. Continue." He nodded to Angel.

Angel looked from Sam, to Bowie, then back to Fletch. "Max is our friend, our family." She looked at Red. "I'm sorry I didn't tell you the truth, that the powerful energy that had been tapped into was mine. But Max had no idea what he was doing. None. He was so shocked and upset when he found out, and, obviously, is punishing himself in his own way, by trying to trap his cousin, no doubt."

"That may be so, but he invaded your body, consumed your essence, which is a sin punishable by death. It is our magical equivalent to the pure-souls being raped," Fletch stated in a flat voice.

Angel let out a frustrated sigh. "I know that, but can't we change the rules just this one time? I mean, Max is basically innocent. And don't forget, he is also one of us!"

Fletch stared at Angel emotionlessly, as if she'd just spoken a foreign language and he hadn't understood a word of it.

He looked across at Tom, then Jess, Bowie, and Michael. "You are all to attend High Council this evening. But before then, go about your regular day. Until tonight, may you keep the souls safe,"

"With every breath that we take," the room chorused.

With that, Fletch spun on his heel and exited the room, which fell silent.

"Classes? After everything?" Sam asked incredulous.

Bowie sighed, draining his cup before meeting Tom's and Jess's eyes. "I know," he said, exhausted at the thought. "I know."

"Let's all just get through this day and have a calming afternoon before the Council require our presence tonight," Jess said as he got up to take his dishes to the kitchen. "Come on, Angel," he called. "We've got surgery."

Angel pulled a hairband out of her jeans pocket and hastily pulled her hair up into a high ponytail before grabbing her cup and plate, the muffin untouched, to follow Jess out into the kitchen.

As she walked past Bowie, he grabbed the muffin and, walking backwards with his eyes on hers, took a bite.

"Mm, delicious," he said before spinning on his heel and heading to the front door. "Come on, Michael. You don't want to be late on your first day."

"Right behind you." Michael dropped a kiss on Red's cheek as she stood silently with her tea, watching Sam, who was still sitting at the table.

"How about I get Jane to accompany us tonight?" she asked Sam.

Sam's eyes brightened. "Would you, Red?"

"Of course."

Sam flushed guiltily. 'I'm so sorry for all the trouble I've caused. Max really is a good person."

Red ran a hand over Sam's silky hair. "I know that, love."

"Are they really going to kill Bowie, over and over?"

"I'm afraid so."

"It's not fair!" Sam cried.

Red sighed. "It's the way things are done, my dear. And the way it's been done for a thousand years, whenever one of our own break the rules."

Sam shook her head. "That doesn't make it right."

"So many things in our world aren't right, Samantha, but these are our laws."

Sam nodded begrudgingly. "I know."

"Come now, let's get this day done with so that, tomorrow, we can focus on the healing."

Sam nodded. "Red?"

"Yes, dear?"

"What are they going to do to Angel and me, for breaking the rules?"

"That, my dear, I do not know."

Sam's eyes met Red's. "Well, whatever it is, I'm ready."

Red smiled sympathetically, hoping that were true. "I'll see you later, with Jane."

"See you then," Sam whispered as Red left, then, ran her hands over her face with a sigh, and went to face the day without Max by her side.

Chapter Twenty-One

"Hey, Angel-cakes!" Gary called as Eddy and Angel finished up their lunch. They'd sat out in the sun near the fishpond in front of the cafeteria.

"Oh, this will be good," Eddy chuckled, getting up.

Angel stood, looking up at him with doe-eyes, begging, "Please, don't leave me."

"What's up, Gazza?" Eddy beamed at his friend. He knew Gary could be painful occasionally, but deep down, he was a nice guy.

"Where's Max at today?" Gary asked as he reached them. "He's not returning my calls."

"He's gone to Melbourne for a while, taking care of some family business," Angel replied, while, across the quadrangle, she watched Bowie talking to another student. He really did fit in well as a counsellor, guiding and supporting both the teachers and students.

Bowie sensed her watching him, and his gaze met hers. It felt like they were only one foot apart with the chemistry that jumped between them, not one hundred.

"Angel?" Eddy had been trying to get her attention.

She pulled her eyes away from Bowie, flushing pink. "Sorry, what was that?"

Eddy pointed to Elizabeth, who was standing a few feet away, and had apparently called out Angel's name more than once. "She's been calling you."

"Oh, yeah, thanks." Angel nodded as she headed towards Elizabeth.

"See you at the lecture in a few," Gary called out as he followed Eddy to the bins to dump their lunch trash.

Angel waved behind her as she stopped in front of Elizabeth. Dark, refreshed, and stunning, as always. "Hi Beth, how are you?"

"I'm good. You look tired, you all right?"

"Oh, yeah. Just…bad dreams, is all." *If only Beth knew…*

Elizabeth nodded. "Listen, I'm going to ask Michael to move in with me. What do you think his response will be?"

"Oh, well, um, he's only just come back home, Beth, I'm not sure what he'll say." How could she tell Beth that there was no chance in hell Michael could move in with her? He needed to be close to Bowie, and the college grounds. The Soul Keepers' life was here in Glenormiston South, not in Terang. And Beth couldn't move in with them; there was no way Michael could keep their precious way of life a secret from her. She was no Mrs. McGoldrick, she was nosy, persistent, and demanding, in a loveable way.

Beth ran a hand through her hair, sighing, "I don't know, Angel. I think, if he loves me, and he says he does, then he'll move in with me."

Angel nodded, checking the time. "You can only ask, there's no harm in that."

"Agreed. I'll see you later." Elizabeth nodded before turning on her heel to go teach a class.

Angel sighed before hurrying off to her afternoon lecture, sitting up near the back as Jess walked to the front of the hall.

She ignored Gary, who was twenty seats away, trying to get her attention by waving madly. Eddy was trying not to laugh at both Gary's persistence and Angel's unhidden annoyance as she sat beside her good friend, Lisa Evans.

"Good afternoon, everyone," Jess began. "I want you to listen to this paragraph and think about what we can do, as farmers and horticulturalists, to restore the soils and reverse the damage done to the land."

Jess read aloud from the book in his hands as he paced the atrium, packed full of both college students and visiting high school students from Terang College.

"'Half our fertile land on Earth is now farmed. More often than not, we have abused it. We overload it with nitrates and phosphates, overgraze it, burn it, overburden it with unsuitable varieties of crops, and spray it with pesticides, so killing the soil invertebrates that bring it to life. Many soils are losing their topsoil and changing from rich ecosystems brimming with fungi, worms, specialist bacteria and a host of other microscopic organisms, into hard, sterile, and empty ground. Rainwater runs off it as it does pavement, and so contributes to the excessive floods that now so frequently submerge the heartlands of many countries that practise industrial farming.'"

Jess snapped the hardcover book shut as his gaze met the hundreds of students. "It should be a crime," he said. "That was a section from David Attenborough's mission statement in *A Life on Our Planet*. What are we going to do about it?"

A year-eleven student from Terang raised his hand.

Jess smiled, pleased someone was that quick off the mark, and nodded, "Go ahead, Marcus."

"We basically need a giant worm to come and piss all over our soils." This stirred some laughter from his mates.

Jess nodded, folding his arms. "Righto. That would be interesting to see, to say the least, and certainly would be helpful. Anyone else?"

Angel sat, enjoying the light banter, and, as always, appreciated how Jess ran his lectures. People absorbed knowledge more readily when it was presented in a non-lecturing way.

A year-twelve student raised her hand. Jess pointed to her, giving her the floor.

"We could start by zoning our cattle when they graze, so they can fertilise the land, and then move on to the next acre. Then we'd leave enough grass roots in the ground so that the microorganisms can continue enriching the soil."

Jess applauded her. "Yes, vigorous plant growth maintenance of ground cover through strategic grazing actually helps improve our soil's structure, by contributing to surface organic matter, which continues to encourage root growth. I know many farmers who do use this method, not just in our country, but around parts of the globe." He nodded to her before looking out at the other faces. "Does anyone know the names of some green fertilisers that are necessary for soil health?"

Angel nudged Lisa, who put up her hand. Jess smiled. "Yes, Lisa?"

"Broadleaf plantain, chickweed, lambsquarters, white clover and dandelions," she answered shyly. Only Angel knew that she'd had a crush on Jess from the day she walked into his classroom during orientation twelve months ago.

Jess nodded. "Correct." He smiled at the pretty, glossy-haired woman beside Angel. Wanting her to continue, he asked. "What do you suggest we need to do in order to return parts of our world to the wild again?"

"We need to restore nature, naturally. Only then can we turn the biodiversity loss that we have caused into biodiversity gain. We need to allow nature to do its thing, and we need the entire human population to do their part right now."

Jess nodded, impressed at the passion in her voice. She may not have been a royal-soul, but her heart held the notes of one. A healer of sorts, for sure.

"Is there anyone here who does not understand the term 'biodiversity'?" He looked around the auditorium. About thirty hands raised in the air.

Jess opened to the back and read from the Glossary, "'Biodiversity. Biological diversity, a term that attempts to sum up the variety of life in the world. It is a function of the number of species, all the different animals, plants, fungi and even microorganisms like bacteria, and the number of or abundance that exists of each of those species.'" Jess glanced up from reading, making sure he had their attention before resuming.

"'In more abstract terms, the planet's biodiversity encapsulates not only millions of species and billions of individuals, but the trillions of unusual characteristics that those individuals have.'" He snapped the book shut once more. "Make sense?"

A hundred heads nodded back at him.

One boy raised his hand. "Yes, Adam?"

"So, basically, it is in the human species' best interest to keep as many other species alive as possible?"

"That's correct." Jess was impressed. "The greater the biodiversity, the more the *biosphere* is able to deal with change, maintain balance, and support life. Our species, the human species, needs to respect Mother Earth, and respect her right now. Otherwise, in sixty- to ninety-years' time, we will be what the dinosaurs once were. Here for now, and then… gone. Fossils."

Angel's left wrist suddenly burned in a way that frightened her. She gasped aloud when it throbbed painfully, as if fire flowed in her veins. Someone was self-harming. Her thoughts swirled with utter darkness and misery as her stomach lurched. She fought against the urge to burst into tears as the pure-soul's desperation filled her completely.

She swallowed the bile that wanted to rise, and her eyes met Jess's over the top of the other students' heads.

Can you make it out? he asked, concern filling his thoughts.

She nodded, gathering her books as Lisa put her hand on her arm.

"Are you okay?" her friend asked.

"Must have been something I ate," Angel whispered as her hearing faded in and out. "I'll see you later."

She stood and excused herself as she made her way along the row of seated students before finally reaching the aisle, stumbled towards the exit and out towards the dormitories. Angel trusted the energy of the one who needed her help to guide her. She rounded the corner and slammed into a figure racing in her direction. Bowie caught her as she went down, frowning at the sight of her pale, sweaty face filled with pain.

"Angel?"

"Someone's self-harming...I need to get to her before it's too late," she whispered, feeling woozy.

Bowie swept her up effortlessly in his arms and followed the direction she was pointing.

In a matter of minutes, they arrived at the dorms on the west side of the college, and he ran up the stairway leading to the second-storey rooms. He placed Angel on her feet and kept one arm firmly around her waist as he gripped the locked door handle, and, with inhuman strength, popped the door open. Then he guided Angel inside, softly pushing the door shut with his foot. He led her into the bathroom, and there, lying in a bath of bloodied water, her life slipping from her wrists, was a fourth-year student named Luna.

The room reeked of Vein influence.

Bowie helped Angel sit on the floor and stepped back, allowing her space to do her thing.

Angel placed her hand on her chest as she gripped Luna's wrist and whispered to the angels above. Her amulet shone, filling her heart with loving intention to heal and cleanse the darkness and remove Luna's depressed thoughts.

Angel could feel the Vein-influenced murk swirl within Luna's mind.

"You can smell it." Bowie scowled, folding his arms.

Angel nodded as she focused on the healing.

"Brimstone," she whispered as the blood in the bath flowed back into Luna's slit wrists, and then, finally, the flesh gelled back together. Bowie turned his back as the water cleared, so as to not see Luna naked.

Angel focused on the girl's mind, clearing it of negative thoughts and returning the girl's normally-rosy disposition. Luna was a high achiever. Granted, she'd always placed pressure on herself to succeed at all she did, but she was a mental health advocate, too. She'd been on the student council ever since she'd first enrolled at the college, to aid and support the wellbeing team with every student that reached out for help.

Angel steered a positive thought to flow into Luna about the need to take a self-care bath before her approaching exams.

Bowie found a couple of healing candles and lit them. Keeping his gaze away from Luna, he placed his hand in the water, heating it up to a perfect temperature.

Angel smiled. "Thank you."

He looked down at her, grateful the pain had left her face. Although, after the night and morning she'd experienced, exhaustion marred every lovely feature.

"You're welcome," he said. "Let's get you home to rest before tonight's unknown."

She nodded. They left as Angel chanted for Luna to wake up.

Luna awoke to candles scenting the air with their uplifting aromas, and warm water filled with calming oils. She smiled, feeling the most refreshed she had in a long time, grateful she hadn't drowned in her celebratory bath. She sighed happily and took a deep breath before plunging under, excited about the month ahead as she neared graduation.

Chapter Twenty-Two

Johanna and Crow Storm stood amongst the hundreds gathered in the old fortress. Water dripped down its decaying walls, and the ceiling had crumbled to nothing a lifetime ago. It stood on the cliff facing the ocean, with an impenetrable forest at its back.

Angel shivered as she stood beside Sam, Michael, and Bowie in the centre of the gathering. Like her blood- and soul-siblings, she was not looking forward to what was to come.

Jane had hugged both the girls hard when she'd seen them, and she'd been glad Red had called her back home to Glenormiston, as she'd been attending a crisis in Inglewood.

Bowie looked over the top of Sam's head to see Angel wrap her arms nervously around herself. Like Sam, she was chilled to the bone. He waved his fingers towards the girls and heat surrounded them instantly.

Angel met his worried eyes. *Thank you.*

Bowie returned a tight smile.

Why didn't I think of that? Sam thought, grateful for her blood-sibling's consideration.

After all, they were here right now, in this mess, because of the decision she and Angel had made to take matters into their own hands.

Michael was anxious, his arms folded tight against his chest, feeling as anxious as his blood-sibling; his jaw clenched in anticipation.

It's going to be okay, mate. Relax. Bowie pushed towards Michael's mind.

Angel peeked at Red, who smiled. Jane looked grim beside her aunt. She was worried about her friends.

How long are they going to make us stand here like this? Angel asked Michael.

I don't know, Angel, this is a first for us all.

Is this part of the punishment, do you think? Sam asked them all.

Bowie almost laughed. Almost. Movement at the far end of the castle's walls startled them as ten elemental-souls, dressed in near-blinding white outfits, proceeded towards them, and stood around them in a circle.

Bowie frowned, wondering why the girls and Michael weren't asked to move aside. His stomach knotted in fear of the unknown.

"Michael Cloud, please step out of the circle." A voice boomed from a figure that could not be seen.

Michael looked at Bowie. "You're going to be fine. I've got you, okay?"

Bowie nodded. "I have all faith in you."

Michael stepped out of the circle and stood behind the elemental-souls.

"Samantha Storm. Angel Cloud. You witnessed an illegal act and attempted to conceal the crime."

Angel strained her eyes, trying to see where the voice was coming from, but it seemed to move around the ancient stones, bouncing off one decaying wall to another.

"It is not in our nature to harm, and it is with a heavy heart that we inflict this punishment so close to your essence ceremony. Alas, it is our way." This statement sucked the night air out of the crumbling fortress as Angel and Sam exchanged a look.

"Samantha Storm, you are to send a lightning bolt through Angel Cloud's body for a total of twenty counts."

A gasp echoed around the stoned walls as the impact of the punishment was felt. For Samantha to inflict this kind of pain on her soul-sibling, the one she was born to protect, would be extreme torture for her too.

"By the Angels," Bowie hissed out between his teeth, looking at Sam, then Angel. They were both stark white.

He stepped towards them, placing a large hand on each of their shoulders.

They looked up at him. He nodded solemnly. "It's going to hurt," he whispered. "Try focusing on a good memory you've shared. Twenty counts isn't that long," he tried to reassure them.

Angel placed her hand on top of his as she whispered, "Just make sure you'll be okay too, Bowie."

He forced a smile. "Well, that's your brother's job in all of this." He saw her worried eyes fill with both fright for herself and Sam, and concern for him. "Hey, we'll all be fine, and tucked up in our beds before we know it. Okay?"

Angel nodded.

Bowie dropped a kiss on Sam's head, wishing he could do the same to Angel, but, instead, moved back, giving Sam the space she needed.

"Commence!" the commanding voice called.

"Let's focus on the time when we were gifted the ponies, when we were eight."

Angel nodded and whispered, "That's a good one."

"Ready?" Sam asked.

"As I'll ever be," Angel replied, shaking nervously. *How bad could it really be?*

"I'm sorry," Sam whispered as she looked up to the night sky, drew a deep breath, and focused her energy on an electric charge. She looked at her soul-sibling, the one she was born to protect, raised her hands, and sent a jolt of lightning energy into Angel's body.

Angel gasped. *That bad...*

They'd both predicted pain unlike any they'd ever felt. What neither of them had expected, though, was the pain of empathy that passed between them to be so severe.

Five counts had Angel falling to her knees, crying in pain, which caused a flood of soul-sibling energy to knock Sam backwards, filling her with an empty dread, as though the sun would never rise again. All thoughts of the ponies and any happy memories vanished.

Sam's absolute despair overwhelmed Angel, the pain visceral.

Sam felt a pounding in her skull as if she were about to go blind as Angel fell against the damp stones. She curled into the foetal position, screaming in agony, her head feeling as if it were about to split in half.

Despite the pain shooting into every single nerve cell, Angel focused on pushing a healing, protective incantation towards Sam, to enter into her soul-sibling.

It was working.

Sam felt lighter, less overwhelmed by pain, and, despite the charge she was sending into Angel, she sensed her soul-sibling protecting her.

Angel, stop it. Please!

It's okay, Sam. Angel's response was tiny, filled with agony.

Bowie's hands were in tight fists by his sides. He was quivering in absolute fury to see Sam have to perform this torture on Angel. It was barbaric.

His eyes met Michael's, who was looking ill, himself.

Finally, it was over, and both Sam and Bowie rushed to Angel's side. She was curled tight, whimpering, her body convulsing, tears drenching her face, teeth chattering uncontrollably. Bowie scooped her up, getting her off of the cold, damp stones.

Jess walked towards him, taking her from Bowie to comfort her.

"No healing, Jess Callum. Angel Cloud will be all right in time. Let us resume our next phase for the night," the voice boomed.

Jess held Angel against him, trying to absorb her shaking, wishing he could cast a soothing spell as Tom put his arm around Sam, holding her close. They all turned to watch as the next command was given.

"Bowie Storm, as an elder, and one who has been favoured by Uriel himself, you have shown great dishonour in allowing Maxwell Black to go unpunished, and you've conspired to keep unlawful acts a secret. You will be shocked until your heart stops, once for every year you have lived on this earth. Your soul-sibling will revive you each time you die, then it shall begin again. Commence."

The voice grated on Bowie's nerves, but he didn't have a second to think about it as the first charge of lightning slammed through him. He stood his ground, not wanting to give the Council members any satisfaction, even as the electricity had him seeing stars. *Just like Angel's kiss.* The thought filled him with hope before the pain gripped his Elemental heart and struck it dead. As he dropped to the ground, motionless, his Elemental brethren ceased their action, and allowed Michael to rush to Bowie's side. He placed his hand on Bowie's chest, his other over his heart, and chanted a healing incantation. Within moments, Bowie's eyes fluttered open.

"Well, that sucked," he whispered to Michael, sweat beading on his pale skin.

"Are you ready?"

"Do I have a choice?"

Michael pulled Bowie to his feet and clapped him on the back. "See you soon." He stepped out of the line of lightning.

Angel whispered to Jess, "I'm okay, Jess, I can stand."

"You sure, pet?" Tom asked, holding Sam close.

She nodded to Tom as Jess lowered her to her feet. She was still shaking uncontrollably, but wanted to focus her energy on Bowie.

Sam took Angel's hand, tears streaming down her face. In that moment, she vowed to never, ever break another rule as long as she lived. How could she do nothing but stand here and watch Bowie suffer?

It's okay, Sam, I'm going to try something.

Sam glanced sideways at Angel before turning back to Bowie, who'd dropped to the cold stones once more. She watched as Michael rushed to revive him. She looked across the great space and saw her parents standing as still as stones, their eyes filled with tears, yet not one fell.

Angel squeezed Sam's hand as she concentrated.

Sam could feel Angel's depleted energy and wondered what she could possibly do to help Bowie when she herself was weak and shaken.

Angel concentrated on placing a strong shield around herself, the strongest she'd ever used. There was something in these walls that penetrated her heart, charging her amulet. Something that wanted to bond with her...something good.

She sensed her shield was in place as she watched Bowie drop again. When Michael rushed to his side, getting his heart beating once more, she prepared herself for the next wave.

Bowie stood and faced his temporary-executioners. He took a deep breath and waited for the next unbearable strike of pain to stop his heart. It hit him hard, as expected, and he fell to his hands and knees, groaning in agony yet again, clenching his jaw to prevent a scream.

But suddenly, although the pain was just as intense, and he could feel his heart stop beating, a sense of freedom, of lightness, overcame him. The pain dissipated as his heart stopped and everything else faded.

And that's how it continued, right up until his twenty-four-year count ended. Though surprised at first, and yes, feeling his heart stop was disturbing...the light numbness in between saved him from going mad, he was sure of it.

This force was powerful, but it didn't feel like Michael.

As they pulled him to his feet for the last time, the elemental-souls who'd inflicted the cruel punishment each came to place a hand on Bowie's shoulder, the other against his chest. They each whispered, "Forgive me."

To which he replied, "Duty needs no forgiveness."

"Young Soul Keepers, step forward, please," the voice called.

Sam, still holding Angel's hand, led her across to where Bowie stood.

Michael joined them, putting his arm around Angel. Bowie tiredly pulled Sam into his arms.

"You both okay?" Bowie whispered. Sam bobbed her head, tucking into his chest.

He could see Angel shaking, her arms wrapped tightly around Michael, eyes wide with pain still. He frowned, hating to see her in any discomfort.

The voice broke into his building anger.

"We are sorry to see you suffer, young Soul Keepers of Glenormiston South. In time, you will come to realise that this was a valuable lesson regarding our laws. For eventually it will be entirely up to you to keep our ways safe and secure." The voice paused for a moment, and its next delivery put Sam's and Angel's nervous systems on-edge.

"Angel Cloud, Samantha Storm, in five nights' time, you will stand before your thirteen, and your soul-essence will choose its forever partner, therefore losing the connection you have shared since birth. Use these next few days to cherish your time together."

Sam and Angel exchanged a look before Sam stepped forward and out from under Bowie's arms.

"I have something to say," she started nervously.

All eyes went to her, and she swallowed, flexing her fingers anxiously by her sides.

"Yes, Samantha Storm?"

"I want to know what your plans are regarding Maxwell Black?"

"The descendant of our enemy?"

"But *he* is not our enemy, he is our family; half heavenly soul, and the love of my life."

"Actions speak louder than words. Although this half-Vein does show decent qualities, he has aligned himself with our enemy by consuming your soul-sibling's essence, only to then run away like a coward. Can you so easily ignore his crime? Do you have such little regard for a heavenly soul who will one day be our greatest weapon against the enemy, and our most powerful healer, to save Mother Earth and all pure-souls?"

Well, does he have to put it like that? Angel pushed into Sam's mind.

No, Sam replied. "Maxwell did violate my soul-sibling, yes. But, afterwards, he had no recollection of the attack and felt great remorse. I believe he was being used and manipulated by an ancient Vein."

"Brendan Black. Yes, we have been aware of his trickery before." The voice had a thoughtful note to it, as if contemplating.

Sam jumped in with hope. "Exactly. And Max is *no* coward," she hissed passionately. "He has gone to both his, and our, enemy, placing his own life in danger in order to trap Brendan Black and contribute to our efforts in bringing the Veins down." She was furious that this 'being' had called Max a coward.

"That is yet to be seen. However, we will take all of his future actions, and feedback from the Council, into consideration. Anything else, young Soul Keeper?"

"No." she kept her nasty comment in her head.

A murmur of interest swept around the ancient stones before the voice called out once more.

"It is time to bid you all goodnight. May you keep the souls safe."

"With every breath that we take," the two hundred Soul Keepers chorused as one.

As the purple-robed figures left, Jane, Red, Tom, Jess, Johanna, and Crow crossed over to their young people. Crow crushed Bowie to his chest as Johanna wrapped her arms around Sam's petite body, rocking her back and forth as she whispered, "My sweet, baby girl, are you all right?"

"Yeah, I'm fine, Mama," she replied, using her childhood name for her mother, feeling tears threaten.

Jane hugged Angel hard as Red ran a hand down her damp hair. "Time we got you all home." She addressed Tom and Jess, who nodded.

"Johanna, Crow, are you joining us?" Tom asked.

"Yes, just for a few hours." Crow smiled at Bowie before looking down at Sam and Angel as Johanna reached her arms out to Michael.

"Thank you for saving our boy, Michael."

He returned her hug. "You're welcome. Life would be dull without him."

"I think we could all do with a bit of dull for a while. Let's go, dears," Red said before waving her hand around them. The fortress' stones allowed her to create a portal, as it allowed all elders to conjure. The wild, blue wind that swirled about them collected them and whisked them straight into the homestead's lounge area.

Angel felt ill after the portal ride, and completely exhausted as pain still wracked her body. She turned from the room to head upstairs and into a hot shower.

Halfway up the stairs, strong fingers wrapped around her upper arm, stopping her.

Her exhausted eyes met Bowie's. "Are you okay?" she asked.

As usual, her thoughts weren't for herself. Bowie nodded.

"You know why I am. You are amazing, Angel, to cast a shield that strong *and* prevent the High Council from detecting that you were blocking the extra pain from entering me. How did you do that after you'd been drained?"

His fingers had run down her arm to clasp her fingers, running his thumb over the back of her hand. She looked down at him, wanting to step into his arms and hold him against her, feel his warmth and comfort his exhaustion away. She shrugged. "I don't know, I just did it."

He brought her hand up to his lips and trailed a sweet kiss over the back of her knuckles. "Thank you."

She forced a tired smile. "You're welcome."

"You going up for a bath?"

"A shower, but now that you mention it, a bath would be perfect."

"How about I go pick you some herbs and crush out some healing oils, get Sam or Jane to bring it up to you?"

She nodded, thinking he was being thoughtful, considering his exhaustion.

"That would be nice, Bowie, thanks. Then go spend time with your parents while they're here, I can't imagine they'll be here for too long."

"No, the war in Sudan is out of control. They need to get back within a few hours." He squeezed her fingers before releasing her hand. "My 'mad at you' has lessened."

"Really? Gee, thanks." She smirked. "Just lessened? Not dissipated?"

"Well, you did say some untoward things back at the hay shed." He shrugged, shoving his hands into his pockets.

She sighed. "You know I was just saying that to get you mad, Bowie."

"Well, it sure worked. Maybe don't try it again?"

She nodded. "I don't plan on it."

He smiled. "Good. Run your bath, Angel. I'll go pick your herbs."

She headed up towards the bathroom, relieved to shut herself in, and ran the bath nice and hot. She sat on the tubs edge as the room filled with steam, waiting for the herbs to arrive. A knock sounded several minutes later, and Johanna stepped in, smiling warmly at Angel, fresh herbs clutched in her hand along with a bottle of oils.

"Here you go, darling girl." Johanna sprinkled the herbs into the steaming water, and she popped open the lid of the oils, pouring it into the tub. The room took on a magic scent of healing, love, and good intentions as the oil spread along the water's surface.

Once Johanna had capped the lid on the oil, setting it on the bath's edge, she faced Angel.

"I cannot thank you enough for what you did for Samantha and Bowie tonight, Angel."

"Sam told you?"

"Yes, they both told me. And, after your bath, I think it would help to lie in the healing garden and allow Sam and Bowie to return the favour. Your energy is so low, my dear, and we cannot have that. When you hurt, Mother Earth hurts too. When you glow, so, too, shall she."

Angel took Johanna's hand and squeezed it as her eyes filled with tears. That was something her mother used to say to her; that one day her glow would save them all.

Johanna put her arms around Angel's shoulder and hugged her. "We love you, dear girl."

Angel nodded, not trusting her exhausted voice not to break.

Johanna kissed the top of her head and whispered, "Hop into your bath, darling, relax. Would you like me to send Jane or Sam up with some tea?'

"No, thanks, just go and enjoy being with Sam and Bowie while you're here," Angel said. "I know they've missed you."

Johanna nodded as she got up, smiling. "Thank you, Angel."

Angel watched as she left the room before shedding her damp, uncomfortable clothing and slipping into the healing waters. She let the energy within revive and kiss every inch of her tired, wounded soul.

Chapter Twenty-Three

Max

Max stood in the twilight-kissed courtyard in Venice, his body swirling with a mixture of pleasure and pain. The ruby around his neck pulsated as it absorbed both pain and essence. Max had performed several ghastly feats the past few days to show his cousin he was loyal. He wasn't sure that, if he survived this and miraculously made it back to Sam, he could ever look her straight in the eyes again.

Max retracted his veins and regretfully gazed upon the lifeless husk of the heavenly soul he'd been ordered to drain and forced his tears not to fall. He knew he was being watched. Always watched. Judged. Assessed. Pushed to the limits. He'd not slept in the one-hundred-and-twenty hours he'd been in Brendan's company. The Heavenly blood and essence he'd consumed in that time, along with sinking a cruise ship off the coast and absorbing the devasted energy of the thousand souls, had filled him with both energised, euphoric lust, and self-loathing.

He turned to Brendan, who was watching him through narrowed eyes. "I think it's time we return home and take what's ours."

Max shook his head. "It's not time. There are still two days before Angel's ceremony."

"Yes, it will give us time to settle in, make our preparations, and you can begin your role as someone who has finally earned your cousin's trust. Are you up for that?" Brendan asked.

Max stared at his cousin, black suit moulded to the man like a second skin, his pupils like that of a shark's. "Absolutely, I am." Max nodded calmly. "Let's do this."

Brendan smiled. "You've come a long way. I knew you'd see things our way once you hit a certain age. What do you want to do with young Samantha once we have Angel?"

Max forced himself not to grind his jaw in fury. Instead, he kept his heart calm, nodding as if he'd already given this some thought. "I want to keep her in the cellar, locked up, to use at my pleasure." His cool gaze met Brendan's.

"Excellent. Your father would be proud. Let me make the arrangements and we'll be back in Noorat before you know it. Give me the ruby."

With Brendan's command, the leather strap released itself from around Max's neck and the ruby fell into Max's waiting palm. He tossed it to Brendan, happy to be rid of it.

Brendan caught it in his fist, a hungry glint in his eyes, before turning on his heel and setting off to put their plans into action.

Max picked up the dead heavenly soul and, with a grieving heart, walked across to the edge of the sinking city and dumped her into the sea. "Forgive me," he whispered to the Angels above before heading back to the villa that had been home for the past few days.

He couldn't wait to see Sam, but it terrified him to think that she'd never speak to him again once she learned what he'd done to trap his cousin. Overwhelmed with anxiety, he tried to calm his racing, muddled thoughts before putting himself back in Brendan's company.

"I do love Saturdays," Sam yanked the fridge open, starving after their two-hour horse ride with Kylee and Joanne into Noorat, down Dalvui Lane, to visit Lisa. They'd enjoyed a carefree morning, laughing with their friends and didn't want the day to end; partly because it was the day before the soul-essence ceremony, and both girls were a bundle of nerves.

While making sandwiches, they heard Jess whiz by on the quad bike. He'd gone to check on the cattle down the east paddock as Tom strolled in through the back door.

"Hello." He smiled as he grabbed an egg and lettuce sandwich off the plate.

Sam grinned at him. "Hello, yourself. You sound chipper."

Tom reached into the fridge to grab the jug of freshly-squeezed lemonade with mint. "Oh, you know, it's Saturday, what's not to be chipper about?" He shrugged as he filled a glass.

"Mm, is that a trick question? Let me think...Um, how about an unwanted soul-essence ceremony?" Sam raised an eyebrow before shoving the corner of her sandwich into her mouth.

Tom sighed. "Sam, trust me, all your nerves will disappear. Remember one thing, your soul and his have been created for one another. The moment it happens, everything else will just fade away."

"That's the problem. I don't want 'everything else' to just fade away," Sam mumbled around her mouthful of food.

"How come you haven't had a ceremony?" Angel asked, pouring a glass of lemonade.

A shadow crossed Tom's lean face, making his angles sharp as he met Angel's gaze.

"I have walked this earth for more than a hundred years."

"More than one hundred?" Angel asked, lowering her glass. "How many more?"

He smiled wryly at her. "Nearly one-fifty."

"Impossible," Angel whispered.

"Neat." Sam grinned.

Tom shrugged, selecting another sandwich.

"And Jess?" Angel asked.

"The same, hence our soul-sibling connection."

"You mean to say, you and Jess have been soul-siblings' for one hundred and fifty years?" Sam looked at Angel. "Why the hell can't we do that, and not have to hook up with some soul-essence geezer?"

Angel raised an eyebrow, waiting for Tom's answer.

He finished his sandwich and drained his lemonade. He rinsed his glass and dried his hands on a tea towel before facing them, feeling dreadful, knowing neither of them wanted this ceremony. *If only they knew how complete they will feel. Whole. Happy. Fulfilled in a way that they could only imagine...*

He cleared his throat before the painful memories crept into his mind and focused on the telling of the tale, not the feeling of it.

"When Jess and I were twenty, we attended our ceremony and were both connected to incredible partners. I cannot even begin to describe what it was like; feeling my and Jess's connection slip away was only made bearable by the magnetic force that a soul-partner can bring. As soon as my soul-essence connected with hers... well, it was everything and more."

"Hers?" Sam asked.

Tom shook his head. Pain filtered across his features, and he said in a low voice, "Please do not make me say her name, Samantha."

"I'm sorry," Sam said, hating seeing any trace of anguish on Tom's face. "It's okay Tom, you don't need to say another word."

"No, we've begun now." He looked from Sam to Angel. "I was with my soul-essence for fifty splendid years, as Jess was with his. We ran a school in Rockingham, Western Australia, similar to the college here."

He smiled. "It was the perfect cover to aid both Mother Earth and the pure-souls alike." He folded his arms, not wanting to tell the next part of the story, but knowing he must.

"Unfortunately, our school's wards weren't ancient like the ones here in Glenormiston South, not as strong…and the Veins infiltrated our school. Someone betrayed us, and both my and Jess's partners were killed, along with several of our family members."

The girls exchanged a horrified look before Angel said, "I'm so sorry to hear that, Tom."

He forced a small smile, meeting her eyes. "It was a long time ago," he said. "The point is, we don't know how long we have to do great things for Mother Earth, to protect the pure-souls. But when your soul-essence connects with another, you will be blessed with powers that will help heal our world, especially you, Angel. You are the key to wiping out every vile Vein that has caused every unjust action; every murder, suicide, disease, and natural disaster. You are the one who can finally bring peace to this world."

"How?"

"As you age, your powers, along with your soul-partners, will increase as your bond grows. It won't happen for a few years yet, but, in time, you will be the cure for the world's horrors."

Angel felt an overwhelming sense of responsibility. She only hoped she could live up to what everyone was saying about her when the time arrived for her to heal all.

"Who's going to stop the pure-souls from overpopulating the planet, if not the Veins?" Sam asked.

Tom raised an eyebrow.

"Hey, it's pure curiosity." Sam held up her hands. "I mean, it's already been overpopulated but, without the Veins eradicating so many…?"

"*We* will. We will educate the souls further, steer them to a sustainable future and back to a simpler way of living within a community. There will always be the good and the bad side of humanity, but we can guide them, and so much more, once we wipe out the Veins."

"But how do we wipe them all out? Is it a spell? A war? I don't understand how I'm going to have this incredible power to…what? Just click my fingers and make them all disappear?"

"No, it won't be that easy." Tom smiled. "And your questions will be answered in time, Angel."

"What about the half-Veins?" Sam folded her arms.

"What about them?"

"Well, is Max the only one, and will he be safe?"

"I'd be interested in that answer myself," a voice called from the doorway.

They turned to see Max, who'd been listening to the last part of the conversation.

"Max!" Sam squealed as she raced to the door, jerking it open to throw herself into his waiting arms.

They kissed long and passionately, making Tom and Angel turn away, trying to give them privacy, as Bowie and Michael walked into the kitchen from the hallway.

Bowie froze when he saw Max and turned to look at Tom, an eyebrow raised.

Tom gave his head a half-shake, waiting.

"Samantha," Bowie called.

As Max and Sam broke their kiss, Max ran a hand along her smooth cheek, her amber eyes glowing with happiness as she stared into his green liquid pools.

"I'd be interested in that answer now, please, Tom." Max looked at Tom as he and Sam stepped into the kitchen.

Tom nodded. "Hello, Max. Any half-Veins who have chosen the wrong path will also be obliviated. However, in saying that, the Council believe you are the only half-Vein in existence."

Max nodded, placing his arm around Sam's waist. "We have a lot to discuss."

"Well, let's head into the study?" Michael suggested.

Tom pushed a message towards Jess, asking him to come to the homestead.

"Should we notify Red?" Angel asked.

"No, we've got this for now," Tom answered as he headed out the kitchen door and towards the study.

Angel stayed where she was. She didn't want to spend her last relaxing afternoon as a single heavenly soul discussing problems that, right now, she could do nothing about. The thought of meeting her soul-essence partner tomorrow made her almost as nervous as facing the High Council for punishment had.

"Actually, I think it's worse," she whispered to the empty kitchen, since everyone had followed Tom out to the library.

"It won't be." Bowie's voice washed over her, making her jump.

"Sorry." He laughed slyly, enjoying seeing her eyes light up as heat washed over her cheeks. *She is so pretty.* "It won't be as bad as you think."

Angel shook her head, letting out a nervous chuckle. "How do you know?"

He shrugged, watching her. "I have no clue. I just don't want to see you stressing about something you have no control over."

"I'm feeling anxious for the twelve souls who won't get to walk out of the room afterwards. What if someone loves them? And because my essence won't choose theirs, that's it…they just evaporate into pure-essence?" She shook her head again. "It's too much."

Bowie sighed, feeling her inner struggle. He was feeling torn, too. How was he going to lose her to some other soul tomorrow and have him move in with them, into their home? To have to watch him hold Angel in his arms, kiss her, touch her in intimate ways…

And he'd just have to stand by and watch her like it. Hell, she'd love it.

He hadn't realised he'd made a strangled sound out loud until Angel repeated herself.

"Are you all right?"

He shook his head. "If you want me to be honest. no. No, I am not all right."

She raised a dark eyebrow. Her lips were slightly parted as she watched him, waiting for him to elaborate. "Go on," she offered.

He ran a hand sharply through his hair before placing his hands on his hips just as Jess sailed through the back door.

"Aren't you two supposed to be in on this meeting as well?" he asked as he strolled by.

"Probably," Bowie answered shortly, his eyes not leaving Angel's face.

"Come on, then." Jess grabbed a sandwich off the plate as he headed towards the muffled voices of their family members.

Angel looked back at Bowie, who stared at her solemnly. All the light and fun from his eyes had vanished, replaced by a look of regret before saying, "Why torture ourselves? Come on, kiddo." He turned around and headed out the room.

Angel sighed. So, they were back to 'kiddo'? She'd enjoyed the endearment of 'baby', but guessed with the ceremony tomorrow, it was smarter to put it all back in order now. She followed Bowie down the hall, thinking this was the worst last-free-day she could ever imagine.

Chapter Twenty-Four

Max addressed the men in the room. "I left, firstly, because I thought it would save you all the trouble of having to protect me, and secondly, because I thought I'd be more useful playing into Brendan's hands, to do my part in cleaning up this mess. I believe I have done that."

Tom nodded. "Give us the details, Max. Don't leave out a single thing,"

Max swallowed, nodding as he ran his hands over his thighs. "I won't lie, the things I've had to do over the past few days have been despicable." He looked at Sam. "I don't know if you can ever forgive me."

"Hey," Sam soothed, running a hand over his back, loving the feeling of having him beside her again. "You did what you had to do." She shook her head, hoping it wasn't as bad as all that.

He nodded once before turning to Jess and Tom, as Michael and Bowie stood on the other side of the desk, waiting.

"Brendan plans to abduct Angel the morning after her soul-essence ceremony."

"And how is he going to do that? Does he think he's just going to waltz in here and throw her over his shoulder?" Bowie scoffed.

"Actually, yes, that's exactly what he plans on doing. Except the plan is for me to carry her out, after I've drained her in her sleep, depleted her of her energy, and then get her to the mansion."

"And then?" Michael asked, forcing calm into his voice.

"And then, of course, he plans on doing to her what he'd done to you for years, he'll drain her essence and power the Veins' cause."

"Angel's essence, after her coming of age ceremony, would give the Veins unimaginable power, and could ultimately begin the destruction of the end of the world as we know it." Jess frowned, folding his arms.

"Hey, can we lose the doom and gloom?" Sam forced a bright smile. "Max is here to work with us and plot against his evil cousin, so none of these things are *actually* going to happen, are they?"

The idea of anyone hurting Angel had Bowie seeing beyond red to a disturbing force of sheer black.

"That's right." Angel nodded, forcing cheer, as the temperature in the room had plummeted. She had goosebumps over every inch of her flesh. "Bowie?"

"Yeah, right." He hadn't realised he'd made the room icy with his dark thoughts. The room immediately returned to a comfortable temperature. "Sorry." He pulled out his pocketknife and flicked it open, checking its sharpness.

"Brendan won't be working alone." Michael looked away from Bowie's gleaming blade towards Tom.

"That's true. Ancient though he may be, if he plans on taking Angel, he'll know we'll come after him. He won't be able to take us all on. Max?" Tom scowled, deep in thought.

Max nodded. "I don't know how, or when, they'll be arriving, but he did mention something about an army."

Angel crossed over to the world globe, and, placing her hand on it, spun it once.

Everyone crossed over to watch as the continents amalgamated, before sliding into the bottom of the globe, then vanishing.

It stopped spinning and a darkness swirled under the surface of the glass, like a small, black snake feeling out a crack to escape its confinement.

Tom reached out and tapped the globe once more, and an aerial view of the district came into focus. In the centre of Mount Noorat, black matter swirled continuously like a cyclone, remaining in the mountain's basin, bidding its time.

"What the hell is that?" Bowie spat in disgust.

"That is a horde of Veins getting ready for Brendan's command." Max folded his arms, looking pensive.

"And the command?" Sam asked her lover.

"Apparently, once we have Angel, they have orders to influence every pure-soul throughout the entire Western District."

"Influence them how?" Angel wasn't sure she wanted to hear the answer.

"Mass suicide," Max answered.

Sam gasped as Bowie swore under his breath.

"We have the information, thanks to Max, therefore, we have the upper hand to put an end to it all." Angel searched one worried face after the other, looking for hope. "It's almost too easy."

"What are you suggesting, Angel?" Michael asked, happy that at least his sister wasn't stressing out at the prospect of impending doom.

"I'm suggesting we play right into Brendan Black's hands. But first, Jess, we have an enormous job to do, and it's going to take more than just the few of us to do it. Max, it's time to put your heavenly soul to use." Angel turned to her blood-sibling. "Michael, can you get Red, Fletch, and Vicki and Vanessa Light here, and tell Fletch we need as many heavenly souls' hands on board as we can get, a.s.a.p."

Michael nodded and left to call the Gatekeeper's cottage, where Red would see to everything.

"You going to fill us in, Angel?" Bowie had a hip resting against the side of the desk, arms folded, his eyes unable to leave the dark, swirling mass in Mount Noorat's basin.

"I'd be more than happy to. We are going to influence every pure-soul in the entire Western District that we can, convincing them to treat themselves to a long weekend away, leaving immediately."

"And where are they going?" Tom asked.

"Anywhere in Australia that's safe." Angel nodded. "I'm sure the Light Accords can organise something?" She shrugged, she couldn't solve all of their problems, as much as she'd like to.

"And then what?" Sam asked her soul-sibling, impressed so far. This mayhem was actually great for taking their minds off the looming, unwanted, soul-partner to-do the next day.

"And then, after our ceremony, I will play 'sucked dry' and have Max carry me to the Blacks' mansion, straight to the source itself."

"*What?*" Bowie yelled. "No way in *hell* will any of us allow that to happen. Am I right?" He looked around the room for back up.

"Bowie." Angel stepped over to him, placing a small, warm hand on his arm. They both felt the current that passed between them.

"If I'm supposed to be this almighty, powerful tool for the royal-souls to end the Veins, then surely I can defeat Brendan. Right?" She caught Tom and Jess exchanging a worried look between them.

"Tom, Jess?" She implored.

"It's a matter of you being powerful with your *partner*, Angel… *together*, you make a powerful weapon," Jess corrected. "And only in time will you become our greatest weapon. You are still so young."

"Well, I'll still be powerful enough to stop Brendan, won't I? And whoever my soul-partner is, he'll just have to get on-board with our plan, won't he?"

"God, I hope he's not a schmuck," Sam groaned.

"I hope *yours* isn't a schmuck." Angel raised an eyebrow at Sam before they both burst into fits of laughter, still not believing that tomorrow they would be connected with someone they did not know.

"I think a wee bit of brandy wouldn't go astray." Tom nodded to Bowie.

"Not until missy and the gang do what they have to do with the pure-souls," Bowie suggested dryly, looking down at Angel.

"Quite right, dear boy!" Red breezed into the room, with Jane on her heels, followed by Fletch, Vicki and Vanessa Light, and a handful of heavenly souls Angel had not met before.

"Okay, our dear elemental-souls, please exit the room and prepare some energising herbal remedies. We are going to need a boost after we perform these spells." She clapped her hands.

Angel's hand was still resting on Bowie's bicep. She didn't want to move it, and, evidently, neither did he.

He gazed down at her as the room bustled around them, then placed his hand on top of hers, and exhaled. "Good luck," he whispered, head dropping a fraction so he could stare directly into her aquamarine pools of delight.

Angel's heart accelerated with the intense way he was looking at her. "It's not fair," she whispered, feeling a magnetic energy pass between them.

He nodded, knowing exactly what she was saying. "I know, baby." They'd only just started exploring their feelings, only to have it all change tomorrow, without their say-so.

Her heart smiled. *Back to 'baby', then.*

"I'm sorry, Bowie, dear. Time to go." Red patted his back.

He nodded, running a hand over Angel's silky locks before turning to leave the room.

Vanessa and Vicki hugged Angel 'hello' as Red commanded every-one's attention.

"My fellow heavenly souls, it is time we combine and focus our energy to persuade the pure-souls of the Western District to pack up their families and leave for a few days. Let us gather about the globe, if you will." She hustled everyone around the desk and, tapping the globe, began whispering a chant.

Angel gasped in surprise as the globe expanded until they were all inside of it and could look out through the glass dome to see the study and all of the things within it, and even out through the door to the hallway and the window that looked out into the rose garden. Yet there was nothing but blue sky above them and, beneath their feet, Mother Earth.

Max met Angel's astonished expression and smiled.

Placing one hand over her heart, the other palm facing the ground, Angel joined in with the group of eighteen heavenly souls. Together, they pushed positive, mindful thoughts towards the sixty-three-thousand pure-souls who lived in the Western District, sending them to safety.

They stood there, focusing, chanting, persuading the pure-souls to leave their homes, for over three hours before becoming exhausted, energy waning. Thankfully, Fletch finally nodded.

"It's done."

Red waved her fingers, and in a snap, the globe was back on the desk, and they were back on the outside.

Angel sighed, feeling depleted like Red had mentioned. "Time to recharge. Especially you, dear." Red put her arm around Angel and led her out into the kitchen.

Sam was waiting for Max, and when she saw him, grabbed his hand and silently led him away from the others.

Michael walked over to Angel. "Why don't you go lay out in the sun, Angel? Maybe sit in the healing garden?" he suggested.

Angel nodded. "I think I will." She wrapped her arms around her brother's waist, pushing her face into his chest.

"What is it?" he asked.

"I love you."

He smiled, holding her tight, before dropping a noisy kiss on her head. "I love you, too."

"Michael?"

"Mm-hmm?"

"What happens if you hate the guy my essence selects?"

"It's not about me, Angel. As long as you love him, that will be all that matters."

"But what if he isn't nice to the rest of you?"

"Then we'll kick his arse in private, when you're not around to defend him," Michael joked, trying to lighten her mood. He loosened his hold to look down at her. She looked drained. "Healing garden, now."

She smiled as she nodded, then walked out the back door as the chatter behind her became a buzz as the healing herbal brew was poured and afternoon tea was distributed. She pushed open the white picket gate under an arch of roses and pulled her pink cardigan off, glad for her sheer, yellow cotton dress that would attract the sun's warm rays. Kicking off her sandals, she lay on the bed of chamomile and used her cardigan as a pillow.

She was asleep in a handful of minutes. Moonie wandered into the garden and curled up by Angel's side, protecting her from the unseen.

The following afternoon, the concern that Angel had locked herself in her room filled the entire household. No one had seen her all day.

"Angel," Sam knocked again, trying to coax her out. "You need to eat something."

"I can't even think about food, Sam."

"Well, come out and hang for a bit."

"I really just need to be alone for a while…I'm sorry. I love you, though," she added to soften any hurt feelings.

Sam chuckled as she called, "Love you," before heading downstairs to tell the men Angel was fine.

"Well, if she doesn't eat, she's going to be exhausted for tonight." Michael frowned worriedly at Bowie. "And if she plans on letting Max take her to the mansion at dawn, she won't have the energy for a good defence against Brendan."

"Michael, relax." Jess passed him a coffee. "She's not going anywhere alone, so it won't matter about her energy." He shrugged as Tom raised an eyebrow. "You know what I mean."

Tom gave a half-smile, nodding.

"I am going to ask a question, and I don't want anyone freaking out." Sam took a bite of a banana, chewing while waiting for everyone to agree.

"Out with it, Sam." Bowie flipped open his pocketknife as he snatched an orange out of the fruit basket, running the blade through its juicy centre.

"Has anyone ever skipped out on a soul-essence ceremony, and, if so, what were the consequences?"

The room fell silent as all eyes focused sharply on Sam, who had the decency to flush a little.

"There was one, a long time ago," Tom began. "A heavenly soul, who felt her duty was to more than just one elemental-soul, and she refused to allow the other twelve elemental-souls to become pure-essence."

"So, she ran away?"

"No." Tom didn't want to finish the story, fearing it would only fuel Sam's thought process in the direction she was inquiring about.

"Come on, please, Tom? I need to know if it's possible."

"It isn't, Samantha," Bowie cut in with a stern tone. "Not for you."

"But it's not fair!" she cried.

"It may feel as though it's not fair, Sam, but you must trust the process. Once your soul-essence connects with another, I promise you, anything you've felt for Max will disappear into a nice memory." Jess tried to comfort her.

"Yeah, yeah...I've heard it all before, thanks."

"Sam." Bowie stepped towards his sister. "Red was the heavenly soul who refused her ceremony. She was then posted as the Gatekeeper of Glenormiston South, where she has lived, alone, serving the Council and the rest of us, for close to one-hundred-and-eighty years. It has only been in the past twenty years that the Council have allowed Jane to visit, and now live with her."

Sam lowered the banana, looking up at her brother. "That's so sad."

"It was Red's decision. She's never regretted it."

"You may try refusing this ceremony, Sam," Jess said, "but you will not be permitted to be with Max, especially after his confession about draining those heavenly souls."

"But he did that to gain Brendan's confidence!" Sam cried, frustrated. "You know he would never have done it otherwise."

Jess nodded once. "That may be so, but it is grave indeed, and will require more discussion."

"So, I have got to just suck it up and be with a soul I have not chosen?"

Bowie let out a strained laugh. "That's the whole point, little sister. You already *have* chosen him, you just don't know it yet! Now, can we please stop going around in circles? Why don't you go upstairs and start primping for your ceremony? Your outfits will arrive shortly." Thinking about Sam, and therefore, Angel, getting hooked up with an unknown random was the last thing he wanted to talk about right now, as unfair as that may be.

Sam nodded, finally resigned that she had to go through with it. "Well, it sucks. And, like I said, it was just a question."

Bowie raised an eyebrow, unconvinced, as he brought a quarter of the orange towards his lips to suck on, silently agreeing that the whole thing did, indeed, suck.

"Is Max still with Brendan?" Michael asked.

Sam nodded as she dropped the banana into the compost bin. "Yeah, he is doing everything he can to convince Brendan that they have us all fooled, and right where they want us."

"Great, that's one positive step in all of this." Jess rubbed his hands together.

A knock sounded at the door. "That will be the girls' outfits," Tom called as he went to answer the door.

Sam waited on the bottom stairs as Jane flounced in.

"Look what I've got." She beamed. "You are going to look stunning. Come on!" She headed past Sam and bounded enthusiastically up the stairs. "Where's Angel?"

"Barricaded herself in her room," Sam sighed as she followed Jane.

"Well, I'll fix that." Jane took the dresses up to the next level and into the octagon library. She dropped the boxes onto the long wooden table and turned to Sam.

"This is supposed to be a celebration, believe it or not, and I plan on celebrating with my two girls. Now, I'm going to get champagne, and you are going to go and have a shower, and come back with a bright, positive attitude. Do you hear me?"

Sam raised an eyebrow at Jane before letting out a strained laugh. "Yeah, okay then. Champagne sounds good…and completely necessary."

"Yes." Jane nodded as she walked towards the balcony door, pushing it open, allowing the breeze to dance about the room. Although they didn't need the light, she waved her fingers and set every candle in the room ablaze, setting the ambience, before heading downstairs to get glasses and a couple of bottles of champagne.

Stopping at Angel's door, she called, "Angel? Sam's in the shower. You are next, then I want you up in the octagon, okay?"

Silence greeted Jane for a minute, then she heard a reluctant, "Okay."

Jane nodded to herself, then went downstairs to set up a festive vibe that the girls would thank her for tomorrow.

Chapter Twenty-Five

Angel paced the length of Red's backroom as she fidgeted with the glass dome hanging between her breasts. The orange, frosted glass door had closed thirty minutes ago, after Sam had stepped through it. Not a sound peeped out.

Red, Jane, Tom, Jess, Michael, and Bowie sat along the window seat where Red's splendid fernery filtered out the night noises of the critters who lived within its sanctuary. They watched Angel pace.

Dressed in ceremony attire, her long, moon-white dress flowed around her ankles in soft layers like a silken waterfall with every nervous step. Her tresses were curled and pinned to the top of her head, with loose tendrils falling prettily around her face. Jane had made her up to look seductive and goddess-like.

Bowie sat forward, elbows resting on his knees, fingers steepled, with his chin resting against them, his gaze unable to leave Angel's figure of absolute mouth-watering perfection. Her dress clung to every curve before it swayed about her ankles with each turn as she paced. He wanted to lunge toward her, take her in his arms, and soothe her jagged nerves.

Her eyes met his, after she'd looked away from Michael, eyes that were wide pools filled with anxiety.

Calm down, he brushed against her mind.

She stopped pacing for a moment as she stared back at him. *I feel like I'm about to have a heart attack.*

Panic attack. Take a deep breath, it will be over soon. He watched her pull in a deep breath as she closed her eyes.

Bowie caught Michael's distressed look before the door opened and Vicki Light stepped in. "Can the family come with me please?"

Angel could not help the small cry of alarm that escaped her lips. *Oh, no…I'm not ready!*

Bowie swallowed his frustrated curse as he followed the others as they each kissed Angel's cheek, wishing her luck.

"You'll be fine, pet," Tom said, followed by Jess.

Michael squeezed her hand, smiling down at her. "Mum and Dad would be as proud of you as I am."

She nodded, too nervous to smile.

Red kissed her cheek, and Jane hugged her quickly. "Can't wait to see who the lucky devil is." She grinned.

Angel nodded as, one by one, they rushed through the door leading into Red's open kitchen and loungeroom.

Bowie stood before her and raised her chin until her nervous gaze met his. He smiled, wanting to tell her how beautiful she looked. That he wanted to brush his lips across hers until they were both breathless, he wanted to hold her close and breathe in her scent, which made his head spin whenever he was near her. He wanted too much, that wasn't hers to give him. So, instead, he bent and brushed her cheek with a chaste kiss before saying, "You've got this, kiddo."

Her heart thudded as his scent floated around her, and she sighed, nodding. *So, we're back to 'kiddo' again.* She shielded her thoughts. *Oh, well…probably for the best.* Soon, anything she'd ever felt for Bowie would disappear, because there was a soul right through those doors waiting for her.

Bowie followed the others through the door as Vicki smiled at Angel, saying, "Just a few moments, dear, you'll know when it's time."

Angel nodded as Vicki closed the door between them. Left alone, she wrung her fingers together, forcing herself to clear the dancing black and white spots that greeted her vision. She hoped that, by now, Sam was happy, and the family had welcomed her new soul-partner.

She shook her head. Was this really about to happen? *Get a grip,* she lectured herself. *There's nothing to fear but fear itself...it'll will be over before you know it...breathe...*

With that thought, the room seemed to sigh, and as she looked at Red's connecting door, it vanished, replaced with a waterfall that gushed a roaring torrent of water flowing nowhere.

Angel looked at the carpet under her feet, not a drop was on it. She shook her head and stepped through the streaming water, expecting it to drench her, but all it did was wash away her anxiety. She had a feeling Red's kitchen and loungeroom wouldn't be on the other side of the waterfall door, and she was right. Angel walked into a meadow strewn with moon flowers that smiled up at the Man in the Moon as the stars twinkled in the night sky. Nature's perfume scented the air, and as it caressed her skin, it made her feel as light as a feather, without a care in the world.

Now this is more like it. This sensation was like the one she'd experienced earlier, after consuming four glasses of champagne with Sam and Jane on an empty stomach. Why had no one mentioned this lovely part of the story? She felt she could happily stay there all night as she walked amongst the moon flowers, feeling the most relaxed she had in days.

But then, up ahead, through a forest of trees that hadn't been there a second ago, thirteen looming figures walked towards her. Thirteen elemental-souls all chosen by a higher power, twelve of whom would, soon enough, become nothing more than pure-essence, drifting around the world, gifting the mindful with a sense of more. She wondered if they saw it as a great honour to be selected, or if they inwardly cursed this process as she herself was doing right now.

Angel swallowed hard as her nerves rose once again to fill her with unease. The thirteen drew to a halt ten feet away, then placed themselves evenly in a circle around her. All were dressed in black, their faces hidden in the shadows. She turned in a slow circle, looking at each figure, and sensed a need from every single one of them. One imminent need…the desire to be chosen.

A vibrant energy swirled around her as she continued to turn to each soul with respect, waiting. She'd been given no instruction about what would happen, only that she would know, without a doubt, when her essence connected with its true partner.

She strolled towards the first man, feeling a nice energy flow from him as he grinned down at her. She reached out to take his offered hand, wondering if this was her forever partner.

He whispered, "I thank you for the honour."

She smiled as their hands met and replied, "And I, for yours."

His warm brown eyes twinkled down into hers. He had a sweet face, and he grinned, hopeful they would be a match, as he brought her hand up to his lips to brush a feather-light kiss over her knuckles. His eyes widened, startled, as he sensed his own fading before he had a chance to utter another word. A bright flash of light blinded Angel for an instant as his hand faded, along with the rest of him. His clothes dropped in a pile at her feet and his bright essence flew towards the dark night sky to join the twinkling stars.

Angel gasped, saddened that a beautiful elemental-soul who'd stood before her had departed from the only form he'd known his entire life. And now? Pure-essence. She stared after him, heart heavy with the thought of stepping towards the next soul.

She did so, wanting to apologise, but forced herself not to diminish his integrity.

He had kind eyes and offered her a small smile as he took her hand, and they shared the same ritual words before he too was taken into the arms of the night sky. To experience his fading was as shocking to her as the first. Passionate tears of frustration welled in her eyes; she hated the fact that these souls were being reduced to…well, it felt like dust.

She did not want to take another step towards any other, and glanced over her shoulder at the waterfall door, wondering how far she could make it before someone tried to stop her. Would someone stop her? One way to find out. She took a step backwards, turning.

Don't do it…do not run. You can do this. It's going to be all right. A calm, sweet voice brushed against her mind. Her heart filled with love, happiness, and calm for the briefest of moments. Who was that?

She looked about the circle, unable to see their faces. She didn't know if she was brave enough to take another step closer to any of them.

She shook her head. "I can't *do this*!" she cried desperately to the night sky.

"You must," the night sky answered.

"I don't want to," she whispered, heart heavy.

"And yet, you will. Continue, dear heart."

Was that the Man in the Moon? She felt sure it was. She sighed heavily and stepped towards the next soul, and her heart broke again, and again. Exhaustion seeped into her soul as each light drifted away to join the stars above. It was both a thing of beauty and great loss. She sighed again as she stepped towards the eighth elemental-soul, and her heart plummeted to an entirely new level of despair when he revealed himself from the shadows. She felt her body go cold instantly.

"No," she whispered in shock, covering her mouth with both hands. "Please, no."

Bowie stood before her; a sombre look across his handsome features. He seemed taller than usual. Foreboding, somehow.

She stepped back, shaking her head as one solid tear of fright finally fell from her eyes. How could she take Bowie's hand and watch him fade away? The answer was simple. She would not. They stared silently at each other as the world stilled. She swallowed, feeling a panic attack creep close, waiting just a breath away.

Angel, breathe.

I can't do this, Bowie.

You must.

I won't! She felt, more than heard, him sigh.

They selected me for a reason. If I'm to fade, then it's my destiny. Please.

She remained still, barely breathing, contemplating what to do.

Take my hand…say the words. He held out his hand, waiting.

Another tear dropped from her lashes and broke his heart. *Please don't let my last image be of you crying, Angel.*

She looked into his amber eyes and saw how hard he was trying to keep it together. He was as apprehensive as she was. She rapidly blinked away the tears that wanted to fall.

Take my hand, now.

Terrified of what would happen, she stepped closer to Bowie. *Please don't let him fade.* Anxious, she reached her small hand towards his large, waiting one. His fingers curled around her hand, his thumb stroking the soft flesh of her wrist, attempting to soothe her. He tugged her closer. She tilted her head back so she could look up into his beautiful eyes, that glowed the deepest of golds, terrified that, at any moment, he would be taken from her. Silently, she begged him not to say the words.

"I thank you for the honour," he said with conviction, his sweet breath kissing her face.

She swallowed, staring up at him as he unblinkingly returned her gaze. She would not say the words, and could not stop the tears that fell from her eyes and ran down her cheeks.

Say it, he implored.

Her lips parted, and a small sob escaped.

He squeezed her hand, his heart breaking as he witnessed her devastation. *Angel?*

"And I, for yours," she choked out in a strangled whisper, feeling as if her heart would break as he raised her hand towards his lips.

Angel closed her eyes as his lips brushed her flesh. She would not see him fade. She *refused* to!

A gust of wind tore around her, ripping the pins from her hair and slamming her hard up against Bowie's chest. His arms wrapped around her as it lifted them from the ground and spun them around. She gasped in fright as her eyes flew open. Was she fading into pure-essence too?

"Bowie?" she cried, but before either of them could think another thought, the stars dropped from the sky to dance amongst the wild wind that had now lifted them three feet above the ground. As it spun them about, the moon lowered beneath their feet, holding them on a stage as pure and sweet as anything they'd ever seen in all their days.

Thankfully, they stopped spinning and could look around.

They stood on the disc of the moon. A calming darkness surrounded them as the stars and the moon flowers lay scattered like an alluring carpet on the moon's smooth surface at their feet.

Finally, their eyes met, and that's when it happened.

Chapter Twenty-Six

A lovely, aquamarine glow emanated from Angel's chest as a warm, amber beam drifted from Bowie's. The two essences merged, twisting around the other to become one divine essence, before splitting in half, each combined essence delicately easing back into the chests of the heavenly- and elemental-soul.

Their eyes widened in disbelief, and small gasps burst from their parted lips. Bowie's eyes glowed with amber flames as he looked down into Angel's aquamarine liquid pools. In that moment, he could have happily drowned in them. The feelings within him, the pulsating energy with their combined essence, were a sublimely wonderful feeling, if not overwhelming.

She felt it too, then, the sudden power. Warm, delicious, plain-good, wholesome energy that swirled around her from head to toe. She smiled up at him and her heart beat in the most content way. He cupped her cheek, and she closed her eyes, reeling with the sensation of his touch… it was like her every cell was alive and calling to Bowie's. The connection was deeper than any she'd ever thought possible, and it was almost too overpowering for her to think a straight thought.

Overpowering is an understatement. He smiled down at her as her eyes fluttered open.

"I didn't think that," she whispered.

"No, you felt it, therefore, I felt it."

She shook her head, smiling. "I thought I was going to lose you."

His smile faded. "It broke me seeing you so upset. And now the thought of anything upsetting you is too painful to imagine." He cupped her chin, and his voice dropped huskily as he bent his head towards her. "I think I'll have to make a rule, to never see you sad from this moment on."

"Oh?" she whispered. It was so sweet that he wanted to protect her, more now than he already had in this life.

Excitement sent a flutter of butterflies scattering about her stomach as she watched his lips draw closer, parting a fraction.

"Mm-hmm." His eyes swept over hers before his lips covered hers in a soft, sweeping kiss as he drank from her sweet mouth.

What they felt as individuals in that moment was enough to send them into a passionate spiral…then they were simultaneously flooded with each other's feelings, thoughts, and emotions. It made for a whirl-wind combination of lust.

Bowie couldn't get enough of her soft lips, that parted beneath his, enabling him to press his mouth over hers, deepening the kiss. His tongue showed her what he wanted to do to the rest of her. Her soft, kitten-like sounds of pleasure had the blood pounding in his temples. Everything about her begged to be loved, from her scent, her soul, her skin, her hair…her essence. He felt close to tears that she was, and would forever be, a part of him, and he a part of her.

Every inch of Angel's flesh tingled with Bowie's attentive adminis-trations. His fingers caressed her skin, moulding her against him, his scent cradling her as if she, and she alone, was his entire world. His lips devoured hers as if she were the sweetest nectar on the planet. Each lap of his tongue against her lips, each thrust that slipped into her mouth, made her insides turn to molten lava, much like the heat she could see in his eyes. She felt as if she would both melt and explode at any moment.

They both felt each other's emotions swirl with multiple delicious desires, taking their prelude to making love to a euphoric level.

Sheesh, and all this with our clothes on? Angel thought breathlessly, immediately hearing Bowie's deep, dark laughter.

They broke for air, staring into each other's eyes as they caught their breath. He smiled at her, eyes gleaming with all he imagined doing to her as he ran his hands down her back, holding her close.

She stared at him in wide-eyed amazement with every thought and feeling they'd just shared. His long fingers continued massaging her skin through the sheer material of her dress. How could a simple, innocent touch of his fingers make her knees go weak?

"I think it's time to go home," he said, his voice husky.

She nodded, emotions high with everything that had happened. "Thank you for not fading."

He smiled again, taking her hand. "Oh, you are welcome."

He led her towards the waterfall as the moon returned to the night sky, the stars trailing merrily behind. The other elemental-souls had vanished, honoured to transition to pure-essence and make the world a sweeter place. Bowie led Angel through the waterfall and into Red's backroom, then outside. When she looked towards the backyard, past the tree ferns to Red's shed, where she potted her plants, Angel smiled. She'd spotted Alana slink out and blink at them curiously before daintily stepping towards them.

Bowie reached down to pet the fox's soft fur, whispering, "Hello, girl," before Alana dashed past them to sit under the rose bushes, waiting for Red to return.

Apart from Alana, there was not a single soul around. All was as quiet as the night sky itself.

Hand in hand, they walked under the Glenormiston moon along Black's Road, over the cattle grid, and past the hay shed, the stables, and back to the homestead. Although they didn't utter one word, they did not walk in silence, either, as every thought and feeling was automatically shared. Bowie smiled down at Angel as she wondered how they would keep birthday or Christmas presents a secret if they could hear and feel everything the other was thinking.

"We can shield our thoughts from each other, with effort, but not our feelings."

"Well, this will be interesting, that's for sure."

"Mm-hmm."

She loved the sound of his voice as it caressed her and could feel his inner chuckle at her thought.

"It will take some getting used to, won't it?" Her eyes twinkled as she looked up at him, thinking he was the most scrumptious morsel she'd ever laid eyes on, and she could not wait until his lips were crushing hers again…and more.

He smiled knowingly.

She blushed.

He laughed, wrapping his arm around her waist as he led her inside the front door and down to where the lights were still on.

As they stepped into the parlour together, several things happened simultaneously. Sam burst into tears of relief that Bowie hadn't turned to pure-essence. After returning to the homestead, she'd been informed that, at the last minute, Bowie had been instructed to join Angel's twelve other elemental-souls. She'd nearly wept in fear at the possibility of never seeing her blood-sibling again. Jane cheered and fist pumped the air.

Michael raised an eyebrow, thrilled that Bowie was still with them, but slightly shocked about his soul-sibling now being connected in such an intimate way to his blood-sibling. *Not* my *soul-sibling anymore,* he thought, unsure how to feel about it. But he was happy that, if Angel was going to be partnered with anyone, it was Bowie. Jess and Tom began clapping, and Red raced over to give them both a congratulatory kiss and a glass of champagne.

And standing beside Sam, holding her hand, was a serious-looking heavenly soul whose heart beat protectively for Sam, and Sam alone.

"Bowie, Angel, this is Peter." Sam smiled a bright, beautiful smile as she introduced her soul-partner.

Bowie stepped forward first and shook Peter's hand. "Welcome to the family."

Peter nodded and smiled. "Thank you," he said in what Angel thought was a comforting voice. She immediately missed Max, and pushed the thought aside as Bowie looked down at her. She forced a smile and reached to shake Peter's hand. "Hello, it's nice to meet you."

"The pleasure is all mine."

Sam hugged Angel. "How do you feel?"

Angel smiled, shaking her head in wonder. "I feel great, although, I didn't feel my connection with you break."

Sam nodded, "Neither did I."

"What does that mean?"

Sam shrugged, "I've no idea, but I'm grateful that hasn't changed." They shared a sisterly smile, before Sam pulled Angel into a corner to talk privately as the room filled with conversation around them.

Tom and Jess questioned Bowie about the ceremony as Red grabbed a plate of homemade sausage rolls and vegetable pasties, along with Bowie's favourite apple slice. Michael gave her a hand as Jane poured tea and Milos for those who didn't want champagne. Sam looked about the room, grateful Jane had pulled Peter into a conversation, and watched as he stood, holding his cup of Milo, listening to Jane before responding enthusiastically.

Angel followed her gaze as Sam said, "I feel so strongly for a man I've only just met, but what's horrid is, although I feel this overwhelming love for Peter... Angel...I still have feelings for Max."

"What?" Angel gasped, quickly glancing around the room. No one seemed to have heard, as she steered Sam further away. "Our connection didn't break, and you're still in love with Max?"

Sam's eyes filled with confused anguish as she nodded.

"How can this be?"

"I have no idea,"

Angel shook her head, "Well, all the legends clearly aren't true, are they?"

"Bonds breaking and connections dissolving?" Sam sighed. "I don't know how I'm supposed to juggle all my feelings, Angel. What am I going to do?"

Angel met Sam's worried gaze. "You're concerned how Max is going to react?"

Sam frowned. "Of course. I shouldn't be though, should I?" She chanced a quick look in Peter's direction, who was still engaged in a conversation with Jane.

Angel shrugged. "You're a kind, considerate soul, Sam—of course you don't want to see Max hurt."

"He's going to be hurt, though, isn't he? No matter how I feel," Sam whispered.

Angel rubbed Sam's arm, "It's all going to work out..."

"You sound so convincing, thanks." She looked towards Peter again, to find him staring at her, and flushed a becoming pink and quickly looked away. She whispered to Angel. "This is all a bit overwhelming, huh?"

Angel nodded as a comforting warmth settled over her, soothing her concern for Max and Sam. She turned her head to see Bowie staring at her, a small smile on his face as he answered Jess's question.

"May I have everyone's attention please?" Red called.

Sam squeezed Angel's arm before heading over to join Peter. Bowie was suddenly beside Angel. She looked up at him, trying to shield how desperately she wanted to kiss him right now and ask him a million questions. The warmth from his body, his scent…she could feel a vibration in the air between them when he was close. She sighed internally, leaning closer, praying it wouldn't be long until they could be alone.

He put his arm about her waist and drew her close. *Soon.*

She smiled as Red began. "It has been a big day, and I understand how tired everyone is. But we must prepare for the next stage of our mission. Bowie, you need to make sure Angel gets some solid sleep; a rested mind, you will need, before we allow Max to cart you off to the Blacks' mansion."

Bowie nodded, feeling calm and relieved; it was a miracle that he'd ended up being Angel's soul-partner, the added bonus being that he would have more control over protecting her.

Control? Angel kept her eyes on Red as she continued discussing what they may be up against in the following hours.

He grinned. *Don't take it like that, baby.*

Her heart filled with happiness. *Good, we're back to 'baby.'*

A knock sounded at the door. "That will be Max," Tom said as he went to answer it.

All eyes landed on Sam. "It will be okay." Bowie soothed his blood-sibling.

Sam looked worriedly at Bowie. "Will it?" she whispered as Tom and Max walked into the room.

It was uncomfortably silent as Max's face reflected the same pained look as Sam's before he cast his eyes in Peter's direction. The air was thick with the tension of the unknown. Angel felt a flutter of deep regret well in Max's heart and reached out, pushing love and family towards him.

He turned quickly, feeling Angel's brush against his mind, and stopped the cruel comment about to escape his lips; she'd always been kind to him, and he knew she meant well. He would not allow his hurt, this pain of seeing his love by another's side, to twist him. He forced a smile as he headed towards Bowie, hand outstretched.

"Congratulations to you both."

Bowie shook his hand, his arm still around Angel's waist, as Max bent to drop a kiss on her cheek. She placed a hand on his shoulder, squeezing lightly, and said, "You are still part of our family, Max."

He nodded, replying, "Thanks, Angel." He took a deep breath before turning around to walk over to Peter, hand outstretched. "Congratulations to you both, too."

Peter shook Max's hand, feeling a little confused. After reading all of Sam's emotions and thoughts, the confusion became clearer regarding the relationship his soul-partner and this 'Max' shared.

"Thank you." Peter released his hand as Max forced a small smile towards Sam and dropped a quick kiss against her cheek.

"Thank you, Maxwell," she whispered, overwhelmed with pain as she saw a flicker of hurt deep in his gorgeous green eyes.

Peter looked down at her, feeling her apology and the thought that Max had gorgeous eyes.

She looked up at Peter with love, and his heart settled.

"That's going to be unusually tricky," Bowie whispered against Angel's ear.

She nodded, wishing he'd continue to say something else, as his lips close to her ear caused his breath to tickle her hair, stirring sweet energy deep within her.

"Your wish is my command." He did it again.

She stopped the chuckle that almost slipped out. Guilt filled her, because glee flooded her senses while Max and Sam stood not ten feet away, both apparently in a world of pain.

Bowie squeezed her waist as Red turned to Max.

"Max, can you share the plan with the others?"

Max nodded, thanking Michael for the tea he handed to him. "Brendan knows I am here, congratulating the happy couples." He couldn't meet Sam's eyes again and, instead, focused on Red, Tom, Michael, and Jess when he spoke. "The plan moving forward is for me to absorb Angel's essence during the night, somehow getting her away from you, Bowie."

Bowie's fingers, which were massaging Angel's hip in a soothing, hypnotic circle, froze at the thought of Max taking Angel away from him, guise or not.

Angel reached up and cupped his chin, dragging his steely gaze away from Max, down to her.

"That will be fine, and easy." Angel smiled softly at Bowie as she replied to Max.

"Even heavenly souls need a human moment in the middle of the night."

Her fingers stroked the smooth skin of Bowie's flesh, wishing she could kiss him right there, along his jaw, right now. But, instead, she turned her gaze back to Max, nodding.

"Surely Brendan will be waiting for our retaliation, Max?" Michael said.

Max nodded. "He will be, which is why he plans on releasing the entire horde of Veins at three a.m. to begin the mass suicide across the Western District. He thinks that will keep you all occupied until he has Angel hooked up to begin the draining process, retrieving both her, and her soul-partner's, essence from within her."

"And if he finds out we have evacuated the entire countryside of pure-souls?" Jess asked, running his fingers through his wavy locks, feeling anxious about the unknown.

"I think we have that covered, dear." Red nodded to Jess. "We have plenty of royal-souls shadowing the pure-souls routines, so it will appear as if the pure-souls are going about their day-to-day business. They, too, will be ready when the Vein horde attacks."

"I almost wish I could be part of that action." Bowie sneered, fanta-
sising about blasting bolts of lightning into as many of the evil bastards
as he could.

Tom grinned. "I'll give you a play-by-play once we're done."

Bowie nodded. "Cool."

He is, Angel thought. *So darned cool, and so hot at the same time.*

Bowie's eyes dropped to Angel, who flushed and shook her head. This
really was going to take some getting used to. As much as Bowie wanted
to drag Angel upstairs, pin her across his bed, and have his way with her,
he knew they only had a handful of hours before Max had to take her
away.

Angel shivered, thinking about Bowie pinning her to his bed, covering her with his body, and devouring her. Her eyes met Sam's, who was
grinning, too. Angel rolled her eyes, shaking her head…it was time to
start shielding her thoughts from everyone.

Michael shifted uncomfortably, and Jane laughed. "This is better than
a game of charades."

"You think so?" Michael grimaced, making Sam and Jane laugh
loudly.

"All right, dears, let's focus please." Red went to a side table where the
decanters sat amongst thick, white candles, and poured herself a small
glass of red wine. She took a mouthful and turned to the others. "Continue, Max."

Max cleared his throat, wishing this entire operation was already over.
Then he could consider his next move with a clear head, and get on with
the rest of his sorry, sad existence without Sam by his side.

"Right, well, I have considered a couple of things. I think it would be
in Angel's best interest if she were actually unconscious when I take her
to Brendan."

"No way in hell," Bowie snapped.

Max held up a hand in explanation. "As much as Angel may be a brilliant actress, if she is conscious when Brendan gets his hands on her to extract her remaining essence, then he'll know I didn't do my part in capturing her."

"You can always say you didn't have time?" Michael shrugged stiffly, not liking all this talk of anyone sucking Angel's essence. The years they'd used him for his power still filled him with dread and anxiety. He'd been grateful when the Council had informed him that they were giving him time to mentally heal before he would have to enter into any soul-essence ceremony.

"That's a better idea," Sam agreed. "I mean, is he really going to interrogate you on the method you used to abduct her? Surely he will just be thrilled you have her, no matter her state of consciousness?" Her words forced Max to look at her. When he did, she wished she'd kept her mouth shut. His eyes were pools that reflected all the emotions of regret, hurt, sorrow, and loss. And a sexy hint of anger. She flinched before Peter put his arm around her shoulder to comfort her.

What a mess. She shielded her thoughts from Peter, with effort, and sent them directly to Angel, who offered her a small, sympathetic smile.

"I think I can be useful in this scenario if I am conscious, Max," Angel said. "It will give us more time to distract Brendan while we wait for the cavalry to arrive. We can trap him with the illusion that he is in control."

"We don't want to trap him, we want to fry him," Bowie snarled. Michael agreed.

Red nodded. "That's the plan, eventually. When you enter the mansion, I, along with the Light Accords Council, will place a powerful binding spell around the property so that Brendan cannot escape."

"And then?" Angel asked Red.

"And then we will end him, in the hope of eradicating them all."

Angel felt the weight of the world on her shoulders for a few moments, heavy with all she wished she could do right at this second to save Mother

Earth and the pure-souls. Anxiety threatened, before Bowie pushed a calming intention towards her, enveloping her in love.

"Can we go now?" she blurted, wanting to be alone with Bowie before the next stage began.

Tom checked his watch. It was nearing midnight. "Yes."

Angel felt relief sweep through her. *Finally!*

"Bowie, I need to speak to you for a second. Good night, Angel." Tom was dismissing her.

Angel nodded and raced around the room, kissing all of them good-night before she stopped in front of Bowie. She looked at him and said softly, "I'll see you in a minute?"

He cupped her chin and brushed the sweetest kiss across her lips. "You will."

Her stomach clenched in excited anticipation, and she skipped out of the room as she headed upstairs.

"Angel," Max called after her.

She turned from the top of the staircase to look down at him, standing in the shadows of the foyer.

"I'll see you in a couple of hours." It wasn't a question.

She nodded. "I'll meet you down here at a-quarter-to-three."

It was his turn to nod before he said, "I won't let him hurt you."

Poor Max. Her heart broke for him. "I know, Max. Thank you."

"Get some sleep."

She smiled. "I think you should, too, even a couple of hours will help."

"Sure."

She smiled again before heading up to the landing and into the bathroom to freshen up, hoping Bowie would be right behind her.

Chapter Twenty-Seven

S mooth, sweet lips swept across hers, sweeping her up in a dream that she did not want to wake from. His warm body pressed heavily against hers, and she almost wept when he moved away.

"No," she pleaded, eyes still closed, fingers reaching for his warmth. "Come back."

Bowie obliged, placing his body against hers, the twisted blankets shifting between them as he covered her mouth with his, kissing her awake, evoking a deep desire within them both.

"Wake up, baby…" he sighed against her lips.

She opened her eyes to see the room lit by the glow of one candle. And that's when the realisation came to her; they'd not had one minute together since she'd come upstairs. In fact, she was still fully dressed in her ceremony dress. The last thing she recalled after leaving the bathroom was coming into her room to grab her pj's, planning on going into Bowie's room. Moonie had been curled up on the bed before stretching out for a tummy rub. She'd obliged, and could not resist the temptation to bury her face into his soft fur before he'd reached out his paw and tapped her nose. She'd fallen asleep in a second.

"*Moonie*," she whispered, exasperated. How had he done it again? She shook her head, staring at Bowie with a mixture of frustration and desire.

He laughed, sliding his arms around her, and pulling her up against him, holding her close as he buried his face into her neck, breathing her in. "Sleep was necessary, and important for what's to come." He nuzzled her neck before trailing a gentle kiss along her flesh, causing goosebumps to follow and ignite a fire within her loins.

It was Tom's firm words, commanding Bowie to allow Angel to sleep, which had prevented him from coming up directly after her, to have his wicked way with her. He brushed his lips against her ear, his tongue flicking inside, making her shiver. She moaned softly, winding her arms around his neck as she pushed her body closer to his; her lips found his chin, seeking his. He collected her mouth hungrily, feeling his entire body react to her in the most pleasurable of ways.

My God, it would only take a minute, and it would feel so darned good... Yes...

Cursing, he got off the bed and pulled her to her feet. He would not allow their first time to be 'wham, bam, thank you, ma'am'.

"We can't do this right now, baby. It's time to go."

Angel sighed regretfully, her body tingling all over. "I know." She pushed her hands through her hair, gathering it up in a high ponytail, and tying it back.

"I miss you already," she whispered, staring at him wide-eyed.

He sighed, reaching out to cup her chin. He didn't need to tell her he felt the same way; she felt it.

A knock sounded at the door before Sam called out, "It's time."

Angel nodded, looking into Bowie's amber eyes, which glowed a burnt orange as he said, "Here we go, show time."

"To say 'I love you' right now doesn't seem like enough," she whispered.

He took her hand, kissing it before leading her to the door, his stomach in knots as he brushed against her mind. *You are my universe.*

Her heart melted as she looked up at him, his profile, pure male beauty, as he looked down at Sam. "Everything set?"

Sam nodded. "Max is waiting."

They headed downstairs to where the hunting party had gathered in the foyer. Max stood in the open front door, standing slightly away from the group, a frown marring his features.

Angel walked towards him. "You okay?"

Max almost laughed. "Sure," he replied.

Angel didn't have time to worry about the glint in Max's eyes as Michael reached out for her.

"Time to go, Angel." He hugged her briefly before turning to Max. "You'll be okay, we won't be far behind you."

Max nodded before looking back at Angel. "Let's do this."

She turned to Bowie, gave him a brief kiss, and smiled up into his eyes. "I will definitely be seeing you soon."

"Save some action for us," Sam said brightly, in a way of farewell to them both.

Max looked over his shoulder at her before opening the boot to the sports car Brendan had gifted him.

Angel sighed as she walked to the open boot, and, turning around, aimed her backside into the boot and rolled into it, tucking her legs behind her. The last thing she saw before Max dropped the boot closed on her were the faces of those she'd loved since forever.

Angel

Angel gasped as Max sped out of the college grounds and over the speed bumps, with no apparent concern for her getting slammed around in the boot. She felt the tyres ricochet over the cattle grid before they raced out of the front entrance and along Glenormiston Road, heading towards Noorat and the Blacks' mansion.

She reached out to Max. *Are you up for this, Max?* They both knew she could have called it out, and he would have heard her. But it was her way of reminding him he was one of them.

I am, don't worry.

Of course I worry, I love you like a brother.

She felt his smile, felt his heart warm a little.

I'll be fine. I'm approaching the driveway. I'll need you to put on a good struggle.

I will. Forgive me if I hurt you.

This time she heard him laugh aloud as he turned into the driveway. The car bumped over the pot-holed gravel towards the mansion.

Once Max turned off the engine and lights, he opened the car door. Angel took a deep breath, hearing his feet crunch on the gravel as he walked towards the boot.

"Good timing, Max." Angel cringed, hearing the grating voice of Brendan Black call out from the front door. Seven years hadn't been long enough.

"Three a.m. on the dot."

"It was almost too easy, cousin."

Angel shivered upon hearing Max's reply. He sounded cold and aloof, so like his cousin in that moment. She prepared herself to lash out and put on a good show. When Max opened the boot, she surprised them both as she aimed a solid kick right into the middle of his six-pack, which sent him flying backwards, landing hard on his backside.

Max cursed as Angel leapt out of the boot and flew around him. She raced over the gravel and towards the soft grass, heading towards the main road.

Brendan's laughter floated after her.

Creep much? Angel pushed towards Max, who was, by now, running after her.

Angel, you mustn't go past the next tree! he implored. *Let me catch you!*

They'd both underestimated her speed down the hill, and his not being able to catch her in time. As Angel flew by the tree Max had tried to warn her about, she wished she'd never been born.

The black force-field felt as though it had sliced her body in half. She felt sick to her core and collapsed in a heap; ice-cold needles drove through every inch of her being, probing her flesh, burrowing into her essence. The pain was beyond unbearable, depleting her of everything. She could not even gasp, let alone scream, as the blackness took everything from her.

Max

Max looked over his shoulder at Brendan, who raised his hand and beckoned with his fingers before walking back inside the house. He cursed as he looked about. The others wouldn't be here for another five minutes. Just as well…Bowie would go insane if he'd witnessed this incident.

"Shh," he whispered to Angel as he scooped her up, trying to offer her some comfort. Her body was in complete shock due to the debilitating pain inflicted upon her when she'd run through the containment barrier. Her fingers were stiff and unnaturally-bent, as if she'd experienced shock therapy. Max checked her feet as he hurried back towards the mansion, noticing her arches were bent and her toes were curled.

Shit! He knew he couldn't heal her, otherwise Brendan would notice. This was a catastrophe!

He pushed the front door open, then kicked it shut behind him as he hurried into the lounge area. The door slammed as he strode into the front room, where Brendan stood by the roaring fire. He placed Angel down on the couch.

"I thought you were going to drain her?" Brendan walked over, looking down at the pretty little thing, who was as stiff as a piece of three-day-old roadkill.

Max tried for casual. "Too boring. More fun this way."

"Mm, well. Let's get her attached to the drains, start pumping that juicy essence out of her."

"You know, her essence won't be half as delicious if she is left in this condition…" Max raised an eyebrow.

"Too right. Straighten her bends out, then by all means, have a feed before we hook her up. I will release the horde. Good teamwork." He laughed, clapping his hands together in joy as he walked out of the room and up towards the attic windows, so he could project his will towards the swirling mass in Mount Noorat's basin.

"Thanks, Brendan, can't wait," Max called after his cousin's retreating footsteps before rolling his eyes.

Once he knew he was alone, he knelt by Angel's side and, placing a hand over his heart, his other over Angel's forehead, he whispered a healing incantation.

"With vile a force and shock bar none, I beg thee, cruel fingers, to come undone." Nothing?

He tried it again, and again, desperately trying to heal Angel. If Bowie and the others arrived, and Angel was in this condition? He didn't want to think about it.

"Come on, Angel, come on!" he whispered fervently before removing his hand from her forehead and placing it over her heart. He whispered the incantation for several minutes before finally, blessedly, Angel's eyes flew open, followed by a God-almighty scream escaping her lips, deafening him.

She slapped Max away from her as she launched to her feet, eyes as wide as Lake Corangamite.

"Hey, hey, hey, Angel. *Relax,* it's okay." Max's heart raced as he looked at her closely.

Her eyes were wild and feral, and he realised that she had no recollection of who he was. This wasn't going the way it was supposed to... although, perhaps that could work to their advantage?

But no, it wouldn't. Because she now assumed he was nothing more than a vile Vein who was out to get her essence. The shock of the force-field must have done something to her memory, and although she might not know who he was, her essence felt it. At least, felt his evil half, judging by her reaction. Did she even know who *she* was?

"Angel Cloud," he tried. *Hang on, do heavenly souls take on their ele-mental-soul's surname when they, well...when they became an item?*

"Angel Storm," he tried this time.

She blinked at him as she took a step back, her body shivering uncontrollably with little spasms. So, he'd healed her enough to enable her body to function, but the force-field held a power he'd never seen before.

Brendan's footsteps drew nearer as he headed towards them down the long, dark corridor, before he strolled into the room.

"What's this?" he seemed confused that Max was not filling his body with her essence.

"Well, the force-field has had an impact on her, she's more confused than afraid. So, knowing that essence tastes all the sweeter with either fear or euphoria, I thought I'd wait for you." Max thought that sounded good enough. Surely the others would be here soon? He sent up a silent prayer to the Angels that that would be the case.

"Good thinking." Brendan grinned and crossed over to the mantel. He reached inside a small, wooden box and pulled out a syringe with a wicked-looking needle, before heading across to Angel.

She instinctively went to run, but Max grabbed her, holding her in place. Brendan advanced and slid the needle into her arm, watching her wide eyes quickly drift shut, and a soft sigh escaped her lips before she sagged in Max's arms. Max sighed in relief himself as he scooped her up and walked to the couch to lay her down again.

"Who's going first?" Brendan asked.

Max thought he'd better, because, knowing Brendan, he would drain her dry without giving her amulet a chance to recharge her heart before the gang arrived.

"Well, considering I brought her here, I will, thanks."

"Of course." Brendan pulled Max's ruby out of his pocket, and tossed it across to Max.

"Put it on. It will absorb and hold her joint essences and, let me tell you, there may come a time you will need the aid of a royal-essence."

Max frowned down at the ruby that had created so much trouble for him.

"Go on, put it on." Brendan challenged after Max stood there for a moment, looking down at it in his hand.

Meeting his cousin's eyes, he unwillingly dropped it around his neck before turning to stand over Angel, who was lying limply on the couch. He took a deep breath and opened his arms, willing the others to get here already.

"What are you waiting for?" Brendan raised an eyebrow. Why was his cousin, who'd been so keen earlier, and doing what he was born to do over the past week that they'd been together, now suddenly hesitant to hurt the girl?

Max forced a smile, sensing Brendan's doubt in his ability to do what he must, and answered, "Just revelling in the anticipation."

Brendan nodded as Max held in his curse, and forced his thin, black veins to pierce through his skin and slide toward Angel. He could have wept with both absolute terror at what he was about to do to her, and pure joy at the anticipation of her delicious essence, which would soon run through his body.

The tips of his veins caressed Angel's flesh, sending a thrill within him, before he forced them to penetrate her skin, burying themselves deep within her, sucking greedily on her blood, her soul-essence. He closed his eyes in bliss, halting the laughter about to spill from his lips. She was pure divinity. As he focused on trying not to absorb too much, yet putting on a good show for his cousin, the ground suddenly shook beneath the house, startling them.

"What the devil?" Brendan spat. He looked about them as the house shook again. He stumbled back a few steps as the floor beneath his feet lurched. Glancing across at Max, he yelled, "Release from her, we're under attack!"

Max snapped his veins back into his arms, thinking, *finally,* before the front door crashed open, and every single window in the house imploded.

Chapter Twenty-Eight

Max

What happened next was no real surprise to Max.

Bowie, Sam, Peter, and Michael stormed through the front door, and, from the looks on their faces, they'd seen Max through the window, consuming Angel's essence. They'd all been aware of the possibility of that happening, to keep Max undercover, but it didn't ease their revulsion all the same.

Bowie and Sam were both filled with fury. The air whipped around them, wildly charged with their anger.

Brendan laughed; not exactly the reaction they'd anticipated.

Michael frowned as he and Bowie exchanged a quick glance.

"Welcome royal-souls, to your own funeral! Maxwell—*assorbire tutto!*"

Before Max could blink, the ruby shone brightly, casting a blinding red glow out and towards the royal-souls, including Angel, and began absorbing their energy. Confusion filled their faces, followed by shock, then despair as each felt as if their life were being drained from them, weakening them, leaving them defenceless. That was one of the ruby's tricks: making the victim feel powerless.

Peter grabbed Sam and thrust her behind him as the ruby absorbed his essence.

"Peter. *No!*" Sam yelled, and went to step around him. Her heart thumped miserably to feel his pain.

Be still, I've got this. He flung a hand towards Max. With the combination of his Heavenly, and Sam's Elemental essences swirling within him, he flung a small cyclone in Max's direction, forcing him to slide backwards along the floorboards before slamming him against the wall.

Max saw stars as his head cracked against the brick wall; his back felt as if it had broken. Still, the ruby shone, and continued absorbing their energy.

Brendan watched, highly entertained, as Bowie staggered across to where Angel lay, unresponsive. What did the boy possibly think he could do in this situation?

Bowie lay a hand over Angel's heart, trying to remain calm as a black rage filled him at having to feel the agony swirling within her. His eyes raised to meet Brendan's before a wicked grin broke over his pale, handsome features. Before Brendan could grow curious about his intentions, Bowie flung his hand towards Brendan, sending a massive energy surge of white lightning straight into his chest.

The ancient Vein cried in both surprise and pain as he staggered backwards. There was no way the young royal should have the amount of power required to inflict this kind of pain.

Bowie continued charging the lightning bolt, noticing that the glow of the ruby faded with each thrust of power.

Sam felt a spark of hope as she saw the ruby's glow dim. Bowie's electric charge was weakening it. She rushed around Peter and towards Max. "Sorry, Max!" she yelled before forcing a surge of lightning straight towards the ruby, attempting to short-circuit it and not burn Max to a crisp at the same time.

The house rumbled as the ground beneath it shifted once more, causing the floorboards under their feet to buck and groan. They heard an eerie, unfamiliar sound in the distance as the horde of Veins attempted to destroy the earth.

It was in that moment that Angel's eyes flew open. Despair and grief filled her as Mother Earth beneath them screamed in pain.

Bowie sensed it, the moment she woke, but kept his focus solely on Brendan as he continued to send both the energy surge into Brendan, and force healing energy into Angel's heart.

Angel blinked rapidly as she tried to take in the scene before her. After noticing the situation at hand, she placed her hand on top of Bowie's. Feeling his essence swirl within her, dancing beside hers, she whispered to Mother Earth and the Angels above for the strength to assist Bowie in whatever needed to be done.

Bowie could feel the divine energy within Angel surge up into his palm, which was pressed against her chest. What happened next made all the things the Light Accords had whispered about Angel throughout all these years suddenly make sense.

Complete power filled his body as their combined essences beat between them. It passed from Angel and shot straight to his core before bursting out of his extended hand, which was pointed towards Brendan Black. It slammed into the Vein with a current of electrified, searing light. Brendan screamed in both surprise and agony, before he suddenly exploded into a bloody puddle of pulp and bones that hissed and sizzled in an abominable, wet pile on the floorboards.

The ruby's glow diminished, and Max rolled over onto his side, breathless, as relief and pain simultaneously swept through him.

Apart from the hissing of Brendan's remains, and the heavy breathing from everyone, the room was silent.

It was then that the quiet chanting outside filtered through the broken windows and, looking out, Michael saw that the royal-souls were guarding a clear dome with an electric blue outline. The ruinous horde trapped within it swarmed desperately about, seeking escape, only to get vaporized when they neared the outer rim of the dome.

Outside of the dome, above and in the distance, the dawn sky was lit with a disturbing red glow that made little sense at that moment.

His gaze scanned the crowd until he spotted Red, Tom, Jess, and many other royal-souls containing the horde as Fletch turned and headed over towards the house. Stepping inside, he nodded to Michael as he took stock of the room, noticing the remains of Brendan Black. Looking over at Angel and Bowie, he said. "We need you outside, quickly. We have most of the horde contained, but we need you to perform an eradication spell on them, and then a healing spell to the earth."

Bowie's eyes widened in alarm as he looked down at Angel, before taking her other hand and pulling her to her feet. "You okay, baby?"

She had no idea how she was in that moment; she squeezed his hand in answer instead.

"Sam, Peter, get Max to the homestead. He has cleared himself of all charges." Fletch turned to Michael. "Let's go."

Peter reached a hand down to Max, who graciously took it as he looked up at Sam. Concern filled her amber eyes, and, as Peter pulled Max up, she grabbed the ruby necklace and ripped it from his neck, tossing it to the floor in disgust.

"Thanks," Max whispered, immediately relieved to have the thing gone.

"You're welcome." She tucked herself under his other shoulder, and, together with Peter, helped him out of the room, towards the front door, and outside.

Michael followed Fletch, joining the circle of Soul Keepers containing the vile mass, more than ready to pour his energy into removing this filth from Mother Earth and the pure-souls, hopefully once and for all.

Angel

Angel took a deep breath, relieved that most of the pain within her had faded. To know Brendan was nothing more than a dripping mess on the floorboards filled her with some sense of justice. She met Bowie's cool gaze and brought their joined hands up to her lips, then kissed his knuckles. "Thank you."

He smiled, before he whispered with such tenderness, "You…are welcome. Are you ready, my love?"

Her heart melted. "I am."

They stepped outside, and Angel sucked in a breath as the wild wind nearly knocked her over. Bowie held her hand tight as he led her into the centre of the gathering. They were both alarmed to see the sky lit up as though it were on fire. Mount Noorat was putting on a spectacular show, sending molten lava shooting towards the sky.

Now, at least, they had the answer as to why the ground had been shifting beneath them; the Veins had activated the dormant volcano that had been sleeping for twenty-thousand years.

The Light Accords Council had their arms raised high, holding the swarming Veins within the dome as they chanted. Sheer love for all the royal-souls filled Angel as, once again, they were doing all they could to ensure Mother Earth and all her pure-souls would be kept as safe as they could be.

"The horde is feeding off the mountain's energy!" Fletch yelled. "You need to contain the eruption before we can bring this mass down!"

Bowie nodded, squeezing Angel's hand as the wind almost blinded them. "Shield," he whispered. Instantly, he and Angel were in their own protected sphere, cutting them off from the wild wind, enabling them to hold their focus on the spewing mountain and their mission.

One hand clasped firmly in the other's, they each raised their free hand towards the mountain as they softly chanted as one:

"Ash and fire from deep within,

sleep again and cause no sin;
evil fingers raised you high,
light and love bids you goodbye."

Over and over they chanted, their voices rising higher above the wild wind outside their sphere until they were shouting, forcing their will and power towards the hissing mountain that shook the ground beneath their feet once more.

As Angel continued chanting with Bowie, she was aware of his fingers wrapped around her hand. His thumb brushed her flesh, backwards and forwards, as he focused both on the mission and making sure she felt his presence. She was filled with love, and, despite the surrounding chaos, she couldn't have been happier. The voices of the Light Accords contained the filth within, and, as she and Bowie continued, she prayed to Mother Earth and the Angels above:

Hear me now, I beg you please,
Let me put your heart at ease.
Trust me now, for I alone,
Will heal and restore the final tone,
Re-wild our world to put all right,
My tears will heal all before end of night.

Bowie could feel her prayer vibrate within him. She did not falter once, as she chanted along with him, trying to soothe the mountain. It amazed him that she could do both with so much power.

The moment the last word left Angel's thoughts, a deep, resonant sound permeated the air around them as the dome shattered into a million pieces. The horde were sucked through the air with such force, such violence, along with the volcanic ash, lava, and smoke, it was a wonder the royal-souls weren't ripped to pieces themselves. But Bowie had whispered to the wind and surrounded them all in a force field of protection.

They stood silently, exhausted and relieved, watching the black mass of Veins vanish into the mountain's mouth as the sky cleared of the volcanic residue. One final rumble shook the earth, and an eerie gurgling permeated the air as Mount Noorat consumed the horde, before sweet silence ensued as morning broke.

Angel looked up at Bowie and smiled through her tears of exhaustion. He wrapped his arms around her, tucking her against his chest, brushing a kiss on the top of her head.

Michael approached them with Tom and Red. "We'll need to perform a cleansing spell," Red said to Michael, who nodded.

"Aunty." Jane slipped her arm around Red's tiny waist. "We can take care of the healing. Why don't you head home, put the kettle on and your feet up?"

"That sounds like a good idea, Jane." Vicki Light smiled. "Come on, Red." She offered Red her arm, not giving the wilful lady an option, and led her to the waiting portal that would whisk them back to the cottage.

"How are you feeling?" Michael asked Bowie, dropping a hand on his shoulder.

Bowie reached out and placed his hand on Michael's shoulder and smiled. "Like I could sleep for a decade."

"Yeah," Michael replied, looking around them as the heavenly souls began blessing Mother Earth with healing spells. "I hear you there."

Fletch approached them. "That was a great effort. Well done."

"Thank you," Bowie and Michael replied together.

"The royal-souls who shadowed the pure-souls around the District have had great success in their mission, also. Although some of our enemy did escape, our elders have reported low activity of negative energy, the lowest they have felt in a decade."

"That's a relief." Michael raised an eyebrow. "Is that worldwide, or just the Western District?"

"At the moment, it is worldwide. According to Max, Brendan commanded the entire European army, so we believe the majority have been wiped out."

"That's a start." Bowie tiredly ran a hand through his wind-swept locks, pushing it out of his eyes.

"Now we can really focus on restoring the stability of Mother Earth without continual interference," Angel muttered against Bowie's chest, not wanting to leave his warmth, his scent, the safety of his arms.

"Yes," Fletch answered, hearing her despite her talking into Bowie's shirt.

"If we can restore the planet's biodiversity, then the pure-souls have a chance to avoid mass-extinction," Michael stated.

Bowie met Angel's gaze as she tipped her head back to look up into his amber eyes.

She nodded. "If they are intelligent enough to learn from their mistakes, to finally listen to their one and only planet, to stop the greed and pay attention, and celebrate the simple things in life again. But will they?"

Bowie smiled as her jewel-like eyes glistened with hope. He could also see how depleted of energy she was. "It will be up to us to help them work it all out, in time. But first, I think a few hours' sleep is in store, don't you?"

She yawned and nodded. Even Moonie's assistance would not be required this time around. She would come back to the mountain later this afternoon and pour her healing love into the soils, as promised, and grow the wild around Mount Noorat, as it had once been. Growth that would then continue to spill out into the District and surrounding areas to stabilise Mother Earth and restore her biodiversity in their domain.

It could be done. *It will be done*, Angel silently vowed. And, she vowed, she would not stop, not until every inch of Mother Earth was once again restored to the wild. She'd give the pure-souls a final chance to prove that they were, in fact, a kind and intelligent species that deserved the gift they'd been born into…the world.

And you won't be doing it alone. Bowie dropped a sweet, quick kiss against her lips before he said to Michael, "Let's go home."

Angel wrapped her arms around his waist as they followed Michael to the wild wind portal that would take them directly back to the homestead. She was so looking forward to falling into bed.

Inside the Blacks' mansion, shattered glass lay in every room; the curtains performed a slow, macabre dance as the breeze playfully whispered its secrets of what was to come.

Silence dominated, until Brendan's blood, which had pooled thickly on the floorboards amongst sinew and bone, dripped down into the thin cracks in the floorboards, falling to the damp cellar. As the last drop splattered into the bloody puddle below, the ruby activated and sent a surge of the royal-souls' energy down towards the pool of blood, charging it, creating a pulsing beat.

With each beat, the blood stirred, before moving itself in a circular motion. And as the beat increased, so, too, did the swirl, raising itself from the damp stones of the cellar until it was a glistening red vortex, spinning in a frenzy.

Hours passed before the mass halted, freezing mid-air, before stretching, forming, becoming the shape of a human as skin grew to spread along the red mass. Once formed, the naked figure turned towards the cellar stairs, and, with jerky movements like that of a toddler, learning to walk, staggered to the rooms above.

Locating a bedroom, it opened a drawer and pulled out items of clothing. It pulled on jeans, boots, and a shirt. It glanced at its reflection in the mirror and raked long fingers through the thick, blonde hair that fell into its amber eyes…eyes that shone with flames. It smiled a handsome smile before turning to leave the room, to prepare for its next phase of terror.

Chapter Twenty-Nine

Angel was grateful for the soothing heat of the shower, though it did little to replenish her energy levels. Still tired, she opened her bedroom door and her eyes widened in surprise at the sight before her.

Healing clear quartz lay scattered amongst the bowls filled with chamomile and lavender that had been placed around the room. The open window welcomed in the breeze to carry the soothing scents towards her. Calming music tinkered at the quietest volume and there, lying in her bed on fresh sheets, was the most delicious sight of all, soothing to her soul.

Bowie lay on his back, hands behind his head, eyes closed, the sheet covering just enough to make him decent. Yet it revealed tantalising narrow hips, and a trail of golden hair under his belly-button that led down a mouth-watering path, pointing under the sheet. She moved her gaze up, swallowing her drool as her eyes glowed hungrily at the sight of his firm six-pack and chest sculpted to perfection. Bowie Storm, in her bed. Waiting for her.

Despite all Bowie's golden glory, her body needed as much rest as his, and with care, willpower, and consideration, she pushed her wanton desire to claim him aside, and slipped into the bed beside him. She turned on her side to watch him, tucked her hands under her cheek, and kept her eyes on him as long as she could. The rhythmic sound of his breathing, his comforting scent, and the tinkering music had her asleep within thirty seconds.

Angel stretched her body, yawning as she flexed her arms above her head before rolling onto her tummy, burying her face into her pillow. It was then, when long, soothing fingers worked on the knots along her neck, down her back, and lower, that she remembered she wasn't alone in her bed.

She felt him smile before he dropped his face into the back of her neck, pressing his warm, naked body up against hers. Her heartbeat accelerated and her blood beat against her eardrums as he kissed slow, lazy kisses along her neck, towards her ear. His fingers hypnotically drew circles over the soft flesh of her back as he whispered into her ear, making her shiver, "Good afternoon, Angel Baby."

She smiled, loving the sound of that, and rolled over to look up at him, beaming. "Good afternoon, Bowie." *My God, was she really lying naked with Bowie Storm?*

"Yes, you are," he grinned.

She smiled.

Bowie leaned up on an elbow, his fingers continuing to stroke her side, his amber eyes glowing. She had no idea about the amount of control it had taken him, lying there beside her for over an hour, to keep his hands off her. He'd watched her sleep, imagining all he wanted to do to her. He would have taken his time exploring her soft, sensual body, and every kiss, every touch, every stroke, every thrust, lick, lap, and suck would have been entirely with her pleasure in mind.

She flushed red as she felt every detailed thought he'd wanted to do to her whilst she'd slept. Her body pulsed eagerly. His expression, suddenly so serious, stole her breath away as his eyes met hers, before dropping to her lips, then back again. Her eyes widened as her body grew heavy in anticipation of their joining. So did his.

She shook her head, reaching out to touch his face, to run her fingers through his silky hair. Her gaze dropped hungrily to his lips before meeting his eyes, which had turned a deep gold with lust. Her body was pulsating, ready, feeling as though she would explode at his single touch. She whispered breathlessly, "How can it feel this good when we haven't done anything yet?"

He smiled, predatorily, as his hand slipped against her lower back, drawing her flush up against his firm, throbbing body. He held her against him so she could feel his desire for her, filling her with a river of molten lava that pooled between her thighs. She moaned softly, her eyes drifting closed, thinking she would go out of her mind…and he hadn't even kissed her yet.

He cupped the back of her head, loving the feel of her silken tresses against his fingers. He wanted to bask in every inch of her being. Bowie leaned down, his lips a breath away from hers, and waited for her eyes to open.

With his wishing it, she opened her eyes, lips slightly parted as she tried to catch her breath, every cell and nerve ending on fire. She slipped her leg over his hip, bringing them even closer. When he felt her moist flower open for him, he took a deep breath, trying not to lose control, as his hot arousal for her wanted immediate entrance to her core.

When she heard his reaction to their proximity, she grinned and pulled him the remainder of the way down, so they could finally have their way with each other. His lips sank into hers, drinking deeply as his hand on her back ran lower, to cup her firm bottom, massaging it before his finger swept along her peach split and stroked her slick opening.

She gasped against his mouth as delight flooded her, and they smiled together as she wiggled closer.

Her fingers stroked along his neck, loving the feel of his silky hair as it tickled the back of her fingers. She could feel his throbbing shaft nestled warmly against her beating core, slick and ready. He moved against her, and she moaned again, seeing stars as the pleasure built.

He angled his head, deepening the kiss as his fingers circled the stigma of her flower, over and over again, butterfly soft, then just a touch harder. She melted beneath him and gasped as delicious sensations had her shivering in pure euphoria, which had him doing the same. He sucked in his breath, breathing her in as he buried his face against her neck, trailing hot, wet kisses over her flesh, driving them both insane.

She rocked against him. "Now, Bowie…" she groaned, pushing her breasts against his chest. She ran her hand down his back and grabbed his buttocks to push him closer to her centre. "Please, right now."

With their shared desires, each throb, each thrill, had them reeling out of their minds before he'd even thrust himself into her moist core. He guided the tip of his throbbing shaft to her entrance, and they both nearly lost it. And then, finally, blessedly, he glided inside her, filling her completely.

They saw stars and felt the universe around them shift as he rocked in and out and against her in a hypnotic dance. She wanted to cry with all the pleasurable feelings building; it was almost too much to bear. Every stroke, breath, and touch were driving her over the edge, she didn't know anything so beautiful could exist. It was mind-blowingly overwhelming as each movement had her heart beating with love for her soul-partner.

When he sensed her love, her need, Bowie claimed her lips once more and joined her on their passionate journey, letting her know she would never, ever be alone. He pumped his hips, hitting her core, sending ripples of pleasure throughout her body, causing a wave to ebb and flow. She sighed happily as he drank from her, and then, as he thrust again, she sucked on his tongue, wishing she could suck on all of him.

That thought had him almost surging over the edge, and he quickly rolled her onto her back, covering her body with his. Her legs wrapped around him, opening her wider as he thrust into her deeply, again and again.

She almost cried at the intensity of his lovemaking as he pumped against her, hitting her moist core and pulsating stigma repeatedly. With each thrust, a gentle wave peaked and swelled, causing multiple sensations within her to crest higher and higher, before reaching a shattering climax, sending them both over the edge and into pure euphoria.

Bowie crushed her possessively against him as he dropped his face into her neck, trailing his nose along her flesh. Breathing heavily, he whispered, "My beautiful Angel..."

Her arms wound tightly around him, and tears of love and pure joy spilled from her eyes as she unintentionally sent a rainbow wave to burst around them. He rolled them over, so she lay on top of his chest, and he smiled up into her aquamarine liquid pools, appreciating the soft glow of colours before the rainbow faded.

She bit her bottom lip as she dropped her chin onto his chest, looking into his eyes as he put a hand behind his head, making it easier to look at her.

"So..." she smiled.

"So?"

"Here we are."

"Indeed." He grinned, running a finger along her cheek before tucking a strand of hair behind her ear.

"I had no idea it would be like that, did you?" she asked, almost shyly.

He shook his head, his expression serious. "All I ever want for you is your happiness."

She smiled and brushed her lips over his. "As long as I have you by my side, I'll be forever happy."

He smiled, then kissed her, lingering on her lips, nibbling. He moaned as she sat astride him, not breaking the kiss. Bowie read every thought she intended as she nestled her moist centre over his already throbbing tip, and slid down onto him, pushing him deep inside her once more. He wanted to laugh it felt so darned good, and he felt her smile beneath his lips.

She rocked against him, moaning in pleasure before he sat up, putting his arms around her and holding her tightly as she moved against him, her arms circling his neck. She glided up and down, building the most delicious wave as she rocked against him, faster, taking him in harder as they drank sensually from each other in every way.

Angel arched her back, crying in delight as his lips ran down her smooth neck to her breast to suck on a plump nipple. It drove a wave from deep within her belly, rising to crash and spread in her core as she ground against him harder and faster.

Bowie could not get enough as he kissed and sucked her soft flesh, pumping his hips harder to send himself deep within her. As he grazed her nipple with his teeth, his shaft sliding in deeply, hitting her core, she cried out as her orgasm tightened around him, screaming out his name in pure ecstasy, which sent him falling over the edge into paradise.

Their laughter filled the room as their eyes met, and he shook his head, smiling. "If it's going to be like this every time, I'm not sure I'll survive."

"I'm not sure we'll be able to leave this room," Angel said as Bowie tucked her in his arms and snuggled them both back under the covers. Tiredness overcame her.

"Sleep," he whispered.

"I need to be at Mount Noorat around nine p.m.," she replied.

"Okay, I promise to have you there by then. But first, sleep." He kissed her closed eyelids, and she was asleep in seconds.

Chapter Thirty

The dining room was abuzz with chatter, ranging from the menu choices to the eradication of Brendan Black. They also discussed activities for the following day, and an event the college was holding in a month's time for the WWF—the Worldwide Fund—for nature, featuring their special guest speaker; Sir D. A. The pure-souls saw him as a legend who defended the planet and its innocent creatures, but the royal-souls knew him as he truly was; an imperial honoured member of the Light Accords for over five-hundred years.

"I think it will be my second-favourite thing to celebrate this year," Angel said to Tom as Jess placed a bowl of minestrone soup in front of her.

Bowie smiled, knowing their soul-essence joining ceremony was her favourite thing.

"Thanks, Jess." Angel smiled up at him.

Jess patted her on the back as he made sure everyone had a plate of food before sitting next to Tom to butter a piece of bread. Sam and Peter were sitting opposite them at the table, and Max was sitting near Michael, hardly eating a thing.

Angel felt his silence, and, to her, it was the loudest thing in the room. "Max, are you feeling okay?" She worried about him, and she wasn't the only one.

Max met her concerned eyes. "I'm sorry about what happened back at the mansion. The force-field barrier, taking your essence..." He shook his head, dropping the piece of bread into in his bowl of soup before propping his elbows onto the table, his head in his hands.

Angel and Sam exchanged a worried look before Tom cut in.

"Max, you'll need to come with Jess and I to the Council meeting tonight."

Max looked up, staring at Tom before saying, "I thought I was in the clear?"

"You are, but rules need to be laid down, and some of the murk needs to be cleared up."

Max caught Jess's eye, and he offered him a sympathetic look. "It won't be so bad, mate, they're just wanting to tie up loose ends is all."

"Yeah, okay," Max replied resignedly, picking up his spoon to stir the soggy bread about his bowl; he had no intention of eating it.

Angel got up from her chair and walked around the table. She touched Max's shoulder and waited for him to look up at her. When he did, tears welled in her eyes, but she kept them at bay. She'd never seen him look so devastated. "Let's go for a walk."

He looked across at Bowie, who smiled. "It's okay, Max. You just need a bit of time to process everything. It's going to be all right."

"Yeah," Michael chimed in. "It is."

Max nodded as Angel linked her arm through his and led him from the room. She heard Bowie call after them, "You've got one hour, baby."

"Okay," she called before leading Max out the front door and off in the direction of the college's footy oval, so they could sit in the bleachers.

They crossed over freshly-mown lawns and passed through the small gate to reach the bleachers.

"I don't know where I belong anymore," Max said after they'd been sitting for a few minutes in silence.

"You belong here."

"I thought I did…I felt like I did, for so long." He shook his head, eyes drifting out to the field beyond the oval, where a frisky herd of horses were galloping about the paddock, ducking under the elms without a care in the world.

"I can't imagine how hard it must be, seeing Sam with Peter, and I wish I could do something to ease your pain. But you do belong here, Max, with us."

He shook his head in frustration as he slid off the seat to pace in front of her.

She waited, watching his frustrated frown turn to grief as he turned his eyes towards her. "I miss her, Angel. I miss being with her. She has been the light and love of my life since we were kids. It's not fair!" he ended on a yell, running his hands through his hair, swallowing tears of regret.

Angel went to get off the seat, to comfort him, but he held up a hand, stopping her as he shook his head. "Don't. I deserve to feel this pain after the things I've done."

Her heart broke a little as she looked at her childhood friend. "Don't say things like that, Max, it's not true."

He looked her dead in the eye. "Isn't it?" he said. "I sucked your essence less than twelve hours ago, which makes that twice in your lifetime. And if I'm honest, Angel, you are the most delicious essence I've absorbed, despite there not having been that many. Even now, your taste lingers within me."

"Are you trying to piss me off?" She got off the seat, folding her arms and facing him in a standoff.

He shrugged. "Just making a statement…"

Before Max could finish the sentence, a gale force wind struck him and knocked him back twenty feet along the oval's grounds.

Angel looked over her shoulder and saw Bowie standing on the hill by the homestead's rose garden, watching, wearing a stony expression. He lowered his hand, the one that had sent the wind to smack Max. He'd tuned into their conversation.

I didn't mean to. Sorry, baby.

It's okay, Max is just…rattled.

He'll be more than rattled in a moment if he doesn't watch his Ps and Qs.

Angel nodded before turning back around to see Max get up and walk towards her, brushing the grass off his bruised backside.

Both of the Storm siblings, and Sam's soul-partner, had struck him down in less than twelve hours, and his body was feeling battered. "I'm sorry." He looked over her shoulder at Bowie in the distance, who nodded and turned to go back inside.

"I think you need to go down to the gym. Ask Eddy for a session, clear your head."

"You're right, as usual." A tear of remorse fell from one startling green eye as he looked at her. "I'm sorry."

She shook her head. "All siblings have squabbles, didn't you know?" She offered him a kind smile and her arm.

He sighed as he slid his arm through hers, and they walked back towards the house. "I think I might move out and into one of the dorm rooms, instead."

Angel nodded. They watched as a flock of black cockatoos filled the sky above them, crying mournfully as they flew towards the tallest tree to settle in for the night.

"You need to make things easier for yourself during this transition period, so I think that's a great idea."

She felt him nod as they walked under the elms and along the driveway. When they reached the front door, she saw Bowie leaning against the doorway.

Arms folded, a displeased look on his handsome face with eyes of steel focused completely on Max, he said, "Go inside, baby."

Angel looked up at Max, who nodded, releasing her arm.

She walked up to Bowie, who hadn't moved an inch, and went to walk by him when he caught her arm, stilling her. Eyes remaining on Max, he whispered, "There's a remedy in the kitchen that I've made for you, drink it all."

"Thank you." She leaned into him, dropping a kiss against his shoulder before heading to the kitchen.

After Angel went inside, Bowie reached behind him and closed the door, facing Max silently for a handful of seconds.

"Look…" Max began, but Bowie held up a hand, cutting him off.

"It's okay. I'm not here to crucify you, mate. I understand how difficult the past fortnight has been, let alone the last couple of days. I get it."

Max nodded, relieved Bowie wasn't going to chew him out. He didn't think he could handle another member of the royal-souls lecturing him right now.

"But," Bowie stepped away from the door, straightening as he looked Max dead in the eyes. "If you ever speak to Angel about her *taste* again, her essence, then you and I will be having an entirely different conversation. One that will not involve words…are you feeling me here?"

Max nodded.

"Okay, then. As for everything else, you are not alone, got it?"

"Sure, thanks Bowie." Max was grateful the conversation was ending. He wanted to go find Eddy and have a session before the Council meeting.

Bowie stepped back, opening the door for Max to go inside. He walked around to the healing garden to have a few moments of peace to recharge and prepare himself to assist Angel in the healing of the mountain and district.

After drinking the herbal concoction Bowie had lovingly made for her, Angel ran up to her room to get changed for the healing ritual. When she pushed her door open, she was happily surprised to see Sam sitting on her bed playing with the end of Moonie's tail. Angel smiled and saw her cat's eyes widen as she approached the bed to run her fingers over his soft, long fur. He purred loudly, blinking his green eyes, before launching himself off the bed and out the open window.

"You look like the cat who got the cream, Sam." Angel ran a hand over Sam's hair before turning to her drawers to pull out a pair of blue jeans and a white shirt with long, flowing sleeves.

She tugged off her clothes to get changed as she waited for Sam. "What's up?" she asked.

"Oh, you know, this and that."

Angel grinned. "Just tell me."

Sam laughed. "Peter and I, our union…"

Angel's eyes softened, and she sighed. "Oh my, I know, it was absolutely divine. Bowie was…"

"Um, absolutely NO!," Sam yelled, covering her ears. "Please, don't say another word, I beg you!" She laughed as Angel launched herself at her, tickling her in punishment.

Once they'd had their fun, Angel retrieved the jeans she'd dropped, and tugged them up as she grinned at Sam. "It was great, though."

Sam shook her head. "What Max and I had was so good, too good…" She sighed, making sure she was shielding strongly enough that her thoughts would stay in this room. "And Peter and I…I don't even know if I have the words."

Angel slid the shirt over her head, reached for her brush, then pulled it through her hair, piling it up into a sweeping ponytail. "Without making you feel ill, I absolutely agree with you on one count, there aren't enough words."

Sam's eyes shone as she leant forward. "My God, he did this thing with his fingers. As soon as I pictured him touching me here, or kissing me there, he just made everything shine, and then, when I went down…"

"Um, no, just *no*!" Angel laughed, shaking her head. "Too much info, my friend."

Sam laughed. "Sorry. It's not really fair that I want to give you details, but can't fathom the thought of you and my brother rolling around in the sheets making magic happen."

Angel chuckled, pulling on a pair of white ballet slippers. "Yeah, there's that."

"Are you heading to Mount Noorat?"

Angel nodded as she opened the door, heading downstairs.

"Angel?" Peter called from Sam's, and now his, room.

She turned, smiling at their new family member. "Hi, Peter."

"Shall I come with you, to help with the restoration?" He watched her with solemn brown eyes.

"No, thank you. Bowie and I will perform this healing."

He nodded. "Well, please, let me know if there is anything I can do."

"Thanks." She didn't know what his role would be here with them, as his cover for the pure-souls, she didn't even know how old he was. And, if she didn't have to rush off, she would have asked those questions. There was plenty of time, she supposed.

She smiled at him, then at Sam. "I'll see you in the morning."

"May you keep the souls safe," Sam said softly as Peter tucked her under his arm.

"With every breath that I take," Angel answered as she ran downstairs, feeling exhilarated by what she was about to do for Mother Earth.

The night sky was soothing, compared to the foul air that smelled like brimstone as they stood at the top of the crater. Angel felt such intense pain, deep within her soul, as she looked down at the one-hundred-and-fifty metre drop inside the basin. Only days ago, lush grass and tiny wildlife had filled it, and now it was a smouldering, black hole, scorched to its core. She felt Mother Earth's devastation. Too many layers of microorganisms had been destroyed. But she would fix that. Her eyes looked across the expanse to meet Bowie's.

Ready? he asked.

I am.

Bowie stood opposite Angel on the other side of the crater's mouth, which stretched roughly six-hundred metres wide. He stirred the surrounding air to carry away the toxic fumes that lingered. Bowie raised his palms outwards, watching as Angel knelt, placing a hand over her heart, the other resting on the scorched soil.

He sensed her whispering to the Angels above, and Mother Earth below, as she pledged and vowed to do everything in her divine power to heal and restore; to educate and share, no matter the cost or time. An hour ticked by, but it wasn't tiresome. He could watch her for an eternity as she performed her heavenly soul duties.

After another hour had passed, he watched the soil below his feet, crisp, dead, and black, fade and drift like onyx dust in the wind he'd summoned. Then, as he felt Angel's words stir deep within him, a carpet of green sprouted from the bottom of the crater and snaked up the mountainside. Like a green lava of carpet, it flowed over the lip of the mountain and down its sides.

He looked across at Angel as she continued to chant, pale but determined, when tiny wildflowers burst through the grass, in patches here and there, promising to please the bees. Saplings, tiny at first, transitioned from shrubs to trees, spreading over the top, then along the mountainside, heading towards the main road. Bare limbs stretched their arms to the night sky before, gloriously, they filled with leaves of gum and eucalyptus, wattle and elm, Their scent filled the air, chasing the smell of death and destruction away.

Tears of angst fell from Angel's eyes, and she felt Mother Earth's tears of gratitude as she continued encouraging the grass, trees, flora, and fauna to grace the entire district and beyond—growth to an extent that it had not seen in decades. She hoped that now, with most of the Veins gone, the royal-souls could focus solely on educating and enlightening the pure-souls on how to reverse the damage they'd caused. To do what needed to be done to restore the stability to Mother Earth, to restore its biodiversity, giving the pure-souls more time to learn how to live as a community again, in harmony and with respect to their one home; Mother Earth.

Not as greedy individuals seeking the highest polluted rungs on their ladders, or hungry corporations that destroyed purely to gain, not caring about the little people or the depredation of Mother Earth. Those who were so focused on taking all they could in the here and now, giving no thought to the future as they relished in their profits and the rape and murder of the air, the ice, the purest of souls, the animals. Such a devastating waste of such majestic creations—of true miracles.

She sighed, feeling exhausted, as she raised her face to the night sky, which rained kisses down over her in the form of droplets that Bowie had summoned to quench the soils.

She smiled, her fingers still pressed to the Earth. She could feel the wriggling of worms and the movements of the millions of microscopic organisms burrowing deeper into the grassroots and the rich soil below, sensing them spread for miles around, enriching the farmers' and gardeners' soils.

Angel thanked the Angels above. Wiping her fingers on her jeans, she kissed them before laying them upon the soft grass at her feet, before rising. She smiled at Bowie across the expanse, which he returned with pride.

It was done.

She watched as Bowie waved his fingers and saw his lips move as he whispered to the wind, before it picked him up and carried him across the crater's mouth and straight towards her.

Angel laughed as his speed increased before squealing in surprise when, instead of stopping as he reached her, he opened his arms wide and scooped her up, holding her close. She wrapped her arms around his waist, her hair whipping madly about them as they sped down the mountainside. She pushed her face into his warm chest as she breathed him in. *I will never get enough of you.*

Likewise. He brushed against her mind as he placed her feet on the ground, brushing a kiss across her temple.

Angel smiled up at him, and her breath caught; he was staring down at her with such an intense look in his eyes. He placed his hands on her hips and steered her backwards until he pressed her against the smooth bark of a ghost gum. "Do you have any objections to me loving you right here?"

She swallowed, shaking her head as he bent towards her. He stepped against her, boxing her in between two hard places that felt like heaven. His lips collected hers in the most decadent kiss of her life, his hands holding her as if she were the most precious jewel. When he removed his clothes, then hers, to worship her like the Angel she was to him, she could have happily turned to pure-essence then and there.

Chapter Thirty-One

Angel watched in appreciation as Bowie disappeared into his office to greet his next client, Elizabeth. She caught Angel's eye and offered her a sparkling smile before following Bowie.

Michael had convinced Beth to take things slow so they could become acquainted with one another once more, after so many years apart. And, so far, Beth seemed happy enough to agree to his terms. They'd filled the last few weeks with date nights, family picnics, and trips along the Great Ocean road.

The Council had officially informed Michael that, for a twelve-month period, no soul-essence ceremony would take place, in order for him to heal mentally. Bowie and Sam had convinced him to enjoy living in the moment with Beth; he deserved some peace and happiness after all he'd endured.

Angel headed across campus to the main hall, reflecting on the hour that had passed since she and Bowie had met their renowned guest speaker. The entire campus were making their way to the hall to listen to him speak.

Every spare minute she'd spent with Bowie this past month had been filled with a thousand shared thoughts, questions, and delicious moments. Moments which left them physically breathless, fulfilled, and always insatiable for more. Their hearts, always aglow, had gifted them with constant healing energy. They'd taken a quick trip overseas to assist in a mission to ease any disputes that arose as consequences of the Veins' transgressions. So much had happened in such a short amount of time, and the intensity of her love for Bowie astonished her most days.

She sighed in appreciation as the image of him, golden and naked above her, worshipping her body and soul, played on repeat in her mind, making her body tingle.

Stop that, he brushed against her mind.

She flushed with pleasure. *Sorry,* she replied, not sounding sorry whatsoever. She heard his voice in her mind give a dry laugh before he turned his attention fully to Elizabeth.

"Hey, wait up!" Eddy called as he jogged up to her. He'd just finished teaching a self-defence class and meditation during the lunch break. "What time did Sir D. A. arrive?"

"A few hours ago." She smiled, thrilled to have spent an hour on her own with the man himself. He had gifted her with his time, knowledge, advice, and guidance about what she would have to do, and continue doing, in the years ahead, if all were to be well. The fact that he was her idol, yet he'd treated her like *she* was his, had been overwhelming and humbling. He'd let her know that, if she needed him, he would be there in a flash. She'd almost cried, but his grace and presence made her compose herself enough to take his hand, bow over it, and thank him graciously.

"One day to go before freedom," Eddy said enthusiastically. "This is the perfect way for the year to end."

Angel beamed at him. "Oh, yes it is, my friend."

This was the last day before the school year finished, which would leave the college dormitories empty of all pure-souls for several weeks. With Christmas and the Light Accords' Christmas party just around the corner, Angel could not have been more content with life.

"Yo, Eddo! Baby-cakes!" Gary yelled out from behind them.

Eddy laughed as Angel cringed, before they turned to watch Max and Gary head towards them.

"Hey, Angel." Max reached out to give her a hug.

She returned his embrace, asking, "Hey, you. Looking forward to this one?" She indicated behind her shoulder, towards the hall.

"Absolutely. To have the opportunity hear him speak in person..." Max shook his head in wonder.

"It will be great." Eddy rubbed his hands together enthusiastically.

"Let's head in and get a decent seat." Max looked down at Angel, an excited glint in his eyes.

Angel nodded, relieved to see his spark return. The past month had, understandably, been difficult for him; he'd avoided the homestead completely, and had been spending his free time hanging out with Eddy, Gary, and a bunch of other classmates, which appeared to have helped soothe his aching soul and shattered heart.

Angel knew he missed Sam desperately, and loved her still. He'd been working hard to hone his skills, and had been taking instruction well from Tom and Red, doing all he could to absorb the lessons required to help assist in the healing of Mother Earth and the pure-souls.

"Come on, Baby-cakes." Gary nodded towards the hall.

Angel avoided Gary's leery grin and led the way.

By the time they walked into the hall, it was packed to the rafters with surrounding districts' high school students, gardening clubs, and environmental supporters. Getting a seat together looked to be a challenge.

"Angel!" Sam yelled out, waving her hand to get her attention. She'd saved her a seat with Lisa and another friend of theirs, Kim K., who was equally as passionate as they were about the topic they were about to hear. They were about to learn how humans could pull their fingers out of their backsides and save the dying planet.

Angel beamed with pleasure, bidding the boys a quick goodbye as she sat with her friends. She didn't miss the look that passed between Max and Sam before he followed Eddy and Gary to a seat a few rows away. Angel patted Sam's knee knowingly, as Jess called everyone to attention. The hall fell silent in seconds, and an excited, high, vibration swirled in the air. Angel and Sam knew it was the royal-souls; all were as thrilled as each other to have Sir D. A. in attendance to gift the pure-souls with his knowledge.

Once Jess introduced the tall man with blue eyes that sparkled brightly, the room held its breath in anticipation of what he was about to say.

Their honoured guest stepped forward; a slight smile fluttered across his lips as his eyes scanned the room, and, meeting Angel's gaze, he nodded before turning his attention to the massive crowd. His voice was hypnotic and potent, in the best possible way, as he began.

"I am older than I look, and in all the years I have been blessed to walk this world, it is only now that I appreciate how extraordinary it is. As a young man, I felt I was out there in the wild, experiencing the untouched, natural wild, but it was an illusion. The tragedy of our time has been happening all around us, barely noticeable from day to day, the loss of our planet's wild places, its biodiversity."

As he spoke, the room absorbed each word, each profound message, each lesson as his soothing voice washed over them. He paused little throughout the two-hour talk, hopeful his messages would not fall on deaf ears. Tears filled eyes all around the hall as many learned for the first time how the impact of their ancestors' mistakes had led them to the demise of the planet's stability.

Angel pushed good intentions to all the pure-souls in the hall, filling them with the need to listen and to act; to do more, give more. To share the knowledge gifted to them this day as their guest drew to the conclusion of his talk.

"We have one, final chance to create the perfect home for ourselves and restore the wonderful world we inherited. All we need is the will to do so. If we act now, we can yet put it right. I thank you for your time."

He bowed to the silent hall before an eruption of thunderous applause filled every ear as the audience stood in absolute awe. Jess shook Sir D.A.'s hand as the applause continued, and, after one final bow and a wave, he left the hall, followed by Jess, Michael, and Red.

Kim shook her head, turning to Sam and Angel as she wiped her tears away. "Best two hours of my life, hands down."

Sam grinned. "As true as that may be, my friend, I think we need to get you a date."

"No, the only man I will ever love has just exited the building." Kim sighed in complete awe, and Lisa had to agree. She hadn't been able to take her eyes off Jess the entire time, and when he spoke, his voice filled her ears like the sweetest symphony.

Angel smirked at Sam as Lisa grabbed her arm, and they followed the crowd out of the hall. It was the perfect ending to the school year, and they each looked forward to the end-of-year Christmas party the following day.

"I think we need to hire more caterers for next year's celebrations, Red." Michael grinned at their petite friend the following afternoon as they finished setting up the tables outside of the cafeteria.

"You may be right there, Michael, but it always works out the way it's supposed to." Red thanked Edna, Mrs. Quick, and Mrs. McGoldrick, who were finishing up the last little touches on the high tea spread, along with the president of the C.W.A., Sue Clark.

"No one will go hungry, that's for sure," Sue beamed at Red.

"We couldn't have done it without you Sue," Red smiled.

Sue tilted her head towards Mrs. Quick and said, "I sincerely doubt that."

"Yet, we appreciate you all the same." Michael slung his arm around Red's shoulder as the crowd began hungrily milling around, looking forward to the feast before them.

Tom and Jess, along with several senior students, had cooked up a storm, including baked potatoes covered in a selection of toppings, along with a BBQ and additional vegetarian options. The weather couldn't have been more perfect for the day, either. The ceremony for the graduating students had gone smoothly, leaving the afternoon free for them all to enjoy the lunch and catch up with their friends for the final time. Most would hit the road first thing in the morning to vacate the college grounds and spend time with their own families over the Christmas break.

"Michael, I'm all finished up." Beth reached him, slipping her arm through his.

"Great. Let's go and get the gifts handed out." He smiled at the ladies before he took Beth's hand, and they headed out towards the back garden to where a small pine tree had been decorated for the students to exchange gifts under. Beth and Michael had purchased different packets of seedling kits and bulbs to suit their students' personalities, as a memento of their days at Glenormiston College.

"Hi, Angel." Beth smiled as she watched Angel handing out her own gifts to her friends.

Angel hugged Kim as she pushed a package into her friend's hands before answering. "Hi there, how's it going?"

"Great, I…"

A squeal from Kim cut Beth off as Angel turned to her friend.

"Oh my God, a signed copy from the man himself!" Kim was jumping up and down, clutching a copy of David Attenborough's '*A Life on Our Planet*' against her chest, the brightest smile of appreciation across her face.

Angel smiled. "You are welcome."

Amidst the joy of the day, as colourful activity swirled around them, Angel froze as an oppressive darkness crept towards her soul, filling her with dread. She did not want to succumb to the crippling sensation that was overpowering her and was disappointed to find herself falling victim to its waiting, murky arms. Eyes widening in surprised shock as she gasped in pain, wanting to keep her composure in front of the pure-souls as her eyes desperately met Michael's.

He frowned, stepping towards her as she swayed.

"Michael," she whispered in anguish. "Something's wrong with Bowie."

"What is it?" Beth asked, worried.

"It's okay, Beth. Angel wasn't feeling well at breakfast this morning, low iron. I'll just take her inside." Michael scooped Angel up.

Kim yelled out, "If there's anything we can do, just call us."

Michael held a deep breath as he took long, brisk steps towards the homestead. *Sam, can you hear me? Bowie? Max?* He prayed one of them would hear his call as Angel wrapped her arms around her waist to stop herself from shaking, both with the sickness and fear.

"It hurts, Michael, I can't *feel* him!" she cried in despair. Where was he? *Bowie! Bowie, please answer me!*

"It's okay, we'll sort this out," he whispered above her head as he pushed the back door open.

He placed her on a kitchen stool. After making sure she wasn't going to fall off, he grabbed a glass, thrusting it under the tap to fill it, and turned, handing it to her.

Her hand shook as she raised the glass towards her lips, spilling a few drops before taking a large mouthful. She was filled with dread, and couldn't stop the sob that burst from deep within her. "I can't feel him… why can't I feel him, Michael?"

His heart thumped uncomfortably as he placed his arm around her shoulders. An uneasy feeling enveloped him; he couldn't feel Bowie, either. He was desperate to start a search, but didn't want to let Angel go.

The back door flew open, and Sam, Max, Tom, Jess, and Peter burst inside. Tom nodded to Sam as he said to Michael, "Sam called us."

Michael stepped back as Tom reached to wrap his arm around Angel's shoulders, which were shaking uncontrollably. "It's going to be okay, pet." He sounded unconvinced.

She looked up at him as a fat tear slid down her face. Jess paced worriedly. "Can anyone feel him?" he asked.

Sam shook her head, clasping her hands frantically together as Peter put an arm around her shoulder, trying to reassure her that all would be well.

"But it won't be!" Sam cried, looking at Peter. "No one here can feel my brother!" She burst into tears of fright, shrugging away from Peter's touch.

Even in all the years that Michael and Bowie were gone, she'd still had a feeling her brother was alive and well. At the moment, nothing but icy dread and emptiness filled that space, and it terrified her.

Max desperately wanted to comfort Sam and knew the only thing he could do was search for Bowie and return him to them all. "What do we do?" he asked Tom before looking at Jess.

Tom and Jess exchanged a look before Tom rubbed his hand over Angel's back.

"There's only one thing to do. For a start, Angel, you must sit in the healing garden and call to him; we'll check out the globe, see if we can't locate him somehow."

Angel nodded as she slid off the stool and stumbled out into the healing garden. She fell onto her hands and knees amongst the smiling faces of the chamomile, hating that this empty feeling was leaving her so deprived of energy. She sobbed once before taking a deep breath and closing her eyes, focused on the earth, the air, and whispered to the Angels above, whispered to Bowie's soul-essence, which swirled deep within her, to search for him and return him to her, alive.

Tom and Jess headed off to the study to check out the globe, as the others stood by the kitchen window watching, waiting, each sending up a silent prayer that they would locate Bowie, and soon.

It took Angel an hour before she leapt to her feet and, turning to them all, cried out, "He's in the cellar at the mansion." She hurried around the front of the house towards the car park. Michael, Max, Sam, and Peter followed her, getting in the car with her, as Jess and Tom raced out of the study.

"Have you got this?" Tom asked Michael, who started the engine.

"Absolutely. You guys get back to the celebrations, so no one notices our absence."

Jess agreed, and they stepped back as the car sped out of the driveway, and towards Noorat and the mansion.

Sam sat nervously between Max and Peter, grateful that neither of them were offering her any sort of comfort. She wasn't in the mood to be comforted, not with the possibility of her brother being dead lurking in her heart. She sat forward and placed her hand on Angel's shoulder, squeezing.

Angel covered Sam's hand with her own, and the car turned up the mansion's driveway minutes later. She was resisting the urge to be violently ill; the icy fingers of doom pinched her shoulders harder the closer they got to the front door.

She threw open her door before the car came to a complete stop and leapt out, racing towards the front door. Pushing it open, she stepped inside. "*Bowie?*" she screamed, running through the house, looking for the stairs that would lead down to the cellar.

"Angel, the stairs are over here." Max called from the kitchen doorway before rushing down, the others right behind him.

Angel ran over and followed them down the darkened steps that led to the damp cellar. An overpowering stench of death greeted them.

"Ew. That can't be good," Sam whispered, fear filling her voice before she flicked her fingers and sent an amber glow over the cellar, to reveal cobwebbed boxes, antique furniture, and dusty crates of wine. And there, in the far corner, lay Bowie, pale and seemingly lifeless.

Angel gasped as she flew towards him, falling to her knees as she quickly placed a hand against his chest, her other over her heart as she whispered frantically to bring him back.

Michael knelt opposite her as Sam warmed up the cold cellar. Peter and Max stood anxiously behind them, waiting for any order that could help.

"Who could have done this?" Sam shook her head. "I thought there were no more Veins in the area?"

"Perhaps Brendan's brethren heard about his demise and sent someone to exact revenge for him and the others?" Max shrugged, folding his arms.

Sam nodded stiffly, looking away from Max and back at Bowie's pale form.

"Michael, we need to get him outside, out of this house," Angel whispered.

He agreed, and scooped Bowie up, frowning at how light he was. Whoever had committed this vile act had almost drained Bowie to a lifeless husk; he prayed Angel's gifts could restore him.

"I think we need to get him off this property," Max advised.

"I think you're right," Sam agreed. "Let's get him home."

Michael drove them back, and they had Bowie lying out in the healing garden in under five minutes. Sam cast a barrier spell around the garden, so if any student or visitor entered the grand gardens of the homestead, they would see nothing untoward.

Michael frowned, noticing Bowie's Mother Earth bracelet was missing as he reached for his own, which held little life in it now, after he'd been abducted for all those years. He wished the tiny amount of life energy within it would enter Bowie's heart as Angel continued chanting in hope of bringing him back to them.

The wind stirred as Sam called to the elements, imploring the pure air to reach Bowie's lungs.

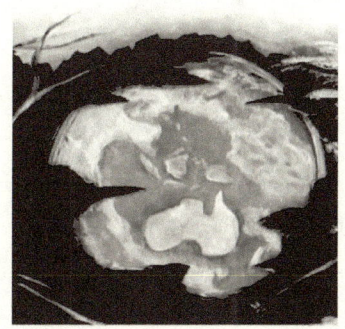

Chapter Thirty-Two

It was a solid hour later, but, finally, Bowie's beautiful, amber eyes fluttered open.

Sam dropped to her knees, and the three of them gripped hands as Angel pushed her face into his chest, sobbing in relief.

"Thanks," he whispered, lying there as a flood of delight swept through him. *This was way too easy. The fools!*

Brendan Black's soul, within the moulded shape of Bowie, wrapped his arms around Angel, holding her close to him, breathing her in. It wouldn't be long before he would absorb every inch of this delightful creature, gifting him with enough power to enable him to make the entire horde of Veins around the globe rise once more.

He wickedly hoped to have the chance to do more to her than simply absorb every ounce of her...

Angel frowned as she sat up, looking down at him. *Why can't I hear you?* She brushed against his mind. He gave no indication he'd heard her.

Sam, Michael? She pushed towards them, keeping her eyes steadily on the 'thing' before her.

My God—it's not Bowie, Michael replied in disgust.

It's Brendan, Max whispered, barely audible. *Act normal.*

"Thank God you found me when you did," Brendan—the Bowie look-alike—said, sitting up before climbing to his feet.

"What happened?" Michael asked, putting his arm around Angel as he led her a step away from Brendan.

Brendan shook his head, which made Angel feel sick, thinking about the monster within, who was wearing Bowie's beautiful face. *If this is Brendan, then where is Bowie? And why can't I feel him?*

The others could hear Angel's rising anguish, and Max replied firmly, *It's okay Angel…Bowie isn't dead, otherwise the link from the ruby's essence, the one that created this skin, would fade.* Max hated the ruby and everything it represented, but right now he was glad he had this knowledge to reassure his family that Bowie was still alive and breathing.

Brendan sighed as he looked at Michael. "I was taking a message to Jane for Red when something knocked me out from behind. The last thing I remember was waking in the cellar before a force sucked the life from me." He raised an eyebrow. "It can't have been Brendan, Angel and I fried him."

He smiled as he reached for Angel, pulling her into his arms, and flush against him. He'd been watching them all for the past month, and knew who was who in this colourful cast of royal-souls.

Angel was trying not to freak out as chills of disgust ran along her flesh. Being held so close by arms that felt like Bowie's but tightened around her with lustful hate, made her skin crawl. *I'm going to be sick.* She whimpered, grateful for Max's insight regarding Bowie still being alive, which gave her the strength to remain standing.

"Hey, Angel wasn't feeling well when we realised you were in trouble." Sam grabbed Angel's arm and jerked her away from Brendan and towards the back door. "We're just going to grab some Panadol." They fled from the men.

"How about we have a drink, celebrate that you're okay before we join the others?" *Red, we need your help,* Michael pushed towards Red as he led Brendan inside and towards the study.

Peter looked at Max as they followed Michael. *Whatever happens, protect Sam,* he instructed Max, who nodded.

Max knew he would protect them all with his life, to bring an end to his filthy cousin. He knew the ruby contained a great deal of power, but to see it in action turned his blood cold. He'd make that his next mission; find the ruby and get it to the High Council.

Michael poured them all a shot of honey whiskey and raised his glass to Brendan. "To family, and keeping the souls safe."

Brendan raised his glass. "Here, here," he replied, not in the 'royal-souls' way, confirming he wasn't, in any way, one of theirs.

"This looks quite the party." Red breezed into the room, followed by Angel and Sam, who stood a few feet away.

"Indeed." Brendan grinned arrogantly through Bowie's gorgeous lips.

Angel was shaking in rage, she wanted to gut the filthy thing here and now. The feeling of hatred was completely new to her, and didn't sit well with her kind soul.

It took Brendan a few moments to realise that the group had placed themselves in a large circle around him, and he wondered if this was something they normally did? He didn't think so. He looked into each of their suspecting eyes; they each wore expressions of disgust.

"Well, well, well…aren't you all entirely too clever for your own good?"

"Where's Bowie?" Angel spat.

He offered her a bitter smile. "You'll never know."

Angel tried not to collapse as Michael brushed her mind with a gentle, calming gift.

Brendan frowned at Max, not having the desire to kill one of his own when so many had been taken from him. His tone was ice-cold as he snarled, "You have disappointed me no end, boy." He shook his head. "You will be punished, despite the role you were born to play."

Max frowned, shaking his head. "You and my father, always talking in riddles. I was born for no one's game, least of all yours." He spat vehemently.

Brendan slowly shook his head. "In time, you'll wish you'd remained loyal to our family and, sadly for you, it will be too late." He shot his hand out, sending a black force towards Sam, knowing her death would be the ultimate torture for Maxwell.

As though he saw Brendan's intention, Peter leapt forward to shield Sam with his own body, the black force slicing into his chest like a hot knife through butter.

Sam's screams as Peter fell to his knees filled Max with anguish. He threw himself towards Brendan, slamming his fist under his chin, sending the man stumbling backwards against the table.

"Shield yourselves!" Angel cried.

Sam put her hand on Peter's shoulder, placing a shield around them both as she watched him bleed profusely onto the rug. She tried to contain the hysterical tears that threatened.

Brendan laughed like a crazed man, having entirely too much fun, as Red waved her hand towards the globe. He regained his balance as he glared at Angel through Bowie's amber eyes. She cried in fright as he shot a handful of veins toward her, hoping to slice through her body and latch onto every organ.

Angel focused on Bowie's essence, which swirled within her, seeking to aid her, and sent all the sickening parasites straight back towards Brendan with an added bolt of lightning. He flew backwards once more, throwing his hands out, and a swarm of veins filled the room, searching for an entrance into all of their flesh.

Unable to penetrate their shields, Brendan then threw his hands towards the windows. The evil parasitic army smashed through the glass and flew outside to invade as many pure-souls as they could, creating a swarm of crazed, inconsolable individuals.

Red waved her hand and spun the globe around the room, expanding its circumference to trap Brendan within its glass dome, as she focused on Angel.

You need to end him, dear girl. Focus on everything of Bowie's that you have, and remove this vermin from Mother Earth, once and for all.

Can I do that?

You can, Red confirmed. *Just feel it, set the intention, and it will flow.*

Michael stepped beside Angel. *I'm here for you if you need me.*

Thank you. She closed her eyes for the briefest of moments before turning them towards Brendan. A lake of aquamarine fury stirred under the surface as she focused on the task before her.

Brendan could see the air stir around Angel, her hair beginning to fly around her as she opened her hands by her sides, facing her palms towards him. He frowned, wondering what the young thing could do to him, and realised he didn't want to find out.

Outside, the delightful screams of the tortured beckoned to him. He needed to get out of here and command his new army. Brendan turned to flee and bounced off the dome wall. He cursed before turning to the tiny, red-haired lady. She shouldn't be too hard to eliminate, surely?

Red focused on holding the globe in position, but as Brendan shot her with a black bolt, her frail body shook.

"Michael!" Angel screamed, as he leapt to Red's defence.

"Max, help Peter!" Sam cried as she leapt to her feet to stand beside Angel. "We've got this, my sister. Come on!" she hissed.

Max knelt beside Peter, who looked lifeless and had lost way too much blood. He placed a hand on the poor man's limp body, the other over his heart, and began a healing chant, pouring everything of himself into his love's soul-partner.

Angel sent a heat blast from within her, calling on Bowie's Elemental-essence to aid her. Within seconds, the face Brendan wore, sagged, and a spine-chilling moan slipped through elongated lips. His long, distorted fingers stretched towards the floor on arms that hung like wet, soggy noodles. He took a jerky step forward, creating an eerie spectacle that made everyone in the room nervous, as laughter spilled from his deformed lips.

Sam had an idea. *Angel, pause the heat for a second…I'm going to freeze him.* Sam felt Angel nod before she blasted him with sub-zero temperature. His astonished scream filled the room, and his shape transformed from a pile of oozing noodles to a frozen figure.

The hairs on everyone's arms stood an inch high with the energy that flowed around the room.

"Now, Angel!" Sam cried.

Angel slammed a violent force of hot, white flames out of her palms and into Brendan's chest. With the collision of fire on ice, he exploded into a thousand glass shards, shattering on the rug and floorboards below. Friction filled the air, and everyone stood silent, frozen in shock. They waited for the army of Brendan's veins to return. Seconds later, they hit against the glass dome surface before fizzing into nothingness.

Laughter resumed outside, and they immediately felt Jess's calming influence wash over the college grounds, soothing all who'd been affected.

Sam rushed to Peter's side and covered her mouth with her hands as his dead eyes stared up at her. "No…" she whispered, horrified. "No, no, no…"

"I'm so sorry, Sam." Max swallowed the lump in his throat. Watching Sam suffer, consumed with grief, was like a thousand knives twisting in his heart. He'd rather be dead himself. "I did everything I could," he apologised.

Michael placed a hand on Max's shoulder. "There was nothing you could do, Max, he was dead the moment the force hit him."

"To save me," Sam whispered with a sob. "To save *me*."

She was in too much shock to notice that the bond she'd shared with

Peter had evaporated; there was nothing in its place but sadness for a heavenly soul who was now lost to them, and not the empty hollowness Tom had described after losing his soul-partner of fifty years.

Bowie, Angel cried, despair filling her heart. *Bowie?*

They could hear footsteps running down the corridor, and they all turned in anticipation to see Tom and Jess race into the room, relief on their faces.

"Everyone outside is oblivious to what's happened," Jess reported, looking down at the glass shards, which were the only remains of Brendan's conduit.

"These remains must be divided into single pieces and distributed around the globe, to be buried in hallowed ground," Red instructed, waving her hand.

The pieces rose in the air and shot out of the window as she sent them to the Gatekeeper's cottage and into the Light Accords' hands, where the Council would deal with them.

"Now, to Bowie." Red turned to Angel. "Back to the healing garden, dear. The rest of you, back to business. The day is about to end and it's almost time for the closing speeches."

"Sam, we must send Peter's body to the Light Accords, so he can be cleansed." Michael said, his hand on the small of her back.

"Why didn't he turn into pure-essence?" Sam whispered.

Red moved Peter's shirt aside to reveal a gaping hole in his chest, and a mass of black maggots burrowing into his already-decaying flesh. Sam gasped in dismay.

"The malevolent energy is keeping him earth-bound. Once he is cleansed, he will ascend," Red assured Sam.

Sam nodded. "I want to help Angel find my brother."

"Me too," Michael agreed.

Tom drew a sheet over Peter as Max stood to the side, feeling riddled with guilt at what his cousin had done, hating that side of his lineage.

"I'm going to head back to the mansion to find the ruby, for the Council," he said quietly.

Red nodded. "A good place to start, Max. Thank you."

Max looked at Sam, who was drying her eyes. Tom lifted Peter's body, and said, "I'll drive Peter to yours, Red, drop Max off, then I'll be back for the speeches."

Red nodded once more as Tom and Max left the room, followed a second later by Angel, who headed outside to the healing garden.

As Sam and Michael went to follow, Red said. "She must do this alone, and you must trust her to do so."

Michael looked at Sam, who sighed dejectedly. "I do trust Angel, with my life and Bowie's, but she might need our help...our healing, after everything that's happened."

Michael agreed, desperate to find Bowie, too. He also didn't want Angel to feel alone.

"My dears, this is the start of Angel's journey. It will be by the grace of Mother Earth below, and the Angels above, that the future of Angel Cloud will evolve. Heartbroken and alone, healing all? Or forever with her soul-partner, gifting the world with mindfulness, joy, and peace? She must face this alone."

Jess could see Red sway and put his arm around her tiny shoulders, gifting her with a healing boost of energy. She smiled up at him as she said to Sam, "It's time to return to the celebrations, dear. Jane will be waiting for you."

"Should I follow Tom? Go and be with Peter?"

"No dear, there's nothing you can do, that Tom won't sort out." Red opened her arms for Sam to step into, as Jess stood aside.

"I feel...weird," Sam whispered against Red's shoulder, as Jess rubbed her back.

Red hugged her hard before saying, "All will be well Samantha, I promise. You are not alone, and Peter will find peace."

Sam nodded, her heart heavy, yet, strangely, not as heavy as it should have been. Why? Her confusion halted her exhaustion, and after kissing Red's cheek in thanks, she followed her family out to the celebrations to find Jane.

Chapter Thirty-Three

Angel lay surrounded by the garden's healing arms, her heart as heavy as she'd ever known. She rested her hands on top of the soil as she glanced up at the blue sky. Scattered with white, fluffy clouds; it had no right to look so cheerful when her soul felt shattered. She could hear the speeches in the distance, and merry makers squealing from the pool. The world continued on, as it always had, and always would, whether her love returned to her or not.

Please come back to me, Bowie…I beg you. Please, don't you leave me. Hear me, feel my love for you, for us, for Mother Earth and the pure-souls. I can't do this without you!

She swallowed her tears, trying not to be too self-absorbed, but damn it! This was the absolute love of her life she was talking about. An elemental-soul who'd done amazing things for the royal-souls, pure-souls, and Mother Earth alike.

A lifetime of memories swirled within her. Bowie giving her and Sam piggy-back rides when they were five. Watching her calmly through amber eyes when she was twelve, getting lectured by Michael when she broke the rules by healing the ewe. When he'd punished her kind soul, trying to teach her to resist her gift as he'd tortured baby Moonie. She almost smiled, remembering slamming her fist into Bowie's stomach before she'd revived her kitten.

His kisses after he'd returned home after several years away...

Every lecture he'd given her, Max, and Sam regarding their actions, to chasing her to the haystack before performing an illegal punishing act on her.

She felt a tear slip from her eyes as she whispered, "I would give anything to have you back Bowie...I'd even go through you zapping me again. Tell me where you are?"

She waited, silently, searching, when a gentle breeze lifted her hair around her face. She sat up, eyes wide, listening. *Please Bowie, help me find you.* She focused on keeping the desperation out of her voice, and pushed calm, loving, healing intentions out into the world.

An energy, dark and intense, slammed into her, causing a pulsating agony within her. She didn't think she could move. When was this all going to end? She leapt to her feet, focusing on a light energy, and ran around to the front of the house, following the pull of the energy. She sprinted down the driveway and over the sweeping lawns towards the blue-stone stables.

Five minutes later, and out of breath, she pushed the old stable door open and stepped into darkness. She closed her eyes and sent a white light to flood the area. Focusing, she sensed his body, barely alive, but alive still. She searched the area, before finding an old trunk, stuffed into the corner of the room, hidden behind several bales of hay. She spied the rusty padlock holding the trunk shut, and grabbed a shovel that stood against the cobbled wall, smashing the lock open in three thrusts. Angel threw the trunk open, and her breath was stolen at the sight before her.

Bowie's long body looked as though something had snapped it in half, his back undoubtedly broken by the odd angle in which he'd been folded into the trunk, his neck too. But life still swirled beneath his pale flesh, rippled in light blue veins of death, dancing under his skin's surface. She wanted to cry, but reserved her emotional energy, grabbing him under his arms and, with all her strength, pulled him out of the trunk. When she straightened his body out, she noticed his bracelet was fading. The tiniest glow danced just beneath the glass surface. It had done what it was made to do, and had kept Bowie's heart beating…

Just.

She ripped the glass marble of Mother Earth's energy from her neck and slammed it against Bowie's chest, trying not to think, how thin and broken he felt, as she pressed her hand firmly down. She placed her hand over his heart and began chanting, pushing all her light, love, and healing energy into Bowie's body;

Elemental-soul, we hold so dear,
Step towards the light, no need to fear.
Feel my heart beat for you,
Filled with love, pure and true.
Mother Earth below and Angels above,
Please hear my prayer, return my love.

Over and over, she whispered her healing incantation. After several minutes, she felt a mass of energy swirl within her. It shot from her palm, which clutched the marble of Mother Earth, pulsating with life, to shoot a charge towards his heart.

She heard his bones snap back into place and watched as his body moved with each stage of the healing. Bones twisting and mending, blood flowing under his skin's surface, his complexion healthy and tanned once more, muscles firm and restored. She leaned closer, desperately watching him, as a long, drawn out breath escaped his lips before his eyes burst open.

The brightest rainbow they'd ever seen spilled over them and around the room, making them shut their eyes for the briefest of moments.

When Angel's eyes opened once again, Bowie was lying very still, staring up at her.

"I can't begin to tell you how good it is to see you," he said, his eyes filled with love.

She launched herself into his arms, sobbing in relief. Every second since his disappearance, everything that had happened between then and now, filtered through his thoughts as he held her shaking body.

He frowned, hating everything that his family had endured since Brendan Black had fooled him into entering the stables, before hitting him with such a force that it had snapped him in half like a pretzel.

That image found its way to Angel, and she gasped in horror.

His arms tightened around her, and he cursed himself for not shielding the unpleasant memory from her. He ran his hand up and down her back, trying to soothe the shock and fright out of her.

"It's okay, baby. I've got you now."

He felt her nod as she sniffed against his crumpled shirt.

"Poor Sam…poor Peter," he whispered.

Angel leaned back as he sat up, and caressed his cheek. "I know. Poor Sam." She looked behind them to the doorway before returning her gaze to his handsome face.

"They all know I've found you."

He nodded. "Michael's asking us to hurry up and return home."

She stood, not letting go of his hand as a car slammed on its brakes outside the stable, gravel flying in every direction, before Sam burst through the door. Tears of relief and joy ran down her face as she bolted forward and threw herself into Bowie's outstretched arm.

Angel went to let go of his hand, so he could fully embrace his sister, but he tugged her against him, so he could wrap his arms around them both.

Angel and Sam joined in the group hug, allowing their tears of relief to flow.

"Come on, loves," Bowie said after a few minutes. "I'd really like to get the hell out of here, if you both don't mind?"

They led him from the stables and towards the car, all of them keen to return to their sanctuary to heal for the next few days in peace and quiet.

Michael and Beth placed the bundle of paper, which held the salty feast of fish and chips, with the other delicious morsels spread along the outdoor table. Red popped the cork on a bottle of wine to share with Johanna. Alana sat under her chair, peeking across the lawn at Moonie through her lush fox's tail.

The family had gathered to finish decorating the outdoor area with fairy lights, lanterns, and other Christmas paraphernalia for the Light Accords' Christmas Eve party the following night. They were all feeling a sense of peace after having Bowie returned to them safely, and once the Light Accords had dealt with Brendan's remains, a calm had fallen over Glenormiston South.

Across the lawn and down the sloping path, Eddy and Jane finished lining the tennis courts with decorations, and were having a friendly game before dinner, umpired by Max.

Sam had been watching Max the past week, noticing that he'd given her plenty of space to grieve for Peter. She felt riddled with guilt that she wasn't completely heartbroken about Peter ascending, but Red had assured her it was perfectly normal not to feel his loss to the point of devastation. The reason being, when the healers of the Light Accords had cleansed Peter's body, his pure-essence had ascended to the sky above, removing their bond. Their joint essence had been divided, and Sam had felt it, the moment his essence had left her body, as hers returned to her.

She was, once more, Sam Storm-elemental-soul, attached to none.

Sam sighed, trying not to become overwhelmed as every feeling she'd once felt for Max swam to the surface, flooding her with longing. She would give herself time…and him, too. Who knew what the future had in store for them both?

"Cheers, guys," Jess said in appreciation, interrupting Sam's thoughts as he grabbed a potato cake and clicked his beer against Crow's bottle.

"Here's to a peaceful Christmas." Crow smiled before taking a long mouthful of the crisp lager.

"With no Vein activity, please…I beg the Angels above," Tom joked, forgetting Beth for a moment.

"Veins?" she asked, licking the salt off her long, elegant fingers.

Bowie internally rolled his eyes as he broke a piece of fish in half, sharing it with Michael as they'd done since they were eight-years-old.

"Is Patricia coming home for the holidays?" Bowie asked Beth, to distract her from Tom's slip up.

It worked. The Kavanagh twins had been separated all year; Patricia had been working overseas in Ireland, and it filled Beth with pride and excitement to share any news of her sister's accomplishments. Beth beamed as she told them she was taking a trip to Ireland the following week, after New Year's Eve.

The conversation flowed around mouthfuls of food, and Max, Eddy, and Jane joined them to delve into the hot, salty chips.

Angel finished decorating the front, with Moonie as her companion, and stood against the smooth bark of the ghost gum, her loyal cat by her feet. She watched her family, with so much love in her heart for every one of them. She smiled as Bowie threw his glorious head back, booming in laughter at something Jess said.

He is so perfect. She tucked a wisp of hair behind her ear, taking in his tanned skin, divine face, delicious body, and a soul that was perfectly pure. She was sure she caught his scent from all the way over here.

Bowie hid his smile as he whispered to the wind to caress her flesh, kiss her with his love. He turned then, unable to avoid her gaze for one second longer as he licked the oils from his fingers before wiping them on his jeans. Eyes unblinking, he focused on her and what he wanted to do to her.

She was grateful for the solid tree behind her, holding her steady as his desires filled her. He stood and walked towards her. *Like I'm his prey.*

You are. And I am going to enjoy taking my sweet time devouring every inch of your flesh. His eyes smouldered with the thought of doing just that.

Molten lava immediately pooled between her thighs as she flushed, heart thudding, lips parting in the softest of smiles as he reached to take her hand, tugging her towards him.

"Come," he whispered huskily, dropping a sweet kiss across her lips before leading her into the homestead and up towards their room.

They were both breathless as the bedroom door closed behind them. They could feel what the other was feeling, sensing, imagining, igniting a raging, pulsing beat of passion, lust, and love within every inch of their fibre.

He reached for the hem of her summer dress and whisked it over her head. She stood before him in a simple, white cotton bra and knickers. He ran a finger along the top of her underwear, tickling the soft flesh of her belly before slipping his fingers down to cup her moist flower. He could feel her stigma pulse against his palm and moaned in pleasure at their combined lust.

Angel pulled Bowie's t-shirt over his head, smiling before dropping kisses along his sweet flesh that smelled like heaven. She ran her tongue around his nipple before sliding her lips back up to sweep along his chin, before his lips dove to claim hers.

Bowie removed his hand, grabbed her around the hips and, lifting her in one swift movement, placed her onto his throbbing shaft, begging to be released from his jeans. Angel purred against his lips as she sucked on his tongue, rubbing herself against the bulge of his jeans, driving him out of his mind.

He stepped towards the bed, and placed her on her back, leaning over her, lips assaulting hers in the most pleasurable of ways. He removed his jeans and her underwear before sweeping sweet kisses along her neck, down her breasts, her stomach, the soft flesh of her thighs.

She moaned in anticipation as his hot breath tickled her centre before he put them both out of their agony and kissed her deeply.

Her fingers gripped the sheets in pure bliss as he lapped at her core, as if she were his saviour. Her hips pumped against his loving lips, searching for release, and she cried out as he inserted a finger inside her dripping mound.

"Sweetest peach I've ever tasted," he groaned, lapping his tongue over her again and again.

She almost cried with the intense desire he was building within her and wanted him inside her—now! Wanted to feel his body thrusting hard, over, and over, as their lips drank from the other. Sliding and pumping, grinding and stroking…giving all and everything until they were spent…

In one swift movement, he slid his engorged shaft silkily into her centre.

She sighed in contentment as he smiled down at her before moving back and pushing into her again. Bodies pressed together, the skin-on-skin contact producing ripples of delight, which washed over them both.

"Angel Cloud," he whispered, eyes ablaze as he skilfully pumped his body in and out in the most hypnotic rhythm.

"Bowie Storm," she whispered, before his lips descended upon hers, stealing any thought she had.

The kiss, the glide, their bodies entwined as their thoughts were flooded with every sensation shared had them spiralling over the edge in the sweetest, pulsating beat of delicious bliss. Angel could feel every molecule in her body throb in pure delight as they lay, entwined together, kissing lovingly, thoroughly, as their fingers swept along each other's flesh.

Bowie looked down upon her beautiful face, smiling in pleasure. "That was nice."

She nodded, unable to speak just yet. The intense love she was feeling in that moment, as her heart beat with everything she felt for Bowie, made her want to cry.

"You can, you know—cry." He swept his lips over hers as he cupped her cheek.

Angel couldn't help the tears that slipped from her eyes, but he kissed each one away before pulling her up against his chest. He cradled her close to his beating heart, sending a calming pulse between them.

"Feel that?"

She nodded.

"That is our forever. You and me. To do all the good we can in this world, to heal all. To nurture. And to love each other for a single day, or a hundred years to come. It's always going to be you and me, Angel. Always."

She smiled softly. "Not always. One day, we'll go to the High Council, and be blessed to carry our first-born."

Royal-souls were born sterile, as they respected the balance and Mother Earth's carrying capacity for humanity. When the time came that a royal-soul couple desired children, they would request to speak to the High Council, who would then ask an Angel to bless the couple who had served in protecting Mother Earth and the pure-souls, and their children after them would do the same. Only Angels had the power to gift royal-souls that blessing.

"Safe sex till then, hey?" he grinned, running a hand along her cheek. "And what a day that will be. When do you envision parenthood? Twenty years?"

She shook her head. "I think fifty years would be perfect. That's when my mother had Michael."

Bowie nodded. "Whenever you are ready, baby." He pushed up on an elbow to look down at her and stroked her silky hair off her forehead before kissing her.

She wrapped her arms around his waist, and buried her face under his jaw, breathing him in appreciatively.

"I wish the rest of the world could be as happy as we are," she whispered into his neck.

He smiled, running his fingers along her smooth back. "And so it shall be, in time, and with our guidance."

She smiled into his eyes, dropping a kiss against his gorgeous lips. "I can't wait to start."

"You already have." He brushed his lips over hers before saying, "And now that we have fed each other." He grinned. "Let's join the rest of our family, before they eat all the chips."

Her stomach rumbled. "Good luck to us."

"Yeah, I don't like our chances. You know, Dad says Terang Fish and Chips are the best in the world." He shook his head, pulling his jeans up as Angel slid her dress over her head, smiling. "He certainly can put them away when he's home."

They finished getting dressed, then, hand in hand, made it down to join their loved ones, and were lucky enough to grab a handful of chips.

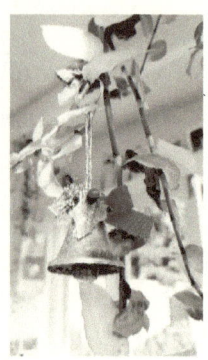

Chapter Thirty-Four

Angel, Sam, and Jane were dressed in summer gowns for the celebration. It was one of the biggest gatherings of the year, that didn't involve Council matters and global talks. Jane was swirling around the dance floor in her vibrant red dress with Eddy, laughing constantly at his light banter. They'd spelled him with a charm, so even if he overheard any royal-soul talk, he would hear it only as any ordinary pure-soul conversation. They'd also cast it on Mrs. McGoldrick and Edna, as they were here as Red's special guests.

Angel's gown was as blue as her eyes, and it dripped over her like a fitted glove, making it hard for Bowie to concentrate on any decent conversation with the hundreds of individuals that filled the homestead's grounds.

Angel was engrossed in a conversation with Johanna regarding a tour to visit all the sacred places around Mother Earth, to dive deep into her crust to heal her.

"I've made sure that you'll be coming along as Sir D. A.'s special guest," Johanna told her.

Angel was glowing with excitement and hugged Johanna hard. "I can't believe you've made this possible for me, Johanna, thank you!"

"Of course, darling."

It filled Bowie with a warm feeling, seeing his mother and his love together.

He sighed. To be here right now, surrounded by light and love, filled Bowie with an overwhelming gratitude for the life he'd been born into. It was his and Michael's first Christmas Eve together since he'd left to search for Michael seven years ago. So much had happened in between then and now.

"Here you go, mate," Michael said after he'd weaved through the crowd to reach Bowie, passing him a round glass filled with punch.

Bowie raised an eyebrow, playfully suspicious. "I don't know if I want to accept any liquids from you at these parties ever again," he joked.

Michael shook his head, smiling. "I deserve that."

"Yes, you do." Bowie grinned before taking the glass. "At least, this time, I have your sister to kick your arse if anything happens to me."

Michael chuckled before taking a mouthful from his glass as he glanced around the packed yard. "I believe she would do an excellent job of it, too."

"Mm-hmm," Bowie agreed through a mouthful of the spicy liquid, which held notes of chilli and sweet berries. He watched Max approach Sam, who looked like a sparkling jewel in her black sequined gown, her blonde hair swept up into a knot with soft curls falling prettily around her face. He desperately wanted her to be happy.

Sam's gaze met her blood-sibling's, and she offered him a smile before turning her attention back to Max.

"It's been tough, huh—watching these two dance around each other like lost souls?" Michael asked.

Bowie nodded. "I have a feeling they'll figure it all out soon enough."

"I hope so. Knowing each other since they were kids has to help the situation."

"Speaking of which." Bowie glanced towards Elizabeth in the crowd. She looked like she belonged in the royal-soul world, more so than some of the royal-souls themselves. "I know I've encouraged you to move forward there, but…" He felt for Michael, and didn't want his soul-sibling to suffer at the thought of breaking Beth's heart.

Michael grinned. "Actually, I have a plan."

"Oh?"

"Yeah, Red and Tom have put it to the Council that I ask Beth to marry me, pure-soul style, and have her blessed with all things royal."

Bowie's eyes widened. "Is that even possible?"

"Apparently, it is. She will have to swear an oath to keep our way of life a secret, and will then be gifted with years to match mine."

"That's unheard of." Bowie took a swallow of the punch.

Michael nodded. "It is. And I've been given my first assignment, to pay back their generosity."

"Oh, really?" he raised an eyebrow.

"Yep. The Council are giving me a month for the wedding and honeymoon, then its sleeves up and diving deep into a new mentoring position—though, I have no idea about the program."

"Mentoring? Sounds neat. They couldn't ask for a better mentor, no matter the program. I'm happy for you, Michael." Bowie smiled at the man he loved like a brother, relieved that he had the chance to be as happy as he himself was, especially considering all the years he had suffered at the hands of the Veins.

Michael met Bowie's eyes. "Thanks. I know I haven't said it out loud, but you really are perfect for Angel. I couldn't be happier for you both."

"That is the sweetest thing, Michael." Angel smiled as she slipped her arm around Bowie's waist. "And I am so happy for you and Beth. Red whispered the news to me."

Bowie put his arm around her, pulling her closer so he could brush a sweet kiss against her cheek.

"Thanks, Angel." Michael squeezed her hand as Uriel called for everyone's attention.

The grounds grew quiet as everyone gathered around. The air held sweet notes of goodness, healing, and love. Uriel started the speeches off by congratulating every soul for their contribution in healing Mother Earth, and the pure-souls, with everything they'd done.

"What's that?" Edna asked Red. "Take a stroll around the pad?"

Red patted Edna's hand. "Yes, dear, after the speeches." She hid her smile; sometimes the art of concealing the royal-souls conversations had interesting moments.

"No, Edna." Mrs. McGoldrick shook her head. "He said, 'help yourselves to the bowl near the lad.'" She frowned, knowing that didn't make sense, and wondered, not for the first time, what Red put in the punch—whenever they had a get together of this magnitude, the conversations, as brilliant as they were, rarely made sense.

"We have much to be thankful for, and I, and the Angels above, thank you all for working so tirelessly over the past several months. The Vein activity is close to nil, and although the eradication of an ancient one has only been recent, we have started to see small signs already that Mother Earth is beginning to heal."

The royal-souls clapped in delight as Angel smiled up at Bowie. "We can do this! We can really save her." Her eyes gleamed like jewels.

Bowie ran a hand over her silky hair, smiling. "Yes, we can." He bent to drop a kiss across her lips.

Uriel continued, "As much as we thank you all for your unwavering service, there are two souls whom I would like us all to thank right now for their major role in the cleansing of Mother Earth's soul, two incredibly special Soul Keepers of Glenormiston South, for their unwavering efforts, despite their young age. Samantha Storm and Angel Clo—"

Before he could get Angel's last name out, the entire crowd erupted in ear shattering applause that floated towards the night sky.

Sam sent Angel a smile of pride and love. *That's us they are thanking.* She grinned.

Angel beamed back at her. *I certainly prefer this attention, compared to the last time we had a big audience.*

Sam nodded as she mock-shuddered, thinking about the terrible pain she and Angel had endured after deceiving Bowie and the Council with the ruby fiasco.

Hearts full of pride and a sense of hope for a sustainable, gentle, non-invasive future for the pure-souls, in which the majority would be saturated in the royal-souls' good intentions, everyone settled back down, listening to Uriel continue his speech..

Now that the Vein activity was close to zero, the royal-souls would have more time to focus on educating and motivating the pure-souls. They'd encourage them to do the right thing in reversing the major damage they'd caused, and to treat the world they'd been gifted with respect, once and for all.

After all, it was only themselves, and the future generations, who would suffer if they didn't heed Mother Earth's warnings and reverse their crimes against her right now.

Once Uriel had finished his speech, the celebrations continued well into the night.

In the early hours of the morning, the four young Soul Keepers of Glenormiston South sat out on the deck of the octagon room, looking out at their precious estate. Beth, Max, Eddy, and Jane had turned in an hour ago, leaving Angel, Sam, Bowie, and Michael to reflect on the past with pride, and look to the future with much hope.

The soulful cry of a black cockatoo rang out, and, in that moment, Angel felt the love from her mother wash over her. From the look on Michael's face, he'd felt it, too. They shared a smile as Michael kissed both girls goodnight and slapped Bowie on the back affectionately before leaving.

"See you in the morning, lovebirds." Sam grinned as she headed to her room.

"Sleep well, hero." Angel smiled after her.

Angel yawned as she snuggled against Bowie's side. "You'll be here in the morning, right?"

Bowie kissed the top of her head. He could feel her exhausted energy despite the attempted joke regarding the Christmas morning seven years ago, when the girls had risen to find the boys missing.

"I'm never leaving your side again, baby."

Her heart swelled as she turned her face, kissing his chest through his shirt. "Good." She yawned again.

"Bed, now," he whispered before waving his hand towards the night sky, which filled with a trillion amber stars, twinkling in the shape of a heart before floating into position, gifting the pure-souls with their milky-way.

Angel's heart melted as she took his hand, kissing it before he swept her up in his arms, kissing her hard.

A gentle rain fell, soaking into the summer soils as the elemental and heavenly soul loved one another completely. With their happy hearts glowing in pure contentment, a healing energy radiated from them both and softly drifted out into the night air, the breeze carrying their healing energy to where it was needed most. They would need the assistance of the pure-souls, as their population was one of such enormity. But it could be done.

If, pray tell, the pure-souls saw the signs before it was too late.

The End

Coming Soon
Obsidian Souls

*S**tars above, why does he wear angry so well?*** Sam Storm quickly looked away as Maxwell Black raised green eyes which glared in her direction; frustration marring his handsome features.

She forced herself not to—one, cringe at his disapproving glare; and two, flush with desire as a flash-back of him poised over her naked body several months prior as he had worshipped her, ignited a steamy memory she knew they would never revisit.

She dropped her eyes to her coffee cup and sighed, reaching for an ornate spoon decorated with intricate details around the Glenormiston College emblem, and stirred in another scoop of sugar. The lunch time noise of the cafeteria was comforting and helped drown out her misery at wanting a man who didn't want her; had told her as much a week ago, when he'd returned from Italy, telling her that what they'd once shared was, and would always be, nothing but a fond memory.

"Hey, you, it's cold enough this time of year without you freezing up the only place that's warm at lunchtime." Angel Cloud, Sam's once soul-sibling, and now sister-in-law, slid into the chair opposite her. Sam raised her eyes and grinned at the pretty woman who had been like a sister to her since the day they were born.

"Sorry, I didn't realise me trying to freeze my heart would freeze the room, too." Sam took a deep breath and focused on returning the room to its normal temperature, noticing a few students and professors briskly rubbing their arms.

Angel shook her head sympathetically before saying softly, "It won't always be this hard, Sam."

"Won't it?" Sam leaned back in her chair, folding her arms as she met Angel's eyes. "I thought that when Max came home, things would be different; that he would have had time to heal. Time to want me again." She raised a dark eyebrow, offset by her blonde curls, as Angel released a humourless chuckle.

"Oh, he still wants you, Sam. Count on that."

"Oh, yeah? Then why was the first thing that came out of his mouth when he saw me, after eight months away, was that he was glad we could still be friends, and nothing but friends? Tell me that?"

Angel shook her head. "I can't tell you what's going on in that mind of his." She cast a look over her shoulder towards Max, who was sitting with his mates, Eddy and Gary, before meeting her sister's eyes. "But what I can tell you is this; that man loves you, still."

"Yeah, well, he has a funny way of showing it." Sam shoved her chair back and grabbed her mug as the bell rang, indicating lunch was over. "I'll see you this afternoon," she called over her shoulder as she headed to dump her mug on the 'returns' counter and head out to a lecture on national soil strategies.

Max sped past the mansions axed, bluestone and wrought iron gates, and along the driveway lined with agapanthus and jonquils. Ancient elms stood guard as their twisted limbs cast shadowy arms over him as he pulled up in the old carriage house. He got out, not bothering to lock the sports car, and headed towards the 1873, Classic Revival mansion. He waved as the last of the tradesmen packed up their vans before driving past him. The site manager, Jason Binery, was waiting for Max.

"We're all finished up Mr Black," he said, passing an invoice to Max, who tried not to cringe at the use of his despised, departed father's name. He'd stopped trying to get Jason, and all the workers on the property to simply call him, Max.

"Thank you." he shook Jason's hand peering past him, keen to get inside and have a look around.

"Building inspector approved everything this morning, so you are good to go."

"The tunnel is secured?" Max asked.

"It certainly is. Very interesting concept there Mr Black." Jason nodded.

"Can't wait to see it. Tell your crew there will be a bonus for all their efforts."

Jason grinned before clapping Max on the shoulder. "Have always enjoyed working for your family, if there's anything I can do for you in the future, give me a call."

"No problems. Thanks for everything."

"Yup. See you around." He waved before he sauntered off towards his vehicle, whistling a merry tune.

Max sighed, grateful to be alone as he looked up at the picturesque Gothic Revival structure, inventively enhanced with its distinctive iron veranda, elaborate gable barges and gothic ornament at its finest. Heading inside, he pushed the heavy, carved door open and stepped into a wide, open arched entrance, leading into a tranquil space of whitewashed walls and open plan living. Max grinned, spotting the large pool table in the main lounge and pushing his hands into his jeans pockets strolled through the soothing interior, taking in the finished space.

Rooms once dark and oppressive, closed off and secretive, were now open and airy. Glass archways that made up the interior walls allowed the afternoon sunlight to stream in through the floor to ceiling windows that overlooked gardens once overgrown and neglected, now abundant in country, springtime glory.

Black iron pendulum lighting stood out, where they hung from thick wooden beams and as Max walked from once space to the next, horse carriage lights softly glowed turning off once he'd walked by them.

Furniture was positioned around the space for both solitary comfort and group conversations. Thick, grey rugs flowed along the polished floorboards and large, indoor plants added a vibrant layer of colour. The largest, solid wall held a deep fireplace with raised hearth for seating and above it, black and white photographs simply framed to celebrate the area's beauty. Mount Noorat, The Glenormiston College, Terang and Camperdown's tree lined avenues. And his favourite directly above the mantel, a scene of an apricot sky kissing five ancient elms that stood proudly in the middle of the Quick's paddock. He stared at it as he listened to the calm silence of the mansion, feeling at peace for the first time in months.

He sighed happily as he ran his hand against the smooth, varnished wood of the mantel.

"I'm home," he whispered. "I'm home."

Turning, he headed towards the open plan kitchen that was designed with a masculine touch. Black Italian marble graced the enormous island bench in the middle, appliances tucked behind streamline cabinets. Locating the door where the fridge was tucked behind, Max grabbed a cold beer before heading out the back door and stepped out onto the decking. Twisting the cap off and tossing it into the fire pit, he leaned against the polished timber railing, before taking a deep swallow of the cool ale as he looked over the sprawling yard. The deep pond strewn with vibrant green Lilly pads, sat beside an old-as-time Weeping Willow where a new swing had been attached, so one could sit amongst the greenery and dangle above the pond. Nursing his beer as the frogs began their afternoon chorus, he glanced beyond his property and towards Mount Noorat. Only then, did he allow his thoughts to turn to Samantha Storm, and what seeing her had done to the solid wall he'd been building around his cold, broken heart the past eight months.

He closed his eyes for a brief moment as her image flooded his senses. Her strawberry blonde waves had grown past her shoulders since he'd seen her last. Her eyes, always warm, amber flames, now liquid pools of honey. Her lips… he remembered the feel of them beneath his all too well. His eyes flew open. "Jesus Christ, if you want to torture yourself, fool of a man, go for a run," he shook his head, turning to go back inside and planned on doing just that. Run his desire for Samantha Storm out of his system. It was the only way to keep her safe from what was coming.

The Victoria Collection

Noorat

Obsidian Souls

Inglewood

A Chilling Summer in Inglewood

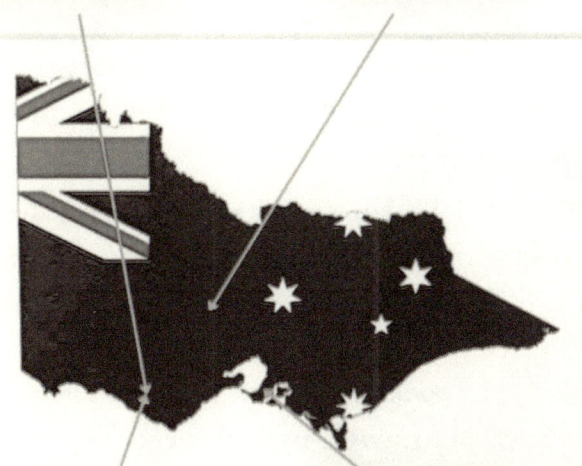

Glenormiston South

SOUL KEEPERS of GLENORMISTON SOUTH

Frankston

Sweet Water Creek

Mickey Martin

Photograph courtesy of Kelly McDonald

MICKEY MARTIN lives and breathes romance into her novels, despite the dark, turbulent situations and plot twists her heroes and heroines must face. Martin is a true romantic writer at heart, who feels it is important to leave the reader with messages of hope and healing. Her books are filled with casts of colourful, resilient characters who thrive and survive, even after enduring hardships and trauma, allowing the reader to draw endless inspiration from memorable faces who have backbones of steel and hearts of gold as they go off in search of their 'happily ever after.'

Martin is also a non-fiction writer under her married name, Michelle Weitering. Here, she seeks to write and make a difference, inviting the reader to question what more they can do to make our world a better place, with acts of kindness.

As a mental health advocate, she uses her writing to become a voice for those living and dealing with issues such as anxiety, depression, and other important social issues surrounding mental illness in order to raise awareness for mental health.

Many new and exciting projects are developing in the pipeline for Mickey as she celebrates her love for her home state, Victoria. Three more novels are soon to follow *Soul Keepers of Glenormiston South*, in her 'The Victoria Collection'. Mickey is hoping to do for Victoria Tourism, what Outlander did for Scotland, with her collection based in the Victorian towns of Glenormiston South, Noorat, Inglewood and Frankston.

Mickey is an author-shareholder with MMH PRESS and is a member of the Romance Writers of Australia, Writers Victoria, and the Peninsula Writers' Club.

She lives in the stunning seaside town of Frankston in Victoria, Australia, with her scrumptious, supportive husband, Jade, and their two gorgeous sons, Jesse and Zane.

Glossary

From David Attenborough's *Life on our Planet*.

Page 365 – Half our fertile land on Earth is now farmed. More often or not, we have abused it. We overload it with nitrates and phosphates, overgraze it, burn it, overburden it with unsuitable varieties of crops, and spraying it with pesticides – so killing the soil invertebrates that bring it to life. Many soils are losing their topsoil and changing from rich ecosystems brimming with fungi, worms, specialist bacteria and a host of other microscopic organisms, into hard, sterile, and empty ground. Rainwater runs off it as it does pavement and so contributes to the excessive floods that now so frequently submerge the heartlands of many countries that practise industrial farming

Page 266 – Biodiversity. Biological diversity – a term that attempts to sum up the variety of life in the world. It is a function of the number of species, all the different animals, plants, fungi and even microorganisms like bacteria, and the number or abundance that exists of each of those species.

In more abstract terms, the planet's biodiversity encapsulates not only millions of species and billions of individuals but the trillions of different characteristics that those individuals have.

Page 359 – *I am older than I look, and in all the years I have been blessed to walk this world, it is only now that I appreciate how extraordinary it is. As a young man, I felt I was out there in the wild, experiencing the untouched natural wild, but it was an illusion. The tragedy of our time has been happening all around us, barely noticeable from day to day, the loss of our planet's wild places, its biodiversity.*

Page 360 – *We have one final chance to create the perfect home for ourselves and restore the wonderful world we inherited. All we need is the will to do so. If we act now, we can yet put it right.*

I can't acknowledge this wonderful man enough for all he has done for our one planet-Earth. I know I am not alone in my adoration of this individual whose knowledge, skills and passion for the living world is limitless.

Sir David Attenborough, I honour you by the choices I make; by stepping forward respectfully and leaving minimal footprints behind me for the rest of my days. As a nature lover, I will continue to be mindful of the magic of the world around me, of the absolute gift that it is, and do all that I can with my two hands to make a positive impact, with minimal damage. We all can, and need to educate ourselves and our children on what needs to be done to reverse the damage we have inflicted upon our earth before it is too late.

Mother Earth is dying. Right at this moment. And that's on each and every one of us.

Protecting our planet starts with you, me, and everyone in between. And it can be as simple as furthering our own education, and educating others on the importance of preserving our natural resources. Plant a tree. Plant something that will attract bees and insects. Let us gift our crucial pollinators with what they need to keep every one of us alive. Choose sustainable, shop wisely—reduce, reuse, recycle. And if you're not sure, Google it, my friends.

Or better yet, read *Life on Our Planet*. It will truly awaken a deep sense of how we all must make a change immediately, for the sake of our children's children, if they are to have a future at all, and have the opportunity to enjoy this wonderous, inherited gift that we have all had the privilege to enjoy—Earth.